GW00503084

BLOOD RED MOON

Written by

Mark Allen

Copyright 2021 by Mark Allen. All rights reserved.

No portion of this novel, with the exception of brief passages for the purpose of review or critique, may be used, edited, reproduced, published, translated, transcribed, or used in any other way, in any language, by any means known or unknown at this time, without the expressed written consent of the copyright holder.

This novel is a work of fiction and the product of a sick, twisted imagination. And though it is set in the Northwest region of Washington state and in real towns and cities on the shores of the Puget Sound, some rather liberal artistic license has been taken on my part for purposes of the story being told.

Any resemblance between names, characters, locations, places, and buildings to real names of actual persons (living, dead, or lycanthrope), business establishments or buildings is accidental, unintentional, and entirely coincidental.

ACKNOWLEDGEMENTS

No author operates in a vacuum. If it takes a village to raise a child, then it takes a village to help, encourage, support and sustain a writer while they actually do the heavy lifting of trying to condense random ramblings into a somewhat coherent storyline, trim it down, get it into some semblance of literacy, and on to publishing, which is akin to watching your child go off to college.

With that in mind, I would like to thank some of those in my personal village who have helped me along the way with this novel.

To Kelly Styles and Kris Wahl, my Beta Readers and first line editors, thank you for seeing the mistakes I missed.

To my mother Dale McCorkle, sister Lisa Henderson, and brother Clark Allen for their encouragement, love, and support.

To my friend, colleague, and fellow horror aficionado, Terry M. West. He's a talented author, and an all-around great guy who helped me when he didn't have to; and helped me when I really needed it.

And to my wife, Fiona Young, an accomplished author in her own right as well as being an award-winning photographer, for always keeping me honest (even when that meant smacking me in the back of the head), keeping my feet firmly on the ground and on the "straight-and-narrow", and helping me (sometimes *forcing* me) to avoid my tendency towards pomposity. She is both my fiercest critic, and my biggest fan.

For Fiona. Always.

"All it takes for evil to triumph is for good men to stand aside and do nothing." – Sir Edmund Burke.

"And behold, I saw a pale horse. And the name of he who sat upon him was Death, and all Hell followed with him" – Revelations 6:8

"Let your plans be dark and as impenetrable as the night, and when you make your move, strike like a thunderbolt" – Sun Tzu, The Art of War.

"For the great day of His wrath has come. And who shall stand against Him?" – Revelations 6:17

BLOOD RED MOON

PROLOGUE

Full dark, no stars. Swirling mist. Muted lights, inky shadows. Fog everywhere. Pea soup, as his *abuelita* would say.

Arturo Sandoval walked, shoulders hunched, down the sidewalk. An icy chill stabbed its way up his spine. He glanced over his shoulder. Nothing there. He tugged at his weathered jacket, zipped it up to his throat.

Mist enveloped him, obscured the familiar street, transformed it into an inhospitable alien landscape. Cold dampness clung to him.

Flashes of old horror movies flickered through his mind. Demented slashers, hacking their way through human flesh. Gore everywhere. Across walls, on the ceiling, the floor.

He had seen worse, of course. In the movies, everything was fake. No one really got hurt. A director yelled "Cut!", and the "dead" actors got up, laughed, and went for coffee.

In the real world though, death was permanent.

Security lights from the small stores and shops shone, pale orbs in the gloom. They coalesced into harder edges as he neared them. Then they disappeared behind him, fading into the night.

That icicle up his spine reached the back of his neck. And he didn't like that familiar gnawing in the pit of his stomach. Having been both predator and prey, he knew what it meant.

He was being followed.

He tried to shrug it off. Nobody lurked behind him. Nobody ventured out this time of night in this part of the city. Except people like him.

Eighteen. No longer a boy; not yet a man. He could be charged as an adult now. That meant hard time, not some bullshit Juvie stint. Time to shape up, walk the straight and narrow, Arturo decided. Find work, make money, help Mom.

But with no degree and no marketable skills, he was staring at a life of minimum wage and poverty, just like his mom.

He remembered that Army brochure he had seen a few weeks ago. Maybe the military would be just the thing. Gain skills, get some training, send some money home. His uncle had been a Marine. He had a solid job, owned a home, had a wife, kids, money in the bank.

Arturo stopped at an intersection, his thoughts churning inside him. He pushed the button, waited for the light to change. No traffic out now, but the way his luck ran, he'd cross against the light and get plastered by some asshole barreling through.

So, he waited. He heard the internal switches click when the light changed. He managed to cross without getting run over or ticketed.

Enjoy life's little victories.

The Great Beast stalked his prey from above, moving silently across the rooftops on padded feet. He had leapt from roof to roof, crossing expanses no human could even dream of making. Claws skittered on shingles, but his sense-challenged prey never heard it.

He had picked up the human's scent six blocks back. He followed close enough for the human to get scared, far enough back to not be seen. He was herding the human along a certain path, forcing him into a kill box.

Arturo heard them before he saw them. Disembodied voices, drifting through the eddying shadows.

"*Hola, amigos,*" he called out.

Amorphous forms materialized as he moved closer.

"*Buenos noches,*" Johnnie Valdez responded, pushing back hanging locks of long, black hair. He grinned, pearly teeth glistening.

"*Que pasa?*" Esteban grunted. In his mid-twenties, he looked hard, like he might explode into violent action at any moment. Arturo never let his guard down around him.

"*Nada*".

"You decided yet?" Esteban asked. "You getting the fuck out?" Hard eyes. Clenched jaw. Mouth stretched into a thin line. Fists shoved into his pockets.

"*Si,*" Arturo replied. Esteban cocked his head slightly, almost imperceptibly. Arturo held his breath.

Esteban nodded. "Good. Get the fuck out while you can. Don't come back."

"I don't want you to think I'm deserting you."

"Live for yourself, *amigo*. People don't like it, fuck 'em."

Johnnie was confused. "Where you going?"

"Military."

Johnnie thought it through. "I'm going to college."

"I'll be out here by myself next year," Regret in Esteban's voice.

"You could still get out," Johnnie suggested.

"Too late, *Juanito*." Esteban shook his head. "I fucked up, did felony time. Nobody wants me. I'm here forever."

None of them sensed the Great Beast sitting on its haunches and huddled low, peering at them from a rooftop across the street, ears hearing every word.

They stood there, mist billowing around them. Arturo knew he was smart enough to get out and stay out. Johnnie, too. He also knew Esteban's choices were nil.

No wonder ex-cons reoffended so often.

Even if they went straight, no one would ever give them a chance to do anything substantive, actually become a contributing member of society like everyone preached about.

But talk was cheap. Sooner or later Esteban would offend again, bounce back to prison, get paroled, then violate again. Esteban's life would become a revolving door until he crossed someone tougher than him and he got ghosted out of existence.

Arturo glanced at his watch. It was late and getting later. He still had that icy feeling.

Esteban noticed. "You got to be somewhere?"

"Home. My baby sister is home alone. Mom's working graveyard at the hospital."

"*Nunca mas importante de la familia,*" Esteban said. Nothing more important than family.

Arturo stepped away, raised a hand. "*Manana, amigos.*"

Arturo swung around and trudged away, hunched against the cold. The fog swallowed him.

Arturo strode down the block, not realizing the Beast was pacing him from above. He was still fifteen minutes from home, and his mom would be pissed that he was late. He had weathered her wrath many times before. One more tirade made no difference to him. He was out in a few months.

The Great Beast grinned, long teeth protruding from his lips. His prey had just turned into the exact alley in which they had set their trap. His packmates were already in place.

Time to tighten to noose.

Arturo filled his chest with dank air. It felt good to have made a decision. A dreamy smile fluttered across his mouth. He went deeper into the alley, taking a shortcut he had taken countless times before.

The two other Great Beasts lay in wait. Their new packmate had done his job. They lurked in the darkness, squatting on powerful haunches in the filth behind a rusted dumpster. They heard the roaches feeding on the detritus inside.

The scout leapt from the rooftop, plummeted to the concrete. He landed softly, almost no sound. Not bad for an animal that weighed close to three hundred pounds. He had considered attacking on his own when his quarry had stopped to talk to the two others. His packmates would have come running. Butcher all three. Split them open. Tear them apart. Gorge on tender meat. Bathe in bright red blood.

Fun times.

But he had followed the plan. One yahoo would invariably wander off on their own. Thin the herd, don't decimate it. Allow the strong and the smart time to reproduce. It strengthened the herd; made the hunts more interesting.

He now dashed across the street, running on all fours into the alley. He slowed, stood up, advanced on two flat feet. He trembled with anticipation.

Like waiting for an orgasm, he thought.

He heard his prey's footsteps now, detected the rhythmic lub-dub, lub-dub heartbeat within his prey's chest. Black lips stretched backwards, exposing rows of sharp white teeth.

A razorblade smile.

Arturo heard a low rumbling up ahead. He stopped, unsure precisely what he had heard, or where it had come from. He held his breath, listening intently. Had it been his imagination? He heard nothing more. He finally breathed out, grinning.

Another rumble, this time from behind! He spun around, eyes wide. Swirling fog and shadow. Then something incredibly large stepped forward, standing just at the edge of Arturo's vision.

Flight or fight kicked in. Arturo spun away to burst into a full run. Then his entire universe exploded.

A deafening roar so loud it ruptured Arturo's eardrums. A massive creature Arturo could not identify in those final milliseconds of life rose up on enormous hind legs, shoved the dumpster aside. The appendage ended in what looked like a combination of an animal's claw and a human hand.

No. That couldn't be right.

Another huge beast rose up on the other side of the alley. What the fuck was that thing?

He back peddled two steps before hearing another rumble come from behind. Three of them, blocking the only ways in and out.

They had him.

Towering above Arturo, the largest of the three beasts bolted forward, roaring and slashing. Arturo's intestines spilled onto the dirty pavement in a steaming pile.

Arturo's eyes widened. He found his voice, mustered up the last of his remaining strength, and screamed.

The last thing Arturo Sandoval saw on this earth was that massive maw opening wider, teeth exposed, large canines like ivory daggers, descending down upon him and clamping over his skull. Arturo felt an incredible viselike pressure. His head caved in with a wet crunch. Then everything went dark.

The other two Great Beasts joined the feast.

"What the fuck was that?" Johnnie asked, eyes wide.

Dread in Esteban's eyes. "Arturo."

They ran towards the terrible, high-pitched scream. Adrenaline surged through their bodies. Esteban in the lead, they bolted across vacant intersections, down the deserted block, careened into the alley. Then they skidded to a stop.

Pitch black. They couldn't see anything, not even the fog dancing around them. Ten feet inside, they moved forward slowly, a cautious creep.

Low-frequency reverberations rumbled up ahead. Sounded almost like a... *a growl.*

Palms sweaty, mouths dry, Esteban and Johnnie continued creeping forward. What the hell was *that* noise? Something new. Different. A sound like cloth ripping, only wetter. It got louder as they advanced.

A wetter sound now, like water splashing across a table. A crunching sound. Like eating celery into a megaphone.

Then gulping something down.

Johnnie and Esteban nearly bumped into the dumpster, the metal dripping with condensation. Now pale white light penetrated from the opposite end of the alley, the streetlight hanging like an artificial moon. Foggy grays. Massive figures hunched over, heavy muscles rippling beneath furry hide. Low to the ground, stooped over something mangled, ripped apart, incredibly dead. Feeding hungrily. Something liquid, so deeply red it appeared almost black in the low light, trickled down the middle of the alleyway.

They inched closer, not comprehending what they were seeing. As big as a bear, but different. The head was all wrong. The snout too narrow, the ears long, pointed, twitching.

Oh shit. There were *two* of them.

Something smacked its lips, dipped its head into the abdominal cavity of the carcass below it, tore something out. Solid and flat, lobed, deeply red. A liver, perhaps. The thing wolfed it down while its partner glared at the interloping humans.

The dining monster swung its head towards them: yellow eyes glowing in the dark, quivering nostrils, furry snout. Two massive creatures glaring at Johnnie and Esteban like they were desert.

Even Esteban's breath caught in his throat. The two beasts rose to their feet, their furry bodies dripping blood. Just as the humans decided to turn and run, a third growl behind them boxed them in.

Checkmate, motherfuckers.

The three Great Beasts lunged at their prey and went to work. Both men slipped into hypovolemic shock within seconds. They bled out quickly, butchered so swiftly and efficiently, the poor bastards never knew what hit them.

CHAPTER ONE

Rain. Again.

In the Pacific Northwest? In late Fall? Wow. Who would have thought?

It came down more than a sprinkle, less than a deluge. It streaked the narrow office window, pattering upon contact. Pulsing rivulets flowed downward. Almost like it was alive.

In a manner of speaking, it was, Caleb Jacobsen admitted. If you took into account the bacteria, viruses, and other single-celled organisms usually present in a single drop of water. A microscopic ecosystem existed within each drop. Living, reproducing, dying. Life cycles measured in minutes.

The rain and iron gray skies sometimes darkened Caleb's mood. He felt pensive now, but the underlying cause was neither the rain nor the cold.

The murders had begun quickly. The first one, in Seattle across the Puget Sound from him. It had first appeared to be an isolated incident.

The mangled body of a homeless man discovered behind a restaurant a few blocks off Pioneer Square. He had been butchered, the reporter on the scene gleefully - and Caleb thought, ghoulishly - described. Dismemberment. Disembowelment.

If it bleeds, it leads, so chanted all the professors over in the Journalism Department.

This was sensationalism, not journalism, Caleb thought. All in the name of ratings, clicks, and ad revenue.

Seattle had typical big city problems, big city crime. Murders, robberies, rapes, drugs, homelessness, hopelessness. Happened every day. But most urban dwellers just kept their heads down and minded their own business, thankful it was not them or anyone they knew.

That first murder had not raised any red flags. Homeless guy in an alley? Who cared, right? Caleb himself had forgotten it initially. But he remembered it now.

It had been the *first* murder. Not the last. The details had not shocked Caleb. God knows he had seen worse. Plus, it happened in Seattle, not in his territory.

Crime in Port Orchard was practically nonexistent. Port Orchard had a population around 14,000 people. Seattle had over 705,000 in the city itself. The Seattle/ Tacoma metropolitan area totaled something like 3.8 million, approximately half the population of Washington state.

Caleb had initially failed to make any connection.

But the signs had been there, plain as day. It wasn't that he had seen the signs and ignored them. No, he had missed then entirely. He had felt safe here for so long that he had gotten comfortable, lazy, complacent.

That was a problem.

Outside, the rain bashed the window unabated. Students huddled under umbrellas as they scurried across campus. Mid-terms were coming up. Tension permeated every classroom, every dorm.

But there was more. Subsequent murders had occurred, marching inexorably down the Puget Sound. Three in Seattle, two in Renton, and one more in Tacoma, all in a period of just six weeks. People on this side of the Sound felt the specter of big city crime on their doorsteps for the first time. They always happened at night, so people went home after sundown. Local bars and restaurants closed early every evening.

Even here on campus, few students ventured out at night. When they did, they moved in packs. He understood the primal concept of safety in numbers. But if Caleb's suspicions were correct, there would be no safety, just a higher body count.

These murders had frightened the police and horrified the public. Six people butchered, dismembered, disemboweled. That they knew of. How many more had simply "disappeared"?

There seemed to be no discernable pattern to the victimology. Both genders, variable ethnicities and ages. The savagery involved was the only constant.

The question was, what was Caleb going to do about it? Indeed, was there anything him *could* do about it?

Caleb closed his brown eyes, stretched in his chair. Chiseled muscles strained beneath his shirt. He sat up and focused, pushed dark hair away from his forehead. He took a deep breath, held it, blew it out. He had work to do. His students' assignments from yesterday weren't going to grade themselves.

A faint, acrid scent wafted past his nostrils. Cigarette smoke. Old and stale, embedded in cotton fabric. The smell grew stronger. The slight thud of someone heavy walking towards his office door. Nanoseconds later, Russell Slater, portly and smiling, filled his doorway. What was left of lank yellow hair hung off his head and across his pale eyes.

"Hey there, handsome man."

Caleb grinned. "What's up, Professor?"

"I love it when you use big words."

Russell lurched inside and headed for the padded chair in front of Caleb's desk. He plopped his considerable weight into the chair. "I just finished my last class of the day. Psyche 101. Tedious. But there's this really hot chick in the front row with a great rack."

"Russell. You know you can't do that, right?"

Russell feigned ignorance. "What?"

"You know what. Banging a student kill your career in a heartbeat. These days, you'd be lucky if that's all that happens."

"It's always been consensual."

"It's not about consent. It's about power dynamics."

"You gonna let me tell my story, or bust my balls?"

This was not the time to push Russell to be a better human being. Caleb sat back in his chair and gestured widely with his hands. "Please. Excuse the inconvenience of my moral compass. Please continue."

"Well, now I don't know if I want to tell you, Mr. High and Mighty."

"Take it easy—"

"Fuck easy. You never banged one of your students?"

"No. Never."

"I was telling you about a hot babe in my class. Is that so fucking bad?"

"For you, it's a step in the right direction."

Russell thought about that. A faint grin whispered across his mouth. "Fuck you."

And just like that, the argument was over, and all was right between them once again. Friendship was a strange animal.

Russell sighed with relief. "So. We still on for tonight?"

"Sure. I've only got one more class."

"Good. I'll be starved by then."

Caleb jutted a forefinger towards his friend's belly. "Stick to the chopped salad and cottage cheese."

"I abhor salad. And I *hate* cottage cheese."

Caleb ignored him. "And lay off the Goddamned cancer sticks. I can smell you a hundred feet away."

"Jesus. You sound like my mother."

"I've met your mother. You should listen to her. She only wants the best for you."

"And you?"

"I don't want you dying before I get that hundred bucks you owe me."

Russell squeezed his eyes shut and slapped his chubby hands over his heart. "You wound me, sir. Are all your motives so mercenary?"

"You bet your fat ass they are."

Russell shook with mirth. "Oh. By the way, you'll like this." He leaned forward. "We need to pick up Marla."

"Marla."

"You remember my cousin, right? She sure remembers you."

Caleb remembered. They had met at a party Russell threw about a year earlier. She had just moved out here to take a research biologist job with a new biotech startup. She didn't even have furniture in her apartment yet. He had detected her musical laughter from outside in the hallway. He picked up her pheromones the instant Russell had greeted him at the door.

Russell introduced them. Caleb hardly heard what Russell said as he kept himself under control as blasts of information bombarded his senses.

Marla was mixed race, white and Hispanic. Tall and slender, she had been born with a body type that would stay height-weight proportionate all her life. She had slugged her way through college on sports scholarships and part-time jobs, she still kept her raven hair short on her neck to keep it out of the way. Delicate feet, strong calves, muscular thighs, flat belly, small perky breasts. Toned arms and shoulders. She still swam laps and ran several days a week.

And she held a Ph.D. in Cellular Biology. Caleb found smart, educated women sexy as hell.

Her pheromone signature, undetectable to modern humans but plain as day to Caleb, trailed after her as they moved about Russell's living room. Naturally, being a red-blooded heterosexual male, he was keenly interested.

Outwardly, Caleb had been a model of self-restraint. He had managed to show interest without alarming her and had conducted himself as a perfect gentleman.

"Yes," Caleb said now. "I remember her."

"You should. You followed around after her all night, sniffing at her like a dog."

"I did not."

"Dude. You practically humped her leg."

"Oh please," Caleb said. He looked out the window a moment, then back at Russell. "Was I that transparent?"

"Saint Bernards drool less than you did."

"Sorry."

Russell waved a hand. "Don't sweat it. She's a grown-ass woman." He winked. "And she is totally *hot*."

Caleb's eyes widened. "Why Russell Slater! Having impure thoughts about your own cousin?" Caleb grinned. "You're a slave to your hormones, pal. You're a sick, twisted, perverted individual. I admire that in a Psychologist."

Russell jiggled as he giggled. "Okay, Stud." He pushed himself out of the chair. "I'll hit you up after your class."

"That's right," Caleb confirmed. "I'll have dinner with you when… when I have no class."

Russell's face turned beet-red, then erupted into laughter. He held his hands across his shaking belly as he turned and caromed out the doorway and out of sight.

Still grinning, Caleb shook his head. He glanced down at his watch. One more class, then his week was over.

He had been hired to teach, but that was not his passion. Teaching allowed him access to some of the finest and most detailed historical documents anywhere at the local museums and libraries. His affiliation with the College opened doors. Caleb's new book was coming along fine, thanks, and the College wanted him to complete it. So, they gave him time and latitude. Once the new book came out, the College could use its visibility as a recruiting tool.

Caleb got to publish, and the school got more students. Win-win.

Reconstruction. That's what his new book was about. Trying to bring his unique perspective to a topic that had already been written about dozens, if not hundreds, of times.

After the end of the Civil War in 1865, major parts of the country had been utterly destroyed. The Union's "scorched earth policy" had been exactly that. The strategy that dated back to the Romans and the Greeks before them. An advancing army would destroy and set fire to anything that might be of use to the enemy. That included houses, clothing, people, crops in the fields. General Sherman's men heaped salt onto burned fields, rendering them incapable of growing food crops for years to come.

In the farthest reaches of his mind, Caleb heard high-pitched screams, echoes of a time long past. He remembered the smells of smoke and salt. Bad times. Bad memories. His pulse raced; his blood pressure rose.

But strong emotion was dangerous for him, especially here. He closed his eyes, took another breath. Calmed himself. Got his mind back on point.

Reconstruction. Right. Once the war ended, everyone was an American again. Everyone was expected to smile and get along; forgive and forget the horrors of war, the lingering memories, the bitter divisiveness war inevitably produces.

Fat chance of that.

Anger thrives in the hearts of men. It eats them alive, twists them into something monstrous, until it rots them out from the inside. Those fortunate enough to survive war carry that darkness with them the rest of their days. The lucky ones learn how to keep a lid on it.

Caleb wondered if those who died were the fortunate ones?

For only the dead truly know peace.

For the living, enduring the Evil of man continued. Caleb had seen it time and again. Post-war xenophobia had given rise to atrocities: rapes, beatings, lynchings. The rise of the Ku Klux Klan. How many black Americans had been terrorized, beaten, murdered? How many black businesses and homes had been razed, burned to the ground?

Bigotry and hatred.

Human nature at its worst.

Caleb forced the memories back into the past where they belonged. He came out of his reverie, opened his laptop, went to a website that streamed local news broadcasts.

Professionally coifed anchors filled the screen. A black man, expensive suit, handsome face, blinding smile. An oriental woman, raven hair, pale face, red lips, slender body. They faded to the background as the titles loomed out at him.

"This KKDA Action News, the Puget Sound's top news station. With Kevin Jones and Diane Yakamoto."

The opening graphics faded away. Diane Yakamoto sat at the center of the desk, prim, spine straight.

"Good evening, Seattle, I'm Diane Yakamoto," she read from the teleprompter. "Our top story tonight: Seattle police made yet another grisly discovery early this morning."

Videotape playback filled the screen as Diane continued talking. It showed the filthy alley, dumpsters pushed askew, three red-stained sheets covering bloody corpses. Uniformed officers, detectives, and technicians in white jump suits sifted through the scene, squinting, bending and stooping, collecting evidence.

"The remains of three young Hispanic men were found after an anonymous 911 call. The bodies were found in an alley in the Industrial District, a few blocks west of the Duwamish Waterway and State Highway 99."

Diane's voice had a soothing effect on Caleb. He picked up his tablet, scanned his notes for his upcoming class. He liked to be in the room before his students arrived. He felt it was professional.

His eyes flicked to the screen. The camera tilted and panned away from the bodies, swept by the crumpled dumpster. That was when he saw it.

In that instant, Caleb Jacobsen's life changed forever.

On the brick wall near the dumpster, about seven feet up. A dried, rusty brown smear.

But not just any smear.

Caleb's eyes narrowed; laser focused on this one image. The smudged center appeared roughly ovoid but elongated front to back. Five tendrils spread out, extending from the central blob. Four close together, one set at an angle and distance away from the others. It resembled the palm print. Not a human handprint, though. Not even close.

The palm print of a werewolf.

Caleb was certain; he had no doubt. Caleb knew all about werewolves. He knew their habits, their methods, understood their mental paradigms.

Caleb Jacobsen had been a werewolf himself for almost one hundred and fifty years.

CHAPTER TWO

The newscast cut back to the studio. Clean, bloodless, sterile. Diane continued speaking directly into the camera, like she was speaking to each member of her audience.

"In related news, the Mayor's Office is responding to growing calls for action by the public. A source at City Hall admitted that the Mayor's Office is pressuring the Police Department to make an arrest as this string of brutal killings continues."

Stupid, Caleb thought. Sure, she could say she was keeping on top of the situation, but she was micromanaging, a sure sign of piss-poor leadership.

He did not hold politicians in high regard. Corrupt, narcissistic egotists out for their own self-aggrandizement and self-enrichment at the expense of others, as far as he was concerned.

"It's rumored local police are considering calling in outside experts."

Caleb turned the broadcast off. The back of his hand was darker, covered with hair now. His finger ended in a long, curved nail.

Like a claw.

He sat back heavily, ignoring the groaning strain coming from the mechanism in his chair. He squeezed his eyes shut, slowed his breathing.

The gruesome handprint, the mutilated bodies covered in sopping red sheets played on a demented loop in his head. Who could have done this? He wished he could visit the scene, try to detect a scent, any scent. All werewolves had their own distinct scent, as individual and as identifying as a human fingerprint. He would know if this was someone he had encountered before, or if this was someone new.

The hair on the back of his neck rose, a primordial instinct. Muscles coiled, tightened. A coldness, a dampness beyond the weather outside invaded the room and pooled around Caleb's boots. Traced its tendrils up his legs, then clambered into his spine.

It had been so long, he didn't recognize the feeling at first. Then it hit him. An epiphany, a lightning bolt of clarity blasted across his brain, crystalline and pure.

Fear.

Caleb strode into the classroom ten minutes early. An old military man, he still operated on a military timetable: fifteen minutes early was on time. On time was fifteen minutes late. The deserted room filled with thirty desks bade him a silent greeting.

He flipped the light switch. Fluorescent bulbs sputtered to white life above him. He placed his computer bag on his desk, pulled out his laptop, opened the clamshell.

He felt better now than before. But he still felt uneasy, out of sorts. Wrinkles creased his forehead. But his only alternative would be to make the Change, and he simply could not do that right now.

Caleb had not made the Change in several weeks. The pull, the lure, already resonated within him like a siren's song. The urge was stronger, growing every day. Soon it would become irresistible, uncontrollable. The Change would overwhelm him whether he wanted it or not. Then he would have to hunt and kill before he could Change back to human form.

He despised that, the loss of control. He lived a life at the mercy of powers within him he did not fully comprehend and would never totally control.

Being a werewolf really sucked.

Muffled voices, squishy footsteps on wet concrete outside. The first of his students entering the building, shaking umbrellas and coats. It would still take them the better part of one minute to reach the other side of the classroom door.

Caleb stabbed a button on his laptop. His lesson plan came up, filling the screen. All he had to do was make it through the next fifty-five minutes. Then at least he could get outside, breathe fresh air.

The door on the other side of the room opened. Half a dozen young men and women of various styles and ethnicities poured through the doorway. Caleb stood tall beside his desk, flashed them a welcoming smile.

"Hey, Teach," one young black man called out.

"Leonard," Caleb responded with a nod of his head.

Leonard pulled a textbook and a tablet out of his messenger bag, placed them both in front of him. Other students did the same. He pressed a button on the screen, opened his book while the tablet powered up. He glanced around the room.

"Hey, Teach. Is this all?"

"We still have a few minutes." Caleb unbuttoned the cuffs on his sleeves, rolled them up to his elbows. He ignored the pheromones emanating from Wendy, the busty redhead in the far corner. A quick glance confirmed she sat in rapt attention, watching his every move.

He had heard someone once say that anyone who looked at you without blinking for more than five seconds either wanted to fuck you or kill you. Wendy had no plans to kill him. Her pheromones telegraphed that much. So that left only one thing, didn't it?

Well, Wendy needed to focus her unrequited lust in other directions. Caleb Jacobsen didn't do students. Period.

"Okay. Let's get started."

Leonard looked around. "Is this all? Why don't you just cancel class? Let us get out of here."

"It's raining out," Lei, a Korean exchange student said. "It's getting dark."

"Are you afraid of the dark?" Caleb asked.

Leonard said, "With all these murders, folks got reason to be afraid."

"You got that right," Lei agreed.

Caleb shrugged. "Okay." Noncommittal.

"You're not scared, are you?" Wendy asked.

"No."

"Tough guy, Teach?"

Caleb grinned.

"I get the campus police to escort me to my car," Tatiana, a smoky brunette chimed in.

"What do you make of all this?" Wendy asked.

The room fell quiet, all eyes on him. Everyone awaited his response.

"Don't know what to make of it," he responded. "But there are certain similarities with other serial murders -- within historical context, of course."

"Like what?"

"Jack the Ripper comes to mind," Caleb said, referring to the infamous murders in Whitechapel, London, in 1887.

"He only attacked white women," Tatiana countered.

"Leonard nodded. "He killed hookers, right?"

"Five of them," Caleb confirmed.

"Kinda like the Manson murders," Wendy added. "He butchered people."

"Actually, Manson was never convicted for any murders that he himself committed", Caleb stated. "He was convicted of masterminding the Tate-LaBianca murders. But other people carried out his orders."

A petite black woman in an orange turtleneck named Rachael sat up. "These things are so gruesome. Like maybe some kind of satanic ritual?"

Caleb folded his arms across his chest and leaned back against his desk. This might actually be interesting after all.

"There needs to be a discernable pattern to it," Leonard said. "Serial killers always display some kind of pattern. There's no pattern here."

Caleb said, "Victims are both genders, various ethnicities. These three latest were Hispanic. But we've had a white victim and an Asian."

"The kills have been all over," Leonard added. "Serial killers establish hunting grounds."

"I hope whoever's doing this never decides to come to this side of the Sound," Rachael said.

"How do we know there's no pattern?" Caleb interjected. "Maybe there's something here no one has seen yet."

"Maybe the randomness is the pattern," someone hypostasized.

"Or perhaps the police have found it, but are withholding it from the public," Caleb countered.

Leonard's face clouded over. "Police do that shit all the time," he said bitterly.

"That sucks." Tatiana again. "We have a right to know."

"Preposterous," Caleb sniffed. Silence fell over the class. His students stared at him in disbelief. "Law enforcement withholds key details from ongoing investigations so if the criminals are watching, the cops don't tip their hand and actually help them escape."

"The people have a right to know," Tatiana replied, glaring at Caleb.

"Preposterous," he said again.

"Why is that preposterous?"

"Because all rights are relative, not absolute," Caleb explained in an even voice. "My rights stop where yours begin. And your rights stop where his begins." Caleb pointed to Leonard. "And the right to know stops when it threatens the integrity of an investigation. It's more important to get it right in court than to feed us every lurid detail."

Another lull as the students digested what Caleb had said. Caleb's mind was already sprinting ahead.

"There's another other possibility here." Caleb looked out at his students. He paused. He alone noticed Russell Slater open the door at the back of the class and move inside.

"What if they're withholding details to protect us from ourselves?" He paused, watching Russell squeeze into a seat at the back of the class. "What if the truth, these 'gruesome details' are so gruesome, so horrifying that they're worried about a tidal wave of fear among the public?"

"You mean a panic?" Leonard asked.

"Historical context, folks. In the late nineteen thirties', Orson Welles does his famous "War of the Worlds" broadcast. At the beginning, they said it was a radio play. But people who tuned in late thought it was real, that the earth was in fact being invaded. Fear led the way to panic. Some people actually fled their homes. All over a radio play."

"Yeah, but I thought the mass panic reports had been overstated," Leonard pushed back. "It didn't happen on a wide scale."

"And yet it still happened," Caleb replied. "What would happen now, with the internet and cell phones and social media, if details so horrifying, so terrible came to light that indicated whoever is doing this, is so dark and twisted, so perverted and sinister, that it could only originate from the purest, deepest Evil?"

Dead silence.

Caleb's favorite line from *The Rhyme of the Ancient Mariner* seemed apropos. "Like one who on a lonely road doth walk in fear and dread; and having once turned 'round, walks on and turns no more his head; because he knows a frightful fiend doth close behind him tread!"

Silence.

The air weighed with tension.

"Maybe it's a ghost of Samuel Taylor Coleridge!" Russell piped up.

Laughter erupted. The tension vanished.

Even Caleb grinned. "Okay. Get out of here."

His students gathered their stuff, closed laptops, zipped backpacks. "Stay safe out there!" Some of them were already heading towards the door.

Russell stayed squeezed into his desk, his rotund belly pressing against the slanted desktop. He grinned at Caleb, looking like the Cheshire cat, ignored the students moving past him.

"Thanks for disturbing my class."

Russell waved his hand dismissively. "Come on, Boy Scout. I did you a favor, and you know it." With some difficulty, he extracted himself out of the desk.

Caleb was not angry. Russell had indeed done him a favor. None of his student had an inkling of what was really going on. And hopefully, none of them ever would. He closed his laptop.

Russell sauntered down the aisle as Caleb shoved the laptop into his bag. He clipped buckles, cinched straps. He threw the bag over one shoulder, dug for his keys.

"Ready?" Russell asked.

Caleb nodded. Russell turned and walked back up the aisle. Caleb silently padded behind him.

Caleb's ears detected a gurgling emanating from Russell's lower bowel. He shifted to the side just before Russell farted, emitting a "silent but deadly" exhibit of Russell's chronic flatulence. Too much drive-through fast food, gutbuster burritos, deep-fried grease.

Moving aside accomplished nothing. Caleb practically gagged. He worried if his friend was on a long slow ride to colon cancer. He squinted reflexively, his eyes tearing like he had been cutting an onion.

Oblivious to Caleb's anguish Russell hummed tunelessly as his hands hit the lock bar and he threw his weight into the door. The door flew back on its hinges, slammed into the cinderblock wall. Russell sailed into the hallway beyond.

Caleb walked into the hallway two seconds behind Russell. His eyes were better, but now his ears were ringing. He slipped through as the door swung back towards the jamb. Caleb sidestepped left and pulled his right foot up and away, barely avoiding painful contact with his shin.

"The chick in the tight sweater wants you," Russell threw over his shoulder.

"Wendy?"

"Dude, she is warm for your form. I'm just sayin'."

"Raging hormones," Caleb said dismissively. "Nothing more."

"Ah!" Russell exclaimed. He turned around, leering. "So you've noticed her."

"I've noticed. So what? It's called self-control."

"Self-control? Where's the fun in that?"

Caleb pushed through the building's outer door. Cold air slapped his face. A drizzle beaded water on his leather jacket.

"Come on, Caleb. Level with me."

"About what?"

"You don't do students. That's… admirable."

Caleb grinned. "It's the right thing to do. Always has been. Plus, with all the social consciousness on sexual misconduct these days, it's a good survival strategy."

Russell overtook Caleb, walked at his side. "But in all the years I've known you, I've seen no evidence you do anyone."

Caleb shrugged. "Maybe I'm celibate. Maybe I'm impotent." Then he added, "Maybe I'm saving myself for marriage."

Russell shook his head. "No. You're just discrete to the point of secretive."

"I like secretive. Keeps everybody guessing"

"Why?"

"Because they always guess wrong. That amuses me."

"Me, I can understand," Russell continued. "I'm over forty and still get zits. Going bald, got a paunch. But look at you: full head of hair, a physique like a Goddamned Greek statue. It makes no sense."

"Mama raised me better than to kiss and tell."

The faculty lot was almost empty. Drizzle came down harder, threatening to become real rain. The wind had kicked up. It was full dark now. The parking lot lights came on around four thirty in the afternoon this time of year.

Russell's dented compact car sat on the far side of the lot. He'd owned it since his grad student days, and possibly had never gotten a tune up or an oil change. The engine coughed and wheezed, threatened to stall every time he hit the accelerator. Rattling doors, squishy brakes, a clutch that slipped with alarming frequency, and a crack that spread laterally across the windshield. But, as Russell repeatedly (and gleefully) reminded Caleb, the heater worked just fine.

"Let's take mine," Russell suggested.

"Let's don't and say we did."

Caleb motioned towards the other vehicle sitting in the lot, a late model Jeep hard top. Four doors, roof rack, painted forest green. The thing sat a good three feet off the ground, supported by oversized, knobby tires and an off-road suspension. Russell knew Caleb had a thing for the outdoors. He just did not understand why. Dirt and dust, ticks and mosquitos. Waking up with grass in your ass crack. Where did that get fun?

"We taking the ferry?" Caleb asked.

"Nope. She's at the Tacoma facility now."

Caleb touched a button on his key fob. The doors unlocked. "How long will she down there?"

"Not sure," Russell responded.

Caleb opened the driver's side door. "Did she piss somebody off?" He slid inside behind the wheel.

Russell clambered into the passenger seat. "Not that I know of."

"I thought that within the Seattle bioresearch community, going to Tacoma was like being banished to outer Siberia. A fate reserved for only those who angered the Biotech Gods."

"If you're sent there permanently. She's not."

Caleb inserted the keys, cranked the ignition. The Jeep came to life. "Good."

CHAPTER THREE

They drove south on Warren Avenue, then turned right onto Burwell. They cruised past the Bremerton police station and gained speed up the formidable hill.

The banter had lulled. Caleb concentrated on driving. Russell turned on the car radio.

Marla was Russell's first cousin on his mother's side. He had told Caleb the story. It was genuinely inspirational.

They had been born into abject poverty in rural Kentucky, Bluebonnet County. No township name, just Bluebonnet County. Caleb was familiar with the region.

Sisters Abigail Moreno and Colleen Slater were three years apart in age. Even as married women, they lived less than a quarter mile from each other in rusted, sagging single-wide trailers. They were connected by a one lane dirt road that got rutted and impassable when it rained and iced over in winter.

Russell was an only child. A tragic tale lurked behind that. Colleen had carried Russell to term with no problem. But two years later, she delivered a stillborn baby. Of course, his parents had been devastated. Colleen had been particularly gun-shy about trying again, but she eventually relented. She miscarried about ten weeks in. After that, Colleen Slater was done trying to have kids.

Caleb and Russell had already crested the hill on Burwell and were now sliding down the opposite side. Eighty-year-old craftsman homes, some sagging from neglect and disrepair, whizzed by as they hurtled down the hill.

Abigail had no problems reproducing. She already had two children when Colleen had Russell. Abbie was always supportive of Colleen, and there was never any friction between the two -- at least, not that Russell knew.

Caleb stopped at a traffic light. His friend was quiet, his chubby chest barely rising and falling. He gazed out the window, contemplating the gas station to their right.

"You okay?" Caleb asked, shifting the Jeep into gear.

"Fine." His tone indicated that he was anything but fine.

They turned left onto Callow. This road would feed them onto State Highway 16 East, and then on to Tacoma.

Both Russell's and Marla's fathers were coal miners. There was barely enough to cover rent and utilities. Both wives took in sewing and childcare to make ends meet. Colleen sold homemade jams and preserves at the local farmer's market. Abbie churned out handmade quilts that she sold off the back of a pickup to rich city folk who came down on the weekends.

Both families pushed their children to excel in academics. They wanted better for their children; wanted them to achieve in this world what they themselves had not. Russell and Marla had obeyed. Both were driven to make good grades, graduate high school, go to college, and get out of the sticks once and for all.

They both succeeded.

Now both were recognized professionals in their fields. Russell had a Master's in Psychology, taught, and consulted. Marla, with her newly minted Ph.D., was a rising star amongst biomedical research crowd. A huge firm, Global BioTech, recruited her. She signed her contract the week before graduation. She had been with them for years, had co-authored several papers that published in peer-reviewed journals and magazines.

That was the nature of the beast regarding academia. Publish or perish. It was as simple as that.

A recognized academic himself, Caleb was subject to the same rules. But rather than publish articles, Caleb had written a scholarly book. He had concentrated on events leading up to the Civil War and had continued through Reconstruction. The book had sold well and was now considered required reading. Several colleges across the country taught from it. He had been complimented by many people who had read the book, saying it had opened their eyes to an 1800's America that they had not contemplated. Some even said the writing was so intimate and knowledgeable that it was almost as if Caleb had lived through those times himself.

Oh, if they only knew…

They continued west. The carrier USS Kitty Hawk, one of the last non-nuclear aircraft carriers sat, pale and hulking, at the dock to their left. They picked up speed, negotiated a mild incline upwards which leveled out, banked smoothly to the left, then shifted to a decline, swinging them around and down to merge with the 16.

Russell heaved a sigh. "I made tenure."

Caleb was stunned. "Congratulations. That's great."

"Pay raise, job security, yeah," Russell moaned. "It just hit me, though."

"What hit you?"

"This is it." He spread his hands out in front of himself. "This is my career."

"And this is a bad thing how, exactly?" Caleb had been passed over for tenure two years ago. He was still pissed about it.

"Because this is it," he reiterated. "I'm a career academic. Not exactly what I had planned."

"What did you have planned?"

"Something more exciting. Forensics. Criminal psychology."

"You've consulted with local P.D.'s."

"I thought I'd be a criminal psychologist for Federal law enforcement, maybe teach once in a while at the Academy, that sort of thing. Be full-time, ass kicking mindhunter." He shook his head. "But I teach at a *junior college,* for fuck's sake -- and I haven't consulted in two years."

"Life is what happens to us when we're making other plans." Caleb glanced over at Russell. "Nothing turns out the way we think it will."

Something about Caleb's tone brought Russell out of his musings about his own disappointments. He looked across at his friend. From where he sat, it looked like Caleb's life was going pretty goddamned good.

But there were some things men did not talk about. Some subjects were taboo, even among friends. Russell bit his lip and stared at the road ahead.

They stayed on Highway 16, heading southeast. The highway forked just south of Sinclair Inlet. The far-left lane funneled to a smaller, two-lane Highway 166. That highway snaked its way into Port Orchard. Caleb had bought a house there a few years back.

Russell had been over once, right after Caleb had bought it, but before he had moved in. He saw blank walls, a buffed hardwood floor, and a sturdy ceiling with exposed natural timber in the rafters. The open floor plan committed over half the total square footage of the house to the main area, which consisted of a smallish kitchen and a large living area, complete with a row of large windows that shot up from about two feet off the floor to just below the ceiling.

The view was absolutely breathtaking. Bremerton twinkled across the bay. Massive white and green WSDOT Ferries chugged along the calm waters, moving back and forth across the Sound. Russell had definitely felt a twinge of jealousy. He had left that day all smiles and well wishes on the outside but felt a bit angry at himself. If he had managed his money better, he could own something like that.

"What are you doing this weekend?" Russell asked, breaking the silence.

"Not much," Caleb replied. "Eat tacos. Read. Eat tacos. Work out. Eat tacos. Watch something on TV."

"And then eat more tacos?"

"Nah. I'm gonna switch to enchiladas."

"Quiet weekend, huh?"

"Except for the farting."

In truth, Caleb planned to drive out to Olympic National Park, trek out into the deep forest, strip naked, hide his clothing for later. Then make the Change.

Hunt something. Stalk it.

Kill it.

Highway signs announced the main exit for Gig Harbor. Just a few more miles to the toll bridge. The next signs announced the toll bridge exit was only one more mile. The highway split into multiple lanes, two going straight to the bridge and three that moved to the right and funneled traffic to the tollbooths.

Caleb signaled, changed lanes and pointed his Jeep at one of open tollbooths ahead. They slowed, stopped behind the car ahead of them.

Waiting his turn, Caleb's eyes drifted down to his arm. Illuminated only by the lights of the dashboard, he noticed the hairs on his hand and forearm appeared coarser than usual. He ran his tongue across his teeth. They felt sharper now than earlier in the day.

His control was dwindling. He had maybe a day or two more, that was all.

Caleb eased forward a few feet at a time until the Jeep pulled up beside the open booth window. The attendant was a Native

American woman in her mid-thirties, dark hair, dark luminous eyes, full lips, high cheekbones.

Attractive, Caleb thought as he rolled down his window. Sounds and smells bombarded his senses in a full-on assault. He wrinkled his nose and blinked, his eyes tearing up a bit.

The attendant smiled at him. "Six dollars, please."

Caleb handed her cash, then rolled up his window without waiting for a receipt. The green light showed. Caleb floored it, getting up to cruising speed. The Jeep veered gently left, then the lanes straightened out in the final approach to the Tacoma Narrows Bridge.

The bridge was enormous, a green monstrosity with three lanes heading into Tacoma, and four lanes heading back into Kitsap County. Affectionately known as "Galloping Gertie", she was designed to sway from side to side when buffeted by the side winds that could come barreling across the water at almost hurricane force, funneled into a relatively tight space by the high bluffs on both sides of the narrow strip of water.

Caleb checked his watch. "Does she know I'm coming?"

"I thought I'd surprise her." A mischievous grin flitted across Russell's lower face.

Caleb's eyebrows went up. "Something you're not telling me?"

"Nope."

They crested the top of the bridge and began a gentle descent towards the other side.

"Take exit 3."

Caleb cocked his head. "Point Defiance?"

"She's at the zoo."

"I thought she did biomedical research."

"The drug they're developing isn't ready for humans yet," Russell said. "They're working with animals. The zoo is working with Global BioTech. Guess they're looking for this drug's veterinary applications."

"Plus a big wad of cash from Global BioTech," Caleb spat, disapproving.

"Don't get your blood up," Russell cautioned. "Corporate partnership happens all the time. It's how things get done."

Caleb eased the car into the far-right lane. "Maybe."

"No maybes about it," Russell said as the Jeep exited the freeway and veered right. "They share the R&D costs now and share the royalties from the patents later."

"It always comes back to money, doesn't it?" Caleb tapped the brakes, stopping at an all-ways Stop sign at the bottom.

"Doesn't everything?" Russell asked, not understanding the bitterness in Caleb's voice.

"Left, or right?"

"Right."

Caleb cranked the wheel, his lips drawn tight. He hit the gas aggressively, gunning the engine and sending the big vehicle lurching forward. The resulting G-force pushed Russell back into the cushions of his seat.

"Good thing these seats have lumbar support," he quipped.

"Sorry," Caleb mumbled, reigning his emotions back under control.

Something in Caleb's voice alerted Russell. His eyes darted left as Caleb maneuvered the vehicle. Caleb's face seemed a shade darker. His beard seemed thicker now, with whiskers creeping upwards on his cheeks and down his neck and throat. But he knew Caleb shaved and trimmed his beard meticulously every day. So what was he seeing now? Russell looked out his own window and tried to shrug it off. It must just be a trick of the light, right?

Caleb and Russell pulled into Port Defiance Zoo parking lot. The rain had let up; wet pavement glittered under the lights. Already closed, about a dozen cars and trucks remained.

"There's Marla's car." Russell pointed to a Subaru Outback to the left. Caleb edged the Jeep in that direction. He parked in the stall next to her.

Caleb and Russell got out, their feet clomping onto the ground. Caleb pointed his key fob, pushed a tiny button. The Jeep went through its lockdown routine: doors clicked locked, lights briefly flashed, alarm chirped once. Then the vehicle went dark.

"This way," Russell said.

Caleb could have easily found the correct path on his own. He already smelled and heard the animals settling in for the night. But Marla was Russell's cousin; it was right to let him take point.

The dark, silent ticket booths loomed ahead. A shadow moved just inside the turnstiles. Russell did not see it, but Caleb did. His back straightened as the shadow coalesced. Man-sized, moving side to side. Soft sounds of a bristle brush. His nostrils flared, picked up the combined scent of sweat, cut grass, and antiperspirant.

Caleb relaxed.

The elderly custodian looked up as Russell and Caleb got closer. He stopped sweeping, leaned on his broom.

"Help you fellahs?"

"We're here to see somebody," Russell responded.

"We're closed 'til tomorrow. Most of the staff already gone home."

"We're looking for my cousin. She's working on the Global BioTech project."

The custodian's eyes widened in recognition. Obviously, everyone around here knew about "the BioTech project".

He reached for a key ring that hung heavy on his belt. It tugged his trousers down on that side. He yanked upwards, held the jingling ring up, began going through the dozen or so keys on the ring.

He inserted the key into a slot on his side of the turnstile, turned it a quarter turn. He stepped aside, lifted his arm towards the interior of the zoo grounds.

Russell stepped through the turnstile, the heavy aluminum bars turning one third of a turn. Caleb slipped through behind him. The custodian turned the key again one quarter of a turn in the opposite direction, locking the turnstile.

Russell and Caleb walked deeper into the dark grounds. Damp pavement reflected light from the occasional lamp strung over the trail. The air remained fragrant with the recent rainfall.

Sights, sounds, and smells bombarded Caleb's senses. His neurons rapid-fired information to his brain.

They walked past the lion enclosure. Two females and one large male sat in the grass. Their eyes locked on Russell and Caleb. Russell glanced their way, felt uncomfortable under their unblinking gaze. He reminded himself they could not get to him.

They came upon the gorilla enclosure. Russell paused, looked. Caleb stopped, knowing Russell had a particular affinity for these close relatives of *homo sapiens*. Within seconds, an enormous silverback male materialized out of the foliage and knuckle walked over to the glass that separated them. His movements leisurely and confident, he stopped inches from them, sat down.

Russell stood there in awe of the magnificent animal sitting quietly, separated by only a few inches of reinforced Plexiglas. His brow furrowed when he realized the great ape seemed to be either unaware or uninterested in Russell. No, all four hundred pounds of the silverback's, attention focused solely on Caleb.

Caleb seemed transfixed, trancelike. He slowly brought one hand up. The gorilla watched intently. Caleb slowly extended his arm out and gently placed the back of his hand, fingers curled, against the glass.

The gorilla looked Caleb in the eye, then looked down and away. He sighed, turned his head, then did something that Russell would remember forever. The great ape lifted his arm and tapped the back of his hand against his side of the glass precisely where Caleb's curled hand rested. The gorilla withdrew his hand, looked around, then looked back at Caleb, who had not moved. The ape tapped the glass again in the same manner. He lurched his mass to his left, moving away from them. He disappeared into the surrounding foliage.

Caleb blinked, let his hand drop to his side. He stepped back from the glass, the psychic connection broken.

"Caleb?" Russell asked. "You okay, buddy?"

"Fine. Why?"

"No reason."

Caleb knew the look in Russell's eyes. He knew something was not right tonight. They resumed walking. New smells assailed Caleb's olfactory senses. New, yet familiar.

"Where are we going?"

"The wolf enclosure."

Could this day get any more ironic?

The wolf enclosure lay at the end of the trail. The pack was outside, lazing the evening hours away. A female lay near the rear of the enclosure, nursing two pups. The rest of the pack lay about halfway towards the partition.

Russell and Caleb stopped.

"Where's Marla?"

"Inside working in the back."

"Let's go."

"Hold on a minute," Russell said. "Just look at them."

Caleb was looking at them, all right. Six in the pack, two females, four males. The alpha pair, larger, darker than the rest.

"Wolves get a bad rap," Russell stated, oblivious to Caleb's plight. "Look at them. Magnificent creatures. Keenly intelligent, at one with their environment. Protective of their young."

Caleb's forehead glistened with sweat. What Russell was droning on about?

"They're not wantonly violent, not the bloodthirsty killers of myth and legend." Caleb looked at his friend when Russell said this. "Did you know that if a parent dies, the rest of the pack raises the pups?"

The pups still nursed near the back of the enclosure. All other activity had stopped. The adult wolves stared at Caleb as if Russell did not exist. Caleb bobbed his head almost imperceptibly, then stepped to the safety rail.

The largest male, the alpha, stood to his feet. He sniffed the air, padded unhurriedly down the slope towards the safety glass. Caleb squatted, dropped his head to the same level as the alpha's. Each still on their respective sides, Caleb and the alpha stared at each other, saying nothing, but communicating, nonetheless.

Caleb cocked his head slightly, pulled back. The alpha did not respond. Caleb ducked his head slightly, looked down and away to the left. The alpha licked his lips and emitted a yawn. Caleb's eyes remained down. The alpha turned, lifted his tail, and dug with his hind paws, similar to a human wiping his feet. Then the alpha climbed the gentle slope back to the center of the enclosure. Only then did he turn and look back at Caleb.

"Caleb? You don't look so good."

Caleb stood and wiped sweat from his pasty forehead.

"Let's find Marla."

CHAPTER FOUR

Attached to the back of the enclosure and hidden from the public, the handler's area was where the work happened. It looked like a cross between veterinarian's office and industrial workspace. Blazing fluorescent lights overhead, concrete floor below. Reinforced cinderblock walls. The builders had spared every expense.

Several metal tables stood arranged end to end, rows laid out about the room. Each table boasted nylon straps and Velcro restraints, sterile medical instruments in sealed packages, and a circular operating light overhead, which hung on a swing arm.

The room crackled with tension. Marla, along with the two handlers, stood clustered in a small knot near the far side of the room. Their eyes were locked onto a huge black wolf. Backed into the corner and frightened, the wolf growled and snapped its teeth. Its head dipped down, level with its shoulders, ears flat against its gigantic head.

"Okay, guys," Marla said, "let's try once more. Get him back into his cage."

Two handlers flanked her on each side. Each grasped a long pole with a nylon loop on the end, and a control mechanism near them to cinch the noose. They glanced at each other, each looking to the other to take the lead.

Ron, young and pale, with blonde hair and frightened blue eyes, was barely out of college. Twenty-three years old; this was his first fulltime job. Was I ever that young? Marla wondered.

Ty stood ready on the other side, frustrated and impatient. Six foot two and over two hundred forty pounds. Middle aged, getting a gut, a foreboding presence. His substandard performance evals told the story. He had worked here for fifteen years, never applied anywhere else. He had never been promoted. Not once.

That told Marla everything she needed to know about Ty. What she did not understand is why she had been saddled with a sullen slug like him.

Ty huffed. "I got this." He surged forward, pole out on front of him. The wolf surged forward himself, lashing out furiously, all claws, teeth, and muscle.

"Fuck!" Ty backpedaled.

"Serves you right," Marla threw at him.

"Fuuuuck you, bitch."

The wolf stood his ground, tired, frightened, chest heaving, in a defensive stance. His front feet spread wide in front of him. He was massive, close to one hundred fifty pounds. Enormous for a wolf. His iridescent yellow eye glowed against black fur. Gray hair sprinkled his muzzle, the top of his head, ran the length of his spine.

"I will report this," Marla warned.

"You won't do shit."

"If she doesn't, I will," came a disembodied voice.

All eyes whipped around behind them, where the deep masculine voice had originated. Caleb stood there, jaw clenched, mouth pressed shut, trying to control his temper. Russell was walking up from behind.

"What did you say, asshole?"

"You heard me."

Ty stared at Caleb, trying to assess if this guy was for real, or full of shit.

"Why don't you come fucking do it?"

The faintest hint of a snarl pulled one side of Caleb's lip upward into a curl, then it was gone. His gaze moved off Ty, whom he knew was all bark and no bite, and settled on the huge male wolf.

Their eyes met.

Ty looked at Caleb, then at the wolf, then back to Caleb. "Who are you? Doctor Fucking Doolittle?"

Caleb never took his eyes off the wolf. He stepped forward, stiff-arming Ty in the chest. "Out of my way," he growled. Ty staggered back, regained his footing. Wincing, he rubbed his chest.

Damn, Ty thought. That guy's stronger than he looks.

The wolf's facial muscles relaxed. His lips dropped back down, covering his teeth. He was interested in this strange newcomer. He sniffed the air and watched Caleb.

Caleb inched forward slowly, careful to not make any sudden moves. His body language projected calm, confidence. He cocked his head slightly to one side. He bent his knees, going into a smooth crouch, squatting on his haunches. He extended his arm, carefully, fingers curled, the back of his hand towards the beast in a form of greeting.

The old male sniffed the air between them, his fear gone. But fifteen thousand years of instinct hardwired into his DNA dictated caution. He moved one paw forward, then another, watching the newcomer, ready to retreat.

The humans in the room tensed as the wolf inched closer to Caleb's outstretched hand. The wild canine sniffed again, this time his muzzle inches from Caleb's outstretched paw. He sniffed again, this time the tip of his nose touched Caleb's hand. The wolf licked his lips, stood alert, ears perked high, tail out behind him.

Calm. Confident.

Caleb gently moved his curled hand downward, until his knuckles pressed flat against the concrete flooring. He dropped his gaze from the wolf's eyes, moved his eyes to the right, acknowledging the wolf's dominance.

The wolf stepped forward on thickly padded paws, claws clacking on the concrete floor. His muzzle filled with sharp teeth hovered mere inches from Caleb's exposed face. Then he licked Caleb's nose and cheek.

Caleb closed his eyes, the kinship engulfing him. He inclined his head, moving his cheek up and down against the wolf's face. He brought his arms up and around, embracing him, pulling him in closer. The wolf sat, rested his head on Caleb's shoulder. He closed his eyes and whimpered, thumped his tail. Caleb stroked the top of his head, scratched velvety ears. One of the wolf's front paws raised and reached out, rested on Caleb's shoulder.

Marla was flummoxed. She had never seen anything like this. The wolf was hugging him! She stood there, eyes wide, mouth open.

Russell was even more confused. Adding this to the events at the gorilla cage and the wolf enclosure, his disquiet grew. He was starting to wonder just how well he really knew his friend.

Tears streamed down Caleb's face. This was the purest love he had felt in a long time. He clucked his tongue softly against the roof of his mouth. The wolf rubbed the side of his face against Caleb's cheek again.

Caleb finally pulled away, looked into the wolf's glowing eyes. He smiled, dipped his head slightly. He stroked the wolf on both sides of his ribs. The wolf licked his face again. Caleb looked beyond the wolf to the open cage in the corner. He looked back to the wolf, ticked his head in the cage's direction.

The wolf followed Caleb's gaze to the cage. He made a sound, something between a whimper and a growl. Caleb sensed the animal's tension rising. He clucked his tongue again, regaining the wolf's attention. He stroked the beast's head again, then ticked his head towards the cage once more.

The wolf padded over to the cage. He hesitated at the door, then stepped inside. He turned around three times, then lay down. Ron closed and secured the door. The wolf growled, just a reaction to the fear he smelled on the human. He did not snap at Ron's fingers. As Ron stepped back, the wolf lay still, glowering at everyone.

For a moment, the only sound in the room was the medium-pitched hum of the electrical current flowing through the lights overhead. It was faint, ambient noise filtered out by the human brain as just so much background. But everyone noticed it now.

Caleb rose to his feet and exhaled softly. He ran sweaty palms down the front of his shirt.

Russell was the first to speak. "Caleb? What did we just see?"

"The power of love and compassion to overcome fear." He glared at Ty with blazing eyes. "You have no business working here."

Ty bristled. "Yeah? Who the fuck are you?"

"Someone who understands this creature better than you."

"Maybe I'll just bust you in the chops. How about that?"

Caleb shifted slightly, squared his shoulders towards Ty. Hands at his sides, eyes unwavering, feet shoulder width apart.

"Come get some."

"What?"

"You heard me."

The gauntlet had just been thrown down. "Somebody needs to teach you some manners."

"I'm waiting."

The moment hung, tension twisting in the air once more. Even the exhausted wolf watched from inside his cage. The silence was in danger of becoming deafening.

Russell's phone rang, piercing the silence, needles to the ears. Caleb winced. One hand instinctively moved up to the side of his head. Russell fumbled in his pocket, pulled the blaring phone out. He pushed a button, threw an apologetic look to everyone as he stepped away.

"You gonna do something?" Caleb asked. Ty gave no response. "I thought not."

Caleb moved diagonally to walk around Ty. Ty grunted and threw a punch, hoping to catch Caleb off guard.

Big mistake.

Caleb ducked fluidly under the arcing fist. Moving in a blur, Caleb growled and grabbed Ty by the throat with one hand. He shoved Ty backwards, slammed him painfully into the cinderblock wall. He pushed upwards, lifting Ty's bulk off the floor with one arm.

"Ty."

Caleb's baritone voice rumbled from somewhere deep within his chest. The single syllable sounded like it had originated inside a well. Human vocal cords had nothing to do with it. Ty opened his eyes, which were squeezed shut in pain.

Caleb stood below him, holding him aloft. His eyes were aglow, an amber yellow not so different from that of the male wolf. His nose seemed wider now. Flat. His beard seemed heavier. He grinned up at Ty. His teeth were longer now, sharper.

The teeth of a carnivore.

Ty's guts turned to liquid. His bowels spasmed involuntarily. He soiled his pants right then and there.

Satisfied, Caleb dropped him, stepped back. He was wearing new shoes, after all.

Ty hit the ground hard, flat on his feet. Pain shot upwards from foot to hip. Knees buckled. He went down hard on his ass, his excrement now pancaked flat within his trousers. The odor was overwhelming.

Marla's plugged her nose. "Jesus Christ, Ty."

"It's all his fault," Ty pointed at Caleb, his eyes brimming with tears at his total and complete humiliation, his emasculation as a man. "I'm gonna kick your ass!"

Caleb turned his back, shunning him.

"Something crawled up your ass and *died,*" Ron said.

Ty ignored Ron, his eyes still on Caleb's back. "You were lucky today."

"You'll be lucky to have a job come Monday morning," Marla interjected. "I *will* be speaking to the Director about this."

Ty pulled himself up. He held both hands behind him, under the soiled seat of his pants. "If it hadn't been for this asshole, this never would have happened."

"If it hadn't been for him, that wolf would have ripped your guts out."

"Go," Caleb said over his shoulder, still turned away. "Your stench is offensive to me."

"This isn't over," Ty shouted.

"Pray that it is." His words cut like shards of ice.

"I'll be seeing you." Ty backed away, moving towards the back exit. "Real soon."

"Pray that you don't."

Ty threw Caleb a poisonous look, which was all he could do. The wolf yawned as Ty left, then sneezed at the lingering odor.

Marla looked over her shoulder. Russell was still on the phone; Ron was busy minding his own business. She noticed the dopey, shit-eating grin on his face from seeing Ty finally get his comeuppance. Smiling a bit herself, she looked at Caleb. She noticed no trace of the creature Ty had come so close to seeing.

"Wow," she said.

"What?"

"What do mean, what? This," she gestured. "That. All of it."

Caleb shrugged, casually, as if this type of thing happened every day. "I'm just glad we didn't have to fight."

"You would have torn him apart."

Yes, he thought. I would have. In front of all of you.

"What was that with Sampson?" She gestured towards the wolf.

"Fitting name."

"He should have eaten your face off."

"That sounds painful."

"You're avoiding my questions."

"Am I?"

Marla appraised him analytically. Mysterious. Hiding something. And why did he have to be so damned handsome?

Russell finished his call. He stabbed the END button, quivering with excitement. He turned towards Marla and Caleb, grinning from ear to ear. His unease from earlier was completely gone.

Caleb grinned. "He looks like the cat that ate the canary."

"That was the police. They want me to consult on this serial killer case!" Russell could barely contain his excitement.

"Marvelous," Caleb said.

"Yeah. Congrats, cousin," Marla said. "When do you start?"

"Right now. They're sending a car to get me. I won't be able to make dinner tonight."

Stunned silence. Marla's mouth dropped open. She looked awkwardly back and forth between Russell and Caleb.

Caleb picked up on this. "No problem," he said. "I'll take Marla to dinner."

Marla stole another glance towards Caleb. Their eyes connected. What she saw there warmed her.

Russell clapped his hands together. "Well. It looks like I won't be missed, eh?"

Still grinning ear to ear, Russell spun on his heel. Buoyed by his own exuberance, Russell floated towards the door. With his hand on the handle, he turned.

"Have fun you two." He opened the door. "Don't do anything I wouldn't do," he added. "And that means the sky's the limit." The door clanged back shut, leaving both Marla and Caleb staring at it, each thinking Russell might pop back in to pitch another witticism their way.

Seconds ticked by. Russell was not coming back.

Awkward.

"Shall we?" Caleb asked.

Marla looked around the room, making sure everything was as it should be. Sampson still lay in his cage. Ron was scribbling on a form secured to a clipboard.

"Ron? I'm outta here."

"Okay, Doc," Ron said, not looking up from what he was doing.

"Have a good weekend."

He nodded as he continued to scribble. "Yeah, you too." Perfunctory, not really paying attention, intent on finishing up so he could go home himself. Caleb heard the scratching of the pencil on the paper.

"Nice to meet you," Caleb called out.

Ron looked up, stopped scribbling. "Yeah, you too."

Marla and Caleb moved towards the door. He glanced at the tables as he went by, wondering how many animals had been cared for on them over the years. They paused at the door. Caleb grabbed the handle, pressed down, held the door open. Marla smiled as she passed through first.

Caleb met Sampson's gaze, ticked his head. Small, subtle. But Sampson saw it, twitched his ears in response. Then the door closed as Caleb and Sampson bade each other silent farewells.

CHAPTER FIVE

Caleb and Marla walked down the pathway, close but not touching. The animals they passed alerted and watched at Caleb. They sensed they were in the presence of an apex predator the likes of which they had never seen.

Of course, Marla noticed nothing. But Caleb, a creature most primal, noticed everything. Bombarded by sounds and smells, Caleb's head swam, threatening full-blown vertigo.

He had to make the Change sometime in the next 24 hours. Maybe he could sneak off later tonight. Get out to the forests --

"Sorry," he spoke. "Did you say something?"

"I said it's a lovely night."

"Yes."

"I love the night," Marla said. "It's peaceful, quiet."

Caleb nodded. "Tranquil."

"Tranquil," Marla repeated. She nodded and smiled. "I like that."

The animal enclosures were behind them now. The front gates stood in the distance, obscured by fog off the Sound.

The gate solidified as they approached. Caleb, ever the gentleman, held the gate for Marla. He noticed the tic of her eyebrows and the look of satisfaction as she moved past.

She likes a man with manners. Good to know.

He stepped through, closing the gate behind him.

"What are you hungry for?" Marla asked.

That's a loaded question, he thought. "Well, I'm a fiend for fried chicken."

"I know just the place. I'll get my car. You follow me."

They moved towards their respective vehicles. Caleb could still hear the zoo animals in the distance. The sounds were faint, yet still distinct. An elephant trumpeted just then.

Marla felt relieved to put some physical distance between herself and Caleb. His manner and his masculinity had impressed her. There were a couple of moments when it was all she could do to keep from throwing her arms around him and showering him with soft wet kisses. The attraction was strong. Purely lust, animal magnetism.

She was fine with that.

She got to her car door, looked across the rooftop to him at his Jeep. She took stock: broad muscular shoulders, tapered torso, narrow waist, tight ass, legs like tree trunks. She assumed six-pack abs. She wondered if she would get to confirm that.

She unlocked her door, slid into the driver's seat, tossed her purse onto the passenger seat. She buckled her seat belt and peered through the passenger window. The Jeep's door was already open, and he was climbing inside.

Inside his Jeep, Caleb sighed. He was already squashing the Change. Now he was going to fight the impulse to pull Marla's clothes off and make love to her for hours.

Primal lust was powerful but distracting.

Human instinct dictated coupling, reproducing, continuing the bloodline. And the nature of the Beast was to do so prodigiously, promiscuously, with impunity.

But there was no true impunity. Every act produced consequences. Some were expected, even desired. Some were not. Even taking no action was an action.

Caleb was responsible for his actions, and their consequences. He did not want to harm, frighten, or offend Marla, and he certainly had no desire to give Russell a reason to be pissed. He needed to walk a fine line tonight.

Caleb slid his key into the ignition, turned clockwise. The engine growled in response. He flipped on his headlights. Intersecting yellow pools illuminated the space in front of him. Gray mist danced on the air, reflecting like tiny bits of glass.

He gazed left at Marla's car. She had not cranked her engine up yet. He waited, engine idling under the hood.

Seconds ticked past. He saw her insert her keys, turn them. The engine did not start up. Something was wrong. A moment later, Marla's headlights snapped on, then off.

Caleb killed his engine, slid out of his Jeep. He walked around the front of her car. Her window was already down.

"It won't start."

"Pop the hood." He moved to the front of the car.

She did. He found the spring-loaded mechanism at the center, moved it, lifted the hood skyward. He pulled out his phone and hit his flashlight app. He checked the battery connections. They were tight.

"Go ahead and try to start it."

He heard her keys turn and heard a persistent clicking sound coming from the back of the engine compartment.

"Okay. Stop." He brought the hood back down, dropped it gently into place. He walked around to her side of the car.

"Your starter has gone out."

"Where am I going to find a mechanic this time of night on a Friday?"

"You won't. Best thing is to call tomorrow."

"But what about tonight?"

"Leave it here. Security will keep an eye on it."

"But--"

"There's nothing to do about it now," Caleb stated. "Let's enjoy the evening. You gotta feed, right?"

Marla had never heard it phrased that way. Caleb stepped back in anticipation of her car door swinging open. She got out, locked her door. He led her to his Jeep's passenger door, held it open as she climbed in. He closed the door, walked around to his side. He felt her eyes on him all the way.

He hauled himself into the driver's seat and buckled up. He cranked the engine, and it roared to life. They crossed the parking lot, turned into the street.

"You said you wanted chicken?" Marla asked.

"Yep."

"Just keep going straight."

Caleb obeyed.

Five minutes and two red lights later, Marla pointed to a restaurant. "Up here. On the right."

Caleb put on his blinker, slowed, and turned. They entered a narrow parking lot. He spied an empty parking stall, pulled in. They got out and strode towards the front door. Caleb grasped the handle, pulled the door open as Marla slipped through first.

It was not a conscious gesture, Marla realized. No virtue signaling, no act. He just did it. Like he would have done it anyway, no matter what. Just part of who he was.

The place was a retro-style diner adorned in vintage décor. The hostess greeted them with a smile on her face and menus in her hand. She guided them to a cozy booth. Caleb paused, allowing Marla to pick which side she preferred. She chose to sit with her back to the entrance.

Caleb felt relieved. With his back to the wall, he had an unobstructed view of the entrance, the entire dining area, and the kitchen entrance/exit to his left. He could see the drink fountain at a small wooden podium in the middle of the room, and the cash register near the main entrance. The only thing Caleb could not see from his were the bathrooms.

Nature of the beast, he thought. Maintain situational awareness.

The hostess handed each of them a menu. "Your server will be right over." With that, she moved quickly back towards the front.

They opened their menus, scanned the offerings. Caleb located the fried chicken plate almost at once. He closed the menu.

Marla's eyes looked up over the top of her menu. "That was fast."

"I hate it when women tell me that," Caleb mumbled under his breath. The comment had been impulsive, past his lips before he realized it. Dread locked him rigid.

Marla stared at him with huge, disbelieving eyes. *Did he really just say that?* Then she burst out laughing. "Oh my God, I can't believe you just said that." Then she dissolved into laughter once more.

Caleb sat there, ears burning. He blew a deep breath out.

"That's a hell of an ice breaker," Marla said.

"Caleb said. "It just slipped out."

"That's what she said," Marla responded, winking at him.

Caleb tilted his head back and laughed uproariously, his whole body shaking with mirth. Marla joined in. They were going to get along just fine.

Their server appeared beside their booth and took their order. Caleb ordered fried chicken. Marla ordered a tuna melt and sweet potato fries. The server scribbled notes on her pad, then walked away.

"So," Marla said, "tell me how you did that."

"Did what?"

"Earlier tonight with Sampson."

"Oh," Caleb waved his hand. "We understood each other."

"That's what I mean."

The smile faded completely from Caleb's face. This was not a topic he wanted to revisit. Then he sat back, casual, as if he didn't have a care in the world. That unguarded moment had been brief, just a fraction of a second, really. But Marla had seen it.

"I have a way with animals."

"If Sampson was a dog, I'd buy that. But he's a wolf. Born in the wild, raised in a pack, not captured until after he was an adult. He's dangerous to work with."

"Didn't seem dangerous to me."

"Sampson's a creature God never meant to be tamed. You had him licking your face."

Caleb raised his eyebrows and shrugged.

"He damn near chewed Ty's face off."

"Ty got what he deserved."

"No argument from me. I meant it when I said he won't have a job come Monday." She paused. "But we're not talking about Ty."

"We're not?"

"There you go again."

The server reappeared and placed their drinks in front of them. She then spun around again, her ponytail whipping around behind her as she pranced off.

Caleb sipped iced tea, grateful for the interruption. She wasn't going to let this go. Easy, he told himself. One question at a time. Dodge, duck, bob and weave. Talk, but don't really say anything.

"Wolves are sensitive animals, "Caleb said at last. "Like dogs and children, they pick up on the emotions of others. I approached in a calm, confident posture. He reacted accordingly."

"That's your explanation?" She picked up her glass. "Well that must be it then."

Caleb's ears twitched. Her vocal inflection belied her words. She had a mind like a steel trap. She wasn't believing a word he said, but she was willing to let it go – for now.

The server came back balancing a tray that looked like the world's largest frisbee. Two steaming plates of food sat atop it. She deftly placed the Tuna Melt with Sweet Potato Fries in front of Marla. Without skipping a beat, she slid Caleb's fried chicken plate directly in front of him.

"Anything else I can get for you?"

Caleb looked at Marla a beat. "No, I think we're good for now."

"I'll check back in a little while." She retreated, leaving Caleb and Marla to their meal.

"Saved by the bell?" Marla grinned.

Caleb looked clueless.

"Never mind. Let's eat while it's hot."

Marla picked up a fry with delicate fingers, popped it into her mouth. Though looking at her food, she watched Caleb. This habit of evaluating men on first dates went all the way back to high school. She had perfected her technique in college. She was so practiced at it, she felt supremely confident he did not realize she was studying him.

Caleb was fully aware she was watching him. She was studying his movements and demeanor, attempting to gain insight.

His mashed potatoes sported a crater in the middle, formed by a cook's ladle and filled with chicken gravy. It looked like a tiny white volcano containing pale lava. He stirred the gravy in, tasted his peas. He then sat his fork on the plate, picked up a chicken thigh. He bit deep, almost to the bone. He held the meat motionless, turned his head to the side, rending flesh from bone in one deft movement.

Marla bit into her sandwich, watched as Caleb flipped the thigh around, bit, and rent another chunk of flesh off the bone with a twist of his head. He smiled rapturously as he chewed.

The man was most definitely a carnivore.

A sharp *CHIRP!* Sounded, piercing the calm. The chirp rapidly repeated. Merciless, the staccato of machine gun fire. Caleb dropped his chicken and grunted, wincing in pain.

Caught off guard, it took Marla a second or two to recognize her ringtone. She plunged her hand into her purse, pulled the phone out. Caleb looked like he was coming down with a migraine.

"Sorry." She slid out of the booth, pushed the talk button and walked away.

The headache and vertigo would pass soon. This had occurred so many times, Caleb could predict how long until the pain subsided.

Caleb turned his attention back to his plate. He really did love mashed potatoes and gravy.

Enjoy every moment.

Standing near the hostess station, Marla put the phone to her ear. "Russell," she greeted. "The police already done with you?"

"No." Russell's voice sounded strained, like someone had replaced his vocal cords with a rusty gate hinge.

"Russell, what's wrong? You sick?"

"Not yet," he replied. It sounded like he was gargling phlegm.

"What's wrong?"

"You need to meet me at the police station."

"What for?"

"I've seen the evidence, all of it, even the stuff they're holding back from the press."

"They're holding something back?"

"Yes, and I agree with their actions."

"Okay," she said. Why was every man she talked to tonight insist on talking in riddles?

"Certain... patterns are emerging." Russell's voice cracked.

"That's a good thing, right? Haven't you told me before that patterns of behavior are how you profile these sickos?"

"Yeah, but this is different. The particular pattern that's emerging, whatever's out there doing this..."

"Russell. Spit it out."

"Marla, I don't think the killer is human."

She looked across the restaurant and froze, eyes glazing over in disbelief. No, that can't be right. Then she remembered she was on the phone with Russell.

"I'll be there as soon as I can."

She ended the call, dropped her hand to her side. She never took her eyes off what she was seeing.

Across the restaurant, oblivious to her, Caleb Jacobson attacked his dinner. He held his prey, the fried chicken, motionless a few inches off the plate. He lowered his head, bit the meat, twist upward, ripping it clean from the bone.

Like a predator devouring his kill.

CHAPTER SIX

Russell Slater sat on a bare silver metal stool. His insides roiled. The pervasive smell of bleach and isopropyl alcohol exacerbated his queasiness.

"I hate morgues." He noticed that the floor tiles matched the wall tiles that covered the lower four feet of the walls. The rest faded to a dull "seafoam green", but in reality, it had no color at all.

Dr. Miriam Melendez shifted on her stool. She was a forensic psychiatrist, not a medical examiner. Instead of wearing scrubs, she dressed in a muted black business suit jacket, white shirt underneath, and heels. She craned her neck, looking up at the stark lighting beating down from above, bathing everything with glaring efficiency.

Any other time, Russell would be ogling her shapely legs or trim waistline. But not tonight. After what he had seen, he was just a frightened middle-aged man with no clue what to do next.

"It's been a while since I've seen someone torn up like that," Miriam said at last.

The main autopsy table squatted patiently behind them. A white plastic sheet covered something underneath.

"We all worked with cadavers in medical school, of course," she continued. "But that was different. Every incision, every deflection was performed rationally, surgically following established protocols." She wrapped her arms around her chest, hugging herself. "But these poor souls were practically skinned alive."

Russell said, "This is something out of a Goddamned horror movie."

Miriam stood, paced slowly. Her heels drilled a dull staccato that echoed back off the walls. Russell decided he hated that sound.

"The whole department's spooked," she said. "Even the detectives won't come down here alone."

"I don't blame them."

She turned, her hair swinging around behind her. Dark eyes, wide with fear. "It's an extremely volatile situation," she said. "Cops are nervous. They don't know who or what to look for. Some of them have itchy trigger fingers."

"With all the shit they have to deal with already, now they have to contend with this," Russell said.

The room fell silent. Russell sat where he was, shoulders hunched, hands trembling. Miriam continued pacing.

The black wall phone rang, making them both jump. Miriam grabbed it. For just an instant, Russell thought he saw a hint of anger in her eyes.

"Dr. Melendez speaking." She listened. "We'll wait here." She hung up the phone, turned to Russell. "Your friends are on their way."

Russell stayed on his stool. Miriam continued pacing. Seconds ticked by.

The morgue door opened, swung inward. A uniformed police officer escorted Marla and Caleb inside. Russell stood, greeted them. Introductions were made as the police officer silently exited, closing the door behind her.

Miriam shook Marla's hand. "Thank you for coming."

"Anything I can do to help."

Caleb's senses came under assault the moment he walked in. Glaring lights pierced like icepicks through his skull. Bleach and disinfectants pummeled his nostrils. He rubbed the back of one fist with the palm of his other hand, an old nervous habit. His nose pulled his head towards the autopsy table.

This was not where he wanted to be.

A 60ish balding black man entered the morgue, spectacles resting low on his nose. He tilted his head back to see through them, giving the impression he was looking down his nose at the entire world. He wore black pleated slacks, black oxford shoes, white oxford shirt, colorful necktie. His unzipped lab smock flapped behind him as he walked. Embroidered above the left breast pocket read CURTIS MILLER, M.D.

"I've asked Dr. Miller to bring us all up to speed," Miriam said.

Miller cleared his throat. "First of all, let me be clear: everything you see and hear does not leave this room."

Marla and Caleb both nodded their understanding. Miller pursed his lips. "When I'm done, you'll understand why."

This morgue, like every morgue everywhere, was kept at around 60 degrees. Cadavers were stored inside refrigeration units regulated to 42 degrees. This retarded bacterial growth and the associated odors. Those were easy to discount.

What alarmed Caleb was something else entirely. Something old.

Something ancient.

Something darker than man's worst nightmares, an evil brought forth from the black and bloody pits of hell itself. And like the smell of death, he was also well acquainted with this.

No way around it. The stench emanated from the autopsy table, from the ravaged corpse lying beneath the plastic shroud. Distinctive, unmistakable.

Now, Caleb was certain.

His heart sank.

Why was everyone else so damned calm? Couldn't they smell it too? How could they not smell it, even with their stunted human senses? Didn't they realize what the fuck was actually going on?

Caleb's hands. Fingernails longer, darker. Pointed. With supreme effort, Caleb remained outwardly calm. If he did not get himself under control – *FAST!* – no one else would walk out alive. Wet stains darkened his shirt under his armpits.

Miller moved to a corner of the room set up for briefings. A wooden podium stood in the center, complete with a laptop, and a half dozen chairs facing it, a blank white wall behind it. Miriam, Russell, Marla, and Caleb followed him. They sat down while Miller edged behind the podium.

"What we have here," Miller began, "is a series of particularly gruesome murders, committed across multiple law enforcement jurisdictions. In all of cases, death was practically instantaneous. Cause of Death was hypovolemic shock, secondary to massive tissue loss, and rapid exsanguination."

Miller pushed a key on the laptop. The wall behind him came alive with an image of an attractive Latina dressed in business clothes, smiling for the camera. "This is Roberta Sanchez," Miller said. "Forty-four-year-old mother of three. Worked as a paralegal at a small firm north of Pioneer Square. She's the second known victim. We believe the first was a homeless man."

Miller pressed another key. The smiling headshot was replaced by a mangled mass of bone and blood atop the autopsy table. The juxtaposition was so abrupt, so jarring, it was difficult to believe this shapeless pile of viscera had ever been a living creature.

Miller turned to the image, used a small laser pointer. A bouncing red dot came to rest on a particular portion of the image.

"Note the puncture wounds and deep lacerations. All have jagged edges with an accompanying rending, a tearing of flesh with extensive damage to the subcutaneous tissue and underlying fascia." The doctor turned to his tiny audience. "This indicates the weapon used was considerably duller than say, a surgeon's scalpel of a sharp knife. The sheer power required to inflict this kind of damage," Miller paused, shook his head in awe, "is almost incomprehensible. What you see here are the only body parts recovered."

Marla sat stoically, examining the photo, her hand held delicately across her mouth. Her eyes were big and bright.

"What do you mean, 'only body parts recovered'?" Marla asked.

Miller looked sheepish. "There were body parts missing," he explained. "Limbs torn off, taken away. Some of them may have been... well, chewed off."

"*Chewed off?*" Marla exclaimed.

Miller nodded. "Some of the internal organs were taken."

"Taken where?" Caleb asked.

Miller paused, looking uncomfortable with the question, like he knew the truth would be insufficient.

"We don't know."

"Perhaps they were eaten," Caleb suggested.

"Eaten?" Russell echoed. "You mean, cannibalism?"

"Why would you propose that?" Miller suddenly seemed keenly interested in Caleb.

"Because it makes sense."

Dr. Miller's seemed pleased. "Indeed, it does."

Miller pushed a key on his laptop. The image immediately changed to a closer view of Roberta Sanchez's abdominal cavity. The cavity gaped open, ripped asunder by unfathomable shearing forces.

The liver, both kidneys, and pancreas were missing

"Upon closer examination, we found what appear to be teeth marks of a large predator," Miller stated. "We also found traces of a clear liquid which we believe to be saliva smeared in all of the victims. Laboratory analysis is still pending."

"Sexual trauma?" Russell asked.

Miller pointed to regions on the wall image with his laser pointer. "No evidence of external sexual trauma to the vulva." He moved his pointer. "The uterus, as you see, is still intact, as is the right fallopian tube and ovary." The red dot moved again. "The left fallopian tube and ovary are gone. We believe this was incidental, secondary to the removal of the other organs."

"Were any of the male victims castrated, sexually mutilated?"

"No."

Miller pressed his favorite computer key again. The wall image changed from a crime scene photo to that of an X-ray. "This is a cross-sectional view of the wound you just saw. What makes this X-ray significant is in what we don't see."

Everyone stared at the image, all shades of black, white, and grays. Denser structures, like bones, showed a pale gray. Gas-filled hollow organs like the stomach and the intestines, showed up darker.

"A blade forged from the hardest steel and honed to the sharpest edge dulls minutely every time it is used. It leaves tiny particles behind." Dr. Miller glanced over his shoulder at them. "This is why we have to sharpen our kitchen knives from time to time." He returned his attention to the X-ray. "These dense particles light up like candles on X-ray." Miller wielded his red dot pointer, punctuating his words. "There should be clusters of bright white in the tissue and along the bone. But there is no indication of that here."

"Maybe whatever did this didn't hit the bone?" Russell asked.

"Oh, it hit bone," Dr. Miller said with authority. He turned back to the image. "The traumatic forces at work here go in this direction, from outside in, at a sixty-degree angle. There are nicks to the ribs here, here, and here." The red dot bounced from detail to detail. "It even scratched the lumbar vertebrae here and here." He turned off his pointer, turned back to his audience. "No metallic fragments."

Marla leaned forward now. "I think I understand why I'm here," she said.

"Something to add, Dr. Moreno?"

"I work in biotech, but I'm a zoologist by training. I worked on the Serengeti Wildlife Preserve in Zambia for three years."

"And?"

"We had trouble with poachers from time to time. But poaching is a deadly business when what you're hunting can hunt you back."

She paused. "Sometimes the poachers were killed by lions, hyenas, leopards. The wounds, the signs of predation – this is quite similar."

Are you suggesting a lion did this?" Miriam asked, incredulous.

"No," Marla replied coolly. "I'm saying someone is going to a lot of trouble to make this look like an animal attack."

Miriam glanced at Russell, who only shrugged. Then she looked to Dr. Miller, whose face was unreadable.

"Why would someone do that?"

"Perhaps to throw the police off the scent."

"Sounds reasonable to me," Caleb said. He had decided he did not like Miriam very much.

"Excuse me, sir, but who precisely are you?"

"Caleb Jacobson," he answered. "I was with Marla when she got the call. Her car is in the shop, so... here I am."

"You shouldn't be here," Miriam said.

"I can personally vouch for Caleb," Russell spoke up.

Miriam looked at him, eyes wide. "Really?"

"Yes," Russell replied, his gaze steady. "Really."

A thinly built Hispanic man quietly entered the room from the back. Short, standing only about five foot six, probably around 140 pounds dripping wet. Thick hair cut short, a moustache on a smooth, handsome face.

Aware of him immediately, Caleb sensed him before he saw him.

The Hispanic man held the door for a six-foot Caucasian woman, broad shouldered, athletically built. She strode into the room.

Dr. Miller noticed them. "Ah, detectives. Please join us."

The two officers approached. They wore conservative clothing, badges hanging from clips on their belts. Jackets concealed powerful firearms worn in shoulder holsters.

"This is Detective Sergeant Sandra Akin, and her partner Detective Jose Martinez." Each detective nodded in turn when their name was called. "They are the lead investigators on the case. Sergeant Akin is Seattle PD, and Detective Martinez is Tacoma PD."

"We're building a multiagency Task Force," Akin announced. "We're grateful for any insight."

"The national news media is running with the story now," Martinez added. "The cable outlets are covering it twenty-four seven, and we're getting pressure from the higher ups."

"We have to build an airtight case so when we make an arrest, we get a conviction," Akin said.

"And right now, we've got *nada*," Martinez said. "No witnesses, no surveillance footage, no clues that make any sense." He glanced at the X-ray image. "This makes the Manson murders look like amateur hour."

Caleb zeroed in on this. "Interesting point."

"Huh?"

"You compared this to the Manson murders from back in the sixties," Caleb said.

"So?"

"What if these murders here are not the only ones like this?" Caleb asked. "What if there have been other murders with similar methodology?"

Akin and Martinez were still not getting it.

"Other murders, other cities, other countries, other time periods?" Caleb explained.

"We can only deal with what's in front of us," Akin said diplomatically.

"And if you concentrate on that to the exclusion of all else, you'll miss the big picture. And maybe you miss the chance to nail whoever is doing this."

Akin and Martinez looked at each other, then back to Caleb. "You really think some kind of historical correlation exists?"

"I won't know until I look."

"And you can do this?"

"I'm a historian," Caleb said. "Historical research is kinda what I do."

"What do you think?" Akin asked Martinez.

"Can't hurt. Might help."

"Then it's settled," Caleb interjected before Akin could say no.

A phone beeped. Akin dug into her pants pocket, extracted her cell phone. She looked at the caller ID.

"I have to take this." She put the phone to her ear and turned away from the group. She spoke in hushed tones. Martinez craned his head, trying to listen in. Caleb concentrated on not jumping up and killing Martinez.

"Dr. Miller," Marla said, "who is that?" She pointed to the shrouded body at the far end of the room.

"Arturo Sandoval," Miller answered. "One of three victims from last night." He smiled. "Want to take a look?"

Dr. Miller led Marla and Caleb towards the table. Russell glanced at Miriam, then got up and followed the others. Having already seen enough, Miriam stayed seated where she was.

Dr. Miller stood at the head. Miller looked at his guests. He glanced at Akin, still on her phone. She seemed in deep conversation. Martinez stood nearby, listening to her side of the conversation.

Standing this close to the kill caused Caleb to shover. The smell made the Beast within him salivate, strain to break free. Blood pounded in his temples as Caleb pushed the Beast back. His heart thudded like a metronome gone wild. The Beast wanted out, wanted to run free. And Caleb wanted to let the Beast loose, oh yes. But he could not.

The scent of a mystery werewolf wafted to his nostrils. Not familiar. Whoever this werewolf was, he (or she) was breaking all the established rules of werewolf etiquette. Killing indiscriminately and repeatedly in the same geographical area attracted law enforcement, the media, Government officials.

Evidence had been gathered. Clues analyzed. Leads investigated. And now, patterns were being detected. The werewolf's anonymity was at risk. And because of it, so was Caleb's.

This was something Caleb could not, *would not* tolerate.

Dr. Miller grabbed the shroud and yanked it back in one deft movement. Ragged remains glistened beneath the glaring light. Russell squeezed his eyes shut. Marla gasped. Caleb simply stared down at the mound of red meat in front of him.

Like Roberta Sanchez, it was difficult to imagine this mangled mass of flesh had ever been a living being, a person full and complete, with hopes and dreams and people who had loved him.

Deep, jagged lacerations crisscrossed the chest and upper torso. Multiple slashes sliced right through flesh and muscle, exposing dull white ribs underneath. The abdominal cavity yawned open. Several organs had been scooped out. The right thigh had been partially amputated. The crushed, severed head had been placed at the top of the open neck, denuded skull showing dull white under the morgue lights.

The boy had been torn apart and partially devoured by an animal of considerable size and unlimited savagery. Only one creature on earth killed in this fashion.

Marla cleared her throat. "Definitely the work of an apex predator," she said. This killer is definitely not human."

"How can you be so sure?" Miriam Melendez had decided to approach the table.

"See these lacerations here?" She curled her fingers to resemble claws and traced them over the wounds. "These are claw marks. And see these indentations here?" She pointed to the edges of the ruptured abdomen. These are teeth marks."

"And you're sure about this?"

Marla turned to Dr. Miller. "This is why there's no metal shards in the wounds. This was done with teeth and claws." She smiled to herself knowing that Miriam was bristling at being ignored.

"See the avulsion here on the thigh?" She continued. "That's a bite. The jaws were so powerful they tore a chunk clean off."

"But why sever the head?" Miriam interjected loudly. "What animal does that as part of its feeding?"

"The decapitation was probably incidental to the attack itself. I won't know more until we can identify precisely what animal did this."

"Sounds to me like there's a lot you don't know," Miriam said.

"She's contributed more to this investigation than you," Caleb said sharply.

Miriam's eyes widened. Her mouth dropped open in mute shock. Then anger took over, flashed in her eyes. Caleb saw it, stood firm. Resolute. Miriam saw a silent warning in his eyes and decided not to say what she wanted to say.

Marla turned to the group. "Animals kill for a reason. They kill to survive, to feed, to protect their young. But this," she waved her hand at the carnage on the table, "this is something else entirely. Whatever did this kills for sport."

At the edge of his consciousness, Caleb partly heard Akin get off her phone. He smelled the nervous perspiration at her armpits.

"Bad news," Akin said. "Another murder. Torn up like the rest."

News of another victim hit them hard. They were all tired from a long week, and emotionally drained by what they had seen. They wanted no more part of this.

But Caleb knew this was not over; it was only the beginning. More was coming. Much more. Things were about to get worse.

A lot worse.

How could he tell them the truth? How could he tell them what was really happening? How could he tell them that Death itself had descended upon the communities surrounding the Puget Sound? How could he tell them that the purest, darkest, most insidious and infectious of all Evils truly did exist?

How could he explain to them that werewolves were real and walked the Earth? How could he tell them that the reason he knew all this was because he was a werewolf himself?

The answer was simple.

He couldn't.

CHAPTER SEVEN

The crime scene was already bustling when they arrived. To Caleb, what appeared chaotic more closely resembled an ant colony – individual workers concentrated on their jobs, but everyone toiled towards a common goal.

Police cars angled across either end of the alleyway, blocking off unauthorized access. An ambulance waited halfway up the block, the EMTs hanging back until they could scoop up the remains and haul them to the morgue.

Yellow crime scene tape encompassed both the alleyway and the squad cars, establishing the perimeter. Uniformed cops pushed curious onlookers back, preserving the scene.

Inside the alleyway, a white plastic sheet enshrouded a corpse resting beside a metal dumpster. It lit up brightly in the stark glare of the work lights. Thick blood trickled out from underneath the shroud, traced its way down the gutter towards a storm drain.

A nondescript dark gray car edged up and stopped. The driver's side door opened with the groan of unoiled hinges. The other doors opened as well. Akin and Martinez got out, clipped their badges onto their belts. Caleb, Russell, and Marla piled out of the back seat.

Martinez looked over his shoulder. "Stay close. Careful where you step. And for God's sake, don't touch anything."

The detectives moved forward, lifted the yellow crime scene tape and held it so everyone else could duck underneath. The civilians stood in a tight knot, waiting. The detectives strode past them, taking the lead. Russell, Marla, and Caleb dutifully fell in behind them.

Spinning red and blue lights danced across building exteriors. Blinding white strobes popped as a crime scene photographer performed her function. Rusty blood on black pavement. Spray patterns across the dumpster. Glaring white lights from the squad cars.

Marla felt a migraine starting behind her left eye.

A young Chinese woman in a lab coat stood near the body, scribbling information on a clipboard. Her eyes were large, dark, almond-shaped. Her thick, raven-black hair tied behind her and away from her face. The label on her coat announced her as Linda Fong, of the Pierce County Coroner's Office.

Linda Fong looked up as the group approached her. "Detectives."

"Sergeant Akin. This is my partner, Detective Martinez."

Linda looked past them. "And who is this?"

"Consultants."

Linda squatted down beside the body. She grabbed the edge of the plastic sheet then pulled the sheet back. Mangled chunks of human detritus lay underneath. Flashes popped anew.

Marla squeezed her eyes shut, turned away. "I can't take much more of this," she whispered to Russell.

"How many of them say that every night?" Russell wondered.

Caleb heard every word with crystal clarity though he was several feet away. He said nothing. Humans needed privacy, or at least the illusion of privacy. Caleb understood the value of minding his own business.

Something at the extreme edge of his peripheral vision caught his attention. It wasn't seen so much as sensed. His spine turned to ice as he scanned the crowd beyond the tape.

Danger was imminent.

He turned full on towards them, scanning the sea of faces. Homeless stood beside housewives. Pimps stood beside professionals. The humans he quickly discounted.

A night breeze kicked up, blowing in from the alley. The scent of death was overpowering. Then the wind shifted one hundred eighty degrees. It now blew from behind the crowd, washing past them.

Caleb detected another of his kind. A male. He locked in on the heartbeat of his quarry. Caleb's eyes narrowed as he searched again. This could be the same werewolf who had committed this murder. He zeroed in right next to the alleyway entrance.

There he was.

Young. Very young. Caleb pegged him at around nineteen. No more than a pup. Smooth skin, delicate, almost feminine features. Long hair flowing away from his face and down the back of his head like a lion's mane. Scuffed boots, faded jeans, black T-shirt, brown leather motorcycle jacket.

A snarl lifted Caleb's lip, creased the side of his nose. Gaze locked, he purposefully moved right and edged forward until he came into the young werewolf's view. Recognition registered in the kid's eyes. Their eyes locked, a predatory gaze, two supernatural creatures sizing each other up.

Both of them mentally shut out the humans. Concentrating, they communicated in the way unique to their kind. Some called it the Mind Talk.

What in the name of God have you done here? Caleb silently asked.

Do not invoke that Name. I do nothing in the name of the false God of simpering weaklings.

Caleb swallowed his frustration. The kid smiled smugly.

Why are you doing this? Why here? Why now?

The kid stifled a laugh.

Who made you?

The kid ticked his head. *The Master.*

Caleb snorted. *Master? Master of what?*

Not a master, the kid mentally replied. The *Master.*

Caleb started contemplating contingencies. None of them were pleasant.

Didn't your Master teach you anything? We kill in secret, away from prying eyes.

You are not of the Pack? The kid asked.

I am my own pack.

Then you are nothing. Strength flows only through the Pack.

You have committed a terrible transgression, Caleb pushed. *This endangers us all.*

You are not my Alpha, the kid pushed back. *This is nothing compared to what's coming.*

Caleb was stunned into silence.

The kid grinned, showing perfect, white teeth. *Do not interfere with us. Join us or stay out of our way.*

Caleb blinked his eyes, swallowed hard. The kid backed away then, wary eyes on Caleb. He dissolved into the crowd and was gone.

This was worse than anything Caleb had contemplated. Struggling to remain calm, he reminded himself to breathe. In through the nose; out through the mouth. In and out.

In and —

"Caleb?"

His mind came back to the here and now. "What?"

Marla. Concern showed in her eyes. "You okay?"

"Fine."

"You look like you've seen a ghost."

"This isn't how I thought the evening would go."

"How did you think it would go?"

"Not like this."

She looked over her shoulder at the crime scene. Two Coroner's assistants were sliding the mangled remains into what looked like a Hefty lawn bag on steroids.

"What's your take?" he asked.

"Animal attack."

Caleb grunted, nodded his agreement.

The two Coroner's assistants had the body in the bag and were about to zip it up. One tapped the other on the shoulder, halting their progress. He pointed at something, turned and signaled with his hand. Akin and Martinez went over, squatted down beside the bag. The Coroner's assistant pointed again.

The two detectives raised their heads, looked around. "Hey!" they waved. "Over here!"

Her tension rising, Marla walked towards them. Caleb tagged along. Russell had even managed to move closer.

Akin pulled out a clear plastic evidence bag. She opened it, nodded to the Coroner's assistant, who reached into a pocket with his gloved hand, pulled out a pair of medical forceps. He guided the forceps close to the raw meat still clinging to the exposed ribs. He gripped something, yanked. A blood-smeared yellowish object, crescent shaped. He dropped it into the bag.

Akin squeezed the top between her thumb and forefinger, drew her fingers across left to right, sealing it. She held it up.

Inside the bag, blood smeared between the two interior surfaces, pushed into odd shapes. A Rorschach test from hell. The yellowish object lay near the bottom. Slightly curved, about four inches long by three quarters of an inch wide, tapering to a sharp point.

Marla recognized it immediately. "Where did you find this?"

The assistant pointed using the forceps. "Embedded in the seventh rib," he said

Marla stared at the blood-spattered face of what had once been a lovely young woman. A hole the size of a baseball plunged through her neck where her throat should have been. One breast had been completely torn away and the other was so deeply lacerated yellow adipose tissue protruded outside the rent flesh. The wound swept down and across her breast, and along the ribs, exposing them.

Claw marks, just like she had seen on the Hispanic victim earlier. She shuddered as she stood back up.

Martinez motioned to the Coroner's assistants, who dutifully zipped the body bag shut. Then he stood up.

"You know what that is." It was a statement, not a question.

An unnaturally pale Marla nodded. "It's a claw, she croaked."

Suddenly nauseous, she felt her gorge rising. Then Caleb was there, putting an arm around her waist, steadying her. Her knees were jelly. Her head swam.

Grimacing, Sandra Akin hung her head. "Fuck me to tears."

"That's not all," the other Coroner's assistant announced.

"What's your name?" Akin asked.

"Pam."

"Pam. What else you got?"

Pam unzipped the body bag just enough for her to grab one of the victim's arms and pull it out without exposing the rest of the body. The hand was encased in a plastic bag, secured with a tie at the wrist.

"It looks like there's something under her nails," Pam said.

"Maybe she scratched her killer?"

Pam shrugged. "There's definitely debris present. We might get lucky."

Marla breathed deeply, regaining her composure. Still wobbly in the knees, she was grateful for Caleb discreetly holding her up. And she had to admit, his arm felt good around her. It made her feel... safe.

Good God. How corny was that?

The first coroner's assistant, the man, cleared his throat.

Akin turned her head towards him. "Something else?"

He nodded.

"And you are?"

Ted," he said.

"Talk to us, Ted."

Ted pointed to the blood around the area. "For such a horrendous death, there's not a lot of blood here," he said. "There should be arterial spray on the walls for ten feet in every direction and there's not. Plus, she has a comminuted skull fracture on the back of her head where she struck the sidewalk."

"She fractured her skull when she fell down," Martinez supposed.

"Not based on the size and depth of the fracture." Ted shook his head. "She was dumped here. She wasn't killed here."

"How could someone dump a naked girl's body in this neighborhood without being seen?" Russell asked.

"Thrown from a moving car?"

Ted shook his head again. "Not based on the bleed patterns and the angles of the broken bones. The directional forces appear pretty flat." He pointed upwards. "These are deceleration injuries. She fell from a height. Like maybe up there."

All eyes turned upwards. They saw the top of the building, an open apartment window over the convenience store on the ground floor.

Akin and Martinez walked towards the building. They said something to a uniformed cop, who pointed to the left. There in the shadows cast by the glaring lights of the investigation, a narrow staircase waited.

Russell watched Ted and Pam pack up their gear. They each grabbed a plastic handle on each end of the body bag. They lifted with their legs, plopped the body bag onto a gurney, secured it with Velcro straps.

Marla stared at the ground. Caleb still stood beside her. He silently took his arm from around her waist, let it hang at his side. Without saying a word, she quietly slipped her hand into his, curling her fingers. He gave her hand a gentle, reassuring squeeze.

Moments later, a shrill whistle sounded loudly, briefly from above. They all craned their necks. Martinez leaned out the window, motioned them up. Then he pulled back, disappearing inside the apartment.

"Why would they want us up there?" Marla wondered.

Russell replied, "They found something."

Marla's eyes widened, her face going ashen once more. She took a step backwards.

"Oh no," she said. "I… can't."

Caleb placed a warm hand on her shoulder. "It's okay," he soothed. "Russell and I will go up. You stay here. We'll be back."

Marla looked terrified. "You're going to leave me alone down here?"

"There's twenty cops down here. You're as safe here as anywhere else."

"That's what I'm afraid of!"

Caleb gave her a smile that he hoped was encouraging. She looked like a frightened child standing there, hopelessly lost in an alien landscape. She crossed her arms across her chest, hugging herself.

Caleb and Russell crossed the street, disappeared into the narrow stairwell. Inside, they climbed claustrophobic stairs, lit by a single naked bulb hanging from the ceiling at the top on the landing. Black and shifting shadows, mobile inkblots, moved like restless specters. Peeling paint on decrepit walls had long lost any hint of color. The stench of decay and urine hung in the heavy air.

"Jesus Christ," Russell muttered. He gulped air as he hauled his massive girth up the stairs. He noticed how Caleb's powerfully muscled legs took the steps in stride. Not only was he not sweating as he advanced past Russell, he wasn't even breathing hard.

Russell figured that gave him the right to hate Caleb just a little bit.

They reached the top of the stairs. Caleb paused. Russell hauled his carcass up the last few steps, relying heavily on the safety rail to keep from falling backwards. His flushed face was beet red and pouring sweat.

Russell put his hands on his knees, gulping air. "Wait a second." Caleb waited. "How the fuck do you keep in such good shape?"

"Good genetics."

The landing was rectangular, wider than it was deep. The glass bulb above them buzzed, an electricity-laden hum. It was already irritating Caleb. Time to move on.

Two hallways branched off opposite of each other, one to the left and the right. Caleb stepped off in that direction, assuming Russell would follow suit.

The hallway tunneled through the building, deep and narrow. Caleb imagined a horizontal mine shaft. Cheap doors lined both left and right, regularly spaced, all the way down to the end. Last door on the left, hanging open. Dull light spilled yellow a few inches into the drab hallway.

A young uniformed police officer, a woman, short, stocky, wavy red hair pulled back, bloodshot blue eyes, stood beside the door, hands resting on the pouches of her tactical vest. Caleb approached, saw her glistening cheeks, smelled the salt, the fear.

She had been crying.

Caleb slowed as he got closer. When he got to the doorway, she put her hand up, gently touching his chest.

In that instant of physical contact, as fleeting as it was, Caleb connected. His brain received an influx of new sensory data – what she had seen inside, heard, smelled.

Her eyes pleaded with him. "Don't go in there."

Caleb's heart went out to her. Her pain, her horror, her overwhelming imperative to squelch it down, to remain outwardly calm, to be professional, touched him. He covered her hand with his, pressed it tighter to his chest. His eyes flickered to her nameplate.

"It's okay, Officer Wahl," he whispered. "We'll be fine."

Her face settled as a peace she did not understand but fully welcomed overcame her. She did not know that as long they touched, her nervous system, her psyche, was connected to his. She breathed easier, felt better. Her bleary eyes blinked and cleared.

"Better?"

"Yeah."

He took her hand off his chest, let it fall to her side. He smiled, went to go through the door.

"Hey."

He paused, looked at her.

"What was that?"

"Magic."

Caleb gave her a slanted Clint Eastwood grin, then moved on. Russell glanced at her as he went past but said nothing. This night had seen so much over the top Twilight Zone material, this latest paranormal exchange seemed downright pedestrian.

Russell entered the doorway and halted as if he had run into an invisible brick wall. He fought hard to keep from puking. The coppery smell of blood mixed with the stench of fresh feces and urine slammed him in the head.

The apartment was barely a one-room studio. A small porcelain lavatory in the corner. No bathroom. No kitchen, either. Just a hotplate and a microwave plugged into an outlet Russell doubted would pass a safety inspection.

Awareness dawned on him as to what he was seeing. The horrific event could be reconstructed by the pattern of the carnage in front of him.

The bare mattress on the Murphy bed seemed to be the epicenter. It squatted on short metal legs across from the impromptu kitchenette. Blood had saturated the mattress and soaked through, pooling on the floor underneath. Spray patterns flung out across the walls, peppered the ceiling. On the side table beside the bed lay a shapeless gray blob of skin and fat cells. He finally realized the brown circle in the middle was a nipple.

The dead woman's missing breast had never left the room.

Russell gagged, feeling acid boil up from his stomach. He stumbled backwards, staggered out the door. He retched in the hallway, forcing Officer Wahl to step out of the way.

Caleb breathed through his mouth, calming himself. The stench in the room was repulsive, yet the Wolf found it intoxicating. His skin tingled. That was always the first sign.

Akin and Martinez approached him.

"Where is Dr. Slater?"

"He stepped out for a minute."

Akin swept her arm back in a large gesture. "What do you make of all this?"

"Nothing you don't already know."

"Please. Let's hear your take on things."

Caleb took a breath. "She was butchered on the bed," he began. "More blood there than anywhere else. The arterial sprays radiate out from there. That thick black goo mixed with blood in the central crease in the mattress is her feces. The poor girl was so traumatized she defecated at the moment of death."

Akin and Martinez were both mesmerized. Caleb continued his analysis with a detached, clinical air.

"See that bright red blood on the ceiling directly above the death bed?" He pointed upward. "That's probably from a ruptured aorta."

"You really think it can get that high on its own?" Martinez challenged.

"Terror drives the blood pressure through the roof," Caleb said. "Basic human evolution. Fight or flight. Blood can travel that far, and everyone in this room knows it." He turned to Martinez, squared his shoulders. "You testing me?"

Akin cleared her throat. "It's odd that a history professor at a podunk community college can hold his own with all this."

"I've seen death before."

"Really?" Martinez now seemed keenly interested. "And where was that?"

"In the war." It slipped out before he could stop himself.

"You're a combat vet?"

"Yes." Careful, Caleb.

"Which branch?"

"Army." One-word answers. No details.

"When were you in?"

"A long time ago."

"Desert Storm?"

Caleb shrugged.

"You don't look old enough for that," Martinez said. "Most of those guys are in their late fifties now."

"I carry my age well."

"Well," Akin chimed in, "maybe seeing all this will motivate you to help us."

"I was motivated already."

They stood there, the three of them staring mutely at each other.

"Well," Akin said, "we have more to do here."

"I'll show myself out."

Akin and Martinez watched him disappear out the door.

"What do you think?" she asked.

"Something's not right about him."

"Like what?"

"Can't say."

"You going to find out?"

Martinez grinned, a bloodhound on the scent. "Oh yeah."

CHAPTER EIGHT

A minute later, Caleb emerged onto the sidewalk. He rubbed his hands together, rolled his head, loosening the tightness in his neck. He located Marla still standing near the alley entrance.

He tried hard not to stagger as he moved towards her. Project calm and confidence at all times. He knew both Russell and Marla were teetering on the edge. They needed his strength to keep from slipping into the abyss.

She looked his way, saw him. She put up a hand that seemed as if it weighed a ton in an exhausted wave. He mouthed the word "Russell". She pointed to the unmarked car in which they had arrived. Caleb's eyes followed. Russell sat in the back seat, one leg out the open door, foot on the pavement.

Marla's eyes searched Caleb's face as he approached. "Russell came down, wouldn't say a word," she reported. "Wouldn't even look at me. He dry-heaved outside the car door."

"I don't blame him."

Caleb walked over to the car. Russell glanced up at him, embarrassed.

"There's no shame in losing your dinner over what we've seen tonight," Caleb said.

"You didn't." Russell's voice sounded weak. He shook his head. "What kind of monster does that? And how could nobody see or hear anything?"

"All good questions."

"I've got no answers."

"I have faith in you."

This brought the slightest hint of a grin to Russell's pallid face. "Fuck you."

Caleb smiled. There was the old Russell.

"Guys," Marla gestured with her head. Akin and Martinez had just reappeared. They spoke briefly, nodded to each other, some kind of silent shorthand. They strode towards the rest of them.

Quite ready to leave, Marla moved closer to the car. She glanced into Caleb's eyes, those beautiful eyes. That rugged face.

How could he be so calm? It was everything she could do to keep from screaming and pulling her hair out. Russell would need a week to recover. But Caleb acted like he saw this stuff every day. She did not know how he did it. Then she realized that, in truth, she did not really know him well.

Hell. She didn't really know him at all.

Akin and Martinez stopped in front of them.

"Everyone all right?" Akin asked.

"Is that a rhetorical question?" Russell quipped.

"We're going to take you all back to the station."

"Good," Marla said. She moved towards the open door.

Russell scooted himself across to the opposite side. Marla ducked in, slid to the middle of the Crown Vic's expansive back seat.

For a moment, Akin, Martinez, and Caleb stood there, stock still, looking at each other. Martinez cocked his head. Caleb smelled Martinez's suspicion on him. Caleb did not trust him, either. They understood each other without speaking.

"Shall we?" Martinez asked.

Caleb heard the challenge in the detective's voice. His dislike for the detective intensified. He outwardly ignored Martinez's tone, squeezed himself into the car. Martinez got in the front seat. Akin slid behind the wheel.

As they inched up the road, Marla craned her neck over her shoulder, watching the crime scene shrink into the distance. She closed her eyes briefly, hoping the horror of that scene would do the same.

It did not.

Akin turned onto a larger street, hit the accelerator. The dreadful scene grew dimmer still in the distance, until it died away completely. The drive back to the police station passed in silence, save for the occasional squawk across the police radio.

Russell stared out the window, morose. He usually just read files and arrest reports, poured over interview transcripts, examined crime scene photos, then formulated recommendations for interested parties. All quite clinical, really. Clean, sterile, far removed from real-world horrors.

Tonight, Russell Slater had ventured into the field and had looked into the face of evil, had gazed into the mouth of madness. And had been found lacking. His anger and disgust with himself seemed more acute compared to Caleb, who had taken everything in stride. Not only had he remained strong, he had provided encouragement and comfort to others.

Russell loved him like a brother. But dammit, sometimes he really just fucking hated Caleb.

Marla sat in the middle, feeling like when she was the youngest of three children. Window seats were a privilege for older children. Here she was again, crammed in on both sides, waiting for the ride to be over.

To her right, Caleb gazed out the window watching the night rushing past them, none the worse for wear. How was that possible?

At that moment, all Marla wanted to do was take his face in her hands and kiss him like she had never kissed any man before. Open her mouth, put her tongue down his throat. Take his tongue into her mouth. And if it led to something else, she was open to the possibility.

Right now, she was open to just about anything to make her feel safe again.

Pheromones radiated off Marla in waves, the scent intoxicating. Caleb tried to ignore it. It was not working. He pushed a button on the arm console. The window lowered; he stuck his head out the window. He inhaled deeply, catching night's fresh scent, that time when everything seemed renewed.

Try as he might to distract himself, he felt a familiar stirring. Now was not the time to be popping wood in the back of a police car. His penis had other ideas.

Damned thing had a mind of its own.

He sat still as long as possible. Eventually, he moved his legs, shifted in his seat.

"You okay?" Marla asked.

"It's cramped back here."

Less than a minute later, Akin cranked the steering wheel and maneuvered into the police station parking lot. Instead, she pulled up near the door, killed the engine.

Everyone piled out. Caleb turned away as he stepped out, quickly adjusted himself inside his jeans, turned back around. No one else seemed to notice.

Akin and Martinez headed straight for the station door. They were serious-minded, had their heads in the game. Caleb respected that.

Russell closed his door, then leaned on the car, elbows and forearms resting on the roof. "Guys." Both Caleb and Marla turned to him. "I've got more to do inside," he said.

Caleb glanced to Marla. She had had enough for one night. A plan of action formed, one that only a wily werewolf like him could accomplish. But he put it aside for now. Take care of Marla first.

"Marla's car went kaput at the zoo," Caleb said. "I'll call a tow truck, make sure she gets home safely."

"Oh, I can't ask you to do all that," Marla said, more out of etiquette than any real desire for him to not help.

"You're not asking. I'm volunteering."

Marla started to speak again but stopped. She allowed herself to be cajoled into something she wanted anyway.

"It's settled, then." Russell pushed his bulk off the car and moved around to the front. Caleb met him in front of the headlights. They shook hands.

"Take care of her, Musclehead," Russell said. There was no levity in his voice.

Caleb understood what Russell was really saying. *She is my family, my loved one. I can't protect her right now. I am entrusting you to keep her safe in my stead.*

"I swear," Caleb replied, equally as serious.

"You'll be safe with him," Russell said to Marla.

"I know."

Russell hugged Marla, then moved towards the door. He paused briefly at the door then turned back to them unexpectedly.

"Hey guys," he said. "Tomorrow we'll put our heads together, see if anything makes more sense then."

He turned, pushed the buttons on the keypad, yanked the door open. He disappeared inside. The door clanged shut behind him.

For an awkward moment, Marla and Caleb stood there alone, staring at each other. The sexual tension was palpable. Both of them felt it.

"Let's get your car towed," he said. He gently took her by the arm. Normally she would have yanked her arm back. But after tonight, she took comfort in it. He led her to his Jeep, unlocked the door. She sat down and buckled herself in.

Caleb closed the door, walked to the driver's side, hauled himself inside. He buckled his seat belt and started the engine.

They turned out of the police lot onto the street. They drove in silence. Caleb noticed the streets were largely empty.

"Do you have Triple A?" Caleb asked as they turned into the zoo parking lot.

"No."

"I do."

He pulled his car close to hers, facing it head on. His headlights bathed it in light, reflective surfaces beaming. He fished his cellphone out, hit a single digit, held the phone to his ear.

He waited, then recited his membership number from memory, gave them the exact location. He dropped the phone back into his front pants pocket.

"They have someone in the area. It'll be about ten minutes."

"Lucky me."

He smelled her fear. Nervous perspiration under her arms, the back of her neck, between her legs. She had been through a lot tonight. He listened to her heartbeat as they sat there, waiting in the dark.

"Talk to me, please," she said.

"About what?"

"Anything. Just talk to me. Where were you born?"

"Missouri."

"Where in Missouri?"

Being careful, Caleb knew the trick to navigating conversations like this was to tell as much truth as possible. Only lie when you need to, therefore the lies become buried in the truth, and will then be believed.

"A place called Jacob's Landing. We were farmers. It doesn't exist anymore," he added, regret in his voice.

"What made you study history?"

"Knowing the past explains the present and helps predict the future."

Headlights bounced towards them. The tow truck materialized out of the mist. Marla remembered a spooky movie she had seen as a kid, something about cars and trucks becoming sentient and intentionally running people down.

The atmosphere in the Jeep grew heavy. She peered at Caleb, saw him sitting ramrod straight, knees bent at ninety degrees, feet flat on the floor. His jaw clenched shut. Muscles flexed near his jaw. His eyes blazed at the tow truck with an almost inhuman intensity. It was like a switch had been flipped inside him. And had his eyes somehow changed color?

The Caleb she saw now, sitting just inches away from her, was someone different from who she had seen throughout the night. A chill ran up her spine.

"Stay here," he muttered, not looking at her. He unbuckled his seatbelt.

"What's wrong?"

"Nothing," he said, trying to sound comforting. "Just stay here."

He opened his door, slid out. His feet hit the pavement a bit too hard. The impact sent an electric jolt all the way up to his knees. He slammed the door without thinking. Hard. The entire Jeep shuddered.

Marla said something from inside the Jeep. It did not register. All his attention, all his senses focused solely on the tow truck. More precisely, on the driver within.

Caleb walked towards the tow truck like he thought it might explode or something. He reacted slightly as the door opened, and the tow truck driver climbed out. He was upwind to Caleb.

The breeze captured the driver's scent. And in that instant the information wafted into Caleb's nose, permeated his nostrils, bolted to his brain, and told him everything about the driver he needed to know.

He surged forward. The driver toted a clip board folded under one arm. His other hand was free, visible. He raised it, waved a greeting.

"Evening," the driver said.

Caleb was still downwind from him as he closed the distance. If anything happened, he wanted to be able to force his way behind the truck, obscure Marla's view.

"So who are we towing?"

Caleb pointed to Marla's car. "That one."

The driver pulled a pen out of his pocket, began scribbling on the clip board.

"Where do you want me to take it?" He was staring at the clip board. All business.

Caleb, now just a few feet away, circled him, his eyes never leaving the driver.

"When was the last time you made the Change?" Caleb asked.

The driver frowned, looked up from the clip board. "Excuse me?"

"The Change."

"Oh. I don't make change, sir. We only take credit and debit cards."

Caleb now moved upwind of the driver. He turned, eyes blazing. Jaw set. No nonsense.

"No. I said, the Change."

Caleb's scent hit the driver, who reacted subtly. Surprise. Apprehension. They locked eyes. Tension rose between them. Caleb's eyes glowed an iridescent yellow. The tow truck driver blinked, looked down and away.

"I'm just here to do a job," he said. "Where do you want this towed?"

Caleb thought for a moment. "Who's the best mechanic around here? Who will do the job right and not rip off my friend?" He motioned to his Jeep. The driver followed the movement, saw Marla sitting in the Jeep.

"You an Alpha Pair?"

"She's human. Doesn't know."

The driver nodded. "I know a guy. One of us."

"Take it there." Caleb pulled his wallet out, handed the driver a debit card.

The driver reached out, carefully, like he thought Caleb would bite his hand off. He took the card carefully, began scribbling again on the paperwork attached to the clipboard.

"You have a pack?" Caleb asked.

"No." Surprise. Fear. "You?"

"You're new, aren't you?"

"Is it that obvious?"

"Look, you don't have to worry about me. I mind my own business. But there's others who will take advantage of you."

The driver nodded. He finished the paperwork. "I'm figuring that out." He held the clipboard out towards Caleb. "I need a signature, please."

Caleb took the clipboard and the pen. "Beware of them," he said. He signed the paperwork, handed the clipboard and pen back to the driver.

"So how did it happen?"

The driver shook his head in dismay. "Picked up a chick in a bar. Took her home. Told me she was a biter, a real animal in bed." He shrugged. "Who knew?"

Caleb grinned, offered his hand. "At least you got laid." They shook. He started back towards his Jeep. The driver tossed the clipboard atop the hood of the truck.

Caleb turned. "By the way, how was it?"

The driver blushed. "Best sex I ever had."

Caleb grinned appreciatively.

"What about you?" the driver asked. "Is that how you got turned?"

"Don't I wish."

Caleb walked towards the Jeep. Even in the gloom, Caleb saw Marla's face with such clarity he could count the pores in her skin. She was relaxed now. Everything had looked like a normal interaction between two humans.

Good.

Still on edge, he felt tingly all over. He chastised himself again for going so long between Changes. But he had been so busy of late with teaching, office hours, fending off attempts by four girls and one guy who were "willing to do *anything* to get a better grade this semester, Professor".

And then there was the book he was trying to write. All the research, checking and rechecking of references, verifying citations, writing footnotes, developing and updating bibliographies. And that of course was all in addition to actually writing the damned thing.

"Everything okay?" Marla asked when he climbed back in.

"Yes."

By now, the tow truck driver had his truck backed up near the front end of Marla's car. He jumped down out of his rig, began operating the hydraulic controls near the back.

Caleb started the Jeep, inched past the driver and his rig. He gave one last look into his rearview mirror. The driver already had Marla's inert auto on a winch, the hydraulics pulling it onto the flatbed in back.

The Jeep stopped at the exit.

"Left or right?"

"Right."

Caleb cranked the wheel, eased off the brake. Once on the street, the vehicle gained speed. The area immediately surrounding the zoo was largely residential. Caleb dutifully kept within the speed limit.

They drove in silence, broken only by occasional directions given by Marla. Turn here, take a right there. They crossed under the highway and continued on into University Place. Upscale, trendy, attracting the young and the affluent.

"So, what do you think about tonight?" she asked.

"I think a lot has happened."

"You seem okay."

"I've seen this kind of thing before." It slipped out before he even knew he had said it. Damn, he hated being an honest man.

"You were in the military? When?"

"Long time ago."

"What unit were you with? Did you see action?"

"I don't talk about it."

Marla stopped. Caleb spoke in measured tones, but she had read about combat vets, how some of them deal with wartime trauma by compartmentalizing events, putting them inside a psychological box and locking it away.

"How close are we?" he asked.

"Around this corner up here."

Caleb came to a stop sign. He edged into the intersection, turning right again.

"Up here on the left," she said. "Park anywhere."

Cars lined both sides of the dark street. He parallel parked the behemoth with surgical precision, killed the engine.

He opened his door, climbed out. He walked around the front of the Jeep as Marla unbuckled her seatbelt. He opened her door. Marla took his offered hand and stepped down. Caleb closed the door behind her, used his key fob to lock the doors and set the alarm.

Caleb escorted Marla across the street. Even though the street was empty and the night quiet, he sniffed the air, scanned the edges of the shadows alert for any danger. They stepped onto the far curb in front of a low profile, well-kept one-story bungalow.

Marla pointed straight ahead. "We're here."

Caleb's eyes, alert and intent, danced as he assessed the bungalow. "Nice digs."

They started up the concrete walkway towards the front door. "The company owns it," Marla said. "One of the perks of my job is I get to use it."

"Nice perk."

They reached the stoop at the front door. A motion sensor light, snapped on, bathing them each in a yellowish glow.

"Thank you for everything tonight."

"Of course."

"Would you—" She coughed, cleared her throat. "Would you like to come in for minute?

"Sure."

She couldn't believe she was actually doing this, inviting a man she barely knew into her inner sanctum. But these were extraordinary circumstances. She felt far from shore, adrift in inky water, drowning and desperate for air, clawing through liquid fear, trying to get to the surface.

Just to breathe again.

She fumbled through her purse for the key, found it. In her nervous haste it slipped from her grasp, clanged onto the ground. Her eyes squeezed shut in embarrassment.

Caleb immediately scooped the key off the cement pad on which they stood.

"Sorry."

"No apologies." He held the key out.

"Maybe you should do it."

Caleb's sharp eyes scanned the night one more time before he turned his back to the street, to the dangers that lurked in the shadows. Marla saw it, understood its import. Caleb was not scared.

Not in the least. No, his keen eyes pierced the darkness with a coldly confident, predatory glare. They sent out an undeniable, silent, primal warning.

Don't fuck with me.

CHAPTER NINE

The door swung inward. Marla and Caleb stood framed in the light above the stoop. Marla stepped through first. He followed. Once inside he closed the door, locked the deadbolt while Marla turned on a light.

"Nice place."

"Thanks." She paused. "Coffee?"

"Please."

The spacious living room was the showpiece of the house. Sofas, easy chairs, coffee table all faced the far wall. A large flat screen TV floated on the wall above the fireplace.

Marla moved off to the right and deeper into the house. Her arm snaked out to the left, turned on a light revealing an eat-in kitchen.

"You want me to turn off the front lights?" He asked.

"I want every light in the house left on."

He stood at the kitchen doorway. "May I?"

"Of course." She watched him pull a chair out and sit down.

She filled the glass carafe at the sink, then set it in its electric base. She touched a button on the handle. A tiny blue light snapped on. She sat down across from him.

"So. What do you really think is going on?" she asked.

"Can't say for sure."

"You have an opinion?"

"I'd rather keep my mouth shut until we know more."

Outwardly, she grinned. Inwardly, her logic chided her. What the hell do you think you're doing? You've invited a man, a quite large, obviously powerful, incredibly attractive man into your house in the wee hours of the morning. You hardly know the guy. Hell, you *don't* know him. What are you thinking?

Actually, she knew exactly what she was thinking, and logic had nothing to do with it.

The water came to a boil. The soft sound made its way into her head, past the internal argument she was having.

"Should we watch the news?" she asked as she stood.

"They won't report anything we don't already know."

She poured hot water into the two ceramic mugs on the counter. She spooned instant coffee from a jar into each steaming mug, stirred.

"How do you like it?" she asked over her shoulder.

"Any way you give it to me."

His tone was neutral, simply answering her question. But she smirked inwardly, thinking, *I'll bet.* She reminded herself not to mutter that aloud.

A mug in each hand, she glided from the counter to the table. She extended one arm, sliding the mug closer to him. Caleb reached out to take it. Their hands touched, softly. Electricity crackled through both of them. She pulled her hand back as she sat down. She cupped her mug, warming her hands.

"Who would have thought I'd be involved in a police case?" She shook her head in amazement. "I'm a scientist, not a cop."

"You've proven your mettle," he said.

"So have you."

Caleb thought about the bloody handprint on the wall. He wished he could have told the police the truth. But if the cops got too close to whoever was doing this, uniformed bodies would litter Northwestern Washington.

Caleb's mission became clear: Find the werewolves responsible and deal with them privately, in the manner that only one of his species could. He saw no other path. When push came to shove, he would rather kill others of his kind than see their secret get out.

Marla was saying something.

"Sorry. Say again?"

Marla grunted a short laugh, surprised. "I said, you seem like a really good guy."

"I wouldn't go that far," he said.

Marla's eyes locked onto him. "Why would you say that about yourself?"

"I'm no paragon of virtue. Nobody is."

"No?"

"We all have our demons, our darker natures. Most people never confront the darkness within them; partly because they never have to. But partly because they don't want to."

"Why is that?"

"They're afraid of what they might find," he said, choosing his words carefully. "So, they pretend it doesn't exist in them."

"But they have it? This darkness?"

"We *all* have it," he stated. "Those who have confronted their darkness spend the rest of their lives trying to keep a lid on it."

"But that doesn't always work?"

He considered how best to respond. "Sooner or later, every Beast has its day."

Marla shuddered, chilled to the core. Something warm enveloped her trembling hands, still clutching her cooling mug. Caleb had reached out across the table, had covered her hands with his.

"This has everybody rattled," he said. "The cops aren't prepared for this. They're looking over the edge, staring into the abyss."

"What do you see lurking in that abyss?"

She saw the guardedness creep back over Caleb. He slowly withdrew his hands from around hers and leaned back in his chair. What was he hiding?

"People are dying. I have a moral obligation to help."

She sipped her coffee. It tasted like battery acid. "Look. I'm not in the habit of inviting men into my home on the first date."

"Okay."

"This whole thing has me scared out of my wits." She looked him in the eyes. "I really don't want to be alone tonight."

"You think I can protect you?"

"You scared the shit out of Ty. Literally." She smirked at the memory.

He grinned. "I live to entertain."

An awkward silence. Caleb considered the pros and cons. It was too risky.

"Of course I'll stay."

Wait. What? What the hell did I just say?

Marla swallowed, blushed. Her eyes were soft. Caleb held his breath.

"Excuse me a minute?" She stood and walked past him, into the gloom of the rest of the house.

Caleb sipped his coffee, which suddenly tasted rancid. He pushed the mug away.

He turned around and looked into the house, past the living room. Down at the end of a hallway that resembled a narrow tunnel, a crack of yellow light peaked through from under a closed door.

This is a mistake, he thought. I should cut and run. But that would be incredibly rude. How could I justify a dick move like that?

Caleb still remembered that night in Portland back in 1880. That night that started out with pleasure and passion but ended in blood and terror. He shuddered at the memory.

But I am so much older in the Wolf now, he told himself. I have learned so much, gained so much more control than I had then. That wouldn't happen now, couldn't happen now. Would it?

Could it?

The bedroom doorknob turned, the metallic click bringing Caleb out of his reverie. He twisted in his seat, looked over his left shoulder.

Marla stood in the open doorway, framed in the light, her hair aglow. She now wore a simple oversized lavender T-shirt that tumbled off her shoulders, down the slope of her breasts, plummeted over her taut belly, cascaded past the round of her hips, and hung loosely halfway over muscular thighs.

Maybe it was the moment, maybe it was a trick of the muted light behind her, or maybe it was purely wishful thinking of his part. But Caleb could have sworn she had just given him a "come hither" look. It took his breath away.

For the first time in a very long time, Caleb felt like a man again.

She reached out to one side; the room went dark behind her. She had turned the switch off. She padded towards him with a step so light even Caleb could only barely perceive her feet on the carpet. She carried a bundle folded under one arm and pinned against her body.

She was in the living room now, gliding closer. He stood as she moved into the light. She stopped at the edge of the linoleum floor, extended the folded bundle out in front of her.

"I know you didn't plan on staying here," she said. "I brought you these."

Caleb accepted the offering, taking the bundle in his hands. Soft cotton beneath his fingertips.

"They're Russell's, she said by way of explanation. "He left them here by mistake the last time he was here."

Caleb turned the boxer shorts and T-shirt over in his hands. "If he wore these, I'll have to make sure my vaccinations are up to date."

Marla laughed out loud. "Don't worry. "They've been washed since then."

"Thank God."

He could smell her as he moved past, and it took every ounce of self-discipline to refrain from dropping the clothes, scooping her up in his arms, and smothering her with kisses.

"Bathroom's on the right," she called after him.

Caleb saw the open door about halfway down the hallway. He steered himself in, flipped on the light, closed the door. A soft coral and seafoam green palette surrounded him.

The bath was actually a three quarters' bath. No tub, just an enclosed stand-up shower. Contemporary design distressed to resemble antique.

He dropped the clothes on the countertop, turned to the mirror. Tired eyes stared back at him. His beard desperately needed a trim.

He unbuttoned his shirt, yanked upwards, pulling it out of his pants. Taut skin stretched across hard muscle as he shrugged out of it. Six pack abs, chiseled chest. Rippling deltoids, cannonball biceps. All side effects of his condition, not endless hours in the gym.

He unbuckled his jeans. They fell to the floor, formed a blue puddle around his ankles. He pulled his underwear off, slipped into Russell's sleep boxers. The elastic waistband had been stretched out. The shorts threatened to spontaneously fall off him at any moment. He pulled the dingy T shirt on over his head. The shirt, about two sizes too big, billowed out from Caleb's body. He looked at himself in the mirror again. He felt like he was wearing a circus tent.

Caleb placed his folded shirt on top of his jeans, picked them up with both hands. He looked around, placed his clothes on the etagere. He placed his shoes and socks in a corner next to the shower.

Satisfied he was being a considerate and respectful guest, his gaze turned back to his reflection in the mirror. He searched his own reflection looking for answers to deep, unspoken questions. He found none.

This is a mistake, he told himself again. This is so not a good idea, for all kinds of reasons. First off, she's human and I'm.... well, I'm *not*.

He opened the door, flipped the light switch off as he stepped into the hall. Directly across from the bathroom he saw the closed door of another bedroom, light seeping through underneath.

He opened the door. Inside, Marla was turning down the guest bed. She looked up as he walked in. Her eyes drank him in. She obviously liked what she saw.

"I left my clothes atop the etagere," Caleb announced.

She smiled. "That's fine. Would you believe, you're the first guy I've met who can properly pronounce 'etagere'?" She stepped away from the bed. She held her own hands in front of her.

Nervous.

Marla's teeth scraped crossed her lower lip. "Well. We need to go to bed –" she stopped herself, blushing mightily. Caleb's eyebrow arched. "What I mean is, it's late."

Caleb checked his watch. "It's closer to 'early'."

"We both need sleep."

"Agreed."

"Well. Ummm, goodnight."

Marla moved forward and at an angle, projected to take her well around Caleb. She made it two steps before she looked at his face, came to a full and complete stop.

Then they were suddenly pressing against each other, arms embracing, hands caressing, mouths exploring. This was what they had both been wanting for several hours. Suddenly, it seemed incredibly hot in the room. And their attire – such as it was – felt terribly constricting.

They stumbled towards the bed. Marla yanked Caleb's t shirt upward. He pulled it the rest of the way off, tossed it aside not caring where it landed.

Marla inhaled. Shirtless, Caleb was a sight to behold. She ran her hands over his torso, fingers tracing the peaks and valleys. She noticed the scars, differing shapes and lengths, all old, faded and flat. The scars did not dampen her mood. If anything, they enhanced it. She was about to be with a rugged man, someone who had felt real pain in his life and had overcome it.

She looked up into Caleb's twinkling eyes, placed her palms flat on his pectorals. She smiled sensuously.

Then she pushed him, playfully. He toppled backwards, laughing as he bounced onto the mattress. She was immediately on top of him, climbing up his body, kissing him lightly along the way, until their lips met again.

She straddled him at the hips, his erection hard pushing against her. His hands, comforting and warm, played across the outside of her bare hips, then snuck underneath her T shirt, up her abdomen until they cupped her breasts.

She pulled away, hiking one leg to move off of him. Like dismounting a horse. She yanked the baggy boxers down, freeing him. She grasped him with featherlight fingertips, gave him a few gentle strokes. Then she climbed back astride him and sat down, easing him into her.

Marla had been to bed with a few other men, of course. The sex had been good enough. But sex with this man, this incredible man, was a different matter entirely. Oh God, was it ever different. In this room with this man at this moment in time, Marla now understood what all the hubbub had always been about.

Caleb craned his head back into the pillow as he arched his hips, lifting her with each thrust. They settled into a steady, piston-like rhythm, complementing each other's movements.

Her breathing came in urgent gasps. She opened her eyes, realized she was looking at the ceiling. She bent her head, looked down at Caleb. Eyes closed, he purred deep in his chest, almost more like a growl, like that of an animal.

She noticed his beard seemed thicker, heavier. His body hair also seemed coarser, darker. Just an effect of the darkness and shadow in the room, she assumed? Then he opened his eyes. His brown eyes. Only now, they appeared lighter, almost amber. They seemed to reflect the low light in the room, almost as if they glowed from some inner source.

But that couldn't be right.

Caleb closed his eyes again and rumbled in his chest once more. His breathing progressed to ragged; his thrusts became more powerful, faster, deeper, lifting her almost all the way off of him. He grabbed her by the hips, his fingernails long enough to indent on her soft skin. He thrust upwards once more, plunging deep, and then sweet release.

She heard him growl again under his breath as he climaxed. She was so close, and him going over the edge sent her over the edge as well. She glanced down at him, saw his lips pulled tight, teeth gnash together. How sharp and pointed his teeth seemed in that brief flicker in time.

Just a trick of the light.

Marla, exhausted and happy, folded over, laid down on Caleb's heaving chest. Her head rose and fell with his breathing. Inside, she distinctly heard that familiar low-frequency lub-dub triphammer rhythm of his heart, pounding away, pumping blood to all the right places. That deep rumbling came again, from inside his chest. She felt the vibrations through her skin.

Caleb took Marla's face in his hands, kissed her. Longingly. Lovingly. She kissed him back, then rested her chin on her hand. His eyes were a chocolate brown once more.

CHAPTER TEN

Marla fell asleep immediately. Exhausted, she lay in a crumpled heap. Caleb lay awake, staring at the ceiling. His eyes drifted to Marla. So soft and sweet and warm, all snuggled beside him. He smiled affectionately. It had been decades since he had felt this level of connection with anyone.

Caleb's condition dictated a lifestyle of superficial acquaintances. He knew people at work, knew people in the haunts he frequented. But knowing someone's name and having a pleasant conversation did not qualify as a true friendship. True friendship was like a marriage. It was a long-term relationship that required a certain level of dedication. Commitment. Sometimes even sacrifice.

True friendship meant having people you could call when the chips were down and they would drop whatever they were doing and show up to help, no matter what. In turn, you had to be willing to do the same for them. No judgement.

Caleb kept his circle of acquaintances small, his circle of friends smaller. Some mistook his reticence for snobbery. But Caleb could never allow anyone to see his true self.

Which brought him back to here and now. Marla lay asleep, relaxed, at peace. One with the universe. He wished he knew that kind of peace. How long had it been? Since before he got bitten? No. Further back. His peace was forever shattered the day his father was beaten to death and his youngest sister gang raped.

Something pure inside a twenty-year-old Caleb Jacobsen died that day. His innocence, really. His naivete, his belief that people were basically good and gentle and kind. Something dark, something reptilian and vengeful grew in its place.

Caleb had gone to war that day in more ways than one. He would never see the world again with the same set of eyes. The tension remained with him, even now over a century later. Sometimes it lessened, but it never completely went away. It was always there, squatting like a malignant toad in the back of his brain.

Marla stirred beside him, sighed in her sleep. She pulled the covers up to her chin. His heart swelled. For in that moment, he saw in the woman the child she must have been. She was pure. Innocent.

She had to be protected at all costs.

Caleb stroked her hair so lightly his fingertips never touched her skin. He allowed himself to enjoy the moment, to be revel in his feelings for her. Then his contentment dissipated, like an iron door slamming shut as reality reasserted itself.

What was he thinking? Marla was an incredible woman. And this had been a wonderful interlude, his first in decades. But it was also a terrible blunder. Caleb wondered how it might play out. Had tonight been just a one-time thing for her? That would solve a lot of problems. He could not envision a scenario that did not end in heartbreak and anger at best, or blood and death at worst.

Nature called. He slid out of bed, slow and quiet. She continued sleeping undisturbed. He crossed the hallway, padded into the bathroom and closed the door with just enough pressure for the latch to catch with a soft click. He turned on the bathroom light. Brightness flooded the room. Caleb winced, clamped his eyes shut. He grunted, then opened his eyes gradually until the light was no longer an electric dagger piercing his skull.

He moved in front of the toilet, lifted the toilet seat up. There was a lady in the house. He urinated, a forceful stream hitting blue water. He resisted the temptation to hike his leg and mark his territory.

The Wolf had already bonded with her, wanted to bond with her for life. But it was not that simple. Humans used their brains to override their hearts. They overthought these things convincing themselves that they didn't feel what they felt, or that the risks somehow outweighed the benefits. He had never understood why they made something so simple so complex.

For being the most intelligent species on the planet, humans could be pretty fucking stupid sometimes.

He finished, closed the lid before flushing, muffling the sound of the water draining into the sewage pipes. Be considerate, he reminded himself. You're in someone else's den – er, someone else's home.

That damn werewolf thing again.

He caught his reflection in the mirror. The light cast garish light and muddy shadows across his face and body. He stared into his own haunted eyes. What would happen when she found out? And she *would* find out, eventually. Truth always had a nasty habit of coming to light.

His gaze drifted downward. Scars crisscrossed his torso and limbs. Old claw marks from that night in Montana showed dull and gray. The bite mark that encompassed his right clavicle and the musculature where the shoulder and neck met still showed pink and raised after all this time, somehow still looking fresh and raw.

Maybe the ancient European myth of werewolves being cursed by God actually had a glimmer of truth to it. But then again, maybe not. After all, they had also believed that anyone with a unibrow was a werewolf, and that left-handed people worshipped the devil, so there was that.

Caleb turned the light off, tiptoed back across the hall. Marla still lay in bed asleep, buried under the covers. Her breathing was so soft and low, even Caleb's heightened hearing could barely detect it.

He eased himself down on the edge of the bed, swung his feet up. He grabbed the covers, pulled some over onto him. Marla stirred a little, shifted her legs. Then she settled back down.

After a while, Caleb slept.

The young werewolf Caleb had seen outside the apartment-turned-slaughterhouse now walked the streets of Tacoma. He reveled in his New Life, senses on full alert. He moved fluidly down the sidewalk, a monster among men. A wolf among the sheep. He tilted his head back and inhaled deeply. A sublime, satisfied smile spread across his mouth, expanded to his entire face.

God, he loved being a werewolf.

Known simply as William, he had fled an abusive home at fourteen and had lived on the streets and by his wits ever since. William had a last name, of course. His birth certificate bore evidence of that. But after bouncing around homeless shelters and soup kitchens, sleeping on skid row for years, he never used his last name.

All that was past. He had a home now. A family. A Pack. He had clothes, money, transportation. While that might have been small things to someone else, they were important to him.

William had always loved the night. When other children hid under their quilts from the darkness, he had embraced it. Perhaps it was because of his home environment. His crackhead parents would leave at night, leave him home alone. His mother was a two-bit whore; his father her pimp. They would be gone until the next morning. And then one day they simply never came home.

When the police cars pulled up outside his front door, William fled, running down the alley with only the clothes on his back and twenty dollars in his pocket. He never found out what happened to his parents.

Didn't matter now. The old life was over; a new one had begun. He had been washed in the Blood. His own blood. He had been shown a new path. A better path.

The Path of Light.

Now if anything bad ever happened to him, at least it would be in service to something greater than himself. All praise and glory be to the Master!

His thoughts wandered back to earlier that night.

Her name was Brenda, at least that was what she told him. William had seen her around. She lied about being twenty years old. William knew she was barely seventeen and had been selling herself on the street for over a year.

William bought her for seventy dollars after talking her down from one hundred. They went to her place to consummate the deal. Once there, they stripped quickly, an urgency flooding William. For Brenda, it was simply time management and cash flow. Get this yokel off, get back out there and make some more money.

They fell across the bed, a tangle of bare flesh. Young and impatient, William was not much for foreplay. He moved straight to the main event, which suited Brenda just fine.

Brenda found this to be a turn on. His urgency fueled hers. His rising passion thrilled her. He kept pounding away at her, skin slapping together with every downstroke. Pain and pleasure mixed for an interesting brew. Brenda liked it rough around the edges.

Maybe this was going to be a good night after all.

As pleasure and passion raced throughout her body, she reached up to stroke William's chest. She frowned. Something was wrong. Instead of bare skin, she touched thick hair. It felt almost like... fur.

Brenda opened her eyes, her brain not processing what she was saw. When it did, terror strangled her. All that came out was a weak croak.

William was gone. Orange iridescent eyes glowed above a muzzle lined with sharp teeth. Long triangular ears. His claws still resembled hands, only bigger, broader and flatter. The long fingers terminated in sharp claws.

Perfect for rending flesh.

In those last moments of her life, William the werewolf orgasmed, exploding into her. He slapped her thin arms out of the way, then slashed savagely at her defenseless body. The first slash filleted her breast clean off her body. He timed each slash with a spurt of his penis.

Brenda finally found her voice. She inhaled and screamed. The Beast slashed laterally, just a flick of the wrist. His claws sliced through her throat, severed her vocal cords.

Blood fountained out. The next slash cleaved through her thoracic cavity. He managed to puncture the heart and sever the aorta. Arterial blood spewed six feet, spraying a pattern on the ceiling above.

She was already quite dead when he finally climbed off her. He stood there, a hulking mass, looking down at her. He felt nothing at all for her.

So much mangled meat. Nothing more.

William made the Change back. He surveyed the damage. This was his third time. Tonight, he had perfected his technique. Some jumbled psychosexual pieces fell into place. Sex was foreplay. Killing sealed the deal.

He padded to the small bathroom and took a hot shower. He dried off using one of her towels, dropped it onto the floor when he was done.

He walked back out into the main room. His clothes were not contaminated with Brenda's DNA, thank God. He dressed quickly, left quietly. Just in case some busybody neighbor heard something and called the police.

And now he prowled the night, replaying the scene over and over, a sadistic porn movie on a never-ending loop in his head. He had years, decades to scratch that particular itch, over and over and over.

Christ. He was hard again.

He turned abruptly, took a shortcut down an alley. Trashed cups and newspaper ads skittered along the cracked pavement, pushed by a brisk breeze. He turned the collar up on his leather jacket.

At the end of the alley he paused, watching multiple lanes of traffic go in both directions. He pushed the pedestrian button and waited. Even as a werewolf, he did not want to get run over.

The white "WALK" icon illuminated across the street. He made it to the other side unscathed, stepped onto the curb, then headed west. He intended to confuse anyone following him. Standard counter surveillance technique. Just like he had been taught.

Being a werewolf could be educational.

He stopped two blocks away. A large Harley Davidson sat parked, its back tire against the curb in front of an all-night diner. He loved the bike's sleek lines, craved the low rumble between his legs. This was not a sexual thing for him; it was spiritual.

William straddled the machine, inserted the key below the gas tank. The engine hummed to life, growling low and powerful. Just the way William felt right then. The way he wanted to feel all the time.

As the engine idled, William donned his helmet and gloves, zipped his jacket up to his throat. He grabbed the throttle, hit it a couple of times. The engine belched and roared. He switched on his headlight, kicked up the kickstand. He surged forward into early morning traffic, keeping pace with the cars around him.

The light ahead turned red. He braked, came to a stop. He had been riding for only a short time. Most people learned on something smaller, easier to handle than a Harley, then graduated up. But William had taken to riding like a duck to water. Once he discovered the Zen "one with the bike" thing, that was it. He would never find satisfaction on four wheels again.

The traffic light turned green. He pulled his feet up and maneuvered the bike easily, keeping pace with traffic around him. He smiled wryly. Blend in, do nothing to draw attention to yourself, they had said.

He put his blinker on, checked his side mirror, turned and accelerated. He swung around over one hundred eighty degrees as he willed the bike to follow the curve of the ramp in front of him. As the road straightened out, he gunned the engine, used his left foot to shift upwards.

William headed north on Highway 16. He moved over two lanes, pushed his speed to sixty-five. He glanced at his side mirror, did a double take. A Washington State Highway Patrol SUV zoomed up out of the night, headlights bright. William's stress level rose as the big American-made SUV pulled up right behind him, then kept pace.

He made certain he was not doing anything else unlawful other than exceeding the speed limit by five miles per hour. He eased off the throttle. The trooper behind him eased back, continued keeping pace.

William turned on his right blinker, eased into the lane on his right. He checked his left mirror again. The SUV's powerful engine roared and the vehicle sped up, blowing past him. The red and blue roof light bar came on; the siren screamed to life as the SUV got smaller in the distance.

CHAPTER ELEVEN

William sighed with relief as the trooper flew past. He was not worried about the cops, of course. If stopped, he would have simply slaughtered whoever he encountered. He was more worried about displeasing the Pack. Their opinion mattered. His place in the hierarchy mattered. Most of all, he feared displeasing the Master.

All praise and glory be unto the Master!

He pushed his speed back up to sixty, followed the gentle slopes and turns. Signage proclaimed the Tacoma Narrows Bridge one mile ahead. Another sign warned him to not change lanes on the bridge itself.

William moved to the far-right lane. Once across, he would take the first exit. He hit the bump in the pavement that signaled the beginning of the bridge. He looked up, caught a glimpse of the orange windsock attached to the bridge. The sock was flaccid, hanging limp.

William accelerated up the incline, the engine easily tackling the convex curve of the bridge. Fifty-four hundred feet across, five hundred ten feet in height at its apex, with a clearance of one hundred eighty-eight feet, connecting Tacoma to the Kitsap Peninsula.

Then he was over the top and descending a gentle slope. He eased off his throttle, looking for that sweet spot that would keep him at a steady speed. He compensated for a gust of wind that came out of nowhere, threatening to push him out of his lane.

He hit the far side of the bridge and the terrain leveled out. The exit appeared almost immediately in front of him. He followed the ramp, eased off the 16. The offramp cut through a hill. Steep earthen walls on both sides rose ten feet above him, shielding him from crosswinds.

The twisting two-lane road paralleled the rugged shoreline. Estates and compounds dotted the coastline, the properties built right up to the edge of the bluffs, which fell straight down to the frigid waters below.

Almost there now.

He eased the throttle, leaned right, turned into a driveway and stopped in front of an immense metal and wood gate. The gate stood seven feet high and close to twenty feet long. Powered by an electric motor, the gate sat on rollers in a metal groove, waiting to move.

William put the bike in neutral, placed both feet on the ground. Hidden in the trees above, a CCTV camera recorded his presence. He grinned and waved. He heard the hum of the motor, then watched as the gate retracted. It moved slowly, requiring William to practice patience he did not feel. But the gate moved at its own pace, no matter what. Perhaps there was a lesson there? William was no philosopher. If there was something esoteric to be gleaned, he didn't give two bat craps.

He blipped the throttle, kicked the gearshift into first and opened the clutch slowly. The motorcycle edged forward through the gateway. As he made his way down the tree-lined driveway, he sensed rather than heard the gate closing behind him.

The house was classic Pacific Northwest. Two sprawling stories, pale exterior, black shingle roof that had been recently replaced. The walls glowed faintly in the moonlight.

Over four thousand square feet inside, not counting the fully finished basement. The basement was not used for living space. No, reserved for one special, specific purpose.

William smiled. He had first been down there for his ceremony. He treasured the memories of his initiation: the biting, the blood, the inevitable sickness and fever, followed by his rebirth. And now, the longer he existed as the New William, the more he marveled at his life before that fateful night and wondered just how he had survived.

All glory be to the Master!

The house served the Pack well. Centrally located with easy access to the highway, the bridge, the rest of the state – hell, the rest of the country! – lay only a few miles beyond. More importantly, it offered privacy. The house sat on a double lot, with nine-foot plaster and stucco walls completely encircling the property. They enjoyed a sense of seclusion, away from prying eyes.

Light emanated from several windows on both floors. The place bustled all hours of the day and night. Of course, that meant the kitchen got used constantly. There was always food available, either steaming hot or something in the fridge he could heat up.

He parked the bike about twenty-five feet from the corner of the house. He dismounted, took off his helmet, placed it on the end of a handlebar. He stretched, ran his fingers through his thick mane. He ticked his head upwards, throwing his long hair back and cascading down his shoulders.

He smoothed his clothes with the palms of his hands. He was proud of what he had accomplished tonight. The Master would be pleased. He rubbed his hands together, walked towards the front door.

William reached out, pushed the doorbell. He looked up and to his right. Another CCTV covering the front entrance stared down at him. The Master had wisely invested in military-grade security. His security forces were exclusively comprised of werewolves with a military, law enforcement, or intel background. Newbies need not apply. These guys were all hardcore. They could go from zero to high-order violence in about a quarter of a second, would kill indiscriminately at the drop of a hat. And each one of them would die with neither hesitation nor regret to protect the Master.

And above all, to protect The Plan.

The heavy deadbolt turned, slid back. The door swung open. Light spilled out, pushing back the darkness. Diane Yakamoto, the pretty Asian news anchor, stood framed in the doorway. The backlight illuminated her; gave the impression she was glowing. He smiled sensuously.

Then he caught a whiff of her. Blood, hers, already clotted. He understood. She was on her period. Oh well, he thought. I'll wait a few days and give her another try.

She eyed him coolly. "William," she said. It was a statement, not a question.

"Hey Diane," he said cheerfully. He walked inside without being asked. After all, it was his house, too.

"Do come in." She pushed the door closed, put the heavy dead bolt back into place. She turned to William.

"The Master is expecting you."

William's face lit up with a childlike exuberance. "Really?"

"Yes," she nodded.

His jaw dropped open. "I get to talk to Him directly?"

"When will you be available?" Snarky. Whether he ignored it, or it simply went over his head, she did not know, but she suspected the latter. William was not the sharpest knife in the drawer.

"Right now." He fought the urge to jump up and down.

She moved at an angle. He fell in behind her, a bit too close for her liking. William was not someone she wanted in close proximity, no matter what form he took.

William identified a second scent caught off her. Sex and semen. Well, that was their business. If the Master wanted to get his blood wings with her, who was William to judge?

As they strolled through the immense house, William noticed several Pack members off to the left gathered around a widescreen TV. They were watching a particularly gory werewolf movie on a cable channel. They all laughed helplessly and uproariously at the faux carnage onscreen.

Real werewolves loved Hollywood werewolf movies. As far as they were concerned, werewolf movies were the funniest damn things they'd ever seen.

They continued gliding through the house, Diane in the lead. Something smelled good in the kitchen. Later, William told himself. They stepped onto the lower landing of the huge wooden staircase. Diane ascended, William behind her. Her scent was intoxicating. His nose was mere inches from her ass.

"Jesus, Diane. If you ever wanna great fuck from a younger stud –"

Diane spun around, furious. She lashed out, slapping William hard across the face. "Watch your mouth." She bared her tiny human teeth.

Surprised, William massaged his jaw. "Fuck you, bitch. There's no call for that."

"You're being disrespectful."

"I just wondered if you wanted to fuck sometime."

"Not with you. Never with you. I am for the Master. For Him and Him alone. Understand?"

His shoulders slumped. Touché. Well played, Diane.

Diane continued her deliberate ascent up the staircase. William followed; eyes fixed on the wooden stairs beneath him.

Social classes, he thought. A caste system. People pretend things like that don't exist anymore, but they do. And women like Diane would always be starfuckers, always bedding the top dog.

Well fuck her. Lots of other bitches out there.

They hit the middle landing halfway up the staircase. The staircase veered ninety-degrees. A wave of fear and dread struck William in the gut just then. Thick and nauseating, an almost solid barrier. He doubled over at the waist. Diane was still moving up the stairs.

Diane sensed he was no longer close behind. She stopped, one leg on the next step and one hand on the bannister. William looked suddenly pale, sweaty. He winced, held a hand across his stomach. It was all he could do to keep from vomiting.

"What's wrong?" Not that she really cared.

William grabbed the bannister, steadying himself. Diane looked him over once more, then turned around. They continued to the second-floor landing. Diane paused once more as William, still weak but putting on brave face, leaned against the wall to catch his breath.

After four or five deep breaths, he tilted his heavy head up. He tried to smile, failed. He mopped his wet forehead with his sleeve. She turned away from him and strode down a hallway. William pushed himself off the wall and stumbled after her.

Another smell, a familiar smell, hit his nose for the first time tonight.

Francois?

Francois, an incredibly large werewolf, waited at the end of the hall, standing guard outside a closed door. His black coat shimmered, punctuated with sprinkles of grey down his muzzle and between his angular ears. But his claws were still just as large, his teeth just as sharp, his own proclivity to high-order violence well known.

The Great Beast rested on his haunches, enormous arms folded in front of him. He sensed someone approaching. With astounding speed for a creature his size, François spun in their direction and stood simultaneously, rearing up to his full height, well over seven feet tall. His ears, which extended beyond the curve of his skull, threatened to caress the ceiling.

A low growl rumbled through his chest. He sniffed the air, recognizing Diane. Then he turned his body towards William. Francois sniffed the air between them, detected something he didn't like. His muzzle crinkled as his lips drew back, exposing long sharp teeth. His yellow eyes narrowed with pure hatred. He growled.

William knew a challenge had been hurled. His fear was replaced by anger. He planted his feet, clenched his fists, began thinking about the Change.

Then something happened that astounded William. Francois, broke off eye contact, took a half step back. Confounded, William's anger dissipated.

Francois stepped to one side. Everyone stood frozen in place for an instant, a real-life snapshot in time. Then Francois moved, ticked his huge head and made a grand sweeping gesture with one arm, pointing to the door.

"What are you waiting for?" Diane asked.

Still nervous, William said, "After you."

"Oh no, after *you*, Mr. Man Of The Hour."

William swallowed, gulping audibly. Diane smirked. She watched as William reached out with a trembling hand, grabbed the doorknob with a sweaty palm. Then he gripped, his knuckles going white. He pushed the door open. Then he stepped across the threshold.

Diane followed him, crossing the threshold without giving it any thought. Francois brought up the rear. He made certain to push the door shut behind him.

The room had originally only been half this size, but an interior wall had been demolished, doubling the space. These stood in the Master's private chambers. They stood in front of translucent gossamer curtains. Beyond them, the well-lit area glowed.

"William," a disembodied voice called out. Deep and gentle. Loving. "Welcome, dear boy." The voice carried the promises of visons not yet seen and deeds not yet done. It was the voice of purest Light.

The Master's voice.

William dropped to one knee, bowed his head in subservience. "M- Master," he blurted. "I am honored to be in your presence."

"But of course you are," the voice responded. "Arise, young William." William stood, dared to raise his head. The curtains were mere inches from his face.

"Come to me, William," the voice intoned.

Obediently, encouraged by the voice's golden throated words, William squared his shoulders. As if gently shoved by invisible hands, he parted the curtains, advanced into the main part of the room.

Into the light.

The Master waited there. Long curling locks, hair the color of honey. Piercing blue eyes, pale, the color of arctic ice, the coldness of glaciers. Thin lips, cruel mouth. High cheekbones. William had heard the Master was over four hundred years old, descended from German nobility right after the end of the Hundred Years' War.

With facial features so smooth they were almost porcelain, he wore no expression whatsoever. He stood motionless. If it had not been for the almost imperceptible rise and fall of his chest, he might have been mistaken for a statue.

His hair flowed away from his face and off his forehead, tumbling down his neck. His robes appeared luminescent, of the purest white. They fell to the floor, held together at his slender waist by a golden sash.

The Master spread his arms, a father beckoning to his child. William stepped closer but stopped short, not feeling confident enough to get too near. He certainly couldn't assume he could actually touch the Master. Both Diane the petite human and Francois the hulking werewolf stopped on each side behind William, forming three points of a triangle.

The Master dropped his arms, disappointed in William for not having the self-assurance to embrace him. Give him time. He's still a child, barely out of his dew claws.

"William. You have news to report."

"I made my first solo kill tonight."

"More satisfying than hunting in a pack, is it not?" The Master glanced to François. Yellow eyes twinkled back at him. "The girl on the news."

"Yes, Master," William replied.

"These pathetic mortals, so frail and fragile. They cower behind puny doors and cheap locks, clutching their guns and their Bibles -- as if that makes them safe from us."

"No human is safe from us," William stated.

"True. But we must also take measures to keep safe from ourselves."

Confused, William uttered, "Master?"

"You threw her body out the window, correct?" William nodded, too terrified to say anything. "What would you have done if someone had seen you, had given a description to the police?"

William now realized the magnitude of his mistake and became immediately petrified at whatever punishment might come his way. He dropped to his knees, head bowed, pressed his palms together in front of him.

"Forgive me, Master," he pleaded. "I'm sorry. It won't happen again."

Secretly appalled by the display of cowardice, the Master simply looked down at his blubbering subject.

"Make certain it does not," the Master said sternly.

"I am sorry about the girl."

"Fear not, young William." The Master smiled with fatherly pride. "You are new to this life. The rules will become easier to navigate as time goes on."

William smiled, visibly relieved. "I live to serve, Master."

Diane stood there, face impassive, taking it all in. Francois, on the other hand, was bored. He turned his head to one side, sniffed. He swung his head back around, ticked his head to one side, stretching his neck like a boxer.

"In the future, remember, we kill in secret."

William's eyes widened. "That's exactly what he said."

Francois turned his ears towards the conversation.

The Master's eyes narrowed. "Who?"

"I met another tonight. One like us."

"Like us," the Master echoed. "Not one of us?"

"No, Master. He is not of our Pack."

"A policeman?"

"He was with the cops, but he wasn't in uniform. I was in the crowd. He found me. We spoke using the Mindtalk."

The Master worked hard to show no emotion outwardly even as the shock of this new information roiled him internally. He smiled at William the simpleton.

"Tell me everything. Leave nothing out. No detail is too small."

William did precisely as commanded. He recounted his surprise encounter with the strange rogue. William did not know his name, but that would be easy enough to decipher later. He left nothing out but was careful to not embellish. He knew anything other than the basic truth would be considered a lie, if not by the Master then certainly by Francois. He had no desire to draw the big werewolf's wrath.

William finished his story, then shut his mouth. The Master stood thoughtfully for a moment; his brow furrowed in concentration as he considered the implications. Finally, he nodded his head.

"Very well, young William. You have performed admirably."

William blushed. "Thank you, Master."

"I must confer with Diane and François," he said. "Leave us now."

"Thank you, Master." William fairly danced out of the room.

The room fell silent after that. Diane could see the wheels turning inside the Master's head. Francois simply stood there, awaiting orders.

The Master finally came out of his reverie. "Francois."

Francois willed himself to Change back to human form. Thick fur changed texture, became thinner, sparser as it retracted back into the skin. His muzzle melted, compressed into a human face. His hulking posture straightened, became more upright. In the span of a few heartbeats, the werewolf was gone. A tall, handsome, powerfully muscled black man stood completely naked in its place.

Diane stole a quick peak at Francois' chiseled chest, flat, taut stomach, and then looked away, but not before sneaking a glance at his impressive manhood.

"What do you make of this?"

"I don't know, Hans," Francois replied. "Not enough information."

"So," Hans the Master started, "what are we thinking? Lone wolf or rival pack?"

"There are no rival packs. I will, of course, investigate."

"I knew you would, old friend."

Diane sighed loudly. "Something to add, my dear?" Hans asked.

"I wish you would Turn me," Diane blurted out with all the patience of a twelve-year-old. "Make me one of the Pack."

Hans glanced at François, who stifled a smirk and looked away. He and Diane had gone around and around about this. Hans took a deep breath, pushed his irritation down. He smiled sweetly.

"My dear Diane. You are far too important to the Cause as you are. You have access to all kinds of useful information through your news anchor position at the station."

"I would still be in the same position afterwards," she pleaded. "My value would not be diminished."

Hans shook his head. "Right now, being human is the greatest value you possess.

Diane knew her words were having no impact. Like using a feather duster to stop a bullet. Once Hans makes up his mind that's it, she thought. She crossed her arms over her chest, stomped her foot, and pouted.

Taken aback by this juvenile display, Hans glanced at François. *Help me here,* he said using the Mindtalk. The big Frenchman simply rolled his eyes and looked to the ceiling.

Hans took Diane in his arms. He kissed her deeply, passionately. She kissed him back, her hands gliding like smoke up his back. When he pulled away, she swooned. He held onto her at an arm's length to keep her from falling.

"Diane. Do you trust me?"

"Of course I do. You know I do."

"Then trust me now," he said flatly. "When the time comes, I will Turn you myself."

Her eyes grew misty. Hopeful.

"In the meantime," Francois interjected, "perhaps your news resources can find this rogue werewolf."

"That's assuming William was telling the truth."

"He was," Hans said definitively. "He wouldn't dare lie."

"The little perv thinks you're a God," Francois said.

They all had a good laugh over that. Even Diane joined in. Hans, like most charismatic leaders, could be many things to different people depending on what they needed to hear. Being a god was not one of them.

When their laughter died down, Hans asked, "Any new business?"

Neither Diane nor François spoke.

"Very well then," Hans sighed. "I would be alone with my thoughts."

Both Diane and François nodded, bowed slightly. They turned and left, closing the door behind them.

Hans tugged at his sash, loosening it until it fell to the floor at his feet. He reached across himself, grabbed the light fabric covering his body and yanked upward. He pulled the long tunic up and off, tossed it aside. It fluttered to the floor, immediately forgotten.

Naked, Hans walked across the room. His antique roll-top desk beckoned him. Dark and lustrous, oiled and stained to a permanent sheen. The desk was sturdy, still as solid as when it had been built almost a hundred and fifty years ago.

His chair was newer. Hans had owned it since the early 1920's. He had been the Wolf of Wall Street decades before that became a thing. He sat down, the leather upholstery cold against bare skin. Leaning back, his feet raised a few inches off the floor. This semi reclined position put his line of sight in perfect alignment with the enormous world map pinned to the wall.

Brightly colored pins skewered cities all over the world. Even Antarctica. But his attention focused on North America.

Canada was simple. He had secured in Toronto, Montreal, Ottawa. Once he secured Vancouver and Winnipeg, he would have werewolf packs in practically every major city in Canada.

The final challenge would be locking down the United States. He had understood this over one hundred years ago when, in another time and another place, the idea that germinated into the "Cause", was first contemplated.

Pins impaled almost every major city in every state. Pins almost rose out of smaller cities, the regional hubs. Unlike modern politicians and the so-called coastal elites Hans had neither ignored nor taken for granted the flyover states.

Earlier, Hans had sent an email to his werewolf brothers in Tokyo. They would spearhead efforts in Hawaii. Of course, securing Hawaii would mainly consist of establishing a Pack loyal to him, and mercilessly butchering anyone stupid enough to oppose him.

Hans would send Francois to Alaska next week to accomplish the same thing.

Pieces were falling into place. Hans reminded himself to be patient, stay disciplined. No need to rush the timetable. Everything was ticking along as planned.

Stick to the plan.

Hans controlled the EU. One of his werewolf delegates currently worked in Brussels, influencing the E.U. President's access to information, which in turn influenced policy. The President had gone against Hans' wishes only once.

Hans had paid a visit to the President's home. He had gently persuaded the errant minister to see the Light and to never, ever cross him again. He had strongly considered eating the man's wife and children in front of him, but ultimately decided that might be overkill. Morphing into a seven-foot-tall, four hundred pounded beast with four-inch fangs had made a lasting impression.

The President had never stepped out of line again. In return, Hans refrained from devouring his family– as long as he answered to Hans.

Hans' contacts in Southeast Asia and Afghanistan controlled the cultivation and export of poppy, which meant he controlled the global heroin trade. He had controlling interest in every link in the pipeline from the cocaine fields in South America, the smuggling routes north through Central America and Mexico, on up onto the streets of the U.S. and Canada.

Then there was China. He had been secretly working with the Chinese Government, through his werewolf intermediaries, to get werewolves or humans sympathetic to the Cause placed into mid-level and high positions within both Chinese business and banks. By influencing the Chinese trade positions and strategy, he was able to keep the U.S. Commerce Department delegates off balance during the recent trade talks.

Hans had encouraged the U.S. President to talk tough and follow through on imposing tariffs on Chinese goods and threaten an all-out trade war. The Chinese, of course, had imposed trade tariffs of their own, and negotiations for a new trade deal seemed deadlocked. The ripple effect had been felt throughout the global stock markets. Investors were nervous, the markets were teetering, closer to collapse than anyone dared admit. Hans stood poised to wreak complete economic collapse upon the world. It would be worse than 1929, worse than 2008. And with everything computerized, the money death spiral would go much faster this time. There would be runs on banks everywhere. ATM machines would quit spitting money out within a week. Then the music would stop, once and for all.

He who controlled the global economy controlled the world.

Hans just needed to give one small final push to bring the entire global market system which was built upon a house of cards to begin with crashing down on humanity's collective head.

Hans left the chair, padded to the window, pushed the curtains back. Looking out across the lawn, he could just make out the precipice that tumbled down to the black waters of the Narrows. Directly below the house, a thin strip of land appeared whenever the tide retreated, only to be swallowed up when the tide swept back in.

Hans had been born into privilege and affluence. He had managed to amass, lose, and then amass again individual fortunes over the years through various business ventures and investments. Stock manipulation, price fixing, the cycle of bubble and burst was nothing new. Times changed, technology advanced, but the underlying principles of wealth tended to remain constant.

Amassing wealth was not the objective. Money, in itself, was not the goal; it was merely a tool, a means to an end. And like any tool, it could be used for good or evil. Everything depended on how one used it.

Dangerous to have something so important as his Plan dependent upon such a delicate balance. All it took was one unknown, one variable to tip that balance, and leave everything in tatters.

This rogue werewolf was working with the police. Why the hell would he do that?

Hans needed to identify this rogue.

He had sat on enough corporate Boards to understand how dangerous one dissenting opinion could be. This rogue could not be allowed to interfere. He would not be the first obstacle Hans had crushed and utterly destroyed. Maybe he and Francois could just gut him and feast on his hot blood and organs.

That thought made him smile.

CHAPTER TWELVE

Caleb's eyes fluttered open. Disoriented, he made out unfamiliar surroundings. Then he sensed Marla lying soft and warm behind him. Memories brought a dreamy smile to his face. Outside, a pale blue glow told him dawn was not far off.

He pushed the quilt off him. Moving on the balls of his feet, he slipped out of the bedroom and into the bathroom.

He closed the door, turned on the light. Pain stabbed like a cattle prod through his brain. He squeezed his eyes shut, grumbling under his breath. He felt his way along the vanity to the privy. He urinated, remembering a time when indoor plumbing was a luxury only for the rich.

He staggered back to the vanity where he peered at his reflection. He looked like shit. A night with precious little sleep would do that to you. Moving back, more of his body came into view.

A latticework of scars crisscrossed his torso. Some interconnected. His own personal roadmap of pain. His eyes settled on the ugly, jagged scar on his left shoulder. a daily reminder of what he was -- a creature caught in a tug-of-war between two opposing worlds.

A small circular scar stared back at him from his right chest, a gunshot wound from that night in Portland. He had a star-shaped scar on his back from the exit wound. Penetrating completely and collapsing a lung, he would have died if he had not already been Turned. The long thin scar along his right abdomen, a memento from an attempted mugging.

Chicago, 1949. Caleb remembered it vividly. His attacker had stabbed him without provocation while stealing Caleb's wallet. If the guy had just asked, Caleb would have handed it over, no muss no fuss.

But no. His attacker had to be vicious about it, so he got what he got. He had the most ridiculous look on his face when Caleb rose from the dirty pavement, a shaggy three-hundred-and-fifty-pound demon dog from hell. Caleb had twisted the man's head clean off his body, then gleefully dined on his liver and heart.

Caleb still found himself in a moral quagmire. He wouldn't deceive Marla, but he couldn't tell her the truth. And he refused to be an asshole and dump her without explanation.

No easy answers.

When he crept into the hallway, he smelled Marla's after-scent. Her bedroom door was closed, a tiny strip of light sneaking out at the bottom.

Stealth mode was pointless now, so Caleb walked into the guest room. He didn't think to close the door. Over the course of his long life, being naked for extended periods of time had become so normal to him that walking around unclothed wasn't even a blip on his radar.

He fluffed the pillows, smoothed the sheets. Pulled the quilt up, tucked it under the pillowcases. He had just pulled his underwear up when he smelled Marla at the door.

Marla stood there already dressed, hair brushed. She was not smiling.

"Morning," he said.

"Hey," she replied. I'll put some coffee on."

"Thanks." His smile was becoming forced now.

"You hungry?"

"Sure." His smile was mostly gone now.

"What would you like?"

"I'm not picky."

She inhaled to say something more, stopped. She disappeared down the hallway, acting like she regretted the night before. He certainly did not. Maybe she had changed her mind about him. He hoped he was reading her wrong, but knew he was not.

He finished dressing, trying to remain calm. If she decided this was just a one-night stand, he would respect her wishes. But casual sex was not really a part of his nature anymore. The Wolf had altered his genetic code, thereby altering his own human nature and therefore, his behavior.

He smelled the coffee as he walked down the hallway. He never got tired of that aroma. Living in the Pacific Northwest and dealing with the cold wet weather, he had become something of a coffee connoisseur. Or maybe just a coffee snob. Either way, he was okay with it.

"Smells heavenly," he announced as he walked in. "And you look absolutely gorgeous."

She smiled in spite of herself. "Thanks." She did not approach him for a kiss.

He made a mental note of this as he sat down. "How did you sleep?"

"Fine, thanks. And you?"

"Like the dead," he fibbed.

Marla fidgeted, rubbing her palms together.

"What's wrong?"

"Nothing," she replied too quickly. She turned to the counter, pulled two mugs down. She grabbed the carafe, poured each mug full. Her hands trembled as she brought the mugs to the table, coffee threatening to spill down the sides as she sat them down. She moved to the fridge, returned with a small container of creamer.

Caleb picked up a spoon, measured out some sugar, dumped it into his own coffee. He added a bit of cream. When the color turned a soft cafe au lait color, he knew he had it right. He was aware of Marla watching every move.

"What?" he asked.

"This is awkward."

Caleb sipped his coffee.

"We just met, thrown together by this murder investigation. We don't really know each other."

"Are you concerned that I am of loose moral character?"

Marla's eyes popped wide. Loose moral character? Who the hell talked like that these days? Her mouth fell open. She then broke into laughter. The tension fled the room.

"That was not what I was thinking," she said at last. She grinned, added cream to her coffee. No sugar.

"Then what?"

"That you might think me 'of loose moral character'."

He looked genuinely hurt. "Why would I think that?"

She stared at him a moment, realizing he was sincere. That had been the last thing on his mind. Time to change the subject.

"Any new theories about the case?" she asked.

"I'm interested in seeing what I can do with historical correlation."

"You mentioned that before."

"Occupational hazard. I look for historical correlation for just about everything." He sipped his coffee, then, "I believe there's few truly unprecedented acts. Serial killers have been documented in every culture throughout history."

"So, nothing new under the sun?"

"I try to avoid absolutes. But a deep dive can't hurt."

They sat in silence a bit. Caleb sensed Marla's tension returning.

She was overthinking it. He had never seen anything good come from overthinking. One of the benefits of his condition was that like a wolf, Caleb could completely live in the moment.

"What happened between us last night was the most natural thing in the world," he said, breaking the silence. "There's no reason to feel bad about it."

"It's not the act; it's the implications."

"Implications?"

Marla's eyes moved right and upwards, a subconscious tell. She was accessing the logic centers of her brain, formulating a response.

"I haven't always had the best luck with men," she said.

Caleb leaned forward, placed his hand over hers. She could feel his warmth, and she reveled in it.

"Relationships aren't about luck," he stated. "They're about trust. You have to put in the work to develop something lasting. It requires daily application."

"None of the others thought that way."

"Wrong men."

"So, you're saying I have terrible taste in men?" She seemed perturbed. "What does that say about me sleeping with you?"

"That your taste is improving."

"The last guy said the same thing," she replied.

"He obviously didn't mean it. I do."

"Oh? And how do I know that?"

"You know," he said with certainty. "I'm not a guy; I'm a *man*. I'm responsible for my words and deeds. I mean what I say, and I say what I mean."

She stared at him again, appraising him. Facial expression and body language indicated no deceit. Could it be he might actually be different?

"You're not secretly married, are you?"

Caleb was genuinely surprised. "No."

"You have kids?"

"None that I know of."

She suppressed her own smile. "You secretly gay and in love with Russell??"

Caleb laughed. "He's not my type."

Her eyes widened. "You have a type? "What is your type, Caleb Jacobsen?"

His eyes twinkled. "I'm looking at her."

She warmed. "Good line."

God, how she wanted to believe this man. She sat back in her chair, eyes never leaving his face.

"No pressure, then," she said. "Let's take it slow, see where this goes."

"Agreed."

CHAPTER THIRTEEN

The functional, aesthetically challenged government surplus clock hung high on the colorless wall inside Homicide Division. White face, black numbers circling the perimeter. The black hour and minute hands, while a bright red second hand swept silently around. It read almost eight o'clock when Akin shuffled in, still wearing yesterday's clothes. Dark circles around her eyes, corners of her mouth pulled down by stress. Pallid skin, hollow cheeks, hair that could only be called a hot mess – not that Akin gave a shit what other people thought.

Martinez sat at his desk, pouring over his notes. He wore different clothes from yesterday. His necktie was already yanked down and the top shirt button popped open. His short wiry hair always looked the same. He could take an hour to dress or just roll out of bed and go. It made no difference.

His face brightened when he saw her. He pointed at the two coffee cups she carried. "Starter fluid?"

She held one cup out.

He took the offered cup. "What's this?" he motioned to a white paper bag she held in two curled fingers. Grease stains soaked the paper brown.

She dropped it in front of him. Holding the top of the bag wide, he peered down to see its contents. He smiled gratefully.

"You always know what I need," he said. He pulled out a cheese raspberry danish.

"You work with someone a while; you get to know them."

He bit into the danish, sipped his unsweetened coffee. "You really are something special."

"Try telling my ex-husband that."

Martinez's face darkened. "I could never tell that arrogant prick anything," he muttered. "He thought we were having an affair, you know."

Akin nearly spewed her coffee all over her desk. "What?" she gasped.

"He pulled me aside at the Christmas party last year, accused me of wanting to sleep with you."

"Did you?"

"Doesn't matter. You were married, and that ends the discussion as far as I'm concerned."

Akin sipped her coffee, stifled her impulse to remind him that she was, in fact, no longer married. But her bare left ring finger served as mute testament to that detail.

A young boy, not more than seventeen, walked in, a manilla envelope tucked under one arm. He stopped, looking around, unsure of himself.

"Can I help you?" Martinez called out.

The boy moved towards them. "I'm looking for –" he checked the name on the envelope – "Detective Jose Martinez."

"You found him."

The lad put the envelope on Martinez's desk. He pulled a receipt and a black ink pen out of his back pocket.

"You gotta sign. Something about 'chain of custody'."

Martinez signed his name near the bottom of the ticket. The kid took his copy, went straight for the exit. He couldn't get out of there fast enough.

"What you got?" Akin asked, pointing to the envelope.

Martinez was stuffing the last of the danish into his mouth. He chewed, sipped more coffee to wash it down. He leaned closer, looked at the name of the sender.

"Medical examiner." He unspooled the string that bound the envelope at the top. Akin got up, moved around to Martinez's side to look over his shoulder.

For several minutes neither one spoke as they read, then reread the wealth of medical forensics in front of them. They occasionally passed a page back and forth to each other, but that was all. As they looked at lab analyses and chemical breakdowns, their minds began to draw conclusions, fill in blanks. And as they did, their emotions, which had started at zero, had moved to confusion, then disbelief, then landed at an, icy fear.

"Wolf saliva?" Martinez breathed at last, fighting hard to keep his emotions in check.

"Look at this." She pointed to a page. "Differing bite radius? Varying maw size ratio?"

"Multiple killers."

"Like a pack of wolves being used to kill."

"Sounds like something you'd see in a bad horror novel." He flipped through the pages, stopped, and pointed to something else. "They found a virus in the saliva."

"Rabies?"

"He shook his head. "They don't know what it is. Not rabies; not distemper. Computer came back with nothing."

"So, we're looking for a wolf pack hunting in major urban areas, eating people, afflicted with some unknown virus."

Akin's mind reeled. Welcome to the Twilight Zone, friends. What the fuck have we stumbled into?" Martinez posed.

"How many diseased animals?" Akin picked up two pages, holding one in each hand. She scanned them, frowning in concentration. Martinez sat waiting.

"The bite radius on victims three, four, and five don't match," she stated. "They're not the same."

"Yeah. Differing bite radiuses. We knew that."

"There's at least three different animals out there." She lay the pages back down on Martinez's desk.

"Here's the scary part," Martinez stated. "If it's an unknown virus, then we've never been exposed to it."

"So?"

"So, if no human has never been exposed, then we have no immunity. I mean zero."

Akins breathed, chilled to the bone. "No immunity means that even if someone survived an attack, this virus could be fatal."

"Or worse," Martinez said.

Caleb sat alone in Marla's kitchen, drinking another cup of coffee. What did he know? What did he merely suspect?

A new pack had established itself in the Pacific Northwest. It was a logical choice. Scenic beauty, four seasons, polite and friendly people who minded their own business. Forests and mountains teeming with wildlife allowed for privacy when one needed to hunt. He had chosen this region for similar reasons.

But Caleb did his thing on his own. He resisted seeking out others like himself, to congregate, establish a hierarchy, build a pack.

They could have it, as far as he was concerned. He had made the mistake once of joining a collective as a young man, years before he ever got bitten. That decision proved a seminal moment, something that altered and influenced everything that came later.

As a result, Caleb despised groupthink. It was dangerous regardless what side of the political or social spectrum from which it sprang. Individuals were capable of mercy, compassion, intelligence, understanding. Put them into a group and mob mentality inevitably took over, spreading like a malignant tumor. Then people became stupid, hateful, vile spewing, dangerous animals. It invariably brought… *unfortunate* consequences.

Marla appeared in the doorway, a concerned look on her face.

"Look. You seem like a great guy –"

"Oh Jesus," he muttered, cutting her off.

"Sorry." Apologetic.

"We just went through this."

"I know. It's just..." She could not quite find the right words.

"You're making this harder than it has to be."

Marla's cell phone buzzed. Caleb winced at the sound, raised a hand close to his ear. The same reaction he had exhibited last night in the restaurant, Marla remembered. She dug in the pockets of her cargo shorts, pulled the phone out pressed it to her ear.

"Hello? Yes. This is Dr. Moreno."

Caleb rinsed his cup out and placed it in the sink. He edged his chair under the table, trying hard not to listen in.

"Yes," Marla said, nodding. "Caleb?" She looked at him. "I'll find him." She pushed the button to end the call, dropped the phone into her pocket. "They need us at the station."

Caleb headed straight for the Jeep while Marla locked the front door. By the time she made it to the Jeep, Caleb had already unlocked the passenger door, gone around and gotten in on the driver's side. The engine roared to life as she adjusted her seatbelt.

The Jeep pulled away from the curb, made a U-turn and headed back the way they had come last night. Caleb turned the corner and hit the gas.

Minutes later, Caleb turned into the Police parking lot. He found an empty stall, pulled in, killed the engine. Marla was opening her door when Caleb reached out and gently grabbed her arm. She froze, turned her head towards him.

"Before we go put our game faces on, I want you to know last night was fantastic."

Marla's eyes softened. She smiled. "We need to get inside."

They climbed out of the Jeep, shut the doors. Marla waited for Caleb as he made his way around the front of the vehicle. She turned began walking. Caleb, already moving, brushed his hand against hers. She blushed, smiled.

He grabbed the door handle. She smiled as he silently held the door. No words were necessary. His actions spoke volumes.

She strode down the hallway, concentrating on the business at hand. Her night with Caleb had to be set aside for now. She felt an obligation to deal with the matter professionally. Their relationship was nobody else's business. And Caleb was no braggart. He wouldn't kiss and tell.

Dr. Melendez waited. Face pale and drawn, hollow cheeks, darkness around her eyes. She looked exhausted.

"Good morning," she said as Marla approached.

"Bad night?"

She grunted. "You have no idea."

Caleb brought up the rear. "Coffee?"

Melendez pointed. "Around the corner."

"Thanks." He turned to Marla. "Want more?"

Marla's mind immediately went back to their nighttime activities. She grinned. Yes, she definitely wanted more. But coffee would do for now.

"Please."

Caleb turned and walked away, a slight spring in his step.

"Anything new since last night?" Marla asked.

"The detectives are going to brief us any minute."

"Russell?"

"I called him before I called you. He's driving down."

Caleb rounded the corner, carrying large cups of steaming coffee. He handed one cup to Marla. She opened the lid, peeked in. He had doctored her coffee just the way she liked it. He had paid attention back at her house.

Don't underestimate this man's powers of observation, she told herself.

Russell appeared in the hallway, waddling towards them. He clutched a coffee cup in one hand, and a half-eaten breakfast croissant in the other. He smiled at them, silently waved with his croissant. He had crumbs at the corners of his mouth, and a smear of something already across his rotund belly.

"Hey there, Scooby gang," he beamed. "What's new?"

"That's what we're here to find out," Marla said.

Melendez glanced at her watch. She sniffed; her displeasure apparent. Dr. Miriam Melendez believed in punctuality. It was professional. It was respectful. She demanded it of herself, and she expected it from others.

A side door opened. Akin strode in, followed by Martinez.

"Ah," Akin said as she approached. "The gang's all here."

Akin and Martinez lead them into a glass-walled conference room off the main area. Martinez flipped the light switch as the consultants found chairs at a conference table.

Akin updated them on the new forensics the lab had provided. She handed out copies of the report, admonishing them to not take the reports outside the station under any circumstances. Then she gave them a moment to look over the details.

As Marla's eyes scanned the documents, fear gripped her. None of this made any sense. In fact, nothing in the entire Goddamned case made any sense.

Wolf saliva, varying bite radii, mutated DNA, and now an unidentified virus. Her eyes darted up to Caleb, who stared intently at his own copy of the report. His face was unreadable, but she noticed an artery on his left temple pulsating. She wondered what was going on behind those eyes.

Akin cleared her throat. "Okay, people. We're open to ideas. Thoughts?"

Russell, Marla, and Caleb all looked around at each other. None of them seemed to be eager to speak. Melendez sat off to the side, watching.

"I'm still not sure what exactly is going on here," Marla said at last. "I've never heard of a wolf the size these animals must be, based on their bite measurements." She looked up from the pages in her hands. "These animals will be significantly larger than wolves that breed in the wild."

"Could a wolf be bred in captivity and then trained to kill on command?"

Marla thought about that for a moment. "Wolves are highly intelligent animals. But as a practical matter, no. Wolves are wild animals, and natural born predators."

Martinez nodded in Russell's direction. "Professor Slater, are there any cults that worship wolves?"

Russell frowned in thought. "The Native Americans believed wolves were omens from the Gods, that they could embody the spirits of their ancestors. But that's different. Modern cults tend to worship whoever sits at the top."

Caleb sat silent throughout, hardly taking his eyes off the copy in front of him. He regulated his pulse, his breathing. Otherwise, things were likely to get…. *hairy* for everyone in attendance.

"Anything new from the girl last night?" Caleb asked.

"Martinez consulted a paper inside the folder in his hand. "Forensics found some hair strands under her fingernails."

"Any roots so we can get DNA?"

"That's very good, Professor Jacobsen," Martinez said. "You've been reading up?"

"I watch a lot of police procedurals on TV."

"Well, it just so happens we did get DNA," Martinez announced. "It turned out to be animal fur. *Canis lupus.*"

"A wolf," Marla said.

"This is where it goes all Outer Limits on us," Akin chimed in. "Somehow the DNA got contaminated. The wolf DNA was combined with human DNA."

Silence in the room. Caleb held his breath.

"The final report isn't back yet," she continued. "But it seems apparent that the samples got contaminated. I mean, a DNA strand that was comprised of wolf and human DNA? That's crazy. That would make the killer a werewolf, right?"

Laughter from everyone in the room except from Caleb. Just as it was dying down, a young Asian woman came in, her open white lab coat swirling behind her. She handed a new folder to Akin and left. Akin opened the folder. Her face contorted as she read it. Martinez knew her well enough to know she did not like what she saw.

She looked up, stared in silence at the assembled consultants.

"What is it?" Russell asked.

Akin's mouth fell open, closed again. She tried to speak, was unsuccessful. Martinez took the folder from her, peeked inside.

"*Madre de dios,*" he mumbled to himself.

Akin and Martinez huddled together, whispered so softly no one but Caleb could hear. He tried to ignore them.

They turned towards the consultants. Akin waved the folder. "They found skin cells on her body. She scratched her killer." She glanced at the folder again. "Maybe it's above my head, but the genetic breakdown of the cells makes no sense."

"Are the cells cancerous? Mutated?" Russell asked.

"No," Akin replied. "According to this, these cells are exactly what the DNA dictates they should be."

Martinez took over. "The cells contain two separate, distinctive sets of chromosomes."

"Impossible," scoffed Melendez. "That amount of DNA would be incompatible with life!"

"I have to agree with the good doctor," Russell chimed in. "This is either a mutation, or the lab botched the results."

"They're rerunning the tests now."

Marla had been keeping an eye on Caleb the whole time. He sat still, attentive in his chair. His left elbow rested on the chair's arm, left hand draped the lower half of his face. Beneath his implacable façade, something lurked behind those eyes.

Something dark. Primal.

Dangerous.

CHAPTER FOURTEEN

It was nearly ten a.m. at KKDA studios. Dammit! They were behind schedule – again! - and about twelve million things had to go right for them to be ready on time. Even though it was a Saturday, both the newsroom and the soundstage hummed with activity.

KKDA was the only local Seattle station with a live weekend news broadcast at noon. All the others scheduled infomercials no one watched.

Production assistants sat in the chairs behind the news desk while lighting technicians adjusted lights that hung from scaffolding above. Camera crews checked their A and B cameras, adjusted focus. The Technical Director grumbled into the microphone on her headset. She complained about something to her boss up in the Control Room.

Off to the side, at the edge of the stage, Janet Mason stood watching it all. She held her cell phone to one ear and the palm of one hand over the other. She frowned in concentration, trying to block out all distraction so she could give her caller her undivided attention.

Almost thirty-five, Janet still had the muscular legs and slender waist of a runner, with the shoulder strength of a swimmer. Her red dress contrasted nicely with her dark brown skin. She wore lipstick, eye shadow, and colorful earrings from Nairobi, Kenya, the country of her parents' birth. She had never been there herself. Born and raised in the U.S., her childhood had been littered with horror stories of life in the Old Country.

She nodded as she listened. "Hold on a minute." She cradled the phone between her ear and her lifted shoulder while her hands snaked into her pockets. They reemerged with a pen and paper.

"Okay. Give it to me, baby," she cooed. Her pen scribbled furiously across the paper. "All right." Her tone had gone back to all business. "You certain about these names?" She listened, nodded again. "Okay, sweetie. Thanks a million. I'll see you tonight."

Janet hit the END button with her thumb, let the phone to fall into her pocket. She headed across the bustling studio floor. She ducked and weaved like a boxer, avoiding calamity as everyone prepared for the broadcast.

"Hey Annie!" she called out. The disgruntled Technical Director turned towards her. "You seen Dragon Lady?"

The Director pointed towards Diane's office.

Diane Yakamoto, aka, the "Dragon Lady", was indeed in her office, leaning back in her chair, her feet on her desk, legs crossed at the ankles. Through reading glasses perched atop her nose, she scanned her rough draft, the stories vying for attention in the upcoming broadcast. She held a felt marker in one hand, occasionally struck out a word and scribbled something better, more impactful in the margins. Her assistant would relay the marked-up copy to the teleprompt controller so the feed could be entered accurately.

Diane had a notorious reputation. Aloof and detached, she was condescending and short-tempered to anyone she did not consider her equal. Her moods and tantrums were legendary. The first thing new hires learned was, don't piss off Diane.

She barely tolerated her fellow anchors, even though they had worked their way up over the years, starting in secondary or tertiary markets just like she had. She ignored the sports guy entirely. He was nothing, a former jock who married the daughter of the station owner. And she absolutely detested the bubbly blonde weather girl. Little Miss "Weather Gurl" wasn't even a meteorologist. She was a communications major who barely graduated from some Podunk University but possessed a flat stomach and perky tits.

Diane knew what everyone called her behind her back. She didn't give a shit. They could say that to her face, and she wouldn't even blink. She simply didn't give a flying fuck what these *people* thought about anything.

Diane was Japanese, and the Dragon was primarily a Chinese symbol. These humans, she thought. They consider themselves educated, yet they don't know the difference between Japanese and Chinese culture. She was cast adrift on a ship of fools.

She had no friends here. No matter. She would be a werewolf soon. She and Hans would become an Alpha pair, the supreme achievement within werewolf hierarchy.

Janet rapped on the door frame outside. Diane looked up from her pages, motioned her in with one hand. Janet stepped inside.

"Janet." Diane laid the pages across her lap. "What did you get?"

"Just the names and backgrounds of the consultants on the case," Janet replied.

Diane cocked an eyebrow as Janet handed the sheet of paper adorned with her scribbling. She scanned the names, not recognizing any of them.

"I tried to get addresses and phone numbers, but that was a no-go," Janet continued.

Diane looked up from the paper. "We wouldn't want to invade their privacy, now would we?"

Janet's mouth split into a grin. "That would be unethical."

"Splendid work."

"Good thing I sleep with a cop, huh?"

"Fuck him good tonight."

"Oh, sweetie. I fuck him good *every* night."

Janet sashayed out. Diane sat back in her chair, looked at the list again, lips silently moving as she memorized the names.

She grabbed her cellphone, stabbed a single button. Speed dial was a wonderful thing. She exhaled, waiting patiently.

"*Bonjour?*" Francois on the other end.

Diane swallowed her disappointment. "It's Diane."

"*Bonjour.*"

"Is Hans there?"

"He is not available at this time. May I be of assistance?"

"I have news to relay. The names of the detectives investigating the case," she said.

"We already possess this information." His tone was neutral, carefully modulated.

"Do you also possess the names of the consultants called in to track you down?"

A long silence on the other end. She grinned, imagining Francois' mouth falling open in surprise, then him recovering.

"Just a moment," Francois said. A rustling of paper on the other end. Finally, he came back. "Okay."

Diane carefully recited the full names and occupations of Marla and Russell. She also relayed the fact about them being cousins. Francois grunted on the other end.

"There's a third one," Diane said. "Sort of an odd choice when taken at face value. A local history professor."

"Name, please?"

"Caleb Jacobsen."

Absolute silence on the other end. The silence continued. Diane frowned, as if François could detect that across the phone line.

"*Mon dieu,*" Francois croaked, his voice sounding strangled.

"Francois?"

"Can you repeat that, *S'il vous plaît?*"

Diane repeated the name. "Francois, what's wrong?"

Francois answered, his voice having slipped back into its well-modulated tone. "Diane, you have greatly advanced the Cause today. Be proud."

Diane warmed. "Thank you."

"Rest assured, I will relay this to Hans immediately. He will be well pleased. *Merci beaucoup. Au revoir.*"

Francois hung up before Diane could say anything else. She pulled her phone away from her ear, tossed it onto her desk.

That had been the least confrontational conversation she'd had with Francois in a long time, and he still cut the conversation short. They each wanted to have Hans's ear as his most trusted advisor and confidant. And both were willing to undercut the other to make themselves look better.

Diane sprung from her chair. She opened her door, leaned on the frame.

"Hey Janet!" she yelled.

"Yes?" came a disembodied voice somewhere amidst the chaos before her.

"Knock on my door in an hour."

"Will do."

Janet was a good egg. Maybe she could talk to Hans, spare Janet's life from the Blood Purge. Janet could work for Diane the Werewolf Queen.

Diane the Werewolf Queen. She smiled to herself. It had a nice ring to it. Conceive, believe, and achieve. Diane the soon-to-be Werewolf Queen was already two thirds of the way there.

She dropped the custom wood venetian blinds from their resting place near the ceiling. She turned a thin plastic control bar, closing the slats. She repeated this for every glass pane in her office.

She walked back around to her chair, plopped down. Diane barely weighed over one hundred pounds. But her weight, combined with the momentum of her drop, caused the springs underneath to groan in protest. She ignored them.

She kicked off her shoes, leaned back in the chair, propped her feet on the desk once again, casually crossing her legs at the ankle. Hands resting behind her head, her eyes drifted over to the closed door. A red dress hung on the back of the door, suspended from a plastic hook. Her wardrobe for later. It contrasted sharply with the faded jeans and plain gray sweatshirt she currently wore.

Diane looked outside. Gray sky, clouds pregnant with rain. She lived in what some referred to as the "rain capital" of the United States. Seattle averaged almost 38 inches of rain based on an average of 152 days of rainfall per year. No wonder Diane owned two rain jackets and four umbrellas.

She hated Seattle. An only child to professional parents who were physically absent for large swathes of time and emotionally distant even when they were home, she had never made friends easily in school. She had always preferred warmer climes, sunny weather. Too bad that evening anchor job in San Diego never materialized. That would have been optimal.

She had known she was not going to have her contract renewed at her last job in Atlanta. She had called her agent and expressed interest in several markets on the West Coast where 300 days of sunshine per year was the norm. Seattle had been her last choice, Diane's own personal nuclear option. But when her last gig ended, no one but Seattle was showing even the slightest interest.

Word was out about Diane Yakamoto: while talented and relentless, she was mercurial, difficult to work with.

The other markets had called Atlanta as part of their due diligence and had been warned off. She could not prove that, otherwise she would have grounds for a lawsuit. But admissible evidence, even in a civil matter where the legal bar was lower, could be hard to come by.

She had dragged her feet on Seattle, even after they had paid to fly her in for interviews. She lived on her savings and investments for three months, hoping that one of the other markets might come around.

None of them did.

Here she was, two years in on a four-year contract, being paid about the same as in Atlanta and resented she was not making more. It was *her* face on the billboards, *her* face on the sides of busses, *her* face featured in the TV promos.

Station management saw things differently. They knew her reputation but had been desperate. Diane had turned out to be precisely as advertised. She showed up on time every day, worked efficiently, practiced due diligence on breaking stories. But they were already tired of her tantrums and the HR complaints they generated. Management had no intention of renewing her contract when it expired in two more years.

Two more long years.

Even if Diane had known all this, she would not have cared. This was her last job. The Werewolf Apocalypse was only days away.

Diane closed her eyes. Thoughts of Hans' kisses floated into her mind, rode across like prancing horses. His kisses, hot and sweet. They never failed to turn her knees to butter as he pushed his tongue into her mouth.

Her body reacted to the memories. She smiled dreamily. She wanted him again, wanted him right now. She would have to wait until later tonight, but that was okay. She would have him again.

After a while, she slept.

The police briefing had ended. The detectives had passed all the new information they possessed. Plausible theories of the crimes continued to elude them.

They were still waiting on toxicology reports and more DNA results. Caleb knew whatever results came back, the police would not connect the dots. He still had to figure out where the werewolves were, why they were killing in public, and most importantly, how to convince them to stop.

Russell and Marla huddled in conference with Dr. Melendez. He thought about joining them, then reconsidered. Better to stay separate and appear to be deep in thought.

The three-way confab broke up with smiles and gentle laughter. Melendez headed for the exit. Russell and Marla, still grinning, turned and moved towards Caleb. Leave it to Russell. That man can find the humor in anything.

"We're going to brunch," Marla announced. "Want to come?"

"Can't."

Marla looked confused, then disappointed. This was not the answer she was expecting. Or hoping for.

"I need to consult one of the Department's computer experts," he said." Start my own investigation."

"Your loss, Beefcake," Russell chimed in.

"Don't I know it?"

"See you later?" Marla asked.

He smiled warmly. "Definitely."

Russell noticed the sparks between them, said nothing. He took Marla by the elbow, pointed her towards the door.

Outside, the rain had stopped. Wet streets reflected bright sunlight that had pierced the cloud cover. Water still beaded on the cars in the police lot. Marla blinked at the unexpected brightness.

"There's an old greasy spoon two blocks down." He pointed in a general direction. "Remember Mama's Country Kitchen back home? It's like that.

"Does it have that same smell?"

He grinned and started walking. Marla followed, caught up, continued walking at his side. They arrived less than five minutes later. Russell held the door for her.

The smell of hot grease hit her like a physical force when she walked in. Childhood memories came flooding back. For all her academic and professional achievements, for all she had accomplished in her life, maybe she wasn't so far from home after all.

They navigated around tables filled with customers, seated themselves in a booth. Russell tossed his phone onto the table. They both grabbed the cheap ceramic coffee mugs resting upside down and turned them right side up. A waitress materialized, carafe of hot coffee in hand. She silently poured them both, then disappeared as quickly as she had come.

Marla looked at Russell, surprised. "Efficient."

"What they lack in manners they make up in speed."

Suddenly the waitress was back to take their orders. Russell ordered from memory. Marla a consulted the menu, made a fast decision. Once they had ordered, the waitress walked away without any extraneous conversation.

Marla sipped of her coffee. Weak swill, not in the same universe as the high-end coffee she usually enjoyed. More childhood memories: Bad coffee, water from the well out back, abject poverty.

Growing up, she didn't understand the concept of rich and poor. Hardships were simply dealt with, worked around, endured, survived. With no other metric by which to measure her life, she accepted her surroundings as normal. She assumed all families lived like they did.

When Marla made her Great Escape to college, the wealth and privilege of other students shocked her. The more she saw the differences and nuances between the students, she came to realize just how dirt poor she and her family really were.

But she refused to be ashamed, embarrassed, or depressed. She was no victim. Marla Moreno would determine her own worth, her own destiny. Where she came from was not her choice. But where she ended up was completely within her control.

Marla Moreno became all about upward mobility.

At college, she finally understood she had been raised for this opportunity all her life. Marla's mom had barely made it through high school before getting pregnant. The hardships of life aged her prematurely, but she was not one to complain.

Marla was very much her mother's daughter. At the same time, she understood how life could beat a person down, whip them into submission to a point where they might think there really was no way out. And when people got beaten down that much, they inevitably gave up. Gave up on hope. Gave up on dreams. Gave up on finding a better tomorrow.

Marla never looked down her nose at them, then or now. She got it. She also got that the same pressures and adversities that broke some people, spurred others on to achieve great things so they never had to live like that again.

She stirred her shitty coffee, her mind a thousand miles away. Russell cleared his throat. Loudly.

She blinked at him, realized he had spoken to her. "I'm sorry. What?"

"I said, 'Penny for your thoughts'".

"Questions. I have questions."

"Fire away."

"About Caleb." She looked up from her coffee. "How long have you known him?"

"A while," he replied. "Several years."

"He stayed over last night."

Russell leered at her. "You sultry minx!"

"Are you done?" She cocked an eyebrow. "Look. I was scared last night. So sue me if I wanted someone around to protect me."

"I ain't judging."

She gulped, nervous. "We um… well we…" Marla blushed, grinned, looked down.

"Ooooooh," Russell breathed. "That good, huh?"

"Can I continue please?"

"By all means."

"So, umm…. Does he date a lot?"

"Until yesterday, I don't think he's dated at all. I know he never forgot meeting you at that party last year."

"He says he's interested, but I just don't know."

"Caleb's says what he means and means what he says. If he says he's interested, then he's interested."

"Simple as that?" She sounded hopeful.

"Simple as that."

"Nothing is as simple as that between men and women."

"It is with him."

"So, if I asked you if he has any deep dark secrets?"

"You mean like, is he a serial killer?"

Marla laughed in surprise. "Something like that, I guess."

"Not that I'm aware of."

"Has he ever been married? Is he hiding some secret family somewhere?"

"Not that I'm aware of." Russell leaned in towards his cousin. "Look. I'm his friend, not his confessor. He plays his cards close to the vest. That doesn't mean there's anything wrong. He's just a private person."

"He just sounds too good to be true."

"Nah. He was just born a century or so too late."

The waitress returned, topped off their coffee mugs. She came back less than a minute later carrying their food. She placed their plates in front of them, asked if they needed anything else. They did not, so she turned and retreated towards the kitchen.

Russell dug in with gusto. He was starved. Marla ate, not really tasting her food. Her mind kept circling back around to Caleb.

CHAPTER FIFTEEN

The front door of the diner opened. Two tall, muscular men stepped inside. One had a salt and pepper hair, black skin. The other sported a blonde mane pulled back in a ponytail secured by black ribbon.

Francois lead Hans to an isolated booth near the back. They eased into thickly cushioned seats, turned their mugs right-side up.

"What's wrong?"

Hans looked like he wanted to be somewhere else – anywhere else - but here. "This place." He shook his head with disgust. "So low-class."

"We can speak freely here without being spied upon."

"We are being spied upon?"

"No," Francois replied quickly. Hans was under more stress than he outwardly showed.

The waitress appeared, menus in one hand, coffee carafe in the other. She dropped menus in front of each of them, poured the coffee expertly, not spilling a single drop. Then she was gone.

Hans looked around, sneering. "A pig trough for the unwashed masses."

"I was born a peasant outside Lyon," Francois said, not perturbed in the slightest. "All my people were unwashed masses." He flashed a jubilant smile. "Of course, the Revolution changed that."

Hans shrugged, stirred the brown sludge in his mug that passed for coffee here. Francois loved to talk the French Revolution. He had participated in that unrest long before it devolved into an orgy of violence and kangaroo courts where anyone of wealth, whether criminal or no, were sent to the guillotine. Francois had been at Ground Zero, had stormed the Bastille on 14 July 1789. He beamed with pride, two hundred and forty years later.

But the Revolution lasted ten years, toppled a monarchy, gave way to a secular republic. It gave rise to Napoleon Bonaparte and an authoritarian government that waged war not only with itself, but with other countries. Francois never mentioned Napoleon's crushing defeat at Waterloo.

Hans felt the French went from the frying pan into the fire. He thought about the various conflicts and civil wars raging across the globe as they sat there. He shook his head. Times change. People don't. Technology advances. War stays the same.

"Hans?"

Hans blinked his eyes, snapped his head. "Yes?"

"The reason we're here is I'm hungry, and you need a break from being the clandestine leader of a global revolution."

"Once we're in power, the first thing I want to do is kill every drug dealer and human trafficker on the planet."

"Good," Francois said. "Stamp out the trade."

"Hell no. We're taking over."

The waitress returned, took their orders for breakfast. She scribbled quickly on her note pad, grabbed the menus, and disappeared. Hans was happy to see her go.

Francois did not like the idea of being complicit in dealing illegal drugs. What did the smart-asses call it? Oh yes. Recreational pharmaceuticals. But it was Han's decision, not his. Francois just had to make the best of it.

"This whole religious cult thing," Francois chuckled. "Sheer genius."

"Simple mathematics, really. The world spawns more sheep than wolves," Hans said. "The lost, the forgotten, the disenfranchised. People of low moral character and spiritual weakness. You know what they all have in common?"

Francois shook his head.

"Hopelessness. It fuels a deep-seated impotent rage they can neither channel nor control. Born followers the lot of them," Hans spat, "just waiting for someone to lead them."

They paused. The waitress came back. They sipped their burned coffee as she placed their plates in front of them. She moved away, heading towards another table as she pulled out her note pad.

Hans lifted some eggs from his plate to his mouth with a fork, chewed, gathering his thoughts. "This new wolf. William."

"What about him?"

"He serves his purpose for now. His sexual proclivities help stoke fear." Hans reached for the ketchup. "Someday we may need to reevaluate his usefulness."

Francois stabbed his fork into his hash browns. "Speaking of increased sex drives, Diane called. Her contacts came through."

Hans grinned. "See why I put up with her?"

"Russell Slater. Psychologist. He's been a consultant for years."

"He's harmless."

"Marla Moreno. Zoologist. Works R&D for Global BioTech."

Hans nodded. "I sit on the Board." He contemplated this. "They think it's animal attacks." Then he shrugged. "None of them have a clue what's really happening."

A pained look on Francois's face. "There's a problem with that."

Hans leaned back and sighed.

"The third consultant, the rogue."

"His name?"

"Caleb Jacobsen."

Hans felt all the air leave his lungs. Indeed, for a brief, hysterical instant, it felt like all the air had left the room. He stared down at his plate, his appetite gone.

"Caleb Jacobsen," he repeated, his voice a husky whisper.

"*Oui, mon ami.*"

There it was.

Confirmation. Terrible, horrible confirmation.

Hans looked briefly at his coffee, no desire to drink more brown water thickened by half-curdled milk. Right now, it looked like a mug of steaming diarrhea.

Hans spoke at last. "Wyoming, right?"

"Montana."

"Right. Montana." Hans fell silent a moment. He exhaled, looking suddenly tired. His entire body seemed to sag, as if he had just become impossibly heavy.

"Javier died that night," Hans wheezed. "Lucky son of a bitch."

"One werewolf died," Francois countered. "Another was born. Fair trade."

Hans grunted. "I wonder."

"You gave him eternal life, *mon ami.*"

"I gave him an infectious disease."

"You bestowed to him an incredible gift."

"But does he see it that way?"

"We must deal with what's in front of us," Francois stated. "What do you want to do about him?"

Hans's mind locked onto the situation. Francois could see the wheels turning behind his eyes.

"We must find him quickly," Hans stated decisively, "before he brings the police down on our heads."

"This I do not understand," Francois said. "Why work with the police?"

Hans leaned forward. "That's his brilliance. He hides in plain sight, points them in our direction. It keeps scrutiny away from him."

Francois's face darkened. "Traitor."

"He's just trying to survive."

"You are too forgiving," Francois observed.

"I'm just keeping my eye on the big picture. Caleb Jacobsen is inconsequential."

"I disagree," Francois warned. "He's dangerous to everything we've worked for. I say we kill him."

Hans shook his head. "I have another way," he stated. "We welcome him, bring him into the fold." Hans smiled. "Accept him for the magnificent Beast he is."

Francois could not believe what he was hearing. "Why would we do that?"

"He's a creature like us. He is clever, resilient, resourceful. The fact he still exists is a testament to his powers of survival." Hans paused, then, "He would make a powerful ally."

"Or a deadly enemy."

"Which is why we must bring him into the fold."

"And if he says no?"

"We deal with him as only we can."

"The prospect makes you sad."

"Mankind has spilled quite enough werewolf blood through the ages without us spilling more."

Francois nodded, knowing the depth of Hans's feelings. He detected movement out of the corner of his eye. He turned to look and saw an attractive Latina walking towards the front cash register, followed by an obese man with thinning blonde hair, sallow skin, and faint smell of decay. They did not notice him watching them, licking his lips like a predator in a nature documentary.

Hans noticed. "What?"

Francois ticked his head towards Marla and Russell. "Those two match the description of the consultants."

Hans focused on the two humans standing waiting to pay their bill. "We have scouts outside?"

Francois leaned back in his seat, pulled his cell phone out, pressed it to the side of his face. He barked a few words in French, stabbed the END button.

"Well?" Hans asked.

Francois looked at his Alpha.

"It shall be done."

Martinez had referred Caleb to a Desk Sergeant well past her prime. Overweight, deeply lined face, with world-weary eyes that had seen too much. She was near retirement, she told him. Just a few more months. Caleb wished her well, asked about computer support. She led him down a long hallway and around a corner to the back of the building. A single closed door awaited them. No nameplate, no placard. Caleb looked questioningly at the Sergeant. She just shrugged.

Inside, the room was small, maybe two hundred square feet. Not much bigger than a glorified broom closet with electrical outlets. Cheap cinder block walls painted a dull white. A single window placed up high on the wall, near the ceiling. Thick glass, opaque, rippled with reinforced crisscross metal strands between the layers. It reminded Caleb of chicken wire. He had just entered through the only way in or out.

One could go claustrophobic in a place like this.

"Can I help you?" came a female voice, slightly irritated.

The voice jolted him. His head snapped away from the window, looking for the source. She stood from her chair in one corner. Tall, slender enough to be called skinny. Brown hair, straight and long, tied into a ponytail that drifted down her back. Dressed in jeans, plaid flannel shirt, hiking boots. She wore a white lab coat over her street clothes. Thin glasses adorned the top of her face.

"I'm Caleb Jacobsen," he announced.

"Oh, yes. I heard you'd be coming by."

"I've heard you're the resident computer genius."

"I prefer Digital Goddess. Call me Jodi."

"Nice to meet you."

She crossed her arms across her whippet chest. "The question remains. Can I help you?"

"I need a deep dive."

"Deep dive is my middle name." She sat back down at her state of the art 21-inch monitor. Caleb walked over and took a position behind her right shoulder.

Her fingers flew nimbly across the keyboard, sending commands to the hard drive built into the screen. "It would be extremely helpful if you told me exactly what we're looking for."

Caleb bristled at her attitude. "Maybe I'll just go tell the detectives you didn't want to help."

She turned towards him in her chair. "What's your problem?"

"You're my problem," Caleb barked, his temper flaring. "I'm trying to stop a serial killer. Now, maybe you had a bad morning, got up late, forgot your coffee, whatever. I don't care. It's no excuse for being rude."

Jodi sat absolutely still. Her eyes searched his face, then drifted over his shoulders, chest, waist. Then her eyes moved back up to his face. Finally, the slightest hint of a smile crossed her lips.

"I like you. You don't take shit from people." She spun in her chair, concentrated on her screen. "So, what exactly are you looking for?"

"I need you to take the specifics of our murders and cross-reference them with every law enforcement agency in the country."

Jodi froze in place a moment, then turned her head at him. her look was incredulous. "Do you have any idea how much work that is?"

"I never said it would be easy."

"Do you have any idea how many law enforcement agencies we're talking about?"

"I'll just tell them you weren't up to the task." He took a step towards the door.

"Hold on a minute," Jodi called out. "It's not that I can't do it. But it's a big job."

"There's five dead people in the morgue right now who strongly suggest you get to it," Caleb said. "How many more need to get hacked and stacked before you cut the shit?"

Fuming, partly because he was challenging her, and partly because she knew he was right, she turned back to her computer.

"Fuck me," she whispered under her breath.

"I'm taken," Caleb muttered.

Jodi looked at him again, this time in shock. How could he have possibly heard that?

"Here's my theory of the crime," he stated. "The parties responsible may have committed similar crimes elsewhere. They've been operating for years."

"A nomadic band of serial killers?" she asked. Before he could respond, she continued. "Most serial killers work alone."

"Your search can prove or disprove my theory."

"And if you're wrong?"

"If I'm wrong, no harm's been done."

"Other than wasting my time."

"You're getting paid, aren't you?" he snapped. "Look. If I'm right, this is bigger than what anyone suspects."

Jodi thought about that for a moment. What if he was right? She would have bragging rights for helping break the biggest case of her career.

"Okay. Just don't expect miracles within the hour."

Jodi squinted at the screen, resumed her rapid-fire keystroke entry. Windows opened, others closed, data downloaded, all following her keyboard commands. She was acutely aware of Caleb watching her, but she did not mind. She was incredibly talented at her job. Some people had used the word "gifted". She finally punched one last ENTER command, then sat back in her chair.

"There you go," she said, holding her arms out.

He looked at the screen. He recognized the computer was running a search, but nothing more.

"I've tapped into the mainframe," she stated proudly. "It's accessing and collating data from similar cases across the country."

"That's great." He meant it.

"But wait, there's more!" she exclaimed, sounding like a late-night infomercial. "I also told it to look for unsolved missing persons cases that had evidence suggesting foul play."

"Foul play?"

"Extreme violence. I told it to go back thirty years."

"Can you search further back?"

"How much further?"

"Two centuries."

Jodi's mouth fell open. "No. That can't be done."

"Why not?"

"Police computer records don't go back that far," she explained. "Some of the bigger cities have digitized their old archival records, microfiche, that sort of thing. The Feds have, of course. But smaller agencies like rural sheriffs and PD's don't have the time or the money. There's still paper files written in pencil sitting in banker's boxes on shelves in musty old basements."

Caleb's mind worked quickly. "How far can you go back?"

"Some jurisdictions, maybe a hundred years," she said. "For most, sixty, seventy years, tops."

"That'll have to do," he said. He paused, thinking. Then, "Lizzie Borden."

"Excuse me?"

"She murdered her parents in Massachusetts in 1892. Sunday morning after they got home from church. Everyone in town knew she did it, but she got acquitted at trial."

"How does she fit in to this?"

"Historical significance," he said. "We know about her case is because of detailed historical records apart from police reports."

"I can't run that broad of a search."

"You don't have to," he said. "My system at the college can interface with history departments, university and public libraries, even newspapers and magazines all across the country."

He turned, headed towards the door. She watched, admiring the rippling muscles beneath his clothes. He stopped and turned, his hand on the doorknob.

"What time do you get off work?"

"Five o'clock."

"I'll back before then."

Jodi watched him disappear through the doorway. The door closed on its own, leaving her alone once in her cramped workspace.

CHAPTER SIXTEEN

Caleb pushed through the exit door, stumbled into bright afternoon sun. Light blasted through his dilated pupils, speared his retinas. He squeezed his eyes shut, then opened them slowly. The daggers stabbing his eyeballs receded. At least he could see the ground now.

He zig-zagged across the parking lot, fished for his keys. He lifted them out, stabbed the key lock button. Ahead of him, the car alarm chirped. A soft *thunk* as the doors unlocked.

Caleb yanked his door open, fell into the driver's seat. He willed his heartbeat to slow. He could not afford a spontaneous Change and he was still dangerously overdue.

He opened his eyes, cranked the engine, eased off the brake. He eased into the street and accelerated, heading towards Interstate 5. He turned on the radio. 70's classic rock blared. He nodded to the beat.

Other werewolves out there did not care about keeping quiet, did not care if they broke cover. Once humans knew that werewolves were real, that werewolves had been in their midst since the beginning of time, panic was certain. Lycophobia and the hatred it would inevitably produce would run rampant. Streets would run red with both human and werewolf blood in cities all over the world.

Caleb Jacobsen had been on the wrong side of history once in his life, and he still carried that guilt, still felt the shame. He would never make that mistake again.

He stopped at a red light, turned right. He hit the onramp, powering the Jeep up the ramp. He checked his mirror, put on his blinker, merged into traffic.

Russell and Marla had finished at the diner, walked back to the station. Marla looked around for Caleb's Jeep.

"Where did Caleb go?"

"Don't know," Russell replied. "Don't worry. He'll be back soon. He won't want to leave his new girlfriend alone for long."

Marla thought about that. Was she his girlfriend now? And did that even matter to her? Marla Moreno was a successful, powerful and independent woman. She had done quite well without a man to lean on. And yet the idea of Caleb being near, being with her made her feel warm inside. What the hell was wrong with her? She didn't need a man in her life, did she?

Well, maybe she didn't *need* a man, but she sure liked the idea of having Caleb around. And he had made it clear he was interested in her. Not her face, not her body. *Her.* How rare was that?

Russell surged ahead, his considerable bulk gaining momentum. Marla dashed to keep up.

"Where's the fire?"

"Inside."

Russell opened the door, held it open. She stepped through. Inside seemed stark, sterile after the sunlit walk back from the diner. Air blew cold and uncomfortable out of vents near the ceiling. They walked back to where they had participated in the morning update. No one else was around.

"Wait here a minute," Russell said. He walked off, disappeared around a corner. Down another hallway.

He found Dr. Melendez's office. The door was closed. No light on from inside. Nobody home. He reached out anyway, tried the door. Locked.

Where the hell was everyone?

Further down the hall, Russell entered a large open space. Lots of cubicles, all furnished with the same generic laminated desks, computer terminals, cheap chairs.

The Detective Division, completely empty.

Marla was waiting for him when he got back.

"No one's here," he shrugged. "No one working on our case, that is."

Russell and Marla walked back outside. Clouds floated heavy in the sky now. The wind had kicked up. They both looked to the Southeast. Mt. Rainier, which had been gloriously and spectacularly visible earlier, was now completely obscured.

"So much for the sunshine."

"Rain in the Pacific Northwest. Who would have thought?"

She grinned. "If only someone had told me it was going to rain up here." In fact, everyone she knew had commented on how much it rained in Northwest Washington before she moved here. They had also warned to her buy warm clothes because in the winter it actually snowed.

They walked over to Russell's rental car. Marla opened her door as Russell skirted around the front. She was buckling in when he swung his bulk into the driver's seat. The entire car sagged a bit.

Russell buckled up, turned the key. They pulled out, paused at the edge of the road, then turned into traffic. They fell silent on the ride over to her house. There was nothing more to be said, at least for the moment.

They pulled up in front of Marla's house and parked. The engine idled, humming contentedly. Marla and Russell stared at each other a moment.

"How bad is this going to get?" she asked. "No bullshit."

"Hard to tell."

"Are we in danger?"

"I don't know."

"Caleb would know."

"Yes. I believe he would."

She grunted under her breath, opened the door. He watched her climb out, close the door, and walk up the walkway to her front door.

He waited until she had unlocked the front door and gone inside. Then he drove away. He noticed several cars parked along the curb in the neighborhood. Most people here owned more than one vehicle, and often parked one in the garage or driveway, the other on the street. No big deal.

One car stood out. Not because of the make, model or color. There were two people in it, not talking, not looking around, just sitting there, pointed in Marla's general direction. He thought about turning around, going back. Just in case. He decided against it. No need to be paranoid.

He got to the end of the block, gave one last look in his rearview mirror, then turned and sped off.

Caleb had planned to get onto the college web servers from his office. As he watched the green trees on both sides of the highway blur by, he realized he could access everything from his laptop at home. He looked ahead, saw rolling hills green with fir and pine, disappearing into low-hanging clouds. To his left, the snow-capped Olympic Mountain Range jutted towards the heavens.

He smiled. Nature did not care about the concerns or fears of man or beast. Nature simply… *was*. Always had been; always would be. And it would continue on, no matter how these events unfolded.

As he drove, his mind turned to dark questions, frightening possibilities. Just how big was this Pack? He remembered the young werewolf in the crowd. He had said there was something larger afoot, larger than Caleb could imagine.

Problem was, after one hundred and eighty years on planet Earth, Caleb didn't have to imagine. He had seen true Evil rear its ugly head more than once. He had witnessed the atrocities of war, of what men did in war and what war did to them, turning some into cold, amoral vicious killers devoid of compassion or mercy.

He had seen more after the war. The rise of the Ku Klux Klan and the Jim Crow era, gang rapes and lynchings. Police dogs and fire hoses unleashed on unarmed demonstrators who had the audacity to demand equal rights. Then the drug trade decimated urban areas, affecting primarily poor people of color.

It was simply a genocide via different means as far as he was concerned.

He had seen the rise of Hitler and Mussolini. He had wept as he watched them butcher millions in Europe, murdered for no other reason other than being different. Different nationality, different race, different religion, different political and social views, different sexual preference. Anyone different was automatically inferior, the enemy, to be feared and hated, to be stamped out utterly so the glorious Master Race could assume dominion over all mankind.

What a load of horseshit.

Fuck Hitler, Caleb thought. Fuck Nazism. And the modern neo-Nazis and white Supremacists of today? Fuck them, too. And all the extreme Islamic jihadists and terrorists stoning women and decapitating children and journalists? Blindfolding gays and walking them off of rooftops?

Fuck those guys too. They were just as bad as the Nazis. In some ways, they were worse. He was happy to see them get their heads handed to them in the past few years. But they had not gone away, oh no. They had simply gone to ground. Waiting to rise again.

You can kill men, he thought. That's easy. But to kill an idea, to kill a movement? To destroy a perverted worldview fueled by fundamentalist hate, political, social, or religious fervor?

That was another matter entirely.

He passed Sedgewick Boulevard, the first exit for Port Orchard. Tall trees, heavy vegetation all around. He took the next ramp at Tremont. He decelerated, turned right, drove past the Urgent Care, then turned left at Port Orchard Boulevard.

Almost home. Thick old growth forests lined both sides of the road. Moss-covered trees that had stood for hundreds of years spread their branches out and over the roadway, blocking out the sun. The road leveled out near the bottom. The blue water of Sinclair Inlet greeted him.

He stopped at the intersection with Bay Street. Downtown Port Orchard lay to the right. The road that way bent left at City Hall and disappeared into the downtown area beyond. To his left lay the Port Orchard Yacht Club, and several marinas and salvage operations.

He turned left, drove past the marinas. Sailboats and power boats bobbed at their moorings. He motored past a drive-up coffee kiosk built in the shape of a tugboat, painted white with bright blue trim. Whimsical. The sight of it always made him smile.

The turnoff appeared suddenly, a narrow driveway marked by reflectors, framed by trees and vegetation on both sides. He turned, left Bay Street behind him. The trees branched out above him, creating a natural canopy that kept the house cool even in the warmest weather.

Finished in cedar shingles on all sides and a composite roof, the two-bedroom, two- bath home boasted a wraparound porch that ranged from the front, around the side, and widened at the back into a deck easily accessible through the French doors off the living room. The shingles had been stained a medium honey brown, then sealed with a clear protective coating. Windowsills trimmed in white. The porch and deck had originally been wood, but he had replaced the whole thing with a synthetic composite that looked like wood but was almost impervious to rot, mold, and the ravages of weather in the PNW.

He stopped just feet from his door, killed the engine. He looked around, opened the door and climbed out.

That's when it hit him.

The faintest of scents, nothing more than a whiff, really, something too diffuse for a human nose to detect. Tension ratcheted up inside him once more.

He stalked forcefully towards his house. He bounded up the steps. The scent was stronger here. He tilted his head back, sniffed the air. The scents turned his head around. His body followed until he stood facing his Jeep, the driveway, and the road beyond.

HOW DARE THEY!

They had been here. He did not know who, but he damn well knew *what*. Werewolf scouts had violated his property. Nothing had been disturbed, but then, that wasn't really the point, was it? No, they wanted him to know they were aware of him. And they wanted to make damn sure he knew that they knew the location of his den.

Boasting their mere presence here was insult enough. Leaving *their* scent in *his* territory?

HOW DARE THEY!

They were warning him, telling him to back off, retreat to his own territory. Mind his own business and leave the humans to their fate.

But this lone wolf did not take kindly to intrusions into his domain. And this lone wolf did not take kindly to "warnings". Others had foolishly attempted to corral him in the past. Caleb understood why. It was the Werewolf Way. But those warnings had resulted in... *unfortunate* consequences for the other parties involved.

Bottom line: Nobody, but *nobody* told Caleb Jacobsen what to do.

Caleb stood on the porch to his home – *his home!* – rumbling in a deep, primeval rage. He exhaled through his nose forcefully, emitting a soft puffing sound. His brain finally registered pain in his hands. He looked down, realized his fists were clenched, his knuckles white beneath thicker body hair. Uncurling his fingers, longer fingernails halfway to claws presented themselves next to sharp indentations in the flesh of his palms. He ran his tongue over his teeth, teeth that once again seemed too long and too sharp for a human mouth.

Caleb stepped off the porch and stalked forward. Head swiveling from side to side, his senses kicked on high alert. He silently urged any intruder to please, *PLEASE* be stupid enough to attempt something now that he was home and spoiling for a fight.

He lumbered past the Jeep, continued up the dirt driveway. Years earlier he had installed two 4X4 posts on either side at the entrance, painted them a pale brown, and nailed yellow reflective disks on all four sides about four feet above the ground.

He paused by one now, his head still swinging from one side to another, alert for danger, daring it to come. A low rumble resonated within his chest. He unzipped his jeans and urinated on the post. He ignored the cars passing by.

He contracted the muscles in his pelvic floor, shutting off the tap. Though uncomfortable to the point of being painful, he shuffled to the other side of his driveway. He relaxed and let loose once more, spraying the other post with the remainder of his urine.

He squeezed himself back inside his jeans, zipped up. He stood there a moment, flexing his muscles, trying to look bigger, more intimidating. His lip pulled up on one side into a snarl. Eyes of swirling amber darted in all directions. His actions and posture spoke volumes to anything capable of understanding. He was Alpha Male here, master of his domain. Any intrusion would be met with *extreme* violence.

Seconds ticked by. No response. Finally, Caleb took a cautious step backwards, alert for danger. But no attack came. He finally turned his back to the road and instinctively drug and kicked the dusty ground with both feet, leaving his marks. In conjunction with urinating and marking his territory, the scratches further advertised who ruled here.

Caleb stalked back down the driveway, stomped onto his porch. He pulled out his keys, slid one into the lock and twisted. The front door swung inward.

He threw a challenging glare over his shoulder. He emitted a sound, not quite a growl, more a combination between a grunt and a short bark.

Then he turned and disappeared inside.

CHAPTER SEVENTEEN

Caleb threw the door closed, prowled deeper into his house. Late afternoon now. The house sat in shade. It went dark inside relatively early in the day this time of year.

He went around turning on lights. Over the stove in the kitchen. A lamp near his easy chair. A light near his laptop. He sniffed the air as he went. He walked into the bathroom, both bedrooms, his nose up and out in front of him.

They had not invaded the interior of the house.

He moved back through the living room, looked out the large windows. Honey-brown trim accented the panes. French doors opened to the deck.

An afternoon breeze rippled the waters of Sinclair Inlet. To the east, skies were already a darker blue. A boxy ferry plowed slow and cumbersome through the channel, coming from the Seattle terminal at the foot of Pioneer Square. It now turned the expanse of its port side, all white and green trim, heading for Bremerton.

Caleb marched past his computer to the kitchen. He filled an electric water kettle and thumbed the switch on. He grabbed a mug off the hook beneath the kitchen windowsill, placed it on the counter. In the cupboard above him, he found raspberry tea, dropped a bag into the mug.

He sat at his computer desk, hands hovering over the keyboard. His wallpaper exhibited a high definition photograph of a full moon. But no ordinary full moon. This photo showed the moon reflecting a burnt orange and angry red color.

A Blood Moon.

A fairly common phenomenon, Blood Moons occurred due to light refraction and polluted air throwing reddish light at the moon, which the moon reflected back. Astronomers attached little significance to them, but humans had been entranced by them for eons.

Caleb stared at the photo, hit the RETURN button. The screen changed. He typed a new command, hit RETURN again.

The water was boiling now. He went to the kitchen, poured the scalding water into the mug. It immediately darkened, turning red.

The color of blood, he mused. He grabbed the mug and headed back to his workstation.

Typing quickly, he connected his computer to the college's History department database. He commanded the times, dates and locations of similar murders going back two hundred years. He hit the COMMAND button, then sat back.

While his system collated data, he thought back over recent events. These killings were not random. He knew that now. Every action the werewolves had made sent a message. That's how werewolves operated. Had he not just marked his own territory in broad daylight? That action sent a message, too.

A very specific message.

They were after him. Bring it the motherfuck on, he thought. But, if they knew about him, they knew about Russell and Marla, too. Their lives now hung in a precarious balance.

Caleb would protect them at all costs, even if that meant they found out what he was. They would have to deal with it -- or not. Caleb could not control how they reacted. All Caleb could do was keep them alive – even if that meant losing them. At least they would be alive.

And where there was life there was hope.

New windows popped open on his screen, one after another. Matching cases, going back in time. First in months, then years. Decades. Centuries.

Maybe this thing truly was bigger than he could imagine.

As the laptop continued its work, Caleb's thoughts floated back to Marla. His eyes softened. The previous night with her. The sight of her curves. The smell of her skin. The taste of her sweat. The jackhammer beat of her heart as she lay beneath him. He wished he was with her now, holding her, kissing her, making love to her.

Becoming one with her.

Caleb leaned back in his chair, sighed. He turned away from the desk, gazed outside at the dark waters. In that moment, terrified of losing her if (when!) she found out the truth about him, he felt very, very old. So many things he had not done, places he had not seen, goals he had failed to achieve, so many dreams dashed, smashed, destroyed.

He had never married, had never known the warmth and contentment of a good marriage, the joy of adoring children. That normal mortal life with all of its pitfalls and limitations had been wrenched away from him.

Mutated DNA had seen to that. The root cause of his werewolfism was actually a virus. And he shed the virus through body fluids. Blood. Saliva.

Semen.

Caleb's ejaculate was chock-full of his mutant DNA strands. Any child sired would grow up to be just like him. Any woman he loved would give birth to a monster. What a terrifying existence for a child. Puberty would be a beast – literally.

Forcing himself out of this melancholy reverie, he concentrated on the computer screen. Windows opened and closed as the college database accessed other colleges and universities all across the country. Library databases at UCLA, Stanford, Harvard, and Yale, among others, all contained digitized history books, writings, journals, and newspaper articles going back to before this country was formed.

Caleb's stomach growled. He had not eaten since early this morning. He wandered to the kitchen, opened the refrigerator door.

He had not been grocery shopping in a while. Ketchup and other condiments stood at attention inside the door. A half-full jug of chocolate milk sat on the top rack.

He grabbed the jug, put the opening to his lips, tilted his head back. He drank deeply, then wiped his mouth with his sleeve. He recapped the milk jug.

His eyes found a one-pound package of ground beef sitting alone on the bottom shelf. He grabbed the meat tray, tossed it onto the counter. He ripped the packaging apart. He thrust a bare hand into the meat, made a fist, and pulled out a chunk of raw hamburger. He mashed it into his mouth and chewed.

He tilted his head back, creating a straight line from his mouth all the way down to his stomach. He swallowed, sending the half-chewed meat on its way. He looked around, instinctively alert for danger as he smacked his lips. Sensing nothing amiss, he grabbed another handful and shoved it into his mouth. Soon, the package was reduced to pink blood and white gristle clinging to the Styrofoam tray.

He grabbed a paper towel, wiped his mouth. He did not want the smell of blood on his shirt sleeve.

He walked back over to his laptop, sat down. Eyes darting left to right, up and down, he scanned through the pages, digesting new information.

Over the next hour, Caleb worked quietly and efficiently. He collated data: times, dates, places. Jesus Christ, there were a lot of them, all over the country, going back God knows how long. As he plowed through, he discarded anything not werewolf related, ruling out serial killers like Dahmer, Gacy, Berkowicz, Gein, Chessman. Their M.O.'s didn't match up.

But even accurate data is meaningless without context, so Caleb cross referenced pertinent crimes and disappearances to when and where they occurred. At first, he felt no specific emotion; the task was purely perfunctory. Time ticked by, and he still couldn't quite wrap his head around what he was seeing. His frustration rose.

Sometimes all one had to do was step back and look at the big picture. When looking at a situation in its entirety, patterns emerge.

Caleb dug his heels into the floor and propelled himself backwards. He crossed his legs, took a calming breath. His lungs expanded almost to the point of pain. He forced the air out through parted lips.

He propped his elbows on the armrests of his chair, rubbed his palms together as he contemplated possibilities. He rested his face on his hands, his extended fingers resting between his nose and his mouth.

For a long moment, he sat absolutely still. Then, through the mist and swirl of confusion, a pattern began to emerge from the ether. It presented itself, coalesced. Solidified.

Came into sharp relief.

Caleb's eyes slowly grew wider and wider. His mouth fell open. His breathing became labored. He involuntarily put one hand across his mouth as he fought back a rising terror.

No. No, this can't be right!

All the pieces fit together now. He had solved the puzzle, and it enwrapped the immortal creature known as Caleb Jacobsen in an icy sheet of horror.

He had often been told throughout his life that the truth could set one free. That truth was liberating. Truth brought closure. Peace.

Bullshit.

Truth could be a cruel, vengeful, jealous bitch, a brutal, ugly thing unmindful of people's feelings or beliefs. It obliterated people's perceptions of the world around them, of people they thought they knew. Digging through layers of lies to expose truth was an inherently violent, penetrative act. And all too often, truth brought no freedom, no liberation, no closure. No peace.

No, real-world truth often provided neither answers nor clarity. It further confused, confounded, generated more questions. Truth, like nature, simply *was*. Bottom line, the truth could be absolutely horrifying.

Like right now.

What lay before him was a blueprint for genocide. Not just one religion or ethnic group, oh no. This was the methodical extermination of an entire species.

Staring at the screen, his shock slowly receded, replaced by a fierce determination and a growing rage. His conscience, with a wisdom born of a disastrous decision made by an impetuous, enraged young man in 1861, spoke to him loud and clear.

"The only thing required for Evil to triumph in this world is for good men to stand by and do nothing."

With Edmund Burke's famous quote reverberating his head, Caleb's lips pressed together and formed a thin line. His eyes went hard and swirled amber. A slight snarl pulled one side of his lip upwards. No way he would let this happen. They would have to kill him first.

Right. Good luck with that, he thought.

His window of opportunity was no more than a brief sliver of time. He might die trying – hell, he probably *would* die trying – but nothing would deter him. The path ahead of him was paved with violence and blood, pain and death. But he would see it through, no matter what.

He glanced at his watch. *Damn!* He had to get back to Tacoma, touch bases with Jodi. He shoved a thumb drive into a USB port on his laptop, downloaded the data.

He pushed away from his desk, stood up. He yanked the thumb drive out, dropped it in his pocket. He marched across the room, stepped outside, locked up.

Inside, the house went dark and quiet once again.

Marla sat at her desk in the wolf care center. It was late afternoon and the zoo was closed. Russell had dropped her off, then had gone over to her house. He had more work to do. He planned to work remotely and consult with Dr. Melendez via video chat. Their work was almost complete but there were still some nagging gaps left to fill.

The crowds were already thinning out when she arrived. She ducked and dodged exhausted parents with smiling kids. She smiled at them; they smiled back and kept going. She wondered if she would ever have kids. She'd need to meet the right guy first.

Maybe she had already met the right guy. Her skin still tingled from the amazing night before. Hold on, she chided herself. Just about any guy could fire on all cylinders for one night. Short-term was easy. What about the long haul?

She had made her way to the wolf enclosure, slid her ID through a card reader affixed to the wall. The tiny red light winked out, replaced by a tiny green one. A buzzer sounded; the latch on the door clicked. She yanked the door open and disappeared inside.

Marla had fed Sampson immediately, made sure he had fresh water. Seeing the old male reminded her of Caleb again.

There was something different about that man. Something deep, hidden. Primal. He was a throwback to another time, a man's man. He had certainly affected her on a primal level she had not been aware she had. Most of the men in her past had been decent enough blokes. Few had been relationship material; none of them had come close to marriage material.

And then along Caleb Jacobsen comes, in a class by himself. Here she was, educated and accomplished, strong and independent, hitting her career stride. And all she could do was grin like a dopey schoolgirl remembering how she had gotten royally plowed the night before. Her sole desire was to be with him again.

Marla squeezed her eyes shut, screwed up her face as if she had suddenly smelled rotten eggs. Come on, dammit! Quit acting like a virgin with her first crush. You're a grown-ass woman, and you have a job to do. Get on with it!

Movement at the corner of her eye. Nothing distinctive; a shadow really, a wispy wraith, nothing more.

"Who's there?" she called out.

No answer.

Then a soft sound, not a clang or a clash, a sound like someone bumping into a table.

"Who's there?" she demanded, standing up.

Still no answer. She looked at the doorway that separated her office from the main treatment area. She had never looked at a simple open doorway and been so afraid of what might lurk on the other side. Biting her lower lip, she moved around her desk and headed towards the doorway.

She stopped short, emitted a startled yip. Directly in front of her a massive shape suddenly filled the doorway. In the low light, she could not clearly make out any features. The massive body heaved, breathing through its mouth.

"You're not supposed to be here." A male voice.

"Ty."

Marla was alone after hours in a building with a disgruntled employee, bigger than her, stronger than her, standing between her and the exit.

Ty grinned. It was ugly. "What are you doing here all by your lonesome?"

"What are you doing here?"

"Just came to check on Sampson."

"You should be careful around Sampson."

"But now I've found you. What am I supposed to do with you?"

"You should be careful around me as well." She mentally inventoried the objects in the room. What could she use as a weapon?

Ty took a step forward.

Marla stood her ground by the desk as Ty took another step. She fought hard to not panic. She tossed her head back, planted her feet, trying to appear nonchalant.

"So, where's your boyfriend?"

"Who? The guy who made you shit your pants?"

Ty froze in place. The grin on his face fell. "You should watch your mouth."

"You should watch your step."

"Oh?"

"If you hurt me, what do you think Caleb will do to you when he finds out?"

Ty paused, thinking this through. Marla's hand drifted towards her coffee mug beside her on the desk.

"Doesn't matter," he said at last. "You won't tell him anything. You'll never tell anyone anything. *Ever.*"

Ty took another step closer. Marla grabbed the mug and swung. Hard. The mug shattered against Ty's temple, driving ceramic shards into his flesh. He dropped to one knee. Blinded by blood gushing down his face, he reached out for Marla as she rushed past him but was unable to snag her leg.

Marla bolted into the main care area. In his cage, Sampson looked up at the commotion. He smelled blood and fear. Violence was coming.

Dizzy and wiping blood from his eyes, Ty growled and lurched after her. Perhaps her fear slowed her down. Perhaps Ty moved faster because of the adrenaline surging through him. Either way, he caught her halfway across the room. He snagged the back of her shirt collar, yanked her off her feet. Off balance himself, he tumbled to the floor alongside her.

Sampson, agitated and feeding off the fear and aggression, stood up inside his cage. He growled, snapped his teeth. Spittle flecked off his tongue and gums.

Surprised to see she still had the jagged remnants of the ceramic mug handle in her hand, she swung her arm in an arc, slashing Ty across the bridge of his nose. He grunted as more blood poured out of his wrecked face. The gash was deep, white cartilage underneath red tissue.

She scrambled backward, trying to get to her feet. But Ty tackled her, slapped the makeshift weapon out of her hand. Then his enormous hand was at her throat, fingers digging into her in a vicelike grip, strangling off her oxygen.

He grinned, murder in his eye.

Sampson's growls finally caught Ty's attention. His eyes flickered upwards, then back down to Marla, who squirmed helplessly beneath him. An idea formed in his primitive brain.

He stood up, pulling Marla up with him, his hand still wrapped around her throat. Her face was turning blue. Eyes bloodshot. She tried to punch him, gouge him, but she was quickly losing strength. He laughed at her.

"Just like all women. You talk a lot of shit, but you ain't nothing without your man around to protect you, are you, you fucking cunt?" He looked at Sampson in his cage. "You love that Goddamn wolf so much? Go see him."

Ty shoved her hard, sending her sailing across the room. She landed on the concrete with a thud and a grunt. She rolled over, a tangle of arms and legs until she slammed into Sampson's enclosure. Sampson skittered back, instinctively protecting himself from harm.

Marla tried to breathe in great gulps of air. She sat, propped against the front of Sampson's cage. Sampson growled and snapped, pushing himself against the door, trying to get out.

To attack.

Supremely confident, Ty moved casually among the treatment tables, looking for something. He grinned when he found it. He picked something up, turned it in his fingers where it glinted under the light.

A scalpel.

"Well now," Ty said. "What can I do with this?"

Knowing her life was about to end, Marla's eyes rolled around in her head, looking for anything she could use to protect herself. Her gaze finally fell on the cage latch beside her.

Jesus Christ!

The latch was closed, but the lock she had hung back on when she fed Sampson had not locked. But instead of cursing herself for a moment's inattention to animal safety protocols, her heart fluttered with elation.

"Don't worry," Ty taunted. "This won't take long." He smiled.

That was all it took. That smug, arrogant smile, those stained teeth, ugly face, that bullying attitude.

Her fear fled, replaced by anger and a grim calm about what she had to do. As Ty took another step towards her, she pulled the lock up and off, pushed the door open.

Sampson, all one hundred and fifty pounds of muscle and teeth, along with fifteen thousand years of predatory instinct, launched himself at the creature he hated most.

Ty never screamed. He never had the chance. In fact, Ty would never utter another sound in this world.

Ever.

The wolf's maw opened as its head twisted sideways in the air. Powerful jaws clamped shut around Ty's throat and bit deep, crushing Ty's windpipe and severing at least one carotid artery.

The impact of the wolf's weight and momentum took Ty clean off his feet. He hit the ground hard, bounced once, then that was it. Sampson maintained his grip, gnashed his head back and forth, biting deeper, severing more blood vessels and tendons.

Marla sat there, watching. A strange calm fell over her. Her eyes registered no emotion whatsoever as Sampson went to work.

Somewhere in the back of her mind, logic dictated now would be a good time to get the fuck out of there. But somehow, she knew Sampson would not hurt her. So, she sat there, watching Sampson do what Sampson did best.

A small smile of satisfaction finally trickled across her lips when Sampson finally ripped a huge gory chunk of Ty's esophagus away from the rest of the corpse and began gulping it down.

CHAPTER SEVENTEEN

Caleb scanned his rearview mirror as he drove. Something caught his eye. A bright red sports car, two cars back, in the other lane. Custom wheels, running lights. He had seen this car before. It had followed him onto the highway from Port Orchard, then settled in behind him.

Caleb had picked up a tail.

The road in front of Caleb was clear for almost a quarter mile. He pushed his foot to the floor. The Jeep sped ahead. The trailing car responded. It changed lanes, moved up, changed lanes again. They were directly behind him now, keeping pace. They knew he had made them. Now they didn't want to spook him.

Caleb stabilized his speed, changed lanes one last time to the outside lane. The red sports car stayed where it was. He noted the exit signs for Gig Harbor. He passed Wollochet, which would have taken them into the quaint downtown tourist area. The last thing the Gig Harbor waterfront needed was a bunch of werewolves battling to the death by the marina.

A brown sign with white lettering announced the exit to Olympic Drive and Pt Fosdick. The faintest hint of a grin passed across his mouth. But his eyes were deadly serious. He flipped his blinker again, wanting them to follow. The red car signaled, changed lanes, just as he had predicted they would.

Amateurs.

The Jeep eased off the highway. The red car followed. Caleb put his left blinker on. The sports car, directly behind him now, did the same.

Caleb moved with the flow of traffic, turned left onto Olympic. He crested the overpass, drove through another traffic light, then turned into a strip mall. A fast food burger joint sat at the far end of the lot.

He headed for the drive through lane. The red sports car pulled into a parking spot. He would have to pass them on the way out. They probably thought they had him boxed in. Fact was, Caleb had no desire to elude them.

He stopped at the lighted menu board, ordered an unsweetened iced tea. He pulled forward to the drive through window. The red sports car remained parked, its two occupants inside.

The window opened and a plump young woman took his money and handed him his drink and a straw. He put the cup in the cup holder, inched forward into the parking lot. If those in the other car had anticipated him making a break for it, they certainly were disappointed. He parked directly facing them.

Moving slowly, he bit the top of the paper surrounding his straw, tore it open. He pulled the straw out, jammed it through the pre-scored opening in the lid. He drank deeply.

Then he opened his door and stepped out.

The two in the red car did not know what to do, so they did nothing. They watched as Caleb sauntered forward, drink held casually in one hand. He leaned against the warm hood of his Jeep, took another sip.

He stared through the windshield. One black, one Hispanic. Good-looking kids. Under other circumstances, he would have thought them college students. He never took his predator's eyes off them.

Who are you and why are you following me? he asked, using the MindTalk.

The two looked at each other, then back at him.

We are but lowly messengers, the driver said back. *We do the bidding of the Master.*

Do you not have names?

The young black man was Bruce. The Hispanic was Pablo.

Why were you ordered to follow me? Caleb pushed.

It is not our place to ask why, came the response.

Who is your Master? Caleb's mind asked.

He who brings us the Truth, they replied in unison. *He who brings us into the Light and shows us the Way.*

Seriously? You two whelps believe that happy horseshit?

Something about the driver changed. His car door opened, and the young black man stepped out, hand on the door, one leg still inside the car. Caleb's eyes locked on him. They turned from brown to iridescent yellow. His nose flattened. His ears elongated.

Just a bit.

Think before you act, young one.

The scout thought it over, slowly slid back into the driver's seat, closed the door.

I'm leaving now, Caleb thought. *I'm heading for the police station. See you there?*

The red sports car's engine started. The driver revved the engine, a threat. Caleb pushed himself off his Jeep, stood about two feet away from the red car with the revving engine, glared through the glass, piercing the driver's soul with his gaze.

Waiting.

Challenging.

And completely unafraid.

The car shifted into reverse, backed away. The front wheels turned, and the car edged away. Caleb watched it surge across the parking lot, turn onto the overpass road.

Since he did not care what else they did now, Caleb turned his back to them and walked back to his open car door. He took another sip, climbed inside. He dropped his drink into the cup holder, buckled in.

Wait a minute. Maybe he *did* care what they did now.

Caleb threw the Jeep into gear, turned right, then left onto the highway onramp. He accelerated, eyes scanning ahead. There they were, up ahead, four cars between them and him.

Caleb paced them. The green towers of the Tacoma Narrows Bridge rose up in the distance. The red sports car signaled to exit at exit nine, the last exit before the bridge. Why would they do that? They weren't going to the Tacoma Narrows Airport. Were they going to circle back to Pt. Fosdick and head north? Caleb doubted it. These two weren't bright enough to utilize countersurveillance techniques.

Their Master had established his Den in one of the expensive houses dotting the cliffs facing south and east. Caleb grinned as they eased off the highway.

Good to know.

Fear squeezed Jodi's spine. She had been staring at her screen for almost an hour, pupils dilated, mouth open. A cold sweat made her shiver.

This can't be, she kept telling herself. It's fucking impossible.

But empirical data did not lie. Facts, like nature, did not care about people's feelings. They just *were.* The implications here were so wide-reaching, so horrifying, her mind did not want to believe it. But she knew her facts were correct.

She had already bolted for the bathroom, intestines roiling. She had experienced a powerful bout of explosive diarrhea, followed by wave after wave of dizziness and nausea. She had at last unlatched the door and staggered out of the stall on weak knees, completely spent. Then she had made the mistake of taking one look at herself in the mirror. Stringy hair, dark-rimmed eyes, slack jaw, cadaverous pallor. She barely got over the garbage can before she retched, throwing up whatever was left from lunch.

She had run cold water in the sink, splashed it on her face. She gave no concern to being dainty or feminine. The question of what someone might think if they walked in didn't even register as water soaked her face and hair, dampened the front of her shirt.

And now here she sat, legs useless, heart hammering, palms and armpits sweating even though it was only 68 degrees. She had no recollection of leaving the bathroom and getting back here. How had she managed that?

Knowing what the data meant, fear and nausea rose once more. She turned away, pushed her chair sideways to the end of her desk. She opened her mouth over a metal trashcan, holding her hair back. Bile rose again, an acidic Old Faithful. She dry-heaved, abdominal muscles spasming painfully.

She slumped back in her chair, feeling weak. She dabbed at the corner of her mouth with a tissue held in a trembling hand.

The door to her office swung open and Caleb Jacobsen strode in. He immediately smelled fear and vomit. He became instantly guarded but projected an outward calm.

Jodi's haunted eyes focused on him. They cleared. Then they narrowed. Her lips drew together into a thin line across the lower half of her face. The stink of fear was replaced by an unmistakably pungent odor.

Anger.

"Who the fuck are you?" Jodi croaked. Her voice sounded as if she had been gargling with road gravel.

"What do you mean?"

She slapped her hands flat on the arms of her computer chair. Fingers tightened; knuckles whitened. She pushed upwards, painfully drawing herself up into a standing position. But to say she stood would be a euphemism at best; she wobbled, kept her hands on the desk to keep from crashing to the floor.

"I mean, who the fuck are you?" she repeated. She pointed at her screen. "What the fuck is this shit you've had me working on all afternoon?"

Caleb took a step forward.

Jodi pulled a small bottle of pepper spray out of her pocket, stopping him in his tracks. "Stay the fuck over there," she warned.

"Whatever you say."

She kept the pepper spray out in front of her, aimed at him. "I'm going to ask you just one more time. Who the fuck are you?" Caleb made to answer, but she interjected, "And don't try to bullshit me about you being a history teacher."

"Well, point of fact, I really am a history professor. Look me up online."

"I already have," she snapped. "Just because you're listed there doesn't mean that's all you do."

"I see."

"Who do you work for?"

"I'm working with the police."

"No, not that," she countered angrily. "What agency?"

"Agency?"

You're going to try and tell me you're not some kind of operative for one of the alphabet agencies?"

Caleb stifled a smile, tried hard to keep from laughing out loud. No one had ever accused him of being James Bond before.

"I'm really… not."

"What does that mean?"

"Just what I said." Time was getting short.

"Look, Caleb – if that's even your real name –" Caleb started to correct her, thought better of it. Let her get it off her chest. "—I'm not stupid, you know."

"I know."

"Then why treat me like I am?" she demanded hotly. "There's no way a theorist, a rank amateur by your own admission, could come up with such detailed search parameters that hit so close to the mark."

"What have you found?"

"Tell me who you are."

Caleb's patience was at an end. "You already know." He stepped forward and she shrank back. He came around her corner of her desk and she stepped further away. He sat down without asking and studied her screen.

Jodi's prodigious skills had unearthed evidence that closely paralleled Caleb's. As he scrolled down the page, she crossed her arms across her chest, chewed on a fingernail.

"Sorry about going off on you like that," she said.

Caleb barely heard her. "Not your fault."

"This has really scared the shit out of me."

"I'd be surprised if it didn't."

"You don't seem surprised at all."

He pulled the thumb drive out of his pocket, showed it to her. "I found pretty much the same thing."

"How did you do that without access to Government databases?"

"I've got my own resources." He pushed the thumb drive back into his pocket. "I needed yours to fill in any gaps."

"And?"

"You've exceeded expectations. Thank you."

She pointed at her screen. "There's been hundreds, thousands of murders going back decades. Centuries. Big cities, small towns, rural areas. The pattern is nationwide. Look at the dates. The farther back you go, the farther east the locations."

"This started on the East Coast."

"As people migrated west, this did, too."

She did not know how right she was. "Missing persons?"

"Same pattern," she replied. "Unsolved disappearances in the same locations and times as the murders."

"You think the disappearances are unreported murders?"

"Click that link in the upper right."

Caleb did so. The screen reloaded, then displayed new information. Even Caleb was shocked at what he was seeing.

"I got a wild hair up my ass and took the search global," she continued. "FBI, Scotland Yard, Interpol, you name it."

He felt weak. "And?"

More of the same," she said simply. "All over the world, dating back to the eighteenth century."

Caleb stood on wooden legs.

"What am I supposed to do now?"

"Go home. Stay there," he said. "Lock your doors and windows. Don't come out until daylight."

"I'm not coming out until Monday morning."

Caleb did not have that luxury. He stepped away from the chair, staggered towards the door.

"You going to tell me who you really are?"

"No matter who or what you think I am, trust me, I'm not."

"Then what are you?"

"Something... *different.*"

"You understand how big this is?"

"Yes."

"You're not scared?"

"No."

"You could get yourself killed."

Caleb thought about that. "Sooner or later, death comes for us all. I just hope when it comes for me, I can face it with courage."

"But what about your friends?"

Something dark and dangerous shifted behind his eyes. Jodi saw it, shivered involuntarily.

"Anything that wants to do harm them has to get past me."

His words, his tone chilled Jodi to the bone. This guy meant it. He was not bragging, not puffing out his chest, not broadcasting false machismo. No, this man was simply *dangerous,* and dangerous in a way she had never before encountered.

Note to self, she thought. Never piss this guy off.

Caleb had no recollection leaving Jodi's office. Yet here he stood, shivering in the crisp air, sweaty palms staining his pants as he ran them down his thighs.

He tried to focus. He lumbered towards his Jeep like his knee joints had fused together. He put his hands out in front him, pressed them against the hood to keep from falling on his face.

It was his own damn fault. It was time. Hell, it was past time. He needed to make a kill.

Now.

Hunting human prey in urban environs was the highest-risk, most dangerous behavior he could engage in. And it was his only choice now.

Once he discharged some of the virus through his saliva, he could regain control of this *thing* that had lived inside him since 1876. Some called it a curse; some called it a gift. In reality, it was both, and yet neither. Caleb viewed it as an ongoing, chronic medical condition. No cure, but symptoms could be managed.

One just had to understand the rules.

The truth was, lycanthropy was a lot different than what most people thought. Obviously, the Hollywood movies got it completely wrong. It was certainly more complex than what had been published in scholarly tomes and taught to students in med school, more than delusions brought on by a psychiatric ailment. Whatever doctor had come up with this convenient idea must have been a werewolf himself.

Somehow Caleb managed to crawl into the driver's seat, slam the door shut. The entire world tilted on its axis in front of him, about forty-five degrees to the right. Then it all began spinning clockwise. He grabbed the steering wheel to keep from falling over.

He was familiar with the vertigo. It would resolve in a few minutes. When the world righted itself and his vision cleared, Caleb thrust the keys in the ignition, cranked the engine, and hit the gas.

Now. Where to go?

Somehow, he managed to keep the Jeep in his lane. But it seemed as if the vehicle was driving itself and Caleb sat outside his own body. Right now, every bit of his brain, every scrap of self-discipline, every fiber of his being was wholly devoted to one thing: staying in human form just a few more minutes until he could find suitable prey.

He knew precisely where to go.

He pulled into the enormous parking lot at Tacoma Mall just a few miles from the police station. It was a major shopping center that had somehow survived and thrived in this new age of same day drop shipments via the internet. He parked in an empty stall, killed the engine. He damn near fell onto the pavement getting out.

He planted his feet shoulder width apart, took a cleansing breath. It did not help. Caleb zigzagged his way towards the entrance doors. He ran his tongue over his teeth. They were so sharp he nearly cut his tongue. The hair on his hands and arms seemed thicker now, his nails longer. He ran one hand through his hair over the back of his head and onto his neck. His hairline had disappeared now into new growth of dark fur on the back of his neck.

He popped his collar up, hunched his shoulders. He grabbed a handle and yanked so hard the door flew open. Moving forward, he made it to the central hub of the mall: the food court. Almost everyone in the mall would end up here, either eating or passing through. He claimed an unattended table, sat down heavily.

All he had to do now was wait. Let his prey come to him.

Two young Army soldiers, easily identifiable by the close-cropped hair and ill-fitting civilian attire that made them look out of place, passed by near him. He heard them say something about going to the movies. A new action flick was out, and they were in the mood for shoot-outs, car crashes, and "big fuckin' explosions".

Caleb caught the scent of a toddler, along with its mother, on their way through the food court towards the same exit through which he had entered. For an instant, he zeroed in on the toddler. Happily toddling and wobbling, one fist wrapped around her mother's finger. A head full of strawberry blonde curls. Cute. Innocent. Soft skin, tender meat underneath, partially calcified bones, easy to bite through to get to the marrow…

NO!

He would not allow the Wolf to do that. He would never allow the Wolf that level of control over him, to pick his prey for him. There was a difference between being a werewolf and becoming a monster. It was a fine line to be sure, and Caleb Jacobsen was determined to walk. It did not matter how difficult it was. How else could he be able to look at himself in the mirror every morning and not loath what stared back?

Whenever humans gathered in numbers, criminals lurked amongst them, looking for easy targets. Moths to the flame.

If Caleb had to kill a human, why not shred some dipshit scumbag crook? They had made their choice to become criminals, parasites leeching off the suffering of others. They thought of themselves as predators. None of them ever considered there might be something far worse hunting them.

Nobody would miss one less criminal in the world.

A disturbance to his right turned his head. In the distance, an older, unshaven and unkempt man approached quickly, pushing and shoving his way past others strolling slower than he. A balding splotchy scalp. Peppered with age spots. Scant, wispy hair that glistened with grease. He wore dirty jeans, old sneakers, some kind of gray T shirt, a faded Army field jacket.

Caleb became mildly interested.

The old guy shoved one woman aside so hard she stumbled, nearly fell. The contents of her purse spilled onto the concrete floor.

"Hey! She protested. "Jerk!"

"Get the fuck out of my way, bitch," the old man grumbled.

Caleb became keenly interested.

The old man continued forward. The people around him stepped back, parting like the Red Sea as he moved through the middle. As he advanced, he glared and dared anyone to challenge him. No one did. He grinned smugly. Nobody wanted to mess with him because he was a badass.

Until his bloodshot eyes made contact with the hirsute young man sitting at a table by himself. What was wrong with that motherfucker's eyes? And why was he staring and not looking away? Maybe he wanted a piece of him? Well…

"Hey! Asshole!" He changed course and headed directly towards Caleb's table. "You got a problem?"

The young man with the heavy beard and the strange eyes said nothing, just continued glaring at the old codger.

"Hey. I'm talking to you, motherfucker. You got a fucking problem?"

"You're everybody's problem." The voice was low. Rumbling.

Almost like an animal growling.

The old man's fists clenched at his sides. "What the fuck did you say?" The younger man sat there, silent and still. He almost appeared to be smiling.

"You heard me."

The old man flew into a rage, made the biggest mistake of his life. He reached across the table and grabbed a handful of Caleb's shirt, making body contact. The back of his knuckles pressed into Caleb's bare skin.

The psychic connection was made.

Caleb's nostrils flared. He smelled death and defecation on him. But there was more. The stench of stale urine emanated from his crotch, mixed with dried semen. Somewhere in the back of his mind, Caleb saw chains, shackles. He heard squeaking bedsprings, high-pitched pleas to stop, *STOP!,* followed by cries to heaven for mercy.

The voice of a child.

Caleb's amber eyes went cold. A snarl crossed his lips, and the old perv caught a glimpse of sharp teeth just as Caleb grabbed his wrist in a viselike grip.

Pain blinded the old man as this lethal young predator stood up and squeezed harder, practically snapping the bones in his useless wrist. The hand went numb, the fingers opened as they lost their grip. Then he dropped to his knee as the sadistic fuck above him applied downward pressure, forcing him into submission.

Revulsion filling him, Caleb pushed hard, sending the old timer sprawling onto the floor, chairs clattering. Caleb stood there, ready for more, wanting more than anything to just Change and slaughter this piece of shit right now.

Cradling his injured wrist, the old man's eyes registered real fear and he scrambled to his feet. He backpedaled, making sure his opponent did not advance.

"You're one lucky motherfucker," he called as he back further away and pointed a quivering finger in Caleb's direction. "You're lucky!"

Caleb said nothing.

The old man headed quickly towards the exit. He still cradled his wrist as he shouldered the door open. Then he pushed his way out into the cold where night had fallen completely now. Headlights flashed at him, stabbing his eyes. Horns blared. He thrust his middle finger in the air at random.

He hobbled across the parking lot on arthritic knees. Everywhere he looked, he saw young people: couples, groups of friends, families with children. Some were arriving, some leaving. All had smiles on their faces.

Oh, how he loathed them and their happiness!

How come they got all the money, nice clothes, and fancy cars? Why did they have people who loved them, friends who would do anything for them? They had what he had always wanted and yet had always lacked. He hated them for it.

It was all their fault. It had to be. It couldn't be that they had worked hard, gone to school, gotten degrees, and had fucking *earned* what they had. It couldn't be that they had been diligent in school, had made wise and prudent choices for their lives and careers and were now reaping the benefits of what they had sown. It couldn't be that they were solid people with morals. It couldn't be they had nurtured and deserved the happiness, friends, family, and whatever affluency they enjoyed.

Oh, no. It simply *couldn't* be that. No. They were just all lucky motherfuckers.

The old man continued his journey, pain jolting through his legs with every step. His knees had degenerated to the point where they were grinding bone on bone underneath the sagging skin and atrophied muscle. He saw the bus stop at the edge of the road. His uninjured hand snaked into his front pocket. Scrawny fingers curled around his bus pass.

The one thing he did not do was look behind him. If he had, he would have seen the young predator with the blazing eyes and sharp teeth walk out a few moments after him. He would have seen this apex predator watch him hobble away, then climb into his Jeep. He would have seen the Jeep creep across the parking lot and park again across from the bus stop with a clear line of sight to the bench where the old perv now sat.

Then old perv would have known that Death had found him. He would have known that his Judgement Day was at hand, and that there would be no mercy for the likes of him.

His slaughter would be epic.

CHAPTER EIGHTEEN

Heavy clouds, suspended low. Moonless night, black sky above. A mist hung cold and damp, threatening to become a full-on fog.

Francois stepped out the sliding glass doors on the back of the cavernous house. He, peered out into the mist, saw Hans, his back to him. Even at this distance, Hans' silhouette seemed hazy, indistinct. Francois breathed in the night air, exhaled with a snort. He assumed Hans had heard the door open and close, but he wanted Hans to know who was behind him. He moved off the concrete porch into the grass, approaching the Master.

Hans stood under a tree near the edge of the cliff. The drop was precipitous; almost 20 stories straight down to the narrow gravel beach. He could hear water lapping. He wore a bulky cable knit sweater, denim jeans, hiking boots. He also sported a black leather bomber jacket, circa World War Two. He had always loved this jacket, ever since he had stolen it from a downed American pilot in 1944. Then he had wrestled the injured pilot's own service pistol away from him and had shot him point blank in the face.

The spoils of war.

He shoved his hands deeper into his pockets. Why would he remember that now? He had not thought about that pilot in decades. He never knew if Allied Forces had recovered the body. He had never known the Yank's name, had never cared.

Francois stopped a few feet behind him, to his left. "It's time," he announced.

Hans made no effort to move, so Francois stood with him in silence. The Frenchman gazed out into the swirling mist, seeing only pale remnants of the brightest lights making their way through the swirling shadows across the Narrows.

The tranquil moment lingered. Seconds expanded into minutes. If Hans could have had his way, he would have stood there until dawn. But he had obligations to meet, didn't he? He hated the game he had to play next. But the damned thing had taken on a life of its own and even he had created it, he now had to serve it.

Hans turned towards his friend. "Let's go deceive the masses."

Francois fell in behind Hans as they walked back towards the house. Ever the bodyguard and protector, Francois' head swiveled as they moved. He looked left, right, up ahead. He occasionally looked back, making certain the rear was secure.

Hans pushed off with one foot, hopped from the lawn to the elevated concrete porch, landed on the same foot he had pushed off with, continued walking without breaking his stride.

Such grace! Even in human form, he was the Wolf. The Alpha. The King. Francois smiled to himself once more as he easily emulated Hans' movements, hopping to the porch with a similar grace that was somehow unique, all his own.

That was the Gift, the power of the Wolf.

Hans pulled the glass door open and stepped inside. He moved deeper into the house, Francois duty-bound to keep pace.

The house seemed strangely quiet. Usually people came and went, socializing all hours of the day and night. But now, the main floor was deserted. Even the big TV in the den hung black and silent. It made the house seem bigger.

Eyes straight ahead, Hans marched forward with purpose. He swept by an enormous accent wall and headed towards the elegant staircase. He began his ascent, not bothering to grab the handrail. Powerful thighs chugged like pistons, propelling him ever upwards.

They topped the staircase, crossed the landing, and headed down the hallway towards Hans' quarters. Once inside the room, Hans immediately shed his clothes.

"My robes, please?"

Hans' robes hung on a hanger at the far left of the closet, dangling by themselves. Francois grabbed them off the hanger like he was picking fruit from a tree.

Hans was already completely naked, placing his clothes on the end of the bed. His muscles snaked beneath his skin as he moved. Tight chest, strong shoulders, narrow waist, muscular flanks. Francois understood why women fawned over him.

Francois held the robe by the shoulders, arms extended out in front of him. Hans glided up, turned, and slipped his arms through the sleeves. Francois let go and Hans shrugged into it, shook his body to settle the fabric.

He pulled the two halves of the white robe in front of him, wrapped them across his torso. He grabbed the golden sash that hung limp at the waist, kept in place by small white loops. He tied the sash across his stomach, completing the ensemble. He took two steps forward, whirled around towards Francois, and presented himself, arms out from his sides, palms upward.

"How do I look?"

"You could walk out in a burlap sack and they wouldn't care."

Hans chuckled.

"It is the destiny of the few to be exalted by the many. We tell them where to live, where to work, when to Change. And not only do they obey us, they thank us for it." Francois paused, then, "That's *power,* my friend."

Hans loved it when Francois got on a roll.

A soft knock sounded at the door. Diane stuck her head inside. Hans motioned her in. Francois chewed his lip, said nothing. Hans knew how Francois saw Diane. A wannabe, a hanger-on.

A werewolf groupie.

Francois firmly believed her fate should be eternal subservience, or outright slaughter along with the others. Francois envisioned a world where werewolves reigned supreme and ravaged bodies were piled high like cordwood. The streets would run slick with human blood.

Glorious.

As Diane came inside, William stuck his head in, ticked his chin upwards in Francois' direction. Francois excused himself. He walked across the room, passing Diane about halfway across. Her eyes drifted to him. He walked past as if she did not exist.

William retreated; Francois silently disappeared out the door. Diane came closer to Hans. His patience with her was likewise growing thin. He understood it was because she herself was growing impatient with his continued promises to Turn her, followed by his repeated and inventive reasons why now was never the right time.

"Diane. What can I do for you?"

"Turn me."

"Your time is coming. Rest assured, you will get precisely that which you so richly deserve."

He watched her think this over. She was not completely buying it anymore. Then she sighed. Good, he thought. Dodged another bullet.

"I need you with me during the ceremony," he said.

She averted her eyes. "I am honored." She had witnessed the ceremony before but had never been invited to stand with him. Her time for Turning must be close at hand. Why else give her this distinction? And once her Turning was complete, she would take her rightful place as Alpha Female, queen to the global werewolf Pack.

Francois came back in, looking at his watch. "Time," he announced.

Hans surged forward, walking confidently towards the door. Francois and Diane fell in on each side and one step behind him. They did not look at each other. Once I am Alpha Female, Diane thought to herself, the season of Francois shall be at an end.

They exited the room and headed down the hallway towards the landing. As they went, Francois updated Hans regarding the scouts who had shadowed Caleb and then had the tables turned on them in the fast food parking lot.

Hans smiled, a tug of respect. "Bold move. He knows we are on to him."

"He doesn't know anything other than that his friends are in danger."

Hans grunted.

"We've ascertained the whereabouts of the two others, "Francois added. "The female is at the Tacoma zoo. The male is at her house."

"Lovers?"

"Blood relatives."

Hans considered this as they reached the landing. "We can use that." He descended the first step, then the next. Francois and Diane followed suit.

"I've sent William over to the house. Under strict orders to only frighten them."

"Frighten them how, exactly?"

"Cordially explain to them what they're up against. Then he is to advise them – gently, of course – that it is in their own best interests to cease and desist."

"Cease and desist. I like that."

"One glimpse of a werewolf should convince them."

Hans paused, looked at up Francois behind him.

"Who would they tell?" Francois asked. "Who would believe them? And if something were to happen to William, well he is expendable, yes?"

They descended the rest of the way in silence. When they reached the first-floor landing, Hans stopped, turned to Francois.

"Get word to Caleb. I want to meet with him."

"A sit down?"

"Hans nodded.

"Looking to allay his fears?"

"No need. He'd meet us anywhere."

The entourage walked into the cavernous kitchen. Francois flipped the light switch. The kitchen boasted a gas grill and chef's stove, all stainless steel and heavy iron. They walked past it.

Hans opened a door set in the far corner, flipped a switch on the wall. A light came on just inside, illuminating a staircase leading downwards. He grabbed his hems in his hand, then descended one stairstep at a time, keeping one hand on the handrail just in case.

Like many houses in the Pacific Northwest, the estate they had commandeered had a basement. But as with everything else about this house, it was no ordinary basement. It was the same dimensions as the rest of structure, over fifteen hundred square feet, with fully seven feet of headroom.

It had originally been just one large rectangular space, without purpose, design, or utility. Hans had ordered an altar and a raised stage constructed at one end near where he and his friends now stood. The basement had two points of entry, and they had come down the back way.

The room had been converted into a madman's a sanctuary. Rows of cheap folding chairs faced the altar, going back to just within a few feet of the far wall. The chairs had been arranged in two columns separated by a central aisle.

People of both genders, all races, all walks of life milled about. Some stood; some sat, already claiming their seats. The mood was light, joyous. They joked as if they had been friends forever. A gray-haired millionaire wearing Armani hugged an African American street kid wearing threadbare jeans and a ratty T shirt. A trans woman was being welcomed by a group of men and women. Everyone was equal inside the sanctuary.

Everyone.

Hans turned his head towards the altar. He assumed everything would be ready, but he always checked before starting just in case.

The altar itself was crude and perfunctory, just a carved and sanded slab of wood, cut from an oak that had fallen over one hundred years ago. Blood stains, rusty brown, caked thick and cracked dry, smeared several points; remnants of the men and women who had lain upon the altar and endured the Turning.

Pewter candelabras flanked the altar, holding six lit black candles each. They added an air of theatricality. Molten wax had already overflowed and spilled over the sides, dribbling black goo downward until it solidified into knobby blobs.

Hans' eyes drifted upwards. Above the altar and the candelabras hung a carved silhouette of a werewolf's head. Suspended by high-tensile wire, secured into the ceiling joists with heavy metal bolts.

The details of the head were intentionally abstract. Triangular ears, wild blazing eyes, open muzzle, long teeth, sharp points. Not much more than that. People would interpret the image and its meaning through the prism of their own lives, which is precisely what Hans intended.

The hanging head was new. Francois had not seen it since it had been installed. He noticed the two "S" letters embossed on one cheek. Elongated and thin, they almost looked like jagged thunderbolts. But Francois knew his history, saw them for what they were.

He leaned close to Hans and whispered, "Seriously? Nazis?" he pointed to the old SS symbol.

"They made me laugh."

"They were assholes."

"They were amateurs."

Francois shook his head at Hans. Was he insane?

"They attacked Russia in winter, opened a second front. Like I said, amateurs. Professional soldiers should have known better."

"A rational man who wasn't an egomaniacal dipshit would have known better."

"If only von Stauffenberg had succeeded," Hans remarked, referring to the German plot to assassinate Hitler.

"Yes," Francois chimed. "But he failed."

Colonel Claus von Stauffenberg had fought in North Africa. He had lost one eye, one hand, and two fingers on the other hand in service to the Fatherland. He had also covertly become a member of the German Resistance, an anti-Hitler, anti-Nazi movement. When his bombing attempt failed, he was rounded up with his family and his co-conspirators.

All were summarily executed.

"I met him once, you know. Von Stauffenberg, I mean. He was no saint."

"Neither are we."

Hans patted the Frenchman on the shoulder. Then he climbed onto the stage. A hush came over the crowd. People took their seats. A few moved towards the back and quickly removed their clothes. They made the Change. They squatted in the rear, guarding the other door.

Hans tilted his head, looked down at the front row. Four people, two on each side of the center aisle, sat, dressed in red robes. Fidgeting, nervous.

He offered a reassuring smile. "Pain is real," he warned, "But so are the rewards. The pain is temporary. But the rewards can last for all eternity."

The four acolytes tried to smile back up at their leader.

Hans looked past them. Almost two hundred people crammed into this room. He raised his arms out to his sides. His resplendent robes bathed in the glory from the spotlights above and his own charisma.

"Since the beginning of time," Hans intoned, "we have existed. Since this planet was young and the ground still warm, we have walked the Earth.

"We were the Ancient Ones, brothers and sisters. We were the Strong. The Powerful. The Beautiful. Worshiped as Gods. This was right and good, for in the bounty of all of the Great God's creation, what creature under Heaven is more Godlike than we?"

He started slowly pacing across the stage in front of the altar. "We watched the Sumerians create the first civilization. We saw the rise and fall of Babylon. We grieved when Atlantis sank beneath the waves."

He paused. His visage changed. "We laughed at the vanity of man as they built their pyramids. We stood in shock at his hypocrisy as humans conducted the Crusades and butchered each other for centuries, all in the name of their God. If you didn't think their way or worship their way, you were the enemy. You were evil." He paused, smiled wryly.

"Sounds a lot like modern politics, doesn't it?"

An angry murmur rippled across the crowd. Even the werewolves in the back nodded their shaggy heads.

The grin faded from Hans' face. "We have never been as plentiful as the humans. Their sheer numbers allowed them to rise to dominance. But their days are numbered, my brethren!"

Another murmur through the crowd. Hans paused as it died down.

"We have strengths and abilities humans can never possess. We have powers they cannot comprehend. Humans are the weak, brethren."

Heads nodding throughout the room.

"They are childish, self-centered, self-serving, petty, vindictive, possessive. They believe more money or nicer clothes makes them better than others. We are beyond that, aren't we?"

Another murmur rippled through the crowd, right on cue. Hans had them eating out of his hand, and he knew it. Oh well, he thought. Roll with it. Have some fun.

"The humans cannot control or contain us. They do not understand us, and so, they fear us. They hate us. Perhaps if things had been different, our races may have been able to coexist.

"But that is impossible now, brothers and sisters!" he snarled. "They've spent centuries hunting us down, driving us from our homes, burning our property, killing us, killing our mates, our pups. Our history is written in the blood of werewolves who have fallen to the conceit of man!"

Thunderous applause ensued. People stood to their feet, clapping their hands. A few scattered whistles of agreement and encouragement. The werewolves in the back stood on their hind legs, tilted their heads and howled. Their hands tightened into massive sledgehammer fists; they beat their chests.

Hans paced the stage casually, smiling out at his flock. Damn, this was going better than he had anticipated. Drive the divide between them and the humans so deep and so wide it would never be bridged.

Much like the politicians and pundits he saw spouting off their ridiculous talking points on TV, peace and love, mutual respect, unity and understanding simply ran counter to his agenda. His success (like theirs!) depended upon ginning up hatred and resentment and shoving it down the throats of uninformed sheep, the lemmings who lacked the intellectual capacity to think for themselves.

Point out what's wrong, tell them who's to blame, and more importantly, tell them who to fear and who to hate. Always identify the problem, but never, *never* float a solution that stands a snowball's chance in hell of actually working.

"Listen, brothers and sisters. Harken to my words. We are a resilient race," Hans continued when the noise died down. "The humans will never exterminate us. We shall subjugate *them*!"

Once again, pandemonium reigned. The noise was deafening within the enclosed space. It eventually died down once more.

"The Middle ages saw us slip from our rightful perch in the eyes of Man. We became shadows of our former selves, the stuff of legend and folklore. We were reduced to fairy tales told to frighten their children.

"We took their disbelief and used it against them. Their minds say, if they don't believe, then we don't exist. We cloaked ourselves in anonymity. And we have moved quietly among them as we plotted our revenge."

The room was quiet. Everyone sat at rapt attention. Hans pursed his lips, as if thinking of the next thing to say. Then, "Yes, I said revenge. For truly, what is a God without worshipers but an angry, vengeful spirit?"

Yet another murmur of discontent rippled through the audience.

"The season of our decline is over. There are other temples just like this one, all over the country, all over the world. Those Alphas accept me as their Alpha."

A smattering of applause. "We have a global network of werewolf disciples, all working to achieve our goal.

"We have members placed in strategic positions in the areas of finance, economics and investment banking, big business and the Fortune 500, real estate, law and law enforcement, medicine and science, and most importantly, politics, entertainment, and religion. We control the narrative now.

"Their heads of state like to talk about the benefits of globalism. We shall show them a globalism the likes of which they never imagined. Werewolves shall rise once again to their rightful place as the world's dominant species!"

More thunderous applause, accompanied by loud whoops, shouting, hollering. People bounded to their feet as they slammed their hands together. Many, tears streaming down their cheeks, lifted their eyes skyward, praising their Alpha. The werewolves in back howled again.

When the din finally wound down, he said, "We are stronger, more plentiful now than we have been in centuries. We are well organized, singularly dedicated. Our time of renewed greatness is indeed at hand."

He pointed out to the crowd. "I have you to thank for that." He paused, allowing his followers to absorb the vibes and feel good about themselves. "You found human existence to be folly. Shallow, superficial. Meaningless.

"Some we sought out. Some came to us. And we gave you a choice: life eternal, reborn in our image. Each and every one of you answered the call. You are all now part of the Pack.

"We never ask for monetary donations. We don't need your money."

He paused, furrowed his brow as if deep in thought even though he knew precisely what he would say next. He walked towards the front edge of the stage, just a few feet from the first row.

"But we do demand something in return. Your honesty. Your time, commitment, and loyalty. Not to me, but to the Pack. To each other. To the common good of your brothers and sisters."

Silence in the room. Hans pointed to those wearing the red robes in the front row. "Tonight, four brave souls come of their own volition to join the Pack. They have been vetted, examined, instructed in the ways of their New Life. And here they are, ready to take the final step."

He spoke to them directly now. "You will live on, forever young. Forever strong, forever beautiful. You will learn to not measure time in months or years, but in generations and centuries.

"But we are not invulnerable," he cautioned. "We are not impervious to pain or injury. And while we have rejuvenating capabilities like that of a starfish, a large caliber gunshot to the head will finish us. Destroy the brain, disconnect the nervous system, and the game is over."

The four neophytes below him swallowed nervously. "We can also be killed by another werewolf in combat. Our saliva contains certain anticoagulant properties. You might bleed to death if the wounds themselves don't kill you first. So, physical combat amongst our kind is rare and to be avoided. We have other, more genteel methods of resolving disputes."

The four neophytes below him nodded their understanding. Hans stepped back from the edge of the stage. He motioned to Francois, standing silently by the side of the stage this entire time.

Francois climbed onto the stage and began peeling his clothes off. Nudity was a given, accepted as normal and natural within werewolf culture. Francois felt no shame or embarrassment as he stepped out of his pants.

He turned, completely naked, towards the audience. The bright lights above cast deep shadows across his dark skin and chiseled physique.

Francois looked down at the four New Believers. Looking down at them, he noticed one, Sara, staring up at him. Her attention seemed to be focused more on his formidable genitals than anything else. He caught the faintest whiff of pheromones.

But Francois had a job to do. He calmed himself, centered himself. He closed his eyes, controlled his breathing, and concentrated.

Really concentrated.

His lips thinned together, then curled. Not into a snarl, but in a smile. A pleasant smile. A pleasurable smile. A sensual smile.

A sexual smile.

His hands opened and closed, long fingers flexing. Then curled into fists. Thick muscles rippled and coiled beneath his skin. A low rumble began from within him, somewhere between his throat and his chest.

Francois made the Change. Black hair grew, covered his face and body. His nose and jaw jutted forward, created a snout. Black lips pulled back, revealing sharp teeth and three-inch fangs. His hands and feet elongated, nails extended into claws sharp as razor blades and harder than folded steel. Sensitive ears became extended triangles above the crown of his skull.

He stood on his hind legs, reaching his full height of over seven feet. Threw his arms and shoulders back, puffed out his chest, tilted his massive head skyward and howled in pure pleasure and exhilaration.

The werewolves in back joined in. Not only did they want to, but instinctively they had to. Howls had been a part of their communication system for millions of years.

The sound was deafening, but no one cared. The euphoria of the moment was what mattered, and it carried them all. The howl subsided, then faded away. All good things, even magic moments, come to an end. Their fleeting nature is what makes them magical.

Hans stepped forward once again, stood beside Francois. He pointed to Sara in the front row.

"Rise, Sara. Come take your place among us."

Sara stood on legs as brittle as balsa wood. Her cheeks drained of color. Hans reached down, taking her hand in his. She clambered onto the stage.

Hans touched her shoulder, turned her towards the congregation. "Sara, meet your new family. Your friends. Your protectors. Your pack." He looked out at his flock. "Everyone, meet Sara."

"Welcome, Sara!" they chanted in unison. They watched as Hans pulled her red robes open. They fluttered to the floor. She was completely naked underneath. They continued watching as Hans helped her sit on the altar, then lie down on her back, her head closest to them. Hans then secured her wrists and ankles in the leather straps attached to the four corners of the wooden slab.

Sara did not struggle. Weeks of indoctrination had been spent preparing her for this very moment. Yet she trembled in fear, worried she was going to pee herself in front of everyone.

Hans took a step back. "And now, my sister Sara, it is time for you to embrace the power of the Wolf!"

Francois approached the altar. He stopped at her left side, towering over her. Breathing hard, panting, she stared up into his orange eyes. There was menace there, the promise of violence. He could tear her apart right now if he wanted to, and no one would stop him.

Francois had no intention of tearing her apart. He was here to do a job, nothing more. He cocked his head as he gazed down upon her. He reached out, placed his enormous, clawed hand on her far side, careful not to cut her. He lowered his head slowly, deliberately, opened his maw, and bit down as gently as he could into her left shoulder. He was careful to avoid her neck and the major blood vessels underneath.

Blood bubbled up in his mouth and spilled over, down her shoulder and back, spreading across the altar, dribbling off the side. Sara bit her lip, tensed up, determined not to cry out. Human weakness had no place here.

The pain was excruciating, of course; worse than she had ever imagined. It was not simply the bite. That she could handle. There was a heat that pulsated at the wound site, then rippled outwards in waves, engulfing her entire body. Even her hair hurt. How was that even possible?

The fever intensified, became overwhelming. Sweat beaded on her forehead, across her upper lip. A wet sheen slicked across her nude body, glistening under the lights. Her brain felt like it was on fire. Her breathing came in shallow gasps. She arched her back, threw her head back, bringing most of her torso off the altar.

The last thing she saw was the faces of the congregation, both werewolf and human, looking at her with love and kinship. A small smile formed on her mouth just as she fell unconscious.

Francois stood up from his bent over position. Red drool dribbled down his chin and chest. As he stepped back, two men in blue robes silently mounted the stage, one from each end. One applied bandages to the wound. The other securely taped them in place. They loosened her straps, lifted her off the table. They carried her off, moving towards the main exit at the back.

The procedure was repeated three more times. Each time Hans gave a quick, pithy speech, the newbie climbed onstage, stripped naked, got strapped to the altar. Francois did his work just as gently with them as he had with Sara. Each one swallowed their own fear, braved the pain, endured the initial fever as best they could, then passed out.

They all understood there was only so much the human body, the frail, fragile, surprisingly weak human body, could take before it simply shut down.

When the last new werewolf Convert had been carried out, Francois made the Change back to human form. Blood covered him from his nose all the way down to his rock-hard abdomen. As a silence fell over the room, he gingerly picked up his clothes, then leapt off stage, ignoring the steps.

A ripple moved through the crowd. Anticipation built. The ones who had been here before knew what was coming. They licked their lips, excited.

Hans raised his arms out from his sides. "And now, it is done!" he shouted. "This is a joyous moment in the life of the Pack. A cause for celebration. So, celebrate! Take pleasure in each other."

The entire hall erupted into cheers. Hans watched from the stage as people began peeling off their clothes. They paired off, some in groups. People embraced, kissing passionately, lustfully. Their hands and mouths went everywhere. Some of the newbies appeared to be a bit more bashful; they had to be cajoled. Finally, their inhibitions fell by the wayside.

In the shadow of the stage and the raised altar, Diane stood near the back-staircase entrance through which she, Hans, and Francois had descended. She was in a room filled with people, yet she felt isolated, alone. She watched the orgy progress, couples and groups, hetero and homo, human and werewolf, all coming together in a mass of bodies and lust and felt her own longing.

She could join in right now if she wanted. No one in the pack would think less of her for it. There was no slut-shaming here.

Aroused, her pulse beat wildly. Her heart raced. She licked her dry lips; felt weak in the knees, like her joints were made of jelly. And oh God, how she wanted to join in, fling her cares and caution to the wind, just jump in and partake in the wild abandon.

And still she held back. Part of it was inhibition. She had never participated in this type of scene, and she admitted to herself she felt a bit overwhelmed by it all. The sex did not frighten her. But she consorted only with Hans.

The Alpha Male.

She was determined to maintain her own discipline to become Alpha Female. Queen of the Werewolves.

Damn if that didn't have a nice ring to it.

A figure approached her in the shadows. She came out of her reverie when the shadow solidified and grabbed her arm.

"Hans!"

"Sorry. Did I startle you?"

"No," she mumbled, trying to recover her balance and calm.

"Oh, I'm afraid I did." He looked out across the undulating ocean of bare skin and copulating couples. "Do you wish to join in?"

"I do my best work in private."

He cocked an eyebrow. "Indeed, you do."

Without another word, he took her hand in his, headed towards the staircase door. They slipped out discreetly and climbed the stairs in silence. Diane's nervousness receded. Hans had been monogamous to her. It was the nature of the Wolf, and it certainly fit with her plans.

The fact was, Diane truly saw herself as superior to the rest, Francois included. She knew he despised her as much as she despised him. Fine. The less time they spent together, the better. But Francois was a dangerous enemy.

Hans and Francois had been friends for centuries. That would be a tough bond to break. But once she was Queen, she could start driving a wedge between them. Getting Francois banished to another part of the world would be good. Getting him excommunicated from the Pack would be better. That was an attractive notion.

But still, if she was clever, she might be able to rid herself Francois once and for all. Maybe, just maybe, she could orchestrate a scenario where Hans had no choice but to order Francois, his oldest and dearest friend, put to death for some violation of the Werewolf Code.

Hans opened the door for her at the top of the stairs. "You're smiling," he observed.

"Happy thoughts."

He closed the door behind them. They headed through the main floor towards the staircase to the upper bedrooms. Diane noticed Hans himself was silent.

"Anything wrong?" she asked.

He looked surprised. "Wrong? What would be wrong? The Plan has come to fruition," he said as they began ascending the staircase. "The slaughter begins within a matter a days."

She shuddered, quite involuntarily.

He put a protective arm around her. "Fear not. You are safe. So is your family. Nothing will happen to them while I live and breathe."

Diane believed him. She believed him because she wanted to believe, and he said the things she wanted to hear. They climbed the staircase to the second floor, then began down the hallway.

Hans pulled her closer. The orgy below had affected him too. But his excitement went beyond mere lust. The Day of Awakening when werewolves come out of the shadows all over the world and begin the wholesale butchering of the human race was upon them.

He opened the door to his chambers, allowed her to enter first. Hans followed, closed the door behind him. He did not bother to lock it; no one save for Francois would dare to enter unless they had been summoned. And if Francois felt compelled to enter unannounced, it wouldn't be the first time he had found them in heat.

Near the bed, Diane turned to face Hans. He noticed a couple of buttons on her blouse were now undone. Smooth alabaster skin glowed underneath. His nostrils flared as he caught whiff of her pheromones.

He stepped close to her. "Diane. My dearest Diane. Have I told you lately how precious you are to me? How essential your talents have been to the Cause?"

Her eyes drifted downward. "Yes."

"Yet I can't help but wonder," he continued, "if I've truly done everything I can to show you just how much I appreciate your services."

A slow smile crossed her face, a wisp of smoke floating on a breeze. "I have many services."

"And in return, I think it incumbent upon me to serve you fully; to fulfill your every desire."

Her eyes came back up, met his gaze. "Do you really?" She stepped closer. They were only inches apart now. "Fulfill my every desire?"

Diane grabbed Hans by the waist, pulled him to her. She felt his erection squash into her belly. Pressing her breasts into him, she lifted her head up, planted her open mouth over his. Tongues explored. Hans encircled his arms around her, pressed her closer but careful not to hurt her. If he squeezed as hard as he wanted to, he would no doubt break her ribs. Maybe her spine.

Humans. Such fragile creatures! It's a wonder they ever survived, much less proliferated into the so-called "dominant species".

Diane grabbed a handful of his hindquarters. Hans kissed her face, then made his way to her neck and her earlobe. He unbuttoned her shirt, which got tossed off her shrugging shoulders and floated to the floor.

She gasped as he cupped her breasts in his incredibly warm hands. She wrapped her arms more tightly around his neck and shoulders. Even though the majority of their bodies' surface area was in contact, Diane simply could not get close enough to him.

Hans licked at the hollow of her shoulder and her neck. Then he traced his hot tongue slowly down her throat and onto her chest, leaving a trail of exquisite fire.

Diane closed her eyes, craned her neck. It was like Hans had become a walking blast furnace. His mouth might as well have been a sensual volcano, and his tongue the roiling magma within the cone, waiting to erupt.

Oh, he was going to erupt, all right. More than once if she had anything to say about it.

She bent her head down to kiss his forehead. Their eyes met. Sparks flew. He stood back up and pressed her against him. Once again, her attention was drawn to his incredible erection. Her hand snaked into the robes, followed the warmth to its source. Her fingers wrapped around him.

Hans responded, his eyes closing to slits. A small grunt escaped his lips. She calculated her next move. She moved her hand back and forth, making those ice blue eyes close completely at last.

She had him now.

Emboldened, she dropped to her knees in front of him, pushed the folds of his robes aside. Then, getting a visual lock on her target, her head darted forward and she engulfed the length of him with her mouth. Her tongue worked the length of his underside as her head bobbed back and forth.

Hans shuddered. His entire body felt like a dynamo, electric jolts of pleasure sparking underneath his skin. He breathed hard through his nose, practically snorting outward. His knees threatened to buckle. His eyes rolled up in his head. He could not last much longer. He felt himself slipping over the edge, falling into the abyss.

He cried out in astonishment at the power of his orgasm. Seconds became hours. It seemed to last forever, and just kept going. When the rhythmic pulses finally subsided, he swooned. Lightheaded, he had no idea how he was still on two feet.

Diane stood up, her eyes pure smoke.

"Diane. You're on fire."

"You got that right, lover. But we're not done. Not by a long shot – no pun intended, of course." She grabbed him by the buttocks, pulled his hips forward into hers.

"If I only knew what you need?"

They kissed again. Passionately. Lustfully. Hands and mouths everywhere again, just like before. Hans grabbed her under her buttocks, lifted her up. She wrapped her legs around his waist, locked them at the ankles. Their mouths never broke contact as he lumbered forward, carrying her to the bed.

He pitched forward, and they fell onto the mattress in a tangle of arms and legs.

CHAPTER NINETEEN

Russell Slater fidgeted, growing impatient as the night wore on. Then worried, then fearful. He tried calling Marla; it went straight to voice mail. He tried calling Caleb.

Same story.

He had turned the TV on but ignored it as he paced. Knowing the worst would be preferable to knowing nothing. When midnight came and went, he attempted another round of calls.

Dead end.

He finally called Akin's cell and left a message, voicing his concerns. He didn't know where anyone was, no one was answering their goddamned phones, and remorseless killers walked the streets. So, could she or Martinez please call him back right away?

A thumping at the front door froze him in place. Seconds ticked by. Nothing more. Perhaps his imagination was working overtime and he had not heard anything at all.

The thumping repeated, this time louder. Longer. Insistent. Someone pounding a closed fist on the door.

Russell waddled through the house as fast as his exhausted legs could haul his bulk. Damn, he thought. Caleb's right. I need to go on a fucking diet. Maybe join a gym. Join a gym? Don't kid yourself.

Russell approached the door cautiously. "Who's there?"

"Police," came the answer, a disembodied male voice from the other side, somewhat muffled and distorted by the solid oak door. Through the peephole, Russell saw two uniformed officers, one an older white man, lines around his eyes and mouth, gray at his temples, wearing Sergeant stripes and a dour look.

His partner, a young African American woman, stood beside him. In another time, in another place, Russell would have fantasized about having sex with her. Her dark eyes scanned the surrounding area, her cop training deeply ingrained. Situational awareness, they called it.

Russell unlocked the door, pulled it partway open.

"Russell Slater?" the Sergeant asked.

"Yes."

"Come with us, please."

"Why?"

"We're escorting you to Point Defiance Zoo."

Russell's anxiety spiked. "Marla!"

"She's fine, sir," the Sergeant assured.

Russell sighed with relief. "What's happened?"

"Detectives Akin and Martinez are on site," the partner said. "They'll bring you up to speed. I take it you know them?"

Russell disappeared inside, leaving the door open. The Sergeant and his partner exchanged glances once again.

"Weird guy," she remarked.

"Egghead Ph.D. type," the Sergeant snorted. "Weird people." He paused, then added, "Excuse me. Not weird. Eccentric."

His partner grinned. "Idiosyncratic?"

He nodded, pointed at her. "What you said."

The door opened, and Russell stepped onto the porch. He now wore a coat against the chill air. He closed the door behind him, slid the deadbolt into place.

On the short ride over, Russell again asked about what was going on. All they knew was there had been an "incident". Marla was uninjured. Other than that, they were clueless.

They arrived and stopped. Other squad cars parked nearby. Russell recognized Akin and Martinez's unmarked car off to the side. An ambulance squatted in front of them, back doors open, lights flashing silently.

The female officer got out, opened Russell's door. Squad cars were designed so that the internal door mechanisms did not work from inside the back seat. That way suspects could not simply open a door and run away.

Russell got out, stood up, stretched his legs. The young officer got back in the squad car.

"You're not coming?"

"We've got to get back to our patrol."

The sergeant put the car in gear, hit the gas. They sped away. Russell had the feeling the older cop wanted to get as far away from whatever this was as possible. And of course, there was other crime out there to deal with.

Cops there checked his ID at the turnstiles, let him through. A stab of light spilled from a light pole up ahead. Two paramedics appeared out of the darkness, pushing a gurney towards him. A blood-drenched sheet covering something underneath, the edges tucked securely. He slowed as They of the Grim Faces wheeled past him without a word.

Disturbed, Russell pushed on towards the wolf enclosure. He hoped Caleb and Marla could answer the hundreds of questions roiling and tumbling around inside his aching head.

God, he would *kill* for a decent coffee right now.

Another gaggle of uniforms milled about the entrance to the wolf enclosure. They checked his ID again, waved him inside.

Once inside, he paused, taking the scene in. Technicians in white paper overalls and blue gloves took samples from a huge blood stain on the floor. One tech snapped photographs of an unidentifiable chunk of flesh and muscle. His eyes flickered right. Sampson lazed contentedly inside his cage, watching the proceedings. He did not bother to look Russell's way.

Straight ahead, further back, Akin and Martinez stood by Marla. She sat in a chair, a gray blanket wrapped around her shoulders. A dazed, glazed look to her eyes, staring into space and seeing nothing.

"Marla!" he called out. Startled, she looked up. For an instant, she stared right through him. Then her pupils constricted, and relief flooded through her.

"Russell!" She bolted from her chair and into her cousin's arms. The blanket swept away from her shoulders and fluttered to the floor. Akin scooped it up.

"I've been so worried." He squeezed her tight.

"I'm okay."

Russell looked to the detectives. "What happened?"

"Looks like a break-in gone wrong. A disgruntled former employee came back to sabotage the place," Martinez explained. "He wasn't expecting her."

"He attacked me."

Martinez pointed. "Sampson took exception to that."

Russell looked questioningly to Marla.

"Ty," she said.

"Oh. Him. He was an asshole."

"Russell!"

"It's true, isn't it?"

Marla sighed, not wanting to admit Russell was right but… Russell was right.

"Where's Caleb?" Russell asked.

Everyone tensed up. Russell looked from Marla to Martinez to Akin. Everyone suddenly had pinched faces.

"We… don't rightly know where he is," Akin said finally.

Flummoxed, Russel said, "Say again?"

Akin repeated herself.

It did not make sense. This time of night and he wasn't answering his phone? Wasn't here with Marla?

"When's the last time anyone saw him?"

"He touched bases with one of our computer techs around seventeen hundred hours," Akin said. "No one has seen or heard from him since."

Russell pulled his phone out of his pocket. "Ridiculous," he muttered. He found Caleb's number in his phone, hit the speed dial button. Beeps on the other end, almost musical in tone. The buzzing of the ring, then a click. Next was Caleb's voice recording, telling whoever was calling to leave a message.

Angry and worried, Russell stabbed the END CALL button on his phone, jammed it into his pocket. "Ridiculous!" he exclaimed. "How can this be? Where the hell is he?"

They all gave him another collective shrug.

"Marla. You don't know where he is?"

"Why would I know where he is?"

"Well now that you and he—"

Marla gave him a warning look. He shut his mouth. She glanced furtively at Akin and Martinez. They looked at her with renewed interest.

"He was working his own line of inquiry," Marla said.

"And he's been incommunicado for over seven hours now?" No one answered. "Can't you track him down? Ping cell towers, triangulate his location using his cell phone?"

"No. We'd need probable cause." Martinez again. Russell was starting to dislike him.

"Probable cause? Listen. What if something has happened to him? What if he stumbled onto something and got hurt or worse?"

"There's no evidence of that."

"And by the time there is evidence of that, it'll be too late," Russell hissed. "His ravaged corpse would be pretty convincing 'evidence', right?"

"It's called invasion of privacy," Akin chimed in quickly before Martinez exploded. "The fact is, if someone wants to go off grid, they can do that, any time they want for as long as they want. It's not a crime."

"But what we're investigating is," Russell shot back. "And seriously. Does anyone here really think Caleb's someone to go off grid at a time like this?"

Martinez shrugged. Akin said, "I don't know him well enough to guess."

"Well, ladies and gentlemen, I do know him well enough, and I'm telling you he wouldn't do this. It's flaky. It's irresponsible. It's not who he is."

"The important thing is that your cousin is safe," Martinez offered. "She'd probably like a ride home. Right?"

Marla looked up, closed her bloodshot eyes, nodded. Her entire body sagged. Russell's anger receded.

"I'll drive them back," Akin suggested.

Marla stood up. Russell threw a protective arm around her shoulders. He walked her out of her office and around the CSI techs. Akin followed behind them. Russell felt better away from Martinez.

Something off about that guy.

Akin knew this incident didn't have anything to do with their case. But Akin wondered how deeply this had affected Marla. Was she going to be useful to the team after this?

Only time would tell.

The only one not feeling better in the fresh air was Marla. She did not feel in any way responsible for Ty's death. She had thought it over in the time between her calling 911 and the first officers' arrival. Ty had definitely brought it on himself. His reputation preceded him, and he had been hanging onto his job by a thread for quite some time.

Memories flashed before her eyes, quick-cut images and sounds. Ty's strangled screams. Sampson as he went to work.

All that blood.

It's not until you see massive amounts of blood pouring out of someone that you realize just how much blood pumps through the human body at any given time.

She shuddered, willed herself not to throw up. Russell mistook it for her being cold. He pulled her closer to him. And while grateful for his protective instincts, Marla was not shivering from the temperature.

Where the hell was Caleb?

Caleb trailed his prey until the old man got off the bus. Caleb parked, locked up, then darted around the corner just in time to see the guy totter off into the fog. He hurried along, pacing his prey, keeping back far enough to not be noticed. The bald bum clomped along, worn boots slapping against wet cement. Caleb moved silently, wearing rubber-soled hiking boots and walking on the balls of his feet.

Where best to kill this motherfucker?

Up ahead, a pale glow emanated from an all-hours convenience store. As he approached, Caleb made out a garish yellow neon sign over the door. His prey changed course and cruised in. He threw a glance back the way he came. Caleb slowed, veered towards the bus stop to his left. He feigned waiting for the next scheduled pickup. He did not need his eyes to tell him when Old Baldy came back out.

The soon to be slaughtered pedophile emerged from the store, stood on the stoop. He looked both ways as he tore the cellophane plastic wrapper off a fresh pack of cigarettes. He wadded the crinkly plastic in one fist, dropped it on the sidewalk. He saw someone standing at the bus stop.

Curious, he stepped off the stoop, walked towards the bus stop. His eyes strained to make out anything about the man standing there, studiously ignoring him.

"Hey, buddy," the old perv slurred. "You missed the last bus."

"Did I?" came the reply.

"Ain't another one until five o'clock."

The mysterious man never even turned his head.

The old man grunted. "Suit yourself, asshole."

"Asshole?"

"Yeah. I was just tryin' to fuckin' help."

"Really?"

The old man thought about saying something else, then didn't. Having lived hardscrabble all his life, he had seen and heard all kinds of boasts, threats, displays. He knew how to quickly distinguish whether someone was full of shit or the real deal.

The guy in front of him was the real deal, all right. But that wasn't all. He would make guys who were the real deal look like hopeless amateurs. The guy in front of him standing at a dark bus stop was one dangerous fucking hombre, a cold, efficient, amoral killer.

Fear flooded the old man's brain. Adrenaline pumped out of the glands atop his poorly functioning kidneys, squirting into his bloodstream and making him gasp audibly. The old perv took a wary step backwards. He put his hands up in front of him, palms outward.

A small grin passed over Caleb's lips. "You okay?"

"Yeah," the old man said too quickly. "Look. Sorry about earlier. I didn't mean it."

"Yes you did."

"I'm sorry."

"Not yet you're not."

The old man was fifteen feet away now. He turned and moved quickly, almost running, to put some distance between himself and the deliberate stranger at the bus stop. Why was a guy like that out on the streets hanging around a fucking bus stop?

Then another thought slammed into him with the force of a speeding freight train. What if the old man had pissed off the wrong person and they had sent a killer after him?

Darkness and fog enveloped him once again. The coldness crept in, penetrated his multiple layers of clothing, chilled him to the bone. But was that the cold damp air of the night, or was it his encounter with that stranger?

He looked over his shoulder, his street sense or his paranoia, whatever you wanted to call it, getting the better of him. He saw no one, kept going. Yet he could not shake the feeling his was being watched. Being followed.

Being hunted.

What the fuck was that? He came to a full stop. A soft scraping, a scratching somewhere behind him. He looked and listened as he tried to tamp down a rising panic. He caught movement just at the edge of his periphery. A shadow, smoky and ephemeral, shifted and melted into nothingness in the fog when he focused on it less than a full second later.

"Who's there?" the old man called out.

No response.

"Is that you, Bus Stop? Hey, I told you, man. I'm sorry for calling you an asshole." He paused again, hoping to see someone appear out of the fog.

No one did.

His dysfunctional brain finally remembered the small caliber handgun he illegally carried in his pocket. It was illegal because he was a convicted felon, having spent time in prison for an armed robbery of a liquor store when he was twenty-two. Ah, the folly of youth. His hand snaked into his coat pocket. His fingers wrapped around the grip, forefinger inside the trigger guard.

He passed dark buildings, hulks of red brick and gray mortar squatting on foundations poured decades ago, towering four stories high. Cheap restaurants, low-end clothing stores, resale shops shouting about vintage goods occupied the ground floor.

The floors above were tiny apartments, complete with kitchenette and a three quarters bath. Some of them were single rooms furnished with a bed, a mini fridge, maybe a microwave or hot plate. These old buildings had originally been built as tenements or boarding houses. Now they housed the old and the poor, illegals, the jetsam and flotsam of society; disposable human derelicts the well-heeled found convenient to ignore. People who lived precariously, one slight stumble away from eating out of dumpsters.

The old perv passed an alley. Fear forced him to slow his walk and look as he passed. The alley had no light. None at all. It reminded him of those things in space he had heard about on TV. Those things scientists said could swallow entire planets. He struggled to remember.

A Black Hole. That was it.

Across the alley, the next building rested, waiting for daylight and human activity. The first floor was a cheap Mexican restaurant. They had a few tables inside, but the bulk of their business was take-out. They had been here for years. He ate there when he could.

He halted at the narrow door facing the street. Inside, a wooden staircase led upwards. He looked to his right.

Something still out there, he knew.

He turned his attention to the small digital keypad on the wall by the door. He punched in a six-digit code. A buzzer sounded and the door lock clicked a split second later. He twisted pushed the door open.

He anticipated the attack right then. Something big and terrible, something dark and scary slamming into his back, pushing him inside. Or maybe he'd get snatched, disappearing helplessly into the gloom.

But the attack never came. He stepped safely inside, closed the door behind him. The click of the lock reengaging should have made him feel better. It did not. He peered through the glass, searching outside for the source of his unease.

After another moment, he trudged tiredly up the stairs.

When Caleb saw the old perv stop at the door, he immediately crossed the street. By the time the old guy had turned to look back, Caleb was already on the other side working his way at an angle, his keen eyes never leaving his prey for more than a second or two.

Caleb stood in the shadow of the building across the street. He stepped backwards, sinking deeper into the alley. It was dark there, even for one such as Caleb. A dumpster on one side. Rats scurrying. Cockroaches rustling. The smell of decay and despair.

But what struck Caleb was the old-fashioned wrought iron fire escape that wound its way up the slab of red brick and ended in a short ladder that went up and over the ledge to the roof.

No ladder from the second-floor landing to the ground? No problem. Caleb took three steps and leapt upwards. His fists grasped the bottom of the landing fifteen feet above the pavement. He easily pulled himself up, threw a leg over the railing. Without pausing, he fixed his gaze on the roof and raced up the fire escape. Within seconds he was pulling himself up and over the top, tumbling onto the roof.

Caleb loped to the front ledge, the top of which came up to the middle of his thigh. His eyes scanned the windows facing him. Most were dark, the occupants inside asleep.

Let them sleep. I'm not after them.

A light snapped on in the corner apartment on the top floor, directly above the doorway and staircase. Through the grimy window and flimsy curtains, Caleb spied the old perv removing his overcoat. The old guy pulled something out of his pocket. Small. Compact. Metallic.

A gun.

He clearly detected movement in his peripheral vision. Someone else was already in the apartment.

If Caleb had been human, he would not have noticed. But Caleb had the same visual field as wolves. He not only saw in color, but also saw clearly one hundred and eighty degrees, from horizon to horizon. He watched his prey turn and disappear briefly from view. A light came on in the next bedroom. The old perv came into view.

Old perv was the proper term for this sorry piece of shit. For he was not alone, oh no. Also in the room, a naked teenaged boy cowered. Dark hair, gagged mouth, eyes wide and fearful. Chained to a bedframe, lying atop a bare mattress besmirched with multiple stains, the origins of which Caleb but did not want to know.

He had always planned to kill this miserable prick; that much was given. Caleb had enjoyed the chase, had trailed his quarry with a clinical detachment, a morbid fascination.

But now fascination was replaced by deep revulsion and a murderous anger that would not be denied. Not tonight.

Merciful God in heaven, Caleb thought. And people think *I'm* the monster.

Caleb stepped away from the ledge, melted into the gloom. He removed his clothes, folded them neatly. He placed his boots on the bottom next to the wet rooftop, his clothing next with his socks and underwear protected from dampness by squeezing them in between his jeans and his shirt, and then he covered everything with his jacket.

He stood back up stark naked, on a rooftop in Tacoma Washington, in the middle of winter. It was barely thirty-five degrees. Caleb had to admit, it felt a bit chilly. But not for long. Serious business was afoot, and once things started, a minor inconvenience like cold rainy weather in the Pacific Northwest would be the least of his concerns.

He calmed his breathing, emptied his mind. He felt no moral quandary about what was coming. The world would continue spinning through space and time without this piece of shit pedophile.

Hell, this wasn't murder. He was performing a goddamned public service.

Caleb closed his eyes. His face shifted, all the lines around his nose and mouth smoothing out. He slowed his breathing more, listened to his heart beating in his chest. Then he concentrated. Concentrated on willing himself to make the Change.

There was a natural resistance at the beginning of the Change, something that said the body was resisting, even though every fiber of his mind and soul wanted it. Maybe it was because of the pain coming.

He mentally pushed against the resistance, like it was a physical barrier instead of a mental one. Caleb pushed harder. Harder.

HARDER!

And pushed through. The barrier broke like a rubber band pulled to its limits until it snaps. A great wave of peace washed over him. He didn't even mind the pain as the Change happened.

Hair sprouted from his pores along his face and neck. His eyes swirled amber, then darkened to a burnt orange. Claws and fangs grew simultaneously. He grunted as his ribs snapped, reformed, healed. Leg bones elongated. His knees shifted, dislocated, then stabilized with a bend in the opposite direction. His face narrowed, elongated into a snout. His triangular ears protruded outwards, twitching in the night breeze. His teeth protruded over his lips, his canines over three inches long. Looking down at his hands, his claws were roughly the size of steak knives.

Only his claws were sharper.

His penis retreated into a sheath as his foreskin grew back, covering his tip. A thin membrane of skin developed and tightened forming a prepuce, pulling his penis up and out of the way, connecting it to his lower belly.

Shimmering dark brown hair now covered his entire body. His muscles kept growing in mass, gaining strength. He heightened during the Change, going from his human height of five foot nine to just over seven feet. As his mass increased, his weight increased as well. In human form, Caleb weighed about one ninety. Now, he would tip the scales at three hundred fifty pounds of teeth, claws, muscle, and murderous intent.

With the Transformation complete, all pain faded away. He stood there a moment, chest heaving, getting his bearings. In those first few seconds, every werewolf was vulnerable to attack, which is why werewolves were careful to make the Change either by themselves, or with others in a safe environment.

And now, here he was, in full transformation once again, blood, adrenaline, and power pulsing through him. God, this felt good. Why the hell had he waited so long? Why had he denied himself this?

He pushed those thoughts out of his mind. He was in a time crunch, and he had other, more pressing business on his plate.

Priorities, priorities.

He crept forward, away from his hidden clothes and towards the front ledge. He stopped there, crouched down, squatting on powerful thighs the size of tree trunks. He extended one arm, spreading his huge hand flat on the ledge to stabilize himself.

He leaned forward, extending his head and part of his upper torso out over the ledge. His keen eyesight immediately took in the events in the apartment across the street. He sniffed then snorted like a bull. His nostrils flared to pull more air inside. He now had larger lungs to fill. His nose quivered at the smells wafting past him carried on the night air.

His prey was still there, still in the bedroom. Caleb watched as the old perv slapped the boy and spit in his face. Then, he laughed.

Humankind's capacity for cruelty and sadism never ceased to shock him.

Caleb's black lips pulled back into a snarl, baring rows of sharp teeth, top and bottom. A low growl rumbled through him, emanating from somewhere deep within his chest, but felt throughout his entire massive body. It was almost as if his entire frame reverberated with it.

A primal, unrestrainable hatred filled him, overflowed out of him. Caleb's body seethed with primitive instincts: his rage, his desire, his need to kill. And his target was right there in front of him, across the street in the filthy apartment.

But how to get into the apartment quickly and efficiently? His great head swung left and right, down at the pavement almost fifty feet below him. Then his head lifted to gaze across the street.

Caleb had his answer. The fact he had never done what he was about to do held no relevance. He peered intently at the glass window, his mind calculating distance, figuring how much of a running start he would need.

Caleb pushed off with his arm, rose on his hind legs to his full height. He stepped away from the ledge, turned and stalked back across the roof. He stopped midway across, near the air vent by which he had placed his clothes. He turned, eyes tracing a direct path from his own feet, across the mildly sloping rooftop and to the ledge which he would use like a diver on a springboard.

He breathed deeply, lolling his head around on his neck. He rolled his shoulders, up, back, and around.

God, this felt good. Caleb had denied the Wolf for far too long. Now it was time for Human Caleb to step aside for a time, take a nap, let the Wolf run free.

Caleb lurched forward in long, loping strides. Arms pumping like pistons, he leaned into it, gained speed. He was maxed out at a full run when he raised his right leg higher, slapped his foot onto the ledge, and pushed off with all his considerable might.

He flung himself outward and upward across the expanse, legs out and arms flung wide, hurtling four stories above the pavement below.

The wind ruffled through his fur. It felt good.

The pathetic excuse of a human being now sat in a chair that should have been thrown away twenty years ago, watching a TV that should have been recycled about the same time. With his advancing years, it seemed like his sex drive was faltering, his desire for that kind of gratification becoming less important. He had beer in the mini fridge, but the thing was on the blink and didn't chill anything much under fifty-five degrees. He had voiced his complaints, but the landlord steadfastly refused to replace it.

Well fuck him. Maybe I'll put one on layaway, pay it out. Then it would be mine. Or maybe cruise the Goodwill and Salvation Army thrift stores, find one that worked for just a few bucks. Yeah. That sounded like a plan.

He decided to watch a few more minutes of TV, then curl up beside the boy, get some sleep. For the first time all day, his rage receded, and he felt almost content, almost peaceful.

Then his entire universe… *exploded.*

The window shattered inward, sending a barrage of razorlike shards flying. The old man yelped and jumped up from his chair as an enormous dark brown thing landed on the floor. He thought he caught a glimpse of teeth, a flash of claws amid shimmering fur.

Shimmering fur?

The old man stood in mute shock as the monstrosity before him uncoiled and stood. Raising to its full height, this demon glared at him through orange eyes filled with seething hatred. His brain tried and failed to comprehend the creature towering over him, the tips of the ears brushing the ceiling. Rippling muscles, claws like talons.

The great beast took a malevolent step forward. The old man pissed his pants, warm liquid spreading throughout his crotch and down his legs. He was so horrified he did not feel it, just as he had not felt the dozens of tiny cuts on his face and arms from the flying glass.

Orange eyes narrowed. Black lips pulled back. White fangs gleamed as a rumble reverberated throughout the room. The man backpedaled, fumbling in his damp pants for something, found it. He pulled out his tiny little gun.

The beast paused, looked at the gun. A strange noise the man could not quite place emitted from the monster's throat. The corners of the maw turned upwards, almost like a grin. The muscular shoulders shook.

The goddamned thing was *laughing* at him!

The old perv's anger, his rage, his impotent screams against an unfair and uncaring world returned. His rheumy eyes went hard. He raised the handgun, pointed right at the beast's heart, and fired.

The demon dog stopped laughing, looked at his prey. The snarl came back, the low rolling growl, narrowing eyes. The huge paw drifted upwards, rubbed the bullet wound in his left pectoral muscle. The bullet had lodged in the muscle fiber, which was about three times more dense than human muscle tissue. Even at that close range, the bullet did not penetrate his heart.

Sure, it stung like hell, but the hulking beast was not injured. But he sure as hell was pissed now.

Moving forward so fast he could hardly be seen, the werewolf grabbed the man's gun wrist in his giant paw, gripped tight as a vise, and wrenched the wrist back and over. Both the radius and the ulna snapped audibly. The werewolf pushed downward, and the jagged ends of the bone erupted through the skin. Blood from ruptured arteries fountained everywhere.

The old man's eyes grew so wide in pain and fear he looked like a cartoon drawing. Under other circumstances, his expression might have been comical. He instinctively grabbed for his mangled wrist as the gun fell harmlessly to the filthy floor.

Hadn't this asshole ever heard of a goddamn vacuum cleaner?

The beast released his grip on the wrist. His dripping red hand completely encircled the old perv's throat and squeezed, cutting off the windpipe, silencing the screams. He picked his prey up off the ground, surged forward and slammed the him into a wall so hard the plaster cracked. Silt drifted down like a fine snow, dislodged from the ceiling above them. His prey's feet dangled several inches above the floor.

The demon dog swung his head around. For the first time, he had an unobstructed view into the bedroom. He saw everything. Dirty wooden floor, peeling paint around the door frame, rusty bedsprings, grimy mattress. And of course, the adolescent chained there.

Revulsion and hatred swelled anew within the werewolf's psyche. Somewhere inside him, the man known as Caleb Jacobsen was so horrified, he wanted to puke. But the Wolf had other plans.

Let the punishment fit the crime.

The huge head with that incredible maw filled with lethal teeth swung back around to his quarry. His eyes narrowed once again, another growl rumbling like a distant thunder. His jaws snapped shut, spittle flying into the old man's face.

He held his prey where he was. He straightened the fingers on his free hand, extending his claws. In one swift, economic motion, the werewolf swung low and upwards. Four-inch claws buried themselves into the man's groin just at the apex of his thighs, puncturing his shriveled penis and lacerating at least one testicle.

A sidewalk vasectomy.

The old perv's eyes popped wide. His mouth tried to open and close. No words came, only unintelligible sounds. His face drained of color as all the blood in his body appeared to be pouring from his crotch.

The werewolf savored the moment. Then he raked upwards with a terrible force, slicing through what was left of the man's penis, waded through the pubic bone, continued upwards. Four deep vertical incisions appeared, completely opening the abdominal cavity. Intestines exploded forth through the deep rents, gruesome jelly spilling out, dangling down around his knees. But the werewolf was not done. His buzz saw claws ripped upwards until they hit bone.

It was like the werewolf had unzipped the bastard.

From the bedroom, the boy had a front row seat to the entire event. He felt no fear for himself. He knew without question the monster would kill him next. He was fine with that. No way death could be worse than the life he had lived.

The werewolf opened his maw, baring sharp teeth and long fangs. His head plunged downward. Powerful jaws clamped down on the man's neck, snapping the vertebrae underneath, severing the spinal cord.

The boy watched with grim satisfaction as his tormentor died an ugly, agonizing death. He hoped that fucker's last moments on earth were filled with a pain and a fear and a regret that would be unfathomable to anyone else.

The werewolf, still holding the body aloft in his powerful jaws, shook his head back and forth violently, a giant dog with a chopped-up chew toy. Even from where he sat several feet away, the boy heard bones snapping like twigs all the way down the man's spinal column.

The werewolf spat the corpse out of his mouth, a chunk of spoiled meat. It fell like a sack of bricks to the floor, a tangle of arms and legs in a pile of intestines. The old man's head had been turned around one hundred and eighty degrees at some point, and so even though the body lay chest down in the muck, his sightless eyes stared up at the ceiling, into infinity and beyond.

The werewolf stood there a moment, catching his breath in the new quiet that settled like a blanket. The deed was done, and the werewolf had relished it. And inside the Wolf, Caleb Jacobsen really didn't have a problem with what had just happened.

Elated with his kill, relieved of the pressure of not making the Change in such a long time, the werewolf tilted his head back, nose to the ceiling, and howled. It started out softly, then built, sustained, then built again until the decibel level threatened to break glass in a crescendo smashing at the end that finally died out.

Later when the police arrived, the boy would tell them a fantastic story. A story about a demon of vengeance that was sent by God to punish his captor. He would relate how God had heard his pleas and prayers, had looked down from his throne, and had passed judgement.

The boy would survive the night and grow into adulthood. But his life would be spent in various institutions and facilities, with smug doctors convinced he had experienced so many psychotic breaks that any thought of releasing him back into society was something no one could risk.

His days would be filled with empty time doing arts and crafts, and useless counseling sessions where they would attempt to convince him that he did not see what he had in fact seen. His nights would be an endless series of darkness and insomnia, filled with memories of what happened. And in those rare times when his body finally shut down and he did sleep, his dreams would be visions of this night, this scene. Reenactments in his mind's eye of these very events.

He would never successfully reenter society.

The werewolf finally remembered the boy. He turned towards him, dripping blood. He stalked forward, ducked his head, and entered the bedroom. He paused, breathing softly, hands at his sides. He looked down at the boy, suddenly not sure what to do next. It bothered him that the boy looked up at him with such a sense of peace and resignation. That was when the werewolf understood what the boy wanted him to do.

The werewolf slowly extended one red arm, stretched out a forefinger with its scalpel claw. It drifted towards the unmoving boy. The claw hovered near his throat, then drifted upwards, worked its way gently between the nylon strap of the gag and the boy's soft skin. With a quick flick of the finger, the claw sliced neatly through the restraint. The gag fell away from the boy's mouth.

For a moment, they simply stared at each other in silence. Eventually, the werewolf turned to go.

"No!" the boy exclaimed. The werewolf stopped, looked back at him. "Aren't you going to kill me too?"

The werewolf cocked his head in confusion. This was the last thing he had expected. He took a step backwards towards the door.

"Wait! Please! Kill me! Don't leave me here. Not like this."

The wolf's ears twitched He craned his neck. Police sirens in the distance. Growing closer. Someone had called the cops.

He lumbered towards the boy. He grabbed the bedframe in one hand, leaned over and grabbed the chain tether in the other. With one swift, deft movement, he broke the chain from the bedframe, let it fall onto the mattress. He then stepped backwards again, his eyes on the boy. The boy's eyes were vacant. His jaw went slack. He drooled. Like his brain had just shut down.

Somewhere inside the Wolf, Caleb Jacobsen's heart broke. He wept. He wept for this boy, he wept for the torture he had endured. He wept for all children who underwent such torture. He wept for the barbarism man rained down upon his fellow man. He wept for all the human suffering innocent people experienced at the hands of other people.

And once again, he felt guilt for when, as a hot-tempered young man thirsting for revenge, he had joined the Missouri militia during the Civil War.

Distracted, he bumped the back of his head on the door frame. The werewolf snarled, put a hand to the back of his head. His mind back in the game, the great beast ducked through the doorway. He ignored the bloody heap on the floor. He had already spent too much time here. He headed straight for the broken window.

He stepped onto the windowsill, careful not to cut his feet on the broken shards still embedded in the frame. He twisted around and reached up, grabbing hold of a steam pipe that ran from the ground to the roof. He ignored the heat from the pipe, pulled himself out of the apartment.

Once again outside, the werewolf felt better. He felt free. The tiny apartment had been too confining. The night breeze ruffled through his blood-soaked fur, cooling him. He paused there a moment, then the sounds and smells of Tacoma at night spurred him to action.

Using his massive arms and shoulder muscles, he climbed upwards hand over hand, nimble for a creature so massive. He pulled himself easily onto the roof, got to his feet, then scampered away. He melted into the darkness, gone as if he had never even been there.

CHAPTER TWENTY

Russell Slater sat on Marla's sofa, drumming his fingers absently on the fabric. He had not slept. Agitated, he stared out the window. The sky brightened to the east, pale blue with a hint of orange, promising a clear sky when the sun finally cracked over the Cascades.

After being dropped off, Marla had trudged silently to her bedroom, closed the door with a slam. He assumed she had fallen across her bed and had passed out, exhausted.

Seeing a man ripped apart only five or six feet away would turn anybody's brains to scrambled eggs, wouldn't it? Well, just about anyone's but Caleb's. That son of a bitch took everything in stride. How the fuck did he do that?

Around seven thirty, Marla emerged, still in yesterday's clothes peppered with Ty's blood. Zombie-like, lank hair, sunken cheeks, sallow skin, vacant eyes. She shuffled down the hallway concrete legs, stumbled into the living room.

"Morning, sunshine," he said.

She grunted. She looked around. "Caleb?"

Russell shook his head. "The detectives said they'd be by here around eight thirty."

She looked at her watch. "I'm going to take a shower. Get some coffee going. You know where everything is."

He stood up. "You might want to consider burning those clothes."

She looked down, ran her finger over the dry rust colored spots. She grinned at him, and he saw something dark behind her eyes. Then she turned and headed back down the hallway towards the bathroom.

Disturbed by the subtle changes in Marla's demeanor; he made his way into the kitchen. Anyone who did not know Marla would have either dismissed her facial expressions as fatigue or shock or would not have noticed at all.

But Russell had known her all her life. Events were changing her.

Into what, he did not know.

The kettle was already full, so he hit the ON button, then reached over and grabbed the French press sitting at the back of the counter against the wall. He took the top off, peered in to make sure it was clean and that grounds from the last brew had been washed out.

He heard the water from the shower down the hall. He coarse ground some whole bean coffee, dumped the grounds into the bottom of the French press.

Russell opened the fridge and pulled out some bacon. A skillet already sat on the stove. He turned the dial to medium heat.

He checked his watch again. Jesus Tapdancing Christ. Where in the hot and holy fuck was Caleb?

He tossed bacon slices into the hot skillet. He heard the water in the bathroom turn off. He hoped the shower had made her feel better. He poured boiling water into the French press, filling it up almost to the top. The beans expanded as they absorbed the water, forming a convex crown. He stirred with a large spoon, carefully replaced the top.

Let it sit for four minutes.

Marla rounded the corner a couple of minutes later. She had changed into fresh clothes. Her hair was still damp, her face still slack with fatigue.

"Smells good." She plopped down in one of the chairs at the bistro table.

Russell scooped up two pieces of the bacon, placed them on a paper plate. English muffins popped up from the toaster. He grabbed them, tossed one onto Marla's plate, the other on his. He carried the plates to the table, set one in front of her, the other one at his place setting.

"Coffee?" he asked.

Marla nodded gratefully. He pressed the coffee, poured up two mugs, brought them to the table, grabbed the half and half from the fridge. Sweetener was already on the table, next to the butter.

He sat down across from her.

"This is great, Russell."

"My pleasure."

She buttered her half of the English muffin. "So. Where the fuck is Caleb?"

Russell was shocked to hear her drop the F-bomb so casually. "Don't know. Tried everywhere. Nothing."

She nodded, attacked her bacon. She bit down, grabbing it with her teeth, rent it in half with a shake of her head. Her eyes drifted up to Russell. He sipped his coffee, added more half and half.

"Look on the bright side," Russell said. "No news is good news."

She looked at him like she did not understand.

"If something had happened to Caleb, the cops would have called. Just because he's incommunicado, doesn't mean anything bad has happened."

"Where is he then?"

"I don't know," Russell admitted. "But I will tell you. He is tenacious. Once he's on the scent of something, he doesn't stop. I just hope he hasn't done something stupid."

"Like what?"

"Like go after whoever's behind these murders."

"You think he would do something like that?"

Russell looked at the ceiling, then back to Marla. "I think Caleb Jacobsen is a driven, determined man."

Marla sat back in her chair, pushed her plate away from her.

"You're worried about him," Russell said. It was a statement, not a question.

"So are you."

"Yes, but not like you." Silence. Then, "You love him, don't you?"

Marla's head snapped back around. Her mouth dropped open in surprise. Then she regained her composure.

"I… I don't know," she demurred. "We've only been together once. I really like him. He seems trustworthy." She paused, then looked Russell in the eye hard. She leaned across the table. "But there's something else, Russell. I can sense it."

"Woman's intuition?"

She waved her hands. "Call it what you will. But I'm telling you, he's hiding something."

Russell turned this over in his head, bit into his muffin. Melted butter dripped onto the plate below his chin.

She muttered, "Something dangerous."

"Dangerous?

"He didn't get all those muscles and those washboard abs by sitting on his ass eating pizza and watching TV," she stated.

Russell thought about his own lifestyle and eating habits. Maybe it really was time for a change.

"I thought chicks liked the bad boys. Got turned on by dangerous."

"Not this kind of dangerous."

A sharp knock came at the door. They stared at each other bug eyed for a moment.

Caleb!

Marla somehow found the strength to bolt out of her chair so fast the chair teetered on two legs behind her, threatening to tip over. But she was already on the move, heading towards the living room. The chair righted itself, came back down to rest on four legs.

Russell pushed himself away from the table and stood up. He took a couple of cautious steps forward as Marla reached the front door.

Marla grabbed the knob. Her stomach in knots, she stared through the peephole. Her heart sank. Disappointed, she opened the door. Detectives Akin and Martinez stood on the stoop. They each had coffee cups in their hands.

"Come in." Marla stepped back, clearing the way for the detectives to enter the premises. She closed the door behind them.

"I thought you might be Caleb," Marla said as they went deeper into the house. Russell stood at the entrance from the living room to the kitchen. They both nodded and tipped their coffee cups in his general direction.

"So, we still don't know Caleb's whereabouts?" Akin asked.

Both Russell and Marla nodded. The detectives looked at each other, concern evident on their faces. Martinez pulled his phone out, walked towards the front window. He punched in a number, began speaking in hushed tones.

"What's he doing?" Marla asked.

"He's putting out a BOLO on Caleb Jacobsen."

"BOLO?"

"Be On the Look Out," Akin explained. "Every cop in the region will be looking for him. He'll turn up."

"But in what kind of shape?"

Akin had no idea. "I get the impression he knows how to handle himself." Russell grunted. "You disagree?"

"Just something Caleb told me one time," Russell replied. "He said, 'No matter how tough you are, how fast or how strong, there's always someone out there tougher, stronger, faster'," Russell said.

"True enough," Akin conceded. "Thank God most of us never meet that person."

"What if Caleb has?" Marla again.

Still on the phone, Martinez looked out the front window through the gap in the curtains. He saw a red sports car drive up the block, slow, then park and come to a stop. Two young men got out, one Black, one Hispanic. They paused where they were. Looked around. Sniffed the air.

They noticed the unmarked cop car, looked at each other. They did not speak. Their mouths did not move. But Martinez knew they were communicating with each other. The hair on the back of his neck raised.

"I'll call you back," he said into the phone. A sliver of dread crept up his spine. He watched them striding up the walkway towards the door. He backed away from the window, dropped his phone into his pocket.

"You expecting company?"

Then came a sharp rap at the door. Martinez gave a look to Akin, who moved to the center of the room.

Marla peered through the peephole. She saw the two young men, one Black, one Hispanic. What now? she thought.

She opened the door partway. "Yes?"

"Marla Moreno," the black man said.

"Do I know you?"

They surged forward, pushed past her and entered the house.

"Hey!" Marla exclaimed. "What are you doing?"

The intruders strode into the living room where they were met by Russell, Akin, and Martinez.

Marla was furious. "Get the fuck out of my house." She thrust her arm towards the door.

"Ah," the Latino said, ignoring her. "Russell Slater." He looked to Martinez and Akin. "Cops." He said it as if it was a profanity.

Akin spoke. "Who are you and what are you doing here?" She allowed her hand to drift up and rest on the butt of her service weapon.

The Black man grinned. "That's cute."

"I said get the fuck out of my house."

"We will. But we must complete our mission first."

Something new going on here. "Who are you and what do you want?" she asked.

"We are but lowly messengers, here to deliver a message to your love, Caleb Jacobsen."

"My love?" Marla asked.

"Please," the Latino said. "We can smell him on you."

Russell, Akin, and Marla all looked confused. Only Martinez held his place, his face unreadable.

"What are your names?"

"I'm Bruce," the Black man said.

"Call me Pablo," the Latino offered.

"Bruce," Martinez said. "Pablo." The looked at him as if they knew him. "You are messengers. Messengers for whom?"

Pablo sneered. Martinez felt his hackles rising.

Bruce spread his hands, silently asking for calm. "Perhaps if we sat down and had a civilized conversation?" No one moved. "Please?"

That last word worked because no one expected it. The atmosphere cleared; the tension dissipated. Everyone found a seat, sat down facing each other, hands in front of them.

"Okay then," Marla said, "We're all comfortable and acting civilized."

"Yes," Pablo grinned. "Very cosmopolitan."

"What's this all about?"

"We actually carry two messages," Bruce said. "One for Caleb Jacobsen, and one for all of you."

Pablo leaned in. "The Master wishes to meet Caleb. A sit down at Pacers in Tacoma. Tomorrow night, ten o'clock."

Russell knew the place, had been there multiple times. "Why a strip club?"

"Because that is what the Master desires," Pablo said flatly.

"And who, precisely, is this Master?" Marla asked.

"He who rules all," Bruce stated. "He is who shows us the Way, the Truth. He who leads us to the Light."

"Sounds like a cult to me," Akin said.

Pablo pitied her, pitied her stupidity. "He shows us how to control the Wolf," he said. "How to channel it. How and when to unleash it."

No one noticed Martinez tensing up. The right side of his upper lip lifted upward. The white of his canine tooth showed. Pablo saw it, returned a crooked smile.

Arrogant.

"Wait a minute," Russell cut in. "Do you guys know something about the murders we're investigating?"

"We're here to deliver messages. That's all," Bruce answered.

"Well, you've delivered the message for Caleb," Marla started. "What is the message for the rest of us?" She wanted these savages out of her home.

"Stop your investigation," Bruce said coldly. "Leave our kind alone."

"Your kind?"

"Are you two doing the killing?" Akin asked.

"You pathetic humans really have no idea, do you?" Pablo said. "You are dealing with ancient forces of nature you cannot comprehend." He paused. The room was silent. "We're talking about beings that have been around since the beginning of time. We predate recorded history, organized religion. Hell, we predate *homo sapiens*."

Bruce sucked air in through his teeth as if he was suddenly growing impatient. "What my brother is saying is this. Leave. Us. Alone."

Every human in the room was so frightened they struggled to control their bladders and bowels. Bruce and Pablo smelled the fear.

Mission accomplished.

"Wait a minute." Marla spoke through the hand over her mouth. She was working hard to not throw up. "You called us 'humans'". Like it was a dirty word. What the hell are you?"

"Bruce turned to Pablo. "Should we show them?"

Pablo stood up, began removing his clothes. "What the hell?" Akin said.

"If either of you shoot him, we will kill everyone. Right here." He meant it. Akin and Martinez knew it.

Pablo finished removing his clothes. Marla tried hard to not look at his genitals.

"What is this supposed to accomplish?" Russell asked.

"Patience," Bruce said calmly.

Pablo slowed his breathing, took in great gulps through his nose, filling his lungs, expanding his chest. He closed his hands, rubbing his curled fingers across his palms. He closed his eyes, calming himself.

Pablo made the Change. Hair sprouted, lengthened, thickened. Eyes went yellow, then amber. His face seemed to melt, then stretched, extended, becoming a muzzle that ended with a quivering black nose. His claws lengthened, sharpened while his teeth became fangs and his body grew in height and weight.

Akin, Russell, and Marla all stared, wide-eyed, mouths open. None of them were quite able to comprehend the monstrosity in front of them.

Only Martinez seemed to not be slipping on the icy edge of insanity. He saw Akin hand grab her weapon, fingers tightening around it. He placed his hand over hers, keeping her from pulling the firearm free of its holster.

Pablo stood there, almost seven feet tall and close to three hundred pounds. He growled, the rumbling coming from deep in his throat.

"Now maybe you understand," Bruce said. "We are literally the last people on this entire Goddamned planet you want to fuck with."

Pablo growled and took a step forward. Everyone recoiled. Bruce put his hand out.

"Pablo. Heel."

Pablo stepped back. He continued glaring at all of them with menacing amber eyes and a complete, black and abiding hatred for them in his heart. He felt a particular revulsion for Martinez.

"H-how is this possible?" Russell stuttered.

Bruce chuckled. "Ask Caleb Jacobsen."

Oh God, Marla thought. Caleb's involved.

Russell moved forward in his seat. "But what is –"

Pablo lashed out with lightning speed, growling and snapping his jaws, spittle flying. He slashed out with one claw, missing

Russell by mere inches. Russell instinctively pulled back, lost his balance and tumbled out of his chair. He landed in a heap on the floor. His bladder involuntarily let go and emptied.

"Pablo! Heel!"

Pablo stopped. He growled one more time, then made the Change back to human. The process was just like the first one, only in reverse. Hair receded into his skin, his face flattened back to human, his height decreased as his claws shrank back into mere fingernails. Once again in human form, Pablo dressed, completely comfortable with his nudity. He paid the humans no mind. To him, they weren't even there.

But Martinez...

Pablo completed dressing. Bruce stood up, looked down at Russell who still lay on the floor in a wet stain that soaked the carpet. Then he looked to Marla.

"Maybe you should put some newspaper down until you get him housebroken."

"Fuck you." Russell had finally found his voice once again.

Bruce looked at him like a parent who is disappointed in a child. "That's the best you got?" He nodded to Pablo. They both moved towards the door. None of the others moved. The two werewolves stopped at the door, Bruce's hand on the knob.

"Heed our warning."

"If I come back here," Pablo added, looking at Marla, "I'm gonna slice your tits off and rip open your womb before you have a chance to die."

Marla felt chilled. This monster meant it. And he knew where she lived. Oh God, what was she going to do?

The two creatures left without another word.

Marla immediately felt her gorge rising, knew it would not stay down. She bolted towards the bathroom. She barely made it to the toilet before everything came up, out, and into the blue water.

Martinez stood, extended a helping hand to Russell. The professor looked up at the cop, his eyes rimmed with tears.

"I am so sorry," he said. "I'm so embarrassed."

"No need to be," Martinez said. He clasped Russell's hand and pulled, helping him up. "That shit was enough to scare the piss out of anybody."

"You handled it well."

Martinez shrugged, said nothing.

Marla was coming out of the bathroom now. Russell headed down the hallway. He had some clothes here, he remembered.

Akin finally remembered she had legs. She stood up, shaky. Her head spun. She put her hands out to balance herself. Martinez moved close, put his hands on her shoulders.

"Steady, partner," he whispered.

The room finally stopped spinning. "What the fuck was that thing?" she demanded.

"Looked like a werewolf to me." His voice was annoyingly calm.

"Are you out of your mind?"

"What would you call it?"

"I don't know what the fuck to call it," she replied. "And why aren't you freaking like the rest of us?"

Martinez looked at her a moment, then said, "We all deal with stress in different ways."

Russell rejoined them, dressed in baggy sweats and an old Bruce Lee T-shirt. He plopped down, already exhausted, and knowing he still had a long day ahead of him.

Martinez was the first to speak. "Okay. Time for feeling overwhelmed is over. We need to consider these new facts and how they might alter our investigation."

The other three all looked mutely at one another. Russell nodded assent. Akin sighed. Marla stood up, mumbled something about coffee all around, staggered towards the kitchen. A moment later she brought two mugs in, placed them in front of Akin and Martinez. She disappeared again, reappeared with two more. One she handed to Russell, one she hugged to her body as if the warm mug and hot liquid would somehow protect her from the new horrors of her now unbalanced world.

"Okay. What do we know?" Martinez looked at all of them in turn.

"We know that those *things* exist." Akin was the first to speak. "Werewolves."

"Why do you keep calling them that?" she demanded.

"What would you call them?"

"But you went straight to that without so much as a stumble." Suspicion flickered in her eyes. "Why is that?"

"Let's get back on point," he countered. "They want us to stop the investigation. Why?"

"Because they're behind it," Russell concluded.

"Exactly, but we still have a case to close. These two asshats aren't the first criminals to try and warn off the cops."

"You're going to keep pursuing this?" Marla asked.

"What else are we gonna do?" He looked to Akin. "Right, partner?"

She glared at him just a beat too long before, "Right."

"There's still a lot we don't know," Marla submitted.

"Like what?"

Marla sipped from her mug, gathered her thoughts. "Okay. For now, let's forget about things like what are they, where they come from, etc. What we need to know is where are they and how many?"

"And why are they killing in such a public manner?" Martinez added.

"What?" Russell.

"They said their kind had been around for thousands of years, right? Well why haven't we seen cases like this before now?"

"Maybe they're from out of town?" Snarky humor was Russell's method of coping. Martinez did not think less of him because of it.

"Right now, all I want to know is, where the fuck is Caleb?" Marla spat out.

As if on cue, they all heard a powerful, well-tuned engine rumble up outside. They listened to the vehicle come to a stop. Then a door opened, closed.

Marla and Russell bolted upright and rushed to the door. Akin and Martinez looked at each other, stood up slowly. They hovered near where they were, so each had a clear line of fire at the door.

Just in case.

Marla heard approaching footsteps on the walkway outside. She spied through the peephole. She did not know whether to be elated, relieved, or angry. At that moment, she was all three.

She unlocked the door and swung it open wide. Caleb Jacobsen, looking absolutely yummy in clean pants and an oxford shirt stretched tight across his chest, stood there, looking surprised.

Marla flung herself into his arms. "Caleb!"

"I missed you too."

She pulled back from him, suddenly angry. "Where the hell have you been?"

"What?"

"Why didn't you answer your phone? We've been trying to get ahold of you all night."

Caleb looked from Marla to Russell, then peered deeper into the room, seeing Martinez and Akin."

"Can I get inside first?"

Marla huffed, stood aside. Caleb entered. He saw Russell's shell-shocked eyes, caught everyone's scent. But there was something else here. The air itself seemed... *tainted.*

"What's up?"

"Marla's question still stands," Akin said. "Where have you been since yesterday afternoon?"

"I visited your computer guru, Jodi," he stated. He hoped his voice sounded neutral. "After that I drove home, did some research to parallel Jodi's. Then I came back, touched bases with her."

"And where have you been after that, Mr. Muscle Head?"

Caleb sat down. "Personal business."

"That doesn't fly here," Akin stated. "Not anymore."

Everyone sat still, looking at him, waiting for him to continue. His eyes rolled towards Martinez.

"Something happened here. Right here. In this room. What was it?"

"How do you know that?" Akin asked, growing alarmed.

"Things... got hairy this morning" Russell snarked.

Martinez calmly told Caleb about the visit from Bruce and Pablo. He described Pablo's transformation, Bruce's admonition. Then he told Caleb of the specific threat to Marla.

"He said *what?*" His eyes were ablaze. His breathing became hard, audible. "He *threatened* her?" Voice deeper, grumbling. Amber swirling in his eyes.

"They said they'd slice off her tits and cut out her womb before she even had a chance to die," Russell quoted.

Caleb jumped up from his seat, began pacing. Rapidly. His breathing changed, became lower, deeper. He clenched and unclenched his fists as he strode back and forth. With an effort, he slowed, took a cleansing breath, sat back down on the sofa.

He looked straight at Marla, directly into her eyes. "As God as my witness, Marla, none of them will touch you. Ever. Not while I'm alive."

Looking at Marla in that moment, memories of their meeting, their date gone wrong, their lovemaking flooded back to him. His heart swelled. A warm tsunami crashed over him.

Caleb Jacobsen loved this woman with every fiber of his being. Period. Full stop.

He would never leave her. Ever. He would stay with her for the rest of his life, if she would have him. She would be his mate, his Queen. He would kill to protect her.

And he would die if need be, as long as it ensured that she could live. No fear, no regrets.

Akin stared at him, analyzing him. "You're not surprised by any of this, are you?"

And the walls keep closing in, ladies and gentlemen. Tighter. And tighter. Caleb sighed, accepting his fate. It had been inevitable from the start, really.

Checkmate.

"I'm surprised they allowed you to live."

Stunned silence in the room. Good thing no pins were dropping. It probably would have spooked the humans.

"Caleb, you're scaring us." Russell. Pale and pasty.

"You knew?" Marla whispered, frightened that the answer she might hear would drive her over the edge.

Honesty was the best policy at this point. "I knew something was terribly wrong, and I wanted to help fix it."

"You knew something was up from the beginning, didn't you?" Russell asked.

"Okay," Akin piped up. "Here's the million-dollar question. Just how do you know about these things, these... *werewolves*?"

Caleb leaned forward, rested his forearms across his legs, hands clasped in front of him. "How do I say this?" He looked around the room, looking for some kind of support, some kind of encouragement to help him quell his own unease.

He found none.

"Yes. I know about the werewolves," he muttered. "But I didn't know they were behind these killings until yesterday."

"And how did you possess this information that has thus far escaped the rest of the world?" Russell demanded.

Caleb looked at Russell, then to Marla. "Because Russell, my dearest friend… I am a werewolf myself."

Absolute silence in the room. All Martinez would allow himself to think was, *how brave of him come out like that.*

"But how?" Russell asked at last.

"The same as for most of us," Caleb shrugged helplessly. "I was attacked, got bitten, and I survived."

"When?" Marla asked, angry tears rimming her eyes.

"A long time ago."

"When did you get bit?"

"Does that really matter?"

"When!" Marla shouted at the top of her lungs. Her fists raised up, slammed down onto the arms of her chair.

Caleb sat back, cleared his throat. "1876."

Marla exhaled hard. Her chest contracted, collapsed, like she had been hit in the heart with a sledgehammer. Finally, she asked, "How old are you?"

No escape now. In for a penny, in for a pound. He wondered if it would be a pound of his own flesh.

"Next summer I'll be one hundred and eighty years old."

Russell stared at him. "You own stock in Botox or something?"

Caleb grinned. "Or something."

"And how do we know you're telling the truth?" Akin demanded.

"Why would I lie about something like this?"

"How do we know you weren't off killing someone last night?"

"Oh." He remembered the events of last night. "I guess you don't."

"How do we know you're not one of them?"

Caleb looked wounded. "I am not one of them," he said emphatically. "I am nothing liked them." His voice had taken on an edge. "I am definitely not one of their pack."

Martinez believed him. "Why not?"

"You don't know?" He saw Martinez tense up. "Jesus Christ, look at what they're doing." He spread his arms out wide. "Indiscriminate slaughter. Making their kills public. That is not our way. Why would they do that?"

"I don't know."

"Neither do I. The question is, what's their endgame?" He looked around the room, making sure he still had their attention. "This is just a prelude to something else. Something bigger."

"What?" Akin asked.

"I don't know," he answered honestly. "And that scares me."

"Why would it scare you?" Marla challenged.

"Because I still possess this pesky little thing called a moral compass."

"So, you want to help stop them because you think what they're doing is wrong?" Martinez asked.

"This isn't just wrong, Jose," Caleb answered. "This is fucking monstrous. This is something dreamed up by a psychopath so twisted he makes Satan look like a choirboy." He looked at the rest of them. "This will not stand. Not while I'm alive."

The finality of his tone stilled them. It sounded like he had just taken a solemn oath. Fact was, he had.

"Wait a minute," Akin barked. "How do we know you're really a werewolf?"

Caleb had not calculated this particular scenario, but he realized he should have. He looked around the room. Akin and Marla both glared at him, daggers in their eyes. Russell looked confused. And Martinez was going to be no help at all.

"Do I really need to do this?" Silence provided him with his answer. He sighed with resignation. "All right."

Caleb stood up, immediately began peeling off his clothes.

"Aw, Jesus!" Russell exclaimed.

"Quiet," Marla chided.

Shirtless, muscles bulging, scars shiny white under the lights, Caleb kicked his shoes off. He tossed his shirt in the chair he had been sitting in, dropped his pants. They formed a denim puddle around his ankles. He stepped out, tossed them on top of his shirt. Then he worked his way out of his underwear.

Naked, he turned to Akin. "Do me a favor? Don't shoot me. That shit pisses me off."

Caleb made the Change. Hair sprouted, nails lengthened, his face melted and stretched. Most importantly to Marla, his foreskin grew over his penis, then the thin membrane appeared and formed a prepuce, pulling his penis up and out of the way, attached to his lower abdomen. Then it disappeared beneath thick brown fur.

Caleb the Werewolf stood before them now. Bigger than Pablo, taller, more heavily muscled. His orange eyes glowed darker. He stood there, looking at them all. Chest heaving, legs bent at the knees, arms at his sides, lethal hands and claws dangling in front of him. He took care to make no sudden or threatening moves.

Russell stared at his friend, eyes wide, mouth open, face drained of color. He had known – or had thought he had known – Caleb for years. He realized he really didn't know his friend at all. But then again, did anyone really ever know everything there was to know about anyone else?

Marla was absolutely overwhelmed. Tears spilled down her face. She tried to scream, but found she had no voice. All the pieces fell into place for her. She now knew what Caleb had so studiously concealed from her, from everyone. This creature, this *thing* had shared her bed, had been invited into the most intimate parts of her body and her life. How could such a handsome, charming man turn into this beast?

Caleb reared up to his full height. He tilted his head back. His nose floated mere inches from the ceiling of the room. And then, he began the Change back to human form. Hair receded, canines shrank, his height shorted. And, Marla noticed, his penis dropped back between his legs, and his circumcised foreskin pulled back to where it belonged.

For a long time, the room was completely silent.

"Well Jesus H. Christ and fuck me sideways," Akin shouted at last. "Is there anyone here who is not a fucking werewolf?" She looked at her suspiciously calm partner. "Are you a fucking werewolf, too?"

Martinez fumbled for words. "What? Why? Why would you even ask me that?"

Caleb spoke as he dressed. "Here's the bottom line, folks. And you need to listen to me like you've never listened to anyone before." He paused. He had their undivided attention.

"There are things in this world, things you would not believe even after today; things of ancient Evil and malevolence the like of which you have never seen. Things that have existed on this planet and have walked the Earth since the beginning of time. The werewolves are among these things.

"This Pack has been working its way across the country for centuries, moving west over time. Now they've gone global. All their chess pieces are in place. And now they're ready to strike." He looked directly at Martinez. "Checkmate."

"Checkmate?" Akin echoed. "What does that even mean?"

"I'll show you."

"You'll tell us."

"No. I must show you."

"Where?" Russell asked.

"My place."

"Why there?" Martinez asked.

"Because I can't protect them here," he answered, motioning towards Russell and Marla.

"Why not?" Akin asked.

"This isn't my territory."

"But your house is?"

"That's how it works."

"This is just too much," Marla said softly. She stood up and left the room.

"Trouble with your girlfriend?"

Caleb ignored Akin. He followed Marla down the hallway, stepped into her bedroom.

"Stay away from me." Caleb froze in place. "Leave the goddamned door open."

Caleb pulled his hand away from the doorknob.

"I can't believe you," she blurted out. "You're this… this… I can't believe I fucking slept with you."

"I'm still the same guy. Nothing's changed."

"Everything's changed!"

"Your perception of me has changed," he corrected. "Fact is, I'm still the same guy. And I still feel the same way about you."

She started to respond but didn't. She fell silent, crossed her arms across her chest. Caleb was careful to make no moves.

"So how are we supposed to go forward? How am I ever supposed to trust you?"

"What would you have done if I had told you the truth at the outset?" She looked shocked, said nothing, then looked down at her feet. "Yeah," Caleb said. "That's what I thought."

He waited for her to speak. When she did not, he realized she couldn't. She was still overwhelmed, still trying to wrap herself around the reality of what was happening. He wondered what would happen when she found out all of it.

He took a step forward. "Marla –"

"Don't!" Her head snapped up and her hand shot out in the universal symbol for STOP. He froze where he was.

"Understand something," Caleb breathed. "As much as you know, as much as you think you know, you still don't know the half of it. You have no idea of what we're capable of."

"What do you know?"

"Everything."

"That supposed to make me feel better?"

"I'm bringing everyone to my place and present my findings. We need to leave."

"I'm not going anywhere with you."

"Then ride with the cops," he snapped.

"You don't get to order me around, Caleb Jacobsen," she fired back. "And you don't get to be angry with me."

"I'm not angry," he responded, "I'm worried. We need to leave. Now."

He left without waiting for her reply. The others would convince her. In the end, her own curiosity, her human need to know everything would override her fears.

He walked into the living room just as Akin was carrying her empty coffee mug into the kitchen. He looked at Russell, then jerked his head over his shoulder. Russell understood, got up and moved down the hall towards Marla's room.

"You took a big risk," Martinez said.

"No choice," Caleb responded.

"Why not just lie?"

"That damn moral compass again."

"What other revelations are you going to share with the group?"

Caleb smiled. "We all have our secrets, Jose. Yours is safe with me."

"What if it turns out I'm part of this… Megapack?"

The smile left Caleb's face. He stared at Martinez with hard eyes. Hints of yellow danced behind the brown.

"I will rip you apart with my bare hands."

CHAPTER TWENTY-ONE

Caleb drove, his Jeep in the lead, followed by the unmarked car. Akin had balked hard at his plan, but Martinez had used his gentle powers of persuasion. She finally came around, but she was still pissed. Caleb realized her anger was a manifestation of her emotional stress. It was not personal, nor was it really directed towards him. It was the situation, so completely outside the realm of her police training, that she raged against.

As Marla locked up, Caleb had noticed everyone else piling into the police car. He had hoped Russell might ride with him. But it looked like Russell wanted to keep Caleb at a distance, too.

Marla had likewise headed for the police car. Caleb stood by his open door, then huffed out through his nostrils. He slid into the driver's seat, closed the door, buckled in.

When he had looked up, he caught motion in the rear-view. Marla, lips tight, storming towards him on the passenger side. She threw the door open, tossed herself inside, slammed the door shut.

She buckled in, looked at him. "What?"

"Nothing."

"Then fucking drive."

"Yes ma'am."

And here they were, heading north, thick silence an invisible barrier between them. He smelled her nervous perspiration. But the fear was a general all-encompassing thing, not targeting him specifically. Creatures such as Caleb interpreted the world primarily through their noses, not their eyes. They could tell the difference.

Traffic moved smoothly. Caleb glanced in his driver's side mirror. The police car was back there, about one hundred feet back. A couple of cars had slipped in between them. But he figured cops knew how to tail someone.

"Tell me about it," Marla barked.

The Tacoma Narrows Bridge loomed before them.

"About what?" Caleb asked.

"Don't play dumb with me," she snapped. "Tell me about you being a fucking werewolf."

Caleb straightened the Jeep's wheels. He positioned himself firmly in the middle of his traffic lane.

"What do you want to know?"

"How about everything since the day you were born?"

The Jeep's front wheels clumped over the first bridge joint, followed rapidly by the rear wheels. The Jeep inclined as they drove upwards.

"The story of my life is a long one."

"We've got time."

"My story doesn't have a happy ending. Not yet."

The incline lessened gradually. They approached the crown of the roadway's gentle arc. Far below, deep dark waters swirled, the powerful current boiling around the metal stanchions that plunged downward into the sediment at the bottom.

Marla sat there, lips pursed together so hard they blanched white. Arms flung tight across her chest, chin down, furrowed forehead.

"I was born in 1840, the third of four children, and the only boy. I grew up on a small farm in Missouri. When I say, 'small farm', I'm talking forty acres of prime farmland. Good soil. A stream crossed our land, so we had a water source.

"We didn't grow cotton. Cotton meant slave labor. Mom and dad were devout Christians and felt that slavery went against the teachings of Jesus Christ."

"So, you never owned slaves?" Marla asked.

"One human being owning another is a sin against both God and man," Caleb said flatly. "Always was. Always will be."

"Back to your story."

"We grew corn, beans, tomatoes, potatoes. We weren't wealthy, but we got by. We had a barnyard. Chickens, hogs. No cattle.

"As I grew older, I graduated to some of the heavier farm work, took some of the burden off Dad. When school let out for summer, I worked twelve hours a day, six days a week.

"Good God."

He shrugged nonchalantly. "For us, that was normal.

"There was also an immediacy to everything you did. Cause and effect. If the crops failed, you went broke. If you didn't get the hogs to market, you didn't have money to survive winter.

"Every bad decision, every failure resulted in dire consequences. If you're going to do something, do it right.

Excellence in all things great and small. That's what I learned living on a farm.

"Momma was our anchor, our rock. She made sure we were clean and fed, got to school, did our homework, did our chores. We'd bathe on Saturday evening, and she'd get us dressed in our 'Sunday-Go-To-Meetin' Clothes' and made sure our butts were in the pews every Sunday morning.

Every night between dinner and bedtime, Mom read from the Bible. It was there, in the quiet of the night and that orange flicker of the fire I first learned the concepts of Good and Evil, the difference between Right and Wrong.

"Dad was not an educated man. He dropped out of school and went to work at age twelve. He was born out of wedlock, which was a big deal back then. Grandma was branded as a harlot. People wouldn't cut them a break. And there were no Government safety nets back then. So, they fended for themselves.

"Dad's lack of education embarrassed him. Back then, if you moved to a new place, your past was whatever you told people it was. But Dad couldn't read; couldn't write his own name. You can't hide that.

"The point is, like most fathers everywhere, he wanted us to avoid his mistakes. He made Goddamned sure we went to school, did our homework, learned The Three R's – reading, writing, and arithmetic. He made sure that we all understood the value of education and literacy. He wanted better for us."

"Okay," she cut in. "This is all very heartwarming in a 'Little House on the Prairie' kind of way. What does it have to do with you being a werewolf?"

"Fast forward to 1860. Abraham Lincoln is President. The South secedes from the Union. The Civil War begins. I had just turned twenty.

"And I was about to find out there is *nothing* civil about war.

"Let me digress just a moment. Some would have you believe that everyone in the South owned slaves. Not true. About 25% of the people in the South owned slaves. That means about 75% didn't. We sure as hell didn't. Mom and Dad were Abolitionists. That means my sisters and I were abolitionists, too."

Caleb paused. Marla looked over at him. Deep emotions passed across his face.

"I love America," he said at last. "I love what it is supposed be, what it could be, not necessarily what it is. We're supposed to be a nation where all men are created equal. But then as now, sadly, some men seem to be more equal than others. And some just don't count. Hypocrisy at its most cancerous.

"I'll tell you a secret. Lincoln's prime directive upon election was to heal the Union, not free the slaves. In August 1862, Lincoln famously wrote to the New York Tribune newspaper, and I'm paraphrasing, but he said, 'If I could save the Union without freeing one slave, I would do that. If I could save it by freeing all slaves, I would do that. And if I could save the Union by freeing some slaves and not freeing others, I would do that.' And I know he said it. I read the article when it first came out."

"How come I never heard about this in school?"

"Because historians decided long ago that Lincoln be painted as a saint. But he was just a man. Like any other."

"But he freed the slaves."

"Yes he did, and I thank God every day for it," Caleb nodded. "Some of Lincoln's Generals convinced him that sending escaped slaves back to the South was inhumane and helped further the Southern cause. And Mary Todd Lincoln, an outspoken and ardent Abolitionist, had her husband's ear. By 1862, Lincoln had 'evolved' in his thinking.

"This wasn't the first war fought on American soil. The Revolution and the War of 1812 were fought here, not overseas.

"But this was different. This was American against American, friend against friend, brother against brother killing each other in people's cow pastures. In their forests. Their own back yards.

He paused, his forehead lined as he recalled painful memories.

"Fate's a funny thing," he said at last. "You lead a peaceful life, tend your family, mind your own business, do right by your fellow man. Live by the law; don't look for trouble. Problem is, sometimes trouble finds you."

"Uh oh."

Caleb had not heard her. His mind was awash with memories, things he had not thought about in a long, long time. His eyes were rimmed with tears.

"Summer, 1862. I'm in the back acreage prepping to plant pumpkins for a late harvest. I heard distant screaming. High pitched.

Mom. I looked up, saw black smoke rising over the hills. I ran towards the house.

Caleb's vice choked with emotion. They rode in silence a moment, the green trees blurring past their window, the Olympic Mountains to their left, snow-capped blue teeth pointing jaggedly towards the sky.

"By the time I got there," Caleb said at last, "it was too late. Union soldiers were everywhere, darting back and forth on horseback. They had already set fire to the farmhouse, the barn. The house was completely engulfed, Dad lay unconscious on the ground, Momma kneeling over him, crying. My youngest sister was nowhere to be found.

"What about your older sisters?"

"They had already married and moved away. I found out later the Union soldiers had come up, demanding to search for slaves. Dad told them we didn't have any; they could look around. Then they demanded food and water, and that we put them up for the night. That's a violation of the Third Amendment, the Quartering of Troops: No private citizen will be forced to feed and shelter Government troops against his or her will.

"He told them they could water their horses and make camp in the barn, but he didn't have enough food for them all. One thing leads to another, one of the troops started eyeing my sister, and you can guess the rest. Dad tried to protect Sadie. They beat him within an inch of his life, gangraped Sadie, set fire to the place.

"The Union Army's Scorched Earth policy? I saw that shit up close and personal.

"Anyway, I get there and it's mostly over. I'm screaming like a madman, and one of the soldiers buttstrokes me in the back of the head.

"I wake up the next morning. Soldiers are gone, Mom and Sadie have me and Dad around the hearth, the only thing left standing. I wasn't hurt all that bad. But Dad never regained consciousness. He died later that morning.

"Some of the neighbors had heard the commotion. Over the next couple of weeks, they helped me rebuild a smaller cabin around the existing hearth. We couldn't work the land or lease it out. They had salted the fields, making it unable to grow food. At least for the time being.

"The minute I knew Mom and sister had a roof over their heads, I grabbed up a rifle and joined the First Missouri Cavalry under Captain Cyrus B. Webb."

"What?" she demanded. "You fought in the Civil War for the South?"

"Think about it," he said. "I didn't fight for the Southern cause. I didn't fight to preserve slavery. I fought to get revenge for what those Union soldiers had done to my family, a family whose only crime was they happened to live on the wrong side of the Mason-Dixon Line.

Marla frowned as she considered this.

"I'll tell you this right now. Fighting for the Confederacy is the biggest mistake I ever made in my life. To this day, I am ashamed of it. Not only was I feeding my own selfish quest for a vengeance that I never satisfied and a peace that I never found, but I left my mom and sister alone and unprotected.

"But I was a hot-tempered young man, and young men don't always think things through. They just act.

"I should have been smart and stayed on the farm. But no. I got caught up in the lunacy. Our first battle was November 1862. I remember it like it was yesterday. The rifles, the cannons. The screams of men dying. The smell of burning flesh. Of dead bodies left to bake in the sun.

"Until you've been in it, you have absolutely no idea the damage warfighting inflicts on the human body.

"We survived that battle, but others followed. Longer, bloodier. This wasn't smart bombs and UAV's where you kill somebody from half a world away. This was point-blank; knife fights, fixed bayonets, and hand-to-hand. War at its most elemental. Just kill everybody wearing an enemy uniform. We fought battles that generated more casualties in one day than all the casualties in Iraq and Afghanistan combined.

"I had no prior training. There was no boot camp. We learned as we went, if we lived long enough. I took a bullet in my left shoulder, caught some shrapnel in my leg. I continued on when everyone around me died.

"I rationalized it as God's will; that God had plans for me after the war.

"But if I had known then what I know now, I would have known what was coming had *nothing* to do with God's will."

"So how about we get to that?" Marla interjected. She didn't need a history lesson.

"April 1865", he continued. "Lee surrenders to Grant. Just like that, the war's over. We turned ourselves in to the first Union patrol we encountered. They took our weapons, administered a new Pledge of Allegiance, then told us to get out of their sight.

"They didn't have to tell me twice. I headed home. But I learned that memories are snapshots. In time, they fade and curl around the edges. Nothing stays the way you remember it.

"I found Mom and Sadie starving, and the cabin practically falling down around their heads from disrepair. Not surprising when you consider I had been gone for the better part of three years. None of the neighbors had really come around to check on them, but I didn't hold a grudge. They had their own hardships to endure.

"I fixed the cabin up, repaired the roof, put in a wooden floor. In those days, a wooden floor was considered a luxury. They deserved it after all they'd been through.

"Word of my return got around, but nobody much came by. I didn't mind the solitude. In fact, I preferred it. I needed to stay busy, so I kept working around the farm. Put up new fencing, built a new smokehouse. Anything to keep me outside. That way I could see someone approaching from far off.

"Inside the cabin felt claustrophobic. Like the walls were closing in. My tension level was elevated all the time, but the needle went into the Red Zone whenever I stepped inside.

"I lay awake most nights, wondering what the hell was wrong with me. When I did sleep, I dreamed of heads exploding, the screams of friends dying, their eyes looking at me, silently pleading, hands outstretched, begging for help I couldn't give. Most nights, I woke up screaming. I slept under the stars one night. I still had the dreams, but at least outside, the dreams stopped when I woke up.

"Back then, nobody knew anything about PTSD.

"By 1868, Reconstruction came to our little corner of Missouri. I scraped together enough money to buy some cheap Government-issue fertilizer – horse manure, mostly – and I fertilized the land those Union bastards had destroyed. I borrowed a mule and plowed, mixing the manure with the dirt.

Mom, Sadie, and I talked about it. The question was, how to best go forward? I was restless. I had found no peace returning home. The farm had become nothing more than a repository of past horrors.

"With me wanting to leave once the snow melted, Momma grasped the reality of the situation. Mom and Sadie couldn't work the farm alone, and we couldn't afford to hire hands.

"She and I went to town, sat with the County Clerk, and divvied the land into parcels except for a small plot the house sat on. Mom sold the parcels piecemeal and made more money than if she had sold the acreage intact. She and the town banker invested the money wisely. She drew a monthly stipend off the interest without having to touch the principle.

"With what I had saved up myself and with a small stake from Momma, I bought a horse and a worn saddle. I figured I'd work as a cowpoke."

"Are we getting to the werewolf stuff soon?"

"Yes. I drifted west, worked odd jobs, moved on. I wasn't sure if I was running from something or running towards something. All I knew was I had to keep moving.

"People now have this highly romanticized image of the Old West, of what it must have been to be a cowboy. John Wayne movies, Randolph Scott, Clint Eastwood. It was nothing like that. The life of a cowpoke was lonely, solitary, violent, dirty, highly transient. I moved from farm to farm, ranch to ranch, learning everything I could. Then I moved on."

"To where?"

"Montana."

"That's where it happened?"

He nodded.

"Montana was great. I liked the weather, the scenery. I even found myself liking the people. The very first day I arrived, I met a man named Nick Gerard. Seemed nice enough. We talked a bit over beer; he offered me a job. I took it.

"Turned out Nicholas Gerard owned one of the biggest spreads in Montana at that time. What John Chisum was to New Mexico, Nick Gerard was to Montana. Two hundred head of horses, over five hundred head of cattle on close to a thousand acres. The place was called the Lazy G ranch. Nick said it was because he had a lazy streak a mile wide. But that man didn't have a lazy bone in his body.

"So, from 1870 on, I worked the Lazy G. Nick liked the fact I showed up with my own clothes, my own horse, my own rifle. Back in those days, most ranchers had to supply their hands with horses, feed and tack, and firearms. He saw me as someone who came ready to pull his own weight.

"I fell into a routine. Other cowpokes came and went. All part of that highly transient lifestyle. But I stayed, and I learned everything about ranching. He asked me one day why. I told him when he was too old to tend to things personally, I could run the ranch in his stead. I will never forget the smile he gave me from underneath that silver-gray handlebar moustache.

"Months turned into years. I slept better there than I had in a long time. Mom and I corresponded by letter. She was doing fine, getting older. Sadie still lived at home. She had no suitors. She was twenty-four then, an Old Maid by the standards of the day.

"I knew the deal. When those Union soldiers gang raped her, they killed whatever chance she had at a normal sex life. She never went out, never went to barn dances. Whenever young men at church tried to strike up a conversation with her, she would turn away.

"Something got broken inside of her that never healed. I got it. Even those of us who lived, we all died a little bit in that Goddamned war.

He paused, swallowed.

"Summer 1876. We planned to run two hundred and fifty head of cattle from the Northern Ranges down into Billings to auction. We made at least one cattle drive a year, sometimes two. But I was Trail Boss for the first time. If things went well, my future was assured. I could stay on the Lazy G the rest of my days.

We headed early to the Northern Ranges where the cattle free grazed. It took some time, but we herded them without incident. The drive to Billings was starting the next morning right after sunrise.

"I volunteered to take the first watch that night. I had a belly full of beans and bacon, and Cookie kept the coffee hot and flowing. The two other guys on watch were both experienced hands who had worked drives before. We went into it with a high degree of confidence.

"Watching the herd at night isn't usually hard. If all goes well, nothing happens. You're there to make sure they don't stampede, and to sound the alarm in case of rustlers. Mostly, you try to stay awake and not fall out of your saddle. I figured this night would be no different.

"I was dead wrong."

Something about the way he said that made Marla turn her head towards him.

"Everything started out fine," he continued. "Clear night, cool. Thousands of stars sprinkled across the sky. A full moon cast everything with a silver glow.

"As night wore on, something changed. I could feel it. Something was amiss. I couldn't shake the feeling I was in the presence of something evil.

"Around midnight, the mooing intensified from the back of the herd. Louder, higher pitched. Fear. Panic. Then pain. Unrest rippled like an undulating wave through the entire herd. I maneuvered my horse in front of the lead bull to reign him in. If he bolted, the rest would follow.

"The rest of the guys woke up. One of them hopped on a horse and sped up to me. I had him control the lead bull and I hauled ass towards the rear where Kansas Jack had the watch. We called him Kansas Jack because his name was Jack, and he was from Kansas."

"Makes sense," she said.

"About halfway back, I heard Kansas Jack's rifle. Then I heard Kansas Jack screaming. Now listen. I've heard men scream. I heard plenty during the war. This was like nothing I had ever heard. Howls of pain, fear, and the terrible knowledge that you're dying, and there's nothing on Earth that can stop it.

"I had seen bad during the war. But what I saw that night, well… nothing prepares you for that.

"Blood spurted everywhere, spraying across the dusty earth, coming from multiple sources. Several head of cattle lay dead or dying, mutilated beyond recognition. All they could do way lay there, eyes wide, disemboweled, rib cages splayed open. Jack got pulled off his horse. He was thrashing around on the ground, trying to fight back. He was stopped when something big and shaggy sliced his chest cavity open with one swipe of a claw.

"That was when I saw… *them*.

"There were four of them. I froze for a moment. It couldn't be real. I blinked my eyes a few times, but they were still there, continuing their butchery. They looked like wolves. But these things were big, bigger than any wolf I'd ever seen. Six, maybe seven feet long.

"They scampered around on all fours until one of them, this enormous golden Blonde werewolf, bigger than the others, swung his head around and saw me. His orange eyes narrowed, deepened to red. He pushed himself off the ground and stood up on his hind legs. That was when I realized he looked almost human. At the time I thought these things must be demons belched from the bowels of Hell.

"Then that big bastard bolted towards me. I remember thinking, *how can something so big move so fast?*

"My horse reared in terror just as I grabbed my rifle. Reins in my hand, I aimed and fired. He ducked and changed directions so quickly, I missed. I spun around and aimed at one of the creatures devouring what was left of Kansas Jack. I fired. The side of his head exploded, and he dropped where he was.

"The rest of them stopped and turned their attention to me. I could hear the shouts of the other cowboys. They sounded thousands of miles away. All the beasts rose up on their hind legs and stalked forward, spreading out to encircle me and my horse.

"These things were smart. By encircling me, they knew if I turned to aim at one of them, the rest could attack before I could get off another shot. They moved closer, tightening the noose.

"Big Blondie was different from the others. Not just the color of his fur. He was bigger, more muscular. There was this keen intelligence behind his eyes. Manipulative. Cunning. When he moved, the others showed deference. He was clearly the leader.

"He wasn't afraid of me. Not at all. He swaggered as he approached me. I chambered another round in my rifle and aimed at him. He froze. The other werewolves growled, snarled, snapped their jaws. The message was clear: if I shot him, they were going to tear me apart. So, I took my eye off my sights. Big Blondie showed his teeth, but it wasn't a growl. I swear to this day, that son of a bitch was grinning at me. I had no chance of escape, and we both knew it."

Marla frowned in concentration, trying to understand, trying to empathize with what Caleb had felt. She watched his face, knowing this fantastic story was indeed true.

Every word.

"Big Blondie loped up with this strange sense of calm," he continued. "I kept my rifle between him and me. I pulled the reins in tight. If the horse bolted, they would all pile on. Blondie eyed the horse, licked his lips, then glared at me.

"I was next on the menu.

"Before I could react, grabbed me by my shoulders, lifted me off my horse and body slammed me into the ground so hard it knocked the wind out of me. The rest of them attacked my horse.

"I brought the rifle up and around. Blondie knocked it out of my hands like a parent snatching a toy away from a naughty child. He gripped my wrist in one huge paw and squeezed so hard I heard the wrist bones break. I screamed. And I swear to God, I could have sworn the sounds coming out of him were something close to laughter. That's right. The bastard was *laughing* at me!

"Blondie howled, growled, snarled and snapped his teeth just inches from my nose. He could have killed me at any time. But no. Killing me wasn't enough. He wanted to torture me, punish me for killing one of his pack.

"With my head turned to the side and one ear pushed into the dirt, I heard the thunderous hooves of horses approaching. He heard it, too. I saw those long ears perk. Distracted, he looked up. In that instant, I saw my chance. I struggled against him again, trying to wriggle free.

"He snarled, lunged downward at me, jaws opening as he went for a kill bite. But I moved to one side just as his teeth found my flesh. He bit down. Hard. Right into the meaty part of my shoulder above my collarbone.

"I thought I knew what pain was. This was like nothing I had ever felt. Hot agony spread outward from the bite, radiated throughout my body down to my feet. Even my hair hurt. The tingling began immediately. It was like touching a live wire.

"I screamed. Blood poured down my back and pooled across the prairie floor. I heard rifle shots. It sounded like hundreds of them. They seemed to go on forever.

"I heard a yelp catch in Blondie's throat, then suddenly his massive weight was gone, lifted off me. I suddenly felt weightlessness, like I had escaped the earth's gravity. Then I was spinning, falling, falling, headed towards a dark infinity. I wasn't afraid then, because I was in a plane that transcended pain and fear, transcended life and death. And then I descended into sweet, blissful nothingness.

"I didn't come around for five days. Once I did, all I wanted was pass out again. Anything to escape the pain. The bite got infected and I ran a high fever. And my dreams, the nightmares, provided me no respite.

"Werewolves after me, always after me. Right behind me, nipping at my heels. They could have taken me down any time. But they were playing with me, taunting me just like Big Blondie. When they got bored, they would bring me down and feast on me. But no matter what they did or how much of me they ate, I never died. I remember one time being reduced to nothing more than a decapitated head, lying on the ground - still alive, mind you - watching them tear my body apart and suck the marrow from my bones.

"Of course, I had no clue what was really happening. The fever and delirium were just part of the process."

"Process?" Marla echoed.

Caleb nodded. "When a werewolf bites a human, the Change begins immediately on a cellular level. The fever is part of the body's immune response. You either die from the sepsis, die from the genetic recoding that occurs, or you survive.

"And you become... something other than human.

"The trail gang had packed my wounds that night and hauled me back to the Big House. Mr. Gerard sent a rider fetch Doc Morton. Nick had lived a rough life, had seen all kinds of wounds. He figured I was a goner. But he wasn't going to let me die without doing everything he could to stop it.

"Doc Morton was old, close to 60. Overweight, thinning hair. Bulbous petechial nose and ruddy cheeks of someone who drank too much. I'm glad I was out of it because I never trusted his trembling hands.

"He checked me from head to toe, sewed the bite closed. That was a mistake. Anyone who knows anything about medicine knows you don't suture puncture wounds. But that was Doc.

"He ordered strict bedrest and my bandages changed twice a day. He left some Laudanum for when I came to. He thought there was no way I'd live. At least with some Laudanum, which is a tincture of opium, I could at least die quietly.

"The wound suppurated, of course. They told me later how it swelled so bad the sutures ruptured, the wound dehisced, and thick yellow and green pus gushed out like an overripe zit.

"Back then, folks didn't survive infections like that. Of course, if anyone had known what was really happening to me, they would have run the other way.

"Doc clucked over me, tried to sound encouraging. But I saw through the charade. He couldn't understand why I was recovering. I saw fear in his eyes.

"The fever never came back. The swelling went down, and the pain vanished, literally overnight. And by that, I mean I went to sleep one night with a dull and diffuse ache even with the assistance of the Laudanum, and I woke up the next morning, completely pain free and without a touch of opiates in my system."

"That's crazy," Marla said.

"Oh, it gets better. Next morning I'm sitting up on the edge of the bed. I worked my shoulder; certain I was going to be blinded by pain at any moment. But the pain never came. After two weeks in bed, I was regaining full range of motion.

"I was hungry. I ate everything in sight. Everything tasted wonderful. And it smelled wonderful, too. It's like tasting food for the first time, like my sense of taste and smell had been on a dimmer switch my whole life, and someone had come along and flipped the switch to overdrive.

"Even I knew I wasn't supposed to recover so quickly. Not only were my senses of taste and smell more acute, but all my other senses were as well. My eyesight had improved. There was nothing wrong with it before, but now it was… better. And I could hear things now other people couldn't. Higher pitches, lower pitches, softer sounds.

"Sleep came more quickly, but the dreams came back. Crazy like before. Werewolves, death and dismemberment. But I was no longer the victim. Now I was a bystander watching the werewolves ripped anonymous people into gruesome tatters of flesh.

"I know now why I was so ravenous. I was putting on weight. My metabolism was in hyperdrive. I had been thin back then, wiry, about 145 pounds. A normal weight for a guy my height back then. But every day, I noticed more muscle, more definition. I had never had six-pack abs before, but I got them then. I was not accustomed to having that kind of strength or carrying around that much weight. It took some getting used to.

"After all, who the hell lies in bed for a month and puts on thirty-five pounds of lean muscle?"

They passed a green and white sign announcing that they were passing into Kitsap County.

"I'll try to finish by the time we get to Port Orchard, "he said.

"We've still got time. Go on."

"The dreams continued. Werewolves, blood and guts, murder and mayhem. They condensed down into one. One werewolf, running at night, howling at the moon, pacing other wolves in their pack. Slaughtering humans. Then the final revelation came. The great mystery was solved.

"The werewolf in my dream was me.

"By the six-week mark, I was back at work, running things for Nick. Just as I got well, he took ill with influenza that worsened into a full-blown pneumonia. Nick was sick as a dog. At Nick's insistence, I stayed on living in the house in a guest room once they figured I was not likely to relapse.

"There were times when out of the blue, for no discernable reason, my vision would change. My vision was already more acute, but this was different. I not only saw things more acutely, but sometimes I saw them in a different color spectrum. It was similar to human, but different, more intense. Garish.

"I fought dark impulses. I had to control my temper with day to day frustrations that are part and parcel with running a ranch. I had to restrain myself several times a day to keep from killing someone.

"Becoming a werewolf doesn't come with an instruction manual.

"October 1876. We had an Indian summer that year, and October was hot. It had been a rough day. Nick was getting worse. I was running everything. The rest of the hands seemed content with me in charge. As long as the ranch was a going concern, they had jobs and knew they would get paid on time.

"But even as I improved, Nick deteriorated. For all the weight I had gained, he lost. He battled a fever, was weak, could only hold broth down. His skin was ashen pale, sunken and sallow. Black circles under his eyes. His breathing rattled wet in his chest. Green phlegm caked the corners of his mouth. When he tried to speak, he could only get a few words out before being overcome by coughing that spewed more green phlegm and racked his body with painful convulsions.

"Time was running out. We all knew it. Doc Morton had been coming out to check on him, for all the good that did. He told me he had done all he could. Surely there was something else he could do. A new medicine. A new procedure. Consult another doctor. He shook his head sadly, told me to prepare for the inevitable.

"Before either he or I knew what was happening, a growl rumbled from deep in my chest, I grabbed him by his collar, lifted him off the ground and slammed him into a wall. Terrified, he stared down at me, his eyes big as horseshoes. I told him he better do something, because even if he had given up, I had not. I informed him what would happen if he let Nick Gerard die because he was a quack who spent most of his time at the bottom of a bottle.

"I put him back down. Looking at me with pure terror, he scuttled outside. I remember the satisfaction I felt to seeing that worthless piece of shit gawking at me with a terror so palpable I could smell it.

"I think I mentioned we had an Indian summer. Close to a hundred degrees every day. Nights weren't much better. I was laying naked on sweat-soaked sheets. Nick was dying, the ranch might have to shut down, and my guys had no futures of their own. As I lay there, stewing about this, I just kept getting more and more frustrated.

"As I lay there, angry and impotent, I thought I would scream. But what came out of me was a deep growl. My vision blurred, then modified like I talked about before. More color, more distant vision, like seeing the whole world in ultra-high def.

"My skin itched and tingled everywhere, and not in a good way. You know how it feels when you hit your funny bone? It hurts but you have to laugh, right? Imagine that about ten times more intense, everywhere. I felt my knee joints *shift*. That hurts like a bitch, by the way. My heart pounded like a jackhammer, pumping blood through my veins with such force I felt every cardiac contraction. I flicked my tongue over my teeth. They were *sharp*. I curled my fists; my nails dug into my calms. They weren't fingernails anymore. They were *claws*. My muscles contracted with a power and force I had never experienced.

"I bolted from the bed and landed on the floor in one smooth movement. I padded silently over to the open window. I tilted my head and inhaled the fresh Montana air. Smells took on new meaning to me. In the distance, I heard the mournful howl of a wolf. Without thinking, I immediately responded with one of my own.

"Not only had I known the howl was from a wolf and not a coyote, I knew it was a call, a shout-out, acoustic social networking. I realized not only was I having a conversation with a wolf, I had not acted with conscious thought. I had simply reacted based on pure instinct.

"I staggered back from the window. A buzz hummed in my head. I turned and I caught a glimpse of my reflection in a full-length mirror.

"Terrified by what I saw there, I recoiled, tried to scream. Once again, a deep rumbling emanated from my chest. My eyes were a deep burnt orange. My face had elongated and narrowed into a snout that ended with a black quivering nose. My jaws opened; my mouth was lined with sharp teeth. My entire body was covered with a thick brown fur, shimmering in the candlelight. In my reflection I saw the very creature from my nightmares.

"I had made my first Change.

"I stood well over six feet tall. I was remarkably heavier, but my muscles and my weight-bearing joints seemed to compensate admirably. I flexed my fingers, watching my long claws reflect in the flickering light.

"I sensed movement somewhere in the house. I think I actually felt the vibrations through the floor. I knew if anyone on the ranch saw me like this, their first reaction would be to shoot me. I took two steps and sprung, lunging neatly through the window. I landed easily and loped away from the house.

"I roamed the prairie, illuminated by a full moon and a starry night. Various stimuli bombarded me. My brain seemed to be working overtime processing it all. I was a newborn werewolf, and no one had taught me anything. So, I was learning on the fly. Never had I ever felt so... *alive.*

"God help me, I liked it."

This sent a chill through Marla. He liked it? It had looked like Pablo liked it, too.

Caleb went on. "I moved away from the house, didn't go anywhere near the horses. The cattle were spread out across hundreds of acres of land. Near a stream, I came across the scent of deer spoor. A terrible hunger tore through my belly. I picked up the trail and took out after them. It didn't take long.

"In the clearing nearby, two does and their fawns nibbled on the grass. The stag stood not far off from them, keeping watch. I crouched downwind behind some scrub brush, bunching my leg muscles. Then I rushed forward, moving so fast I was nothing but a brown blur.

"The herd bolted, but it was too late. I was committed to the attack. I went for the stag. If I killed a doe, her fawn would die of starvation. And killing a fawn is like killing a baby. I just couldn't do it. So, the stag it was.

"I gained on him quickly, twisting and turning and changing directions, mirroring his doomed attempt to outmaneuver me. I leapt through the air. My claws sunk into his hindquarters. My added weight brought him down. One bite severed the spine. I clambered up over his body and bit him in the throat, killing him quickly.

"Then, I ate.

"That first kill was one of the most exhilarating, satisfying experiences of my life. It was like really great, mind-blowing sex. I'm not trying to be vulgar. There's just not any other human experience that compares.

"Later I would fully realize the terrible price I would pay for this new life that had been dumped into my lap.

"After I fed, I ran back to the stream. I was thirsty, so I drank deeply. I sank down onto my haunches, then keeled over. Exhausted, all my energy spent, I passed out. It was a deep sleep, dreamless, restorative. I would learn later just how much energy it takes to power that werewolf metabolism.

"I woke up, looked around. The sky was brightening to blue. Birds sang. The water in the creek babbled along. I stood there in the early morning air, buck-ass naked, half of my body smeared with blood. I headed back towards the ranch house on stiff legs and wobbly knees.

"It was still early when I got back. everyone was still asleep. I made my way back to my bedroom window and jumped back inside. I felt a huge sense of relief getting back into the room without being seen.

"I had survived my first Change. You would be surprised how many new werewolves don't.

"I got cleaned up, threw my clothes on, went to work. Just another day. Only it wasn't just another day. Things were not the same. They would never be the same again."

"What happened to Nick Gerard?" Marla asked.

"Nick died a week later. The whole ranch went into mourning. I rode with the body to the Undertaker, arranged for the funeral.

"After that, I went to see Mr. Jonas, the town banker. He had already heard, so he knew why I was there. He reached into his desk and pulled out an envelope that contained a letter from Nick that he had written sometime prior. It was a list of instructions regarding the ranch and how to keep it running and keep everybody paid. Leave it to Nick Gerard to take care of "his lads" even after he died.

"The letter instructed me to see the town attorney, Abraham T. Mattox. They had been friends for decades. He welcomed me into his office, had me take a seat. Mattox wasn't one for small talk. He knew Nick was gone. He knew about the instructions left with Jonas.

"Much like Jonas, he pulled some papers out of his desk drawer and without any preamble, began reading the Last Will and Testament of Nicholas J. Gerard.

"I remember it word for word, but I'll spare you the minutiae. Nick left the Lazy G to me. The land, the money, the livestock, everything. I was sole beneficiary.

"I was shocked. I'd had no idea. His death had made me wealthy. But what really bowled me over was the last sentence. 'I never had children in this life, Caleb. But if I ever had a son, I would want him to be just like you'."

Caleb dabbed at his eyes. "Sorry."

"It's all right."

"Weeks turned into months; one season gave way to the next. The Changes still occurred. I was careful to get away from the house. I realized I experienced a prodromal effect before every Change. I knew to make sure I was far away.

"I started to understand that I actually could develop a certain measure of control over the Change. If I kept calm, kept my temper in check, I could delay a Change. First it was just a few hours. But then it became days, weeks. I also discovered if I concentrated, and I mean concentrated really hard to the exclusion of all else, I could trigger a Change.

"I knew I could not stay forever on the ranch. In fact, I would never be able to stay in one place for very long.

"That's been the biggest change from my old life to the new. Since my cells don't really degenerate, they don't build up oxidants and free radicals. My cells don't age, my organs don't malfunction. My brain does not atrophy. I age so slowly now that I have, in human terms, stopped aging entirely. You see the problem, right? Everyone around me, all the people I knew, the banker, the lawyer, my ranch hands, they were all going to get old, wither and die.

"Not me.

"So, in 1888, twelve years after my attack, I sold the Lazy G to an experienced rancher with deep ties to Montana. I made it a condition of sale to keep all the lads employed and living there. I sold the ranch for tidy profit, added it to the money I already had, and moved on.

"I wound up in Seattle. I didn't need to work, so I went to college and got my bachelor's in History. Years went by. Technology advanced. Buildings went up. Babies were born. Old people died. Life went on. Everything and everyone around me changed, yet I stayed the same. By 1898, 58 years after I was born, I still looked and felt like a 30-year-old."

"Did you ever see your family again?" Marla asked.

"Once," Caleb replied. When Mom passed. I hopped the next train headed east, cabled ahead to let my sisters know I was coming. I knew they would be shocked by my appearance, but it couldn't be helped. She was my mother. When I arrived, all three met my train.

"Delia, the oldest, was seventy by then. She wore glasses and hobbled about on a cane. Ophelia's hair was so gray it was almost white. She had gained weight. But after having five children, what do you expect? Sadie, the youngest, still stood slim and tall at 54.

"Their faces registered shock when they saw me step off the train. They put on a brave front, took turns hugging me. Ophelia said something about how good I looked.

"The town had prospered while I had been gone. There were two hotels now. I took a room in the oldest and grandest of them. Delia and Ophelia were staying at the other, and Sadie still lived in the cabin. She had money to live elsewhere, but she never wanted to leave the homestead.

"Over the next few days, we attended the funeral. Few remembered me. Even fewer recognized me. As the pastor droned on about God's will and heavenly rewards, I realized that I had nothing in common with anyone there. That included my sisters.

"That small town in Missouri would always be where I'm from, but it wasn't home anymore. It would never be again.

"Mom's wealth passed to us kids. I informed my sisters that I neither needed nor wanted anything. I had come to pay my respects, nothing more. They could take my share and divvy it amongst themselves.

"The night before I left, I treated all my sisters to dinner in the hotel restaurant. Everyone ate well that night. We laughed, reminisced about the old days. Funny how we always talked about the good times, never the bad. We talked about Dad, but never about how he died. But even in the levity of the moment, I could feel their eyes on me, wondering why I had not aged. And where did all these muscles come from when I had been thin as a kid? None of it made sense.

"They came to the train station to see me off. Hugs all around and promises to stay in touch even though we all knew that wouldn't happen. I waved goodbye as the train pulled away. That moment, all my sisters standing on the platform waving goodbye to me is the last image I have of them. It's like a snapshot in my mind.

"Years went by. My sisters all grew old and died in the fullness of time, which is the natural order of things. The land eventually sold to another family.

"I moved around the western United States. Washington, Oregon, Utah, Wyoming. But I always wound up here. I moved back in the 60's and decided to stay. This is where I'm meant to be."

"Tremont is coming up," Marla announced.

Caleb put his blinker on. The unmarked car behind them did the same.

"So how does a werewolf live around normal people? Simple. You act normal. You hide in plain sight. It's easy. People don't believe in werewolves anymore, so we use that disbelief to move about freely.

The Jeep eased right, exiting the highway. The unmarked car followed.

"That brings us back to our current situation," Caleb said as he turned right at the bottom of the ramp. "I am not responsible for these murders. But someone like me is. His pack will do anything he commands, no matter what, without hesitation. No limits, no rules. And no morality. That makes them dangerous.

"I have to find out who's doing this and get them before the police do."

"Why?"

"Because if the cops tangle with them, there's gonna be cop bodies scattered all over the Puget Sound. And then the secret gets out. It always does. Then people will know once again that werewolves are real and walking the Earth. I can't allow that."

By this time, they had negotiated the two roundabouts, and were approaching the turn to Port Orchard Boulevard.

"These werewolves are killing for sport," he said. They're killing for fun. And they're sending a message."

"What's the message?" Marla was afraid of the answer.

"That the killing has only the beginning. They've put all of humankind on notice. This isn't over; they're just getting warmed up."

The air in the car was suddenly made of lead.

"Make no mistake. They're going to keep killing. And absolutely no one on this planet, not even you, is safe." He saw the fear in her eyes. "I cannot, I will not allow anything to happen to you. They will not harm you as long as I'm alive.

"So here we are, Marla. That's it. There's something out there hiding in the shadows, skulking in the dark, squatting in the fog and the mist. Growing stronger. More malignant.

"Like a cancer.

"Something's happening within the werewolf ranks. Something big that could spell death for millions. And there's one last thing you need to know."

"What's that?"

"I am the only living creature on this planet who has the power to stop it."

CHAPTER TWENTY-TWO

Their sex had been wild. Animalistic.

Orgasmic.

Now they lay naked and spent, sprawled across the enormous bed. Tousled sheets, pillows scattered, pushed onto the floor. Diane lay spread-eagled, half buried under the covers. Hans sat propped against the padded headboard smoking a cigar, sheets covering his waist.

He lazily blew smoke rings, watching them waft on invisible eddies and currents. Gray borders dissipated into shimmering tendrils.

Ephemeral.

He blew a new smoke ring to replace the last, watching the ritual repeat.

Though his body was relaxed, his mind knew no peace. Old memories crashed over him, waves on a beach. Memories of friends and rivals, people he had loved or hated, revered or reviled, supported or vanquished over the course of his life.

Life was a curious term to him. Could he honestly define his immortal existence on this spinning rock in space "Life"? He did the things living people did. He paid bills. He ate, drank, slept, had sex, went to the bathroom just like everyone else.

Like normal people.

But Hans was not "normal people", was he? Normalcy had been ripped out of him that snowy winter day so long ago in his native Germany. He had not been looking for it, but he damn sure got it.

Serves me right, he thought. My own Goddamned fault. Naïve, stupid, arrogant. Who would have thought the wolf I was hunting that day was also hunting me? Luring me deeper and deeper into the forest, into a place where he had me trapped?

Diane stirred, stretched, shifted on her belly, turned her head. He kept pondering fate along with shimmering smoke rings.

Hans felt a deep loss regarding humans. So similar yet so inferior. Physically fragile, mentally weak semi-educated minds locked within a miniscule view of what they considered reality. Insecure children who reacted vehemently, violently whenever confronted with evidence that forced them to question preconceived beliefs.

A half-forgotten quote flitted into his mind. He thought it was Mark Twain who said, "It is easier to fool a man than to present evidence to him later that he has been fooled".

What contemptable fools the humans were! Dismissing anything not drilled into their skulls since infancy as a hoax or myth. Ignorant and arrogant, feeling entitled and privileged without having actually earned it.

But one has to do what others were not willing to do in order to have the things others don't get to have.

Humans had not had to fight for their right to exist in generations. They had degenerated, become fat and weak, listless and lazy, limp-dicked, impotent. They squandered intellect and technological marvels on phone apps that did their thinking for them and choked down blue pills to help their useless penises function again.

They deserved what was coming.

And yet, sitting there on the eve of his ultimate accomplishment, Hans felt empty, unsatisfied, alone. Human had something he no longer had -- a choice. A choice to obey the law or become a criminal. A choice to treat others with respect. A choice to be kind to babies and pets. A choice in how they lived their lives. And sometimes, if they were lucky, a choice in how they died.

His melancholy deepened, a black void that could not be filled. He knew. He had tried filling it in the past with love, lust, sex, violence, depravity of all stripes.

Nothing worked.

The high-def TV on the wall caught his attention. An old black and white movie played. He looked closer, realized it was the 1931 production of DRACULA, starring Bela Lugosi. The story had been told hundreds of times in film and television, but this one held up remarkably well. He watched Bela turn to the camera. A wistful look on his face, the Hungarian actor delivered his famous lines. Hans whispered along with him.

"To die! To be truly dead! That must be glorious."

Hans covered his mouth with his hand. Tears rimmed his eyes. Dammit! Why was he getting so emotional?

Diane stirred again, stretching like a cat. She sighed, rolled over next to him, so close their bodies touched. Her tiny hand landed on his thigh, rested there. As delicate as the wing of a butterfly.

"Did you say something?" she asked, her eyes still closed.

"Nothing important," he said.

Her eyes snapped open. "You sound worried."

"No."

She looked up at him. She wondered if he was becoming paranoid.

He nodded, reading her thoughts. "Perhaps I am being paranoid. But it is now, right now, I am at my most vulnerable."

Diane pulled her hand back, breaking the connection. She hated it when he did that.

"What are you afraid of?"

Darkness passed through his ice blue eyes. "Him." The word came out low and powerful. Like a grunt. Or a bark.

Diane saw a mournful cloud pass behind his features. The lightbulb came on. "You know him."

"Indeed."

"So, what's the story?"

He shrugged, said nothing.

"You're not making this easy for me."

"You're a reporter," he replied. "You enjoy the chase."

She watched him turn away from her, crush out his cigar in a glass ashtray on the nightstand. When he turned back towards her, he lay flat beside her.

"Something happened that made you enemies." Then, it hit her. "You Turned him."

He closed his eyes. Wrinkles creased his forehead. He turned towards her, tears running down his cheeks.

"This is what humans don't see," he said. "The things you regret; the guilt you carry. Five hundred years of people loved and lost; mistakes that can never be corrected. Sins which cannot be forgiven. Five hundred years, searching for something you never find."

"I've already found what I'm looking for. It's right here in this bed, by your side."

"I am not invincible, you know. I can be killed."

"Not you," she responded. "You'll live forever."

The smile left his face. "That's what I'm afraid of," he whispered so low she barely heard him.

Diane had no idea how to respond to that. He did not want to live forever? How could that be? She sure as hell did. No wrinkles, no sallow skin, no bulging waistline or sagging breasts for her, thank you very much.

Give her immortality any day.

The two-car caravan turned left at Port Orchard Avenue, heading down the sloping two-lane road. Old growth forest lined both sides, trees covered in algae and moss, limbs projecting out and over, intertwining above into a canopy. It was like driving through a green tunnel.

Marla had not spoken since Caleb had finished his story. Her view of him, of the world at large, had been fundamentally altered. After what she had seen, she knew his story was true. Their fledgling relationship might be irrevocably damaged.

He hoped not.

He looked ahead. Bay Street, running parallel to the shoreline, waited for them. He braked, looked left and right, turned left. Driving away from downtown, he passed the Boatworks, then turned into the familiar gravel driveway. He stopped, the police car pulling up beside him.

Caleb climbed out. Akin, Jose, and Russell all got out, stretching arms and legs. Caleb walked around the front of the Jeep, aware that Marla had not moved. He opened her door, held out his hand.

She sat there, staring straight ahead, studiously ignoring him. He scanned the area for danger as everyone else moved towards the house. The scent of other werewolves. Faint, but present. No imminent danger. He turned from Marla, left her door open and walked towards the house.

Caleb mounted the steps onto the porch. Akin and Martinez walked past his Jeep, gave questioning looks towards Marla. Russell broke off, walked to the open door.

Akin and Martinez joined Caleb on the porch. "What's with her?" Akin asked.

"She asked me questions. She didn't like the answers."

He unlocked the door, swung it open wide, stepped aside. He motioned for them to enter. He followed them inside, closed the door behind him.

Russell leaned one arm on the car door, striking a somewhat casual pose. She glared resolutely ahead; hard eyes rimmed in red.

"Hey, Pooky," he said, using the childhood nickname he had given her. She had been called "Pooky" until she outgrew it in her teen years.

Marla heard him but gave no outward reaction.

"Look. He's still Caleb."

"Is he? I don't know who he is," she replied. "And neither do you.

"Marla—"

"He's lied to both of us since the beginning. He should have told us."

"Would we have believed him before all this? Come on." He paused. "The man is risking his life to protect us."

"How do we know he's not going to decorate his lair with our intestines?"

"You really think he wants to do that?"

"Look. I'm mad, and I want to stay mad."

"You're not mad. You're scared."

"Goddamned right I'm scared." Her eyes filled with tears. "Fucking werewolves roaming the earth. And to hear him tell it, they're everywhere. All the time."

"Yep."

"I let that man into my life. Into my home. Into my bed. And now I find out he can gut me like a fish anytime he wants."

"Again. Do you really think he would do that?"

She turned this over in her mind. Russell saw her features soften a bit, then saw the curtain fall back down over her face.

"Doesn't matter," she said. "What are we even doing here? How can we trust anything he says?"

"What choice do we have?" he asked. "Overview, Marla. These motherfuckers know who we are. Where we live. Without Caleb, how long will we last? A few hours? A day, maybe? Use your head for something besides a hat rack and think it through."

Marla thought it through. Russell was right. She just wanted him to be wrong. She sighed, unbuckled her seat belt.

"All right." She climbed down, shut the door. "But if he eats my brains out of my skull, it's your fault."

She turned and stormed off without giving him a chance to respond. She stomped up the steps, paused at the door.

"You coming?"

Inside, everyone was waiting for them. Caleb rose from his desk as they entered. His laptop was booting up. Akin and Martinez sat in leather chairs.

"Please come in," Caleb said. "Make yourselves comfortable."

Marla looked around. The view of Sinclair Inlet was spectacular. Leather furniture, medium wood tones, some nautical-themed accessories, all of it antique. She had to admit, it suited him.

"Can I get you anything?"

"I'm good." Not really. She was far from good.

Caleb saw through her façade. But she had to come around in her own time. Forcing the issue was the surest way to push her away forever.

And he couldn't have that.

He sat back down in front of his laptop. Russell moved into the kitchen. He opened the fridge, pulled out a soda. The top popped loudly in the otherwise quiet room.

Marla took two timid steps forward, then stood where she was. She folded her arms across her torso, a subconscious projection of her fear.

Caleb typed quickly as the computer fully booted. He brought up the same map and historical dates he had been looking at earlier.

"Okay. Gather around."

Akin, Martinez, Russell, and Marla gathered behind his chair and gazed at the screen from over his shoulders.

"Composite map of North America. The red dots and dates represent known or suspected werewolf attacks."

"How far back does this go?" Russell asked.

Caleb pointed to New England. "1588." He pointed to numerous red dots up and down the East Coast.

"Werewolves have existed alongside humans, in every age, in every culture since the beginning of time itself. It makes sense that they would expand as man did.

"What about the Native Americans?" Jose asked.

Caleb looked at him meaningfully, then turned his head back to the screen. "They came here twelve thousand years ago along with the first humans. We crossed the land bridge from Asia during the last Ice Age. Most of it is oral history."

"Why would werewolves come here at all?" Akin again.

"Same reason everyone else came," Caleb said. "Fame. Fortune. Freedom."

"Food." Russell.

"We can hunt any prey we desire," Caleb said, an edge to his voice. "We don't have to kill humans,"

"These assholes do," Marla chimed in.

"Which is why we must stop them." Caleb turned back to the screen. "The push West brought them, too." He pointed to red dots and corresponding dates. The farther west, the more recent the dates. He pointed to a green dot, Montana, 1876. "That's me."

"You killed someone there?" Russell asked.

"I was Turned there."

"The attacks move further West over time. All up and down the Coast. Multiple attacks in every state."

"What does this all mean?" Akin asked.

"They're everywhere," Caleb said simply. He pushed his chair back away from the computer. "Something's happening. Something big. This --" he pointed towards the screen -- "is not normal werewolf behavior."

Marla stiffened. "What constitutes 'normal werewolf behavior'?"

"Not this." He turned in his chair to face the group. "This isn't random. It's part of a larger puzzle."

"Like what?"

Caleb thought for a moment, shook his head. "I'll know more after tonight." He knew better than to share with them what he was beginning to suspect. Keep it to yourself until you know, he told himself.

"You can't go!" Marla exclaimed. "They'll kill you just to get you out of the way."

He smiled darkly. "Let them try."

Everyone stood, stunned to silence. Now they understood. Caleb was not afraid. Not in the least.

"More likely they'll try to recruit me," he said. "I don't play well with others."

"What if you're not given a choice?"

"I always have a choice."

"What will you choose?" Marla demanded.

"What's the definition of integrity, Marla? It's doing the right thing, no matter what it costs. It's doing the right thing even when nobody's looking."

He shot up out of the chair, walked to the huge window. He stared out, calming himself. She was still overwhelmed, he told himself. The rules of her existence had just changed drastically for her, and she was still trying to catch up.

Behind him, the little group broke up. Akin and Martinez both pulled out their phones and began making calls. Russell plopped down on the sofa. Marla stayed where she was.

"You got any girlie magazines?" Russell called out.

"My subscription to 'Big Boobs and Bubble Butts' ran out."

"Damn."

The smile faded quickly from Caleb's face. He was in a dangerous situation. His friends were living more precariously. How best to protect them?

Caleb grabbed a faded barn coat hanging on a coat rack, threw it on. He pushed his arms through the sleeves, unlocked the glass door. He stepped out onto the back deck.

Seagulls floated on tufts of air over the water, keeping a sharp eye out for food. Scavengers, Caleb thought. Flying garbage cans, seagulls will eat just about anything.

He looked farther out across the glassy surface. He wind was gentle, intermittent, and the water's surface took on a reflective quality. He looked left and right to see if he could see any Canada geese. They sometimes roosted on the shoreline nearby. But not today.

He buttoned the barn coat, shoved his hands into his pockets. Tonight would be a largely futile effort. They could meet, opposing generals before the outbreak of hostilities, try to negotiate a settlement to prevent unwarranted bloodshed. But there would be no compromise tonight. They would not deviate from whatever plan they already had set in motion. And if he stood aside, millions, possibly billions of human lives would be snuffed out.

All it takes for evil to triumph is for good men to stand by and do nothing, he remembered.

Was Caleb a good man? Not always, he admitted. But he always strived to be, even when he fell short. He didn't harm those who didn't deserve it. He didn't kill children and avoided humans in general when he could. Last night had been an exception.

But telling himself he was a good man was too pat. It's easy to talk lofty principles when nothing crucial lies at stake. Now, everything was at stake. His life, the lives of his friends, the life of She Whom He Loved, the fate of the entire world, the future of humankind as a viable species.

Everything.

Caleb sighed, momentarily unsure of himself. He was not afraid of dying; he had gotten past that long ago. No, he was afraid of what would happen if he failed. He was afraid that when the chips were down, he would not be enough by himself to save his friends.

To save everything.

He ground his teeth, pursed his lips. He turned to his left, looked up into the top of a Douglas Fir about a hundred feet down the shoreline. A bald eagle sat perched near the top, lone, still, majestic, its keen yellow eyes and white head contrasting sharply against its dark body. It stared down at the water, looking for fish caught in the receding tide. Caleb never ceased to be awed by these magnificent birds.

He looked back across the water, trying to calm himself. If he was being honest with himself, he wasn't sure he would survive. But he couldn't get off at the next exit. Everything dear to him would be wiped out of existence. He would do whatever was necessary. That included unleashing the full power of the Wolf.

The full power of the Wolf.

Even after all this time, that still frightened him. He had been told about it, heard rumors, heard stories, he really didn't know anything about it for sure. It was something that each werewolf carried, somewhere deep inside themselves. Most who attempted it died. Few ever used it, and even fewer could responsibly wield the power that came with it. All he knew for certain was, if he tapped into it, somehow found it within himself, no living thing on this planet would stand against him and live.

Behind him, the French door opened. He heard Marla's heartbeat. It had been normal when she had been looking at him through the glass. Once she had stepped outside, it increased.

Marla stood beside him in a matching barn coat about two sizes too big. She fairly swam beneath its folds. The sleeves were too long; the tips of her fingers barely extended below the cuffs. Just for an instant, he had some notion of what she must have looked like as a little girl trying on her Daddy's coat.

"When were you going to tell me?"

"I had no plan one way or the other," he said truthfully.

"Really?"

"We'd only met a few times prior at social occasions, never one on one. We've only had one date, and that got hijacked by all *this*." He gestured, his frustration showing. "I didn't plan on any of this."

"Didn't you?" She immediately felt sorry for saying it.

He pushed himself off the railing. He turned and reached for the door handle.

"So why did you take up with me, anyway, Mr. Lone Wolf?"

He paused, stood at the door, looking at the handle. He heard the pain, the desperation. The loneliness.

"Do you really need to ask that?" His voice was soft, hurt.

Oh crap. This was not what she had expected.

"So, what next?"

He opened his hands, palms up, looked at her questioningly. He was silently asking for more specificity.

"Let's say neither one of us gets killed in the next few days and we continue as a couple. What then?"

"I don't understand the question."

"What if you decided to leave me?"

Caleb looked at her like she had just stabbed him with a knife. "I would *never*."

"How can you be so sure?"

He stepped closer to her. She did not back away.

"Wolves mate for life," he whispered. "You know that."

"Yes. And that's the problem."

"Excuse me?"

"You're pretty much always going to look like this." She gestured towards him with one hand. "Not me. I'll age. My hair will go gray, my skin will wrinkle, my belly will go soft, my ass will get big, my tits will sag."

"You think that shit matters to me?"

"Doesn't it?"

Caleb realized what she was truly asking. This was her deepest fear. Any woman's deepest fear.

He considered his next words carefully. There could be no room for ambiguity.

"Marla, listen to me very carefully." He looked deeply into her eyes. "I. Will. *Always* love you. I will *never* leave you." He took her hands in his. "I will kill for you, and I will *die* to protect you. No remorse. No regrets."

Tears rimmed her eyes. "I just have to know what's going to happen when I'm no longer beautiful."

She saw that confused look again, followed by a warmth and a love she had never seen in any man's eyes when looking at her.

"Oh, Jesus Christ, Marla. Don't you get it?" His voice cracked with emotion. "You will always be beautiful to me."

And just like that, she was in his arms, squeezing him close, unable to speak. She looked up, drew closer, and suddenly his mouth was on hers. She knew now, with every fiber of her being, that this man, this immortal creature, this werewolf truly loved her. He would never harm her, never get drunk and smack her around. He would never forsake her, never betray her, never screw around on her. He would be there, unshakeable and resolute, right by her side until her dying day.

It was a wonderful feeling.

Inside, Akin, Martinez, and Russell watched the display through the glass. Akin and Martinez smiled to themselves. They understood what was going on. But Russell had no smile on his face. In fact, he scowled at them. Something dark flickered behind his eyes.

"Looks like they made up," Martinez whispered.

Caleb stepped inside, closed the door behind him. Marla, still outside, smiled with contentment. She turned her back to the house, leaned easily on the rail. Caleb took his coat off, hung it on the coatrack.

"You break her heart and werewolf or not, I'll fucking break your face," Russell said as Caleb marched across the room. He froze, stared at Russell with silent surprise. Here was a man, a mortal human and his best friend, threatening to kick his ass if Caleb betrayed Russell's cousin.

He nodded solemnly towards his friend.

"I ever do that, you go ahead and swing." Hard. I'll have it coming."

"She's family."

"I know."

"I'm not kidding, Caleb."

"Neither am I."

Russell was about to say something else, but stopped as Caleb froze in place, a look of alarm on his face. He sniffed the air, turning his head this way and that. He swung around to check on Marla; she was still where he had left her. His anger rising, he glared at Martinez, then covered by allowing his eyes to drift to Akin. Then he sniffed again, and his head whipped around. He craned his neck forward, extending his nose in front of his body, pointing towards the front door.

"What is it?" Russell asked.

A look of steely determination flooded Caleb's features. He breathed hard through his nose. His jaw flexed and set.

"Stay here," he barked. Deep. Rumbling again.

Martinez had picked up on it, too. But this was not his property to defend, not his territory to protect. He watched Caleb march towards his front door, ignoring the questions being hurled at him by both Russell and Akin. What was wrong? Where was he going?

Caleb flung the front door open with such force it crashed against the wall, shaking the glass panes. Ignoring it, Caleb stomped onto his porch, paused. Concentrating, he peered into the foliage around his property, seething. Rippling muscles flexed, heaving chest expanded, body hair stood on end, a primal instinctive reaction to make him appear larger and more intimidating. His lip pulled up in a snarl, sending a crease up his face to the side of his nose.

He dashed down the steps and across the small yard. He unzipped his pants, pissed furiously on the hedges, spraying back and forth. He contracted his muscles, crimping off the urine flow. Without bothering to put himself back inside his pants, he hurried over to another area, unleashed more of his stream. He immediately jogged over to the reflective posts at the entrance to his property. He had already pissed here before, but he leaned his head, sniffed again. The scent of his marking was still strong, but Caleb finished emptying his bladder here anyway.

His stream narrowed to a trickle, dribbled to a stop. He quickly put himself back inside his pants, zipped up. When he turned around, Russell, Martinez, Akin and Marla all stood on the front porch, watching him. Completely unashamed of what he had just done, he walked back towards them.

"What the hell you doing?" Russell asked as Caleb stopped in front of them.

"Marking my territory."

"Why?"

"We're being watched."

"How did you know?"

"Can't you smell them?" Caleb asked.

"What if they decide to attack?" Marla asked.

"They won't."

"Why not?"

"I left them a warning." He jerked his thumb towards the wooden posts, then said, "It's a werewolf thing."

Caleb shot one last dangerous glare over his shoulder, then stomped up the stairs, onto the porch, and inside the house. Martinez and Akin followed. Russell and Marla looked at each other.

"It's a werewolf thing," Russell repeated. "No big deal."

Marla sighed, shook her head a little. She turned and wordlessly marched back inside. Russell looked around, an icy stab of fear in his gut. He suddenly realized he was outside all alone.

He turned, went back inside, closed the door. He joined everyone else, huddled in the living room.

"Where are they?" Marla asked.

"Next door," Caleb replied.

"So, we're supposed to sit here and wave goodbye when you drive off into whatever trap they've set for you?"

"Pretty much."

"And what if they kill you, Furball?" Russell asked.

"They won't."

"How do you know?"

He looked back and forth between Russell and Marla. "I haven't lived this long without acquiring some serious survival skills."

Each of them tried to imagine what encompassed "serious survival skills". The only one with a clue was Martinez, and he wasn't talking.

"Now. Make yourselves at home. Grab a bite. Watch some Pay Per View. I'm taking a nap. I need to bring my "A" game tonight."

Caleb disappeared down the hallway to his bedroom, closed the door.

"He still thinks it's called Pay Per View," Russell said. Grins all around. "I'm raiding the freezer."

That seemed to break the ice. Marla realized she was hungry and followed Russell into the kitchen.

"Should we?" Akin asked.

Martinez shrugged. "He said we could."

Akin considered this. It was against departmental policy, she knew. "May as well," she shrugged. "This is going to be a long day."

Caleb was asleep when Marla opened the door and crept in. She closed the door gently, careful to not make any sound. Of course, she made some sounds, but they were soft and brief. Surely, they wouldn't disturb him. She could barely hear them, and she was the one making them.

She looked around the room, taking it in. It was more than just a bedroom. It was what realtors call a "master suite". Night tables with lamps stood on each side at the head of the bed. A small half-bath stood discretely tucked away to the left. A seating bench sat up to and touching the foot of the bed.

A comfortable, worn and scarred leather chair waited in a corner. A throw blanket draped across the back and over the top. A tall reading lamp with a broad brass base, spindly body and upturned light cover stood behind the chair for optimal illumination.

A reading nook.

Tall wooden bookcases stood against one wall, completely filled. She noticed a row of hardcover, leather-bound works of classical literature. Leaning forward, she squinted at the titles. A TALE OF TWO CITIES, RETURN OF THE NATIVE, TESS OF THE D'URBVILLES. There was more. FRANKENSTEIN, THE PICTURE OF DORIAN GRAY. She was impressed.

On impulse, she pulled an old copy of DRACULA. She opened it carefully, the pages yellow and brittle. On the publisher's page, she read, "First printing, 1897". She turned one more page, and read a handwritten inscription, *"To Caleb, with all my admiration and respect, Bram Stoker"*.

Her mouth dropped open. Her eyes snapped over to the person sleeping peacefully in his bed. She closed the book gently and placed it back on the shelf.

The last thing she noticed in the suite was the set of French Doors that opened directly onto the wraparound back deck. Caleb had a view of the water from pretty much every room in the house.

Emotionally drained, Marla peeled her clothes off down to her bra and panties, slid under the covers. Caleb moved his head a bit, sighed in his sleep. She lay on her side, watching him. His back was to her, his head turned away. She gazed appreciatively at his broad shoulders, leading down to a narrow waist, which gave all fit men that V shape to their torso.

Still asleep, Caleb moved his shoulder, turned his head and began licking a spot over and over. He paused, eyes closed, then licked the same spot on his shoulder again several times. His head fell back against the pillow.

Being with this man is going take some serious adjustments.

But the key to any successful long-term relationship was compromise. Marla had always treasured her own space, her own time, her own life separate from her dating. She had enjoyed her men well enough but right now she couldn't even remember their faces. She had never been in love with any of them, certainly not to the point where she was willing to give up the "me" for the "we".

Well.

Things were different now, weren't they? Her life was in imminent danger by incredible Beasts of Legend and this man, this immortal Beast of Legend beside her had professed unconditional, eternal, undying love. For her. Not someone else, not anyone else.

Just her.

And he very matter-of-factly had told her he would kill for her, that he would die, yes *DIE*, to protect her. That's how much he loved her.

How could she not love him back?

He shifted in his sleep, turning over and settling on his back, one arm behind his head between the mattress and the pillow. He looked completely relaxed, like it might take a bazooka blast to wake him up. The entire world was at risk, and he was catching some Z's. She wondered when she had slept so soundly.

Caleb's eyes popped open. His head fell towards her. His eyes warmed.

"Hey you," he whispered.

He reached out with one hand, traced a finger along her jawline to the point of her chin. A touch so light it was almost weightless. She found herself thinking of things other than sleep.

"I could get used to this," he said.

"Get used to what?"

"Waking up to you."

Good answer. She felt a pleasant, spreading warmth throughout her body. It took every ounce of self-discipline she had to keep from jumping him right then. But before she could congratulate herself on her own self-restraint, her hand snaked under the covers, found a resting place on his side just above his hip bone. She watched the desire register on his face.

Her hand drifted further downward, across his muscular flank. In return, he drew that same feather-light fingertip down her cleavage.

Okay. Fuck self-restraint.

She plastered her mouth over his, kissing him hard, tongue exploring. His hands were everywhere. She reveled in the feel. They met around her back and just like that, her bra popped loose. She tossed it aside.

She straddled him, felt him hard against her. She leaned down, pressing her bare skin against his. She gasped as one of his hands cupped her breast while the other grabbed a buttock.

After tonight, Caleb might be dead. By tomorrow night, they might both be dead. That was the path they found themselves on.

But right now, today, they were both *alive*.

CHAPTER TWENTY-THREE

Detective Martinez sniffed the air from the front porch. It was late afternoon, already getting dark. Wind whispered through the trees. Cars passing by on Bay Street had already turned on their headlights.

He smelled the werewolf scouts hidden somewhere in the Boatworks to his left. He had scanned every shape and outcropping to no avail. He could neither see them, nor hear them. But his nose never failed him.

He felt no urgency. Like Caleb, he lived his werewolf life on the down low. He wasn't worried about being burned at the stake. He was concerned with getting recorded on someone's cell phone. If people found out about him, they found out about them all. Most werewolves would not appreciate the notoriety, and would not hesitate to make their displeasure known, in a very real and permanent fashion.

Like Caleb, he had not asked for this. It had been dumped in his lap, too. But he lacked Caleb's strength, that depth of character, and he knew it. Fact was, Jose Martinez, always looked for the path of least resistance, the easiest way to get something done. If that meant cutting a few corners or bending a rule here or there, he was fine with that. He simply worked things to his advantage.

Don't hate the player. Hate the game.

Martinez was a born follower, just another face in the crowd, easily forgotten. That's why his family had been flabbergasted when he announced he was dropping out of college to join the police. They were even more astonished when he did well at Academy and graduated top of his class.

Out of the safety of the classroom environment, Martinez had only been a mediocre performer, going through the motions, phoning it in. He kept his nose clean, never took money that wasn't his, never looked the other way. He occasionally made good collars that resulted in low-level convictions, but he had never blossomed into the stellar, stand-out kind of cop his academy potential had suggested. No citations, no medals. No praise from the Mayor or

Chief of Police. He faded in the crowd once more, just one of the rank and file.

After being bitten, his performance had improved across the board. Top scores on the firing range, and his physical fitness tests. Now that he had made Detective, he planned to cruise along, keep his head down, do quality work but nothing that drew unwarranted attention. He would retire, take the silly gold watch and a ridiculously small pension, then move on. New place. New identity.

And leave no forwarding address.

Footfalls from within the house coming closer. The door opened then closed. He did not need turn his head.

Caleb stood beside him in faded jeans, untucked brown plaid flannel shirt, hiking boots. For a moment, neither one talked.

"They're still over there," Martinez said at last, once the silence became uncomfortable.

"Let them watch."

"Let them watch?" Martinez was genuinely surprised at Caleb's cavalier attitude.

"What are they gonna do? Stop me?" he paused briefly, then grunted a bemused laugh. "Good luck with that."

Fear stabbed through Martinez.

Caleb sensed it. "You suffer from a high level of self-doubt."

"Sort of."

"No, not 'sort of'. You're afraid."

"The question is, why aren't you?"

Caleb turned to meet his gaze. "Here's the bottom line, Jose. Shit's about to get real. When it does, you're gonna have to pick a side."

"What if I don't want to pick a side?"

"You won't have a choice. None of our kind will." Caleb paused, allowing this to sink in. "You really think once they've risen to power, they'll make allowances for Lone Wolves like us? Think again, buddy. It'll be their way or else."

"Maybe they'll –"

"No," Caleb cut in sharply. "You think they'll allow any kind of independent thought amongst the ranks? Did Soviet Russia? Do the Chinese? The North Koreans? Cuba, Venezuela? Iran? These werewolves will be like any other totalitarian government.

Independent thought leads to dissent. And dissent is dangerous. You tow the line, or you get squashed. Hard."

Martinez had never thought of it that way.

Caleb leaned in "And just so you and I are clear, if anything happens to the humans inside my house and I find out it's because you didn't have the balls to do what's right..." He tilted his head, cocked one eyebrow. "Well. I'm gonna take that shit personal."

He glared directly into Martinez's eyes until Martinez broke contact, looked down and away. The younger werewolf gulped.

Caleb stepped back. "I'm glad we had this conversation."

"You really think they'll try something while you're gone?"

"It's what I'd do."

Martinez shuddered. "All I ever wanted was to be left alone."

"Me too."

Martinez swallowed, tried to speak, realized he could not. His heart pounded, a biological metronome in overdrive within his chest.

"I've never fought another werewolf," he croaked.

"It's all right to be scared," Caleb assured. "Just don't be a coward."

"What the hell does that mean?"

"Bravery isn't the absence of fear. It's being afraid and still manning the fuck up." He glared at Martinez, his jaw set hard. "Do not be a coward tonight," he warned, his voice low. "If you do, refer to my earlier statement."

Fear turning to frustration, Martinez said, "And what the fuck does that actually mean, anyway?"

Caleb's face darkened. His eyes went amber. He took a quick step forward, grabbed Martinez up by the collar so fast the werewolf detective had no chance to react.

"You know precisely what the fuck it means," he growled. His voice rumbled, roiling from somewhere south of his human vocal range. He held Martinez there a beat more, wrestled his own burst of anger under control. He let go of Martinez and took a step back to a less threatening, more neutral distance.

When Martinez said nothing else, Caleb turned, reached for the doorknob to go inside. He froze, his hand on the knob when Martinez spoke.

"So, if they do come tonight and pull some kind of double-cross, you expect me to die protecting them?"

"I expect to come home and I either find everyone safe and sound, or your shredded corpse staining my hardwood floors." He gave Martinez one last amber flash of his eyes for effect. Then he went inside, leaving Martinez trembling on the porch.

Inside, Russell read a book on the sofa. He was holding up pretty well. Akin was busy with her phone, swiping across the screen with her index finger. Going over police reports and Medical Examiner findings. A consummate professional, she was looking for anything to bring these people to justice, as if man's justice held any sway.

Marla came walking down the hall, still half-asleep. She smiled dreamily his way. He smiled back, butterflies in his stomach. He wished he was an eagle so he could spread his wings and soar, buffeting on the air currents. He wished he had met Marla under different circumstances.

Akin looked up. "So. What's the plan?"

"I go meet my archnemesis and his nefarious henchmen. You stay here and stay alert. When I'm done, I come back."

"And if something goes wrong?"

"Use every bullet you have. You won't kill them unless you get a headshot, but if you're lucky you might slow them down enough to get away."

Both Marla and Russell felt chilled. This talk of life and death as if it was so casual a thing; making contingency plans in case Caleb got murdered. Marla got nauseated at the possibility. She didn't want her man – and yes, he was indeed her man now – getting hurt.

Russell pushed his fear aside by observing Caleb closely. He detected a glimpse of Caleb's inner turmoil. He was not afraid for himself, of that Russell was sure. Caleb's concern was for everyone else, especially Marla.

"So. Great Dane," Russell said when the conversation seemed over, "what's it like?"

"What is what like?"

"Being a werewolf, Einstein," Russell quipped. "What's it like when you Change?"

Caleb thought for a moment. "My entire body becomes pins and needles, and not in a good way. It's like my skin is on fire." He paused. Then, "Then the internal changes happen."

"It hurts?"

"Goddamned right, it hurts. My rib cage cracks and reshapes, my facial bones break and push forward, stretching my skin. My internal organs reshape, reorder themselves. I grow extra weight-bearing joints in my legs. My knees shift a hundred and eighty degrees, so they bend backwards instead of forwards. Does that sound like fun to you?

"It sounds like being born," Marla said softly.

"Once I complete the Change, the Wolf takes over. There's a euphoria in it."

"What about you?"

"It's still me inside the Wolf," Caleb explained. "I can still think and feel. My mind functions. But there's one big difference."

"What?"

"As humans, we all have hidden thoughts, secret wants and desires, forbidden impulses. But because we're taught to be civilized people, we don't act on them. Right?" He looked around the room. They were with him. "The Wolf has no such inhibitions. If I want to do something, I just do it. No hesitation."

"No impulse control."

He nodded.

"Wow."

"Why does this Change happen?" Akin asked.

"I'm pretty sure it's some kind of infection. The way it gets spread, I think it's viral, kind of like herpes."

"You lost me."

"I'm altered on a genetic level." Everyone nodded in agreement. "This thing replicates inside me over time. Once it builds to a sufficient concentration, it triggers a Change if I haven't Changed on my own. The rest of the time, it lies dormant unless something else triggers it."

"What else triggers it?" Akin asked.

"Extreme emotion," Caleb replied. "Fear. Anger."

"I think I get it now," Russell said.

Everyone turned to him. "The way the animals reacted at the zoo. They knew you were different."

"Yes."

"And Sampson," Marla said.

"Kinship."

Russell shook his head. "Amazing."

Marla had been listening, contributing only in the most limited amounts. But her mind was churning. These implications had lifelong consequences. Then she remembered something, and the pieces fell into place.

"Caleb, can I speak to you in private?"

Marla headed towards the bedroom. Caleb followed. When they heard the door close, Russell and Akin looked at each other. What was Marla saying in there?

Marla whirled towards him, her arms crossing her chest, feet planted shoulder-width apart. Caleb read the body language in a heartbeat. Uh oh.

"Where did you really go last night?"

"I told you."

"Who was it?"

"Excuse me?"

"Don't be cute," she scolded. "I know enough math to put two and two together. You made a kill last night."

"Yes."

Marla sucked in air as her hand flew up to her mouth. Her eyes widened in horror.

"So, you're a murderer."

"No. I'm a killer. Big difference."

"You just randomly picked someone to shred?"

"I never pick prey 'at random'."

"Human prey?" Marla felt a shudder go through her. "So, who was it?"

"Someone who deserved it," he answered. "A pedophile"

"How do you know?"

"The fifteen-year-old boy chained naked to his bed was a big clue."

Marla startled. A fresh look of horror came over her face as she pictured a boy chained like that.

"What did you do to the guy?"

He hesitated a moment. Then, "You don't want to know."

There was a dark finality to his voice that told Marla he had said all he was going to say. She knew he would not describe it in graphic detail. But her imagination was already working overtime.

"What about the boy?"

"I snapped the chains. Then I left."

"And you didn't harm him?"

He looked insulted. "What kind of animal do you think I am?"

She sighed, shook her head. This was still too much. Here she was, standing alone in a bedroom with a creature that shouldn't exist. That's when reality smacked her in the face like a sack of bricks.

She was in love with a man who was also a creature that should not be, a creature who was a cold, amoral killer.

"You're everything I could ever want in a man," she said. "But you're also this other thing. You kill people."

His heart jumped into his throat. "What are you saying?"

"I'm saying I don't know if I can be with you."

Caleb stood in stunned silence, his entire world crumbling inside him. He breathed deeply, bit his lip to keep from screaming. He sighed, feeling very old.

"After everything that's happened, after what's happened between us, and with what's still going on right now as we speak, one less pedophile in the world is what's going to kill our relationship?" He sounded hurt.

She stood there, ran her tongue over her teeth.

"Everything I said on the back deck still holds true. You know what I am, what I truly am." He paused. She was almost afraid to breathe. "I love you, Marla. But I can't force you to love me back, and I refuse to possess you." He gestured, moving a finger back and forth between them. "But we can't go through this every time something new comes up."

"Oh. Something new is going to come up?"

"Ever seen a relationship where it didn't?"

She mentally reviewed every relationship she, or anyone she knew had navigated. Something always did come up, didn't it? The only question was if the couple involved were committed enough to work it out.

Caleb checked his watch. "I can't tell you what to do," he said. "You have to make this decision on your own."

She looked up, but he was already turning away, heading towards the bedroom door. She watched him go, wanting to speak out, wanting more than anything to tell him to be careful, that she loved him just as much as he loved her.

But all she did was watch him open the door and disappear from her sight. She felt more alone now than ever.

She sat down on the side of the bed, brought her hands up to her face and began to cry.

"The time is nigh."

Hans was out of bed, checking some of his investments on his laptop. Francois stood at the foot of the bed. Diane, still naked under the sheets, began to stir.

Hans stood, still naked. "Weather?" he asked, scanning the dark sky through his window.

"Cold and dreary," Francois responded.

"Very well."

Francois exited, closing the door behind him just as Diane pushed herself up onto one elbow. Her hair was messy, eyes still heavy with sleep.

"What time is it?"

"Early."

He padded over to his closet, swung open the door, went inside. A few moments later, he reemerged, with dark slacks, socks, silk briefs, and a beautiful bulky cable knit sweater, imported of course, made of the finest Scottish wool, all draped over one arm. A custom-made pair of Italian oxford shoes dangled from two fingers on his other hand. He tossed the clothes onto the bed, dropped the shoes onto the floor.

Diane watched as he sat down, his back to her. He hunched over as he dressed.

"What's happening tonight?"

"I meet Caleb Jacobsen and assess his threat level."

"Why not just kill him?"

He turned to look at her, a dangerous glare in his eye. "That is not our way," he spat at her. "You say you want to be one of us, yet after all this time, you don't seem to know how we conduct ourselves."

"That's not fair—"

"Shut up," he grumbled. He turned away from her, continued dressing.

Diane's eyes narrowed in anger. "How dare you!" she raged. "Who the fuck do you think you are, talking to me like that?"

Hans stood, unconcerned, pulled his silk briefs up. He adjusted himself inside the pouch, then released the elastic waist band. It snapped to his skin. He glanced over at Diane as he moved. He knew she was outraged. He just didn't give a shit.

He stepped into his trousers, pulled them up.

"I asked you a question."

He stood straight, looked her in the eye. "I am Hans, Alpha Male of the Global Wolf Pack. I decide whether or not you ever become a werewolf. I also decide whether you and your family live or die."

He pulled the sweater over his head as his words finally hit her. In a flash she was up and out of bed, surging towards him, completely oblivious to her nakedness, eyes tearing up, fists raised, face contorted.

He held his leather belt in his right hand. He swung without thinking. The belt caught Diane full on. The right side of her face exploded in hot pain, blinding her. She fell sideways across the bed.

Diane lay there, stunned, an angry red welt already forming. It would get bigger, swollen, bruised as time went on. She tried to think, but her brain was no longer firing on all cylinders.

Hans waited to see if she would charge again. When it became obvious she would not, he threaded his belt through his pants, secured the buckle.

He walked to the door, looked back at her.

"You have a problem with boundaries," he said. "It's one of the reasons why I hesitate to Turn you." She remained silent, but he knew she was listening. "I've tried to be patient. But you can't seem to reign yourself in." He paused again. "Don't ever come at me like that again."

Then he was gone out the door.

Francois met him on the main floor. They walked together.

"There's another anomaly in our Luxembourg accounts," Hans said.

"I thought we had that under control."

"Get the forensic accountants on it," Hans ordered. "I want to know what's happening."

"I'll talk with the Minister of Finance," Francois said. "He's one of us.

"Tell him I will hold him personally accountable."

"By your command."

William sat in a chair in the living room, waiting. He appeared nervous, but he was excited. He had been given a rare opportunity for someone so young in the Wolf. His only fear was that he perform well, execute any orders given without hesitation, and most importantly, avoid doing anything to embarrass himself. He saw them coming. He bolted to his feet.

"Ah, young William," Hans greeted with a smile. "You're coming with us tonight."

"Thank you for this opportunity, sir. I won't let you down."

Outside the front door, the chill wind ripped through their hair and cut at their faces, thousands of tiny ice shards. Hans breathed the air in, relishing the sensation. Francois, ever the tunnel-vision soldier, stared straight ahead and did his best to ignore it.

Werewolf sentries patrolled the inside wall perimeter in the distance. Even in the darkness, Hans's werewolf vision saw them prowling the grounds. Obedient foot soldiers. Every general needs them, he thought. Every army needs cannon fodder.

Expendables.

They all turned towards the small group, sniffing the air. They recognized the Master's scent. They bowed their heads, then went back to what they had been doing.

Francois had trained them well.

A late model Lexus waited in the driveway. Francois pulled a set of keys with a fob, pressed a button. The car responded by a quick *chirp*. Headlights blinked off and on twice. A soft *thunk* as the doors unlocked.

Hans took the front passenger seat. Francois slid in behind the wheel. William crawled in the back. It was all about the pecking order, the hierarchy of the wolves. Alphas invariably led from the front.

William had to earn the privilege of riding up front. Someday. But for now, he had to wait his turn. Besides, it was an honor just to be here. He had been selected for this important mission. He had been the envy of his fellow younglings earlier that evening.

Why was he chosen and not someone else? More than one Wolf had been jealous, envious, angry. But perhaps William was being groomed for great things. Best not to get on his bad side now. It could come back to bite them later.

Francois put the car in gear, turned and crept towards the sliding gate. As the headlights illuminated the heavy metal gate, a motor started grinding somewhere. The gate slid aside, providing access to the street beyond.

Security had been honed to split-second timing. The instant the trunk of the car edged past the opening, the motor ground again, pulling the gate back across, securing the perimeter.

Caleb drove south. He stayed in the right lane, keeping within a few miles per hour of the speed limit. His thoughts were not on the meeting ahead. All his thoughts swirled around to the woman he loved, the woman he had pledged his life and blood to.

He had done all he could. He had been honest with her, had told her the truth. The question was, could she deal with it? The decision would be hers, and he would respect it, no matter what. Even if it killed him inside. After all, what was he going to do? Lock her up? Stalk her? Slap her around until she saw things his way?

Not bloody likely.

People always had a choice in how they acted and reacted, how they conducted themselves, in matters both great and small. The flip side was each person had to shoulder the responsibility for their choices.

That was the tough part.

Caleb tried understanding what Marla was feeling. It was tough for him. Then for some reason, memories of his youngest sister popped into his head.

Sadie had died peacefully, having gone to sleep one night and simply slipped away. After the trauma and tragedy of her life, her passing had been painless.

He had felt compelled to attend her funeral. He had slipped in quietly, sat in the back during the service.

As the pastor droned on, he had looked around the sanctuary. He recognized several old timers, all in their seventies and eighties, that he had known as a child. Sitting in the back, he felt no threat. They all faced forward in their Sunday best, focused on the pastor. His anonymity did not last.

Eventually the church service concluded. Everyone stood up to accompany the pastor and the casket, born by six strong pallbearers to the cemetery behind the church.

He felt their eyes upon him, heard heartbeats accelerate. Heard gasps, saw shocked faces, recognition in their eyes. No, it couldn't be. It couldn't be Caleb. He would be, what, in his eighties by now? If he was still alive, that is. No, that must be a relative. A grandson. Had to be.

Right?

Caleb had stood by himself, separated by much more than the few feet between him and the rest of the mourners. People he knew, people he had played with at school, now tottered on canes. Bald heads, thick middles, eyeglasses perched on wrinkled, tired faces.

He saw fear in their eyes, smelled it on their clothes.

The graveside service concluded. Some people came up to him, introduced themselves, remarked how much he looked like Caleb Jacobsen. He introduced himself as Caleb's grandson. Caleb had passed away several years back, was buried in Seattle.

Greatly relieved, everyone smiled and nodded as if they had known it all along. This was Caleb Jacobsen's grandson, come in from the wilds of the great Pacific Northwest, so far away from these Missourians it may as well have been on a different planet. Out of small-town decorum, some asked if he was staying for a while. He assured them he was leaving on the morning train. He was a businessman and had to return immediately. More smiles and nods.

Perhaps he understood Marla's reaction now. She couldn't smile and nod things away.

Everyone smiles and nods when they hear an explanation that they want to hear, and none of this was what Marla had wanted to hear. Caleb shook his head, felt bad for her, felt responsible for putting her in the middle of this.

And here he was, going to a meeting of a completely different kind. This was dangerous for him, but much more dire for humankind.

He gripped the steering wheel tighter as he crested the Tacoma Narrows bridge. His anger slowly built inside him. There was still such a thing as right and wrong. Like all honorable men and women, Caleb Jacobsen had to live – or die! – by a moral code.

Human genocide violated his moral code. He would not stand aside and let this happen.

No fucking way.

He ground his teeth as he seethed. He would be dealing with creatures such as himself. Just as old, possibly older. Possibly stronger. He knew what had to happen. He knew he had to prepare himself mentally, to slip into "combat mode".

Time to go dark inside. Really dark.

Pitch black.

CHAPTER TWENTY-FOUR

Caleb exited the highway. After driving fast for so long, it felt like he had slowed to a snail's pace. Traffic around him ebbed and flowed.

His mind wandered, recalling werewolf folklore. Though werewolf legends appeared dating back to the Sumerian times, the modern concept surfaced in Europe during the Middle Ages. The illiterate populace looked to the Church for guidance in all things. The Church instructed them to believe anything they could not understand – or anything the Church did not condone - was inherently evil. So, werewolves automatically became the spawn of Satan. Caleb had pondered many times over the years if perhaps the old Europeans had been more correct than they knew.

But they had also been wrong about pretty much everything, too.

No full moons, of course. Since the Change was triggered by viral mutation to DNA, the cycle of the moon had nothing to do with it. Caleb liked to Change during a full moon, though. More light.

Wolfsbane? Please. That shit just gave him a nasty case of hay fever. He would sneeze for days. Antihistamines helped.

Silver bullets? Come on. Silver or not, bullets just pissed werewolves off. But hey. Getting shot *hurts!* It would piss anybody off.

There were ways to kill a werewolf. A shotgun blast to the head, for instance. Landmines, claymores. Even the regenerative powers of werewolf physiology had its limits. Fire was a death sentence, a horrifyingly painful one. And of course, he could be killed in battle by another werewolf.

Caleb turned into the parking lot of Pacer's, an upscale strip club. Not his kind of place. He had no moral qualms with strip clubs; they just weren't his thing. He parked, killed the engine. Still early, only a smattering of cars here and there.

Caleb climbed out of Jeep, locked his door. Keen eyes scanned the area as he prowled forward. He picked up several scents. Axle grease and engine exhaust comingled with asphalt. Cheap perfume, hurried sex, used condoms.

Werewolves.

Something familiar now. He had smelled this before, recently. The long-haired kid at the murder site. What the hell was he doing here?

Two others worried him. Both faintly familiar. Not recent, something farther back. Way back. A sense of real danger filled him as he stalked towards the entrance.

What the holy hell was he walking into?

Dusk painted the sky deep blue with bands of purple and black outside Caleb's house. Lights from the Naval Shipyard glittered, silver stripes across the water.

Marla fervently flipped through a magazine, her mind a raging storm. Russell had his phone out and his ear buds in, watching videos. Martinez sat in a chair, keeping his eye on everyone else.

Akin stood near the glass, looking out across the dark water. Martinez noticed the worry in her eyes. Crow's feet more pronounced. He heard her heart pounding.

Martinez rose, silently padded beside her. Without saying anything, he gazed out across the water.

"How you holding up?" he finally asked.

"Anything happens tonight, we can't stop it. Especially if there's more than one." She spoke quietly, hoping neither Marla nor Russell would overhear.

"Maybe nothing will happen."

"Do you really believe that?" Her eyes swiveled towards him. She saw her partner raise his shoulders, then allow them to drop. A shrug, noncommittal. It always irritated her when he did that.

Tonight, it pissed her off. "What?" she demanded. "What's going through that head of yours?"

Martinez breathed a moment. "Anything happens," he started, "head for the bathroom. Lock yourself inside."

"Why?"

"They won't kill them," he replied. "But we're collateral damage."

"What about you?"

"Don't worry about me."

"You said it yourself. They'll kill you."

"No, they won't."

Akin inhaled, started to speak. The air hitched, caught in her lungs. She took a step back, as if her partner carried some terrible, contagious disease.

Martinez stared at her, his eyes a glowing amber. Then they dimmed, replaced by his normal brown. He put an index finger up to his lips, indicating for her to be quiet. He pointed discretely in the others' direction, then brought the finger back up to his lips. He saw his partner purse her lips as she dug down within herself to wrestle control of her powerful emotions.

She leaned in and whispered, "How long?"

"Twelve years."

They both turned and gazed out at the water again.

"Caleb?" she asked.

"He's entrusted me to protect you while he's away."

"How does that work?"

"Keep close to the hallway so you can beat a hasty retreat at a moment's notice," Martinez said. He had already made up his mind what he would do. "I'll handle the rest."

She saw his head tick. His ears twitched. It was unsettling to see them move independently of each other. Her heart jumped up into her throat.

"Get to the bathroom," he whispered urgently. "Hide."

"But—"

"Hide. Now."

She turned without another word, strode towards the bathroom. Martinez walked across the room, positioned himself near Caleb's computer desk. Russell looked up, took his ear buds out just as Akin closed the bathroom door and locked it.

"What's up?" he asked Martinez.

Before Martinez could answer, the front door exploded inward, splinters flying, the remnants of the door twisting off its hinges with a sharp metal squeal. Marla yelped; Russell screamed. Martinez simply stood where he was.

Wooden shards lay scattered across the floor. Dusty silt floated on the air. They all stared at the open doorway, into the dark hole within the doorframe. Everything had gone silent.

Silent as the grave.

Then several brown *things* came spilling in from outside. Growling. Snarling. Snapping teeth. Frothing mouths. Demonic eyes.

No mercy.

Inside the bathroom, Akin panted in short gasps. She instinctively pulled her firearm, checked to make sure a round was in the chamber. She heard terrible high-pitched screams coming from Russell and Marla. Their voices were drowned out by the werewolves' roars.

The noise, already deafening, got louder. Furniture overturned. Glass broke. She backed away from the door, as if the noise outside was a physical force pushing her away. Somehow, her service pistol came up, pointing at the door. She tried to steady it with both hands. Her calves bumped something, and she nearly lost her balance. She had backed into the side of the bathtub.

A sudden silence registered in her fevered brain. She looked towards the door as if it would answer her unspoken questions. An agonizing moment of suspense ensued.

Akin realized someone – no *something* – had made its way down the hall and was standing right outside the door. She heard snorts as it exhaled, an impossible beast that could not be, and yet was. Her eyes focused on the doorknob as her entire being filled with panic.

The doorknob moved slowly, back and forth, clockwise, then counterclockwise. She inhaled as the doorknob jiggled. The great thing outside was testing the door, realizing she had locked it.

Akin suddenly found herself in the bathtub, hunkered in the bottom. Her pistol remained in her hands, her elbows bent, the gun held close to her face.

If she was going to die, then she was going to die fighting. Maybe take the bastard with her.

An honorable death.

Through the translucent curtain, she saw a huge hairy fist punch a hole cleanly through the hollow door. A blurred hand snaked down to the knob, unlocked the door. The hand and the furry arm to which it was attached retracted through the hole. The door swung open, easily, lazily. The entire house was silent.

Was anyone left alive?

A huge dark brown shape suddenly filled the room. Her wide eyes saw the blurry image as the werewolf swung its head from side to side, sniffing the air. Then the head swung back to the front, looked down.

Directly at her.

The great beast took one slow step forward, paused, then another. A low, guttural series of sounds came from the beast's throat. Not growls, not snarls. It sounded more like… *laughter.*

Laughter? Yes, laughter! The goddamned thing was laughing at her.

Outrage replaced fear. Her eyes hardened. Her jaw flexed, set. Resolute, she aimed her weapon as the werewolf took another step forward. Only about two feet away now, with nothing but a gossamer plastic shower curtain separating them.

Good enough for her.

She looked down the barrel of her weapon, sighting the spot between the huge ears, slightly above those goddamned glowing eyes. She calmed herself. Breathed in. Breathed out.

Then she fired her weapon, the report booming within the tiny room. The beast jerked back, crying out in pain and surprise.

Akin fired again, then again.

Over and over and over.

Until the hammer clicked and clicked on an empty chamber.

Caleb paid his cover fee. The bouncer looked like he could arm-wrestle Bigfoot. He informed Caleb of the two-drink minimum. Caleb nodded, pushed past the black curtain, then stepped over the threshold. The curtain fell into place behind him.

Just inside the entrance, he took it all in. Blaring music that hurt his ears. Lots of mirrored surfaces. Rotating lasers creating dazzling patterns across walls, the ceiling, the floor. The glare hurt his eyes.

The room was large, built around two separate stages, where at least one naked woman danced around each pole. Gawking men sat in club chairs, watching with bright eyes and slack jaws.

Dumb shits, Caleb thought. If any of these losers could actually develop a relationship with a real woman, they would be at home with the real thing. As it was, the only thing these yahoos were going home with would be a case of blue balls after the ladies had relieved them of all their money.

The place was only about half full. Tables near the stages, booths farther back. Some kind of half-assed buffet with hot dogs and barbequed meatballs. VIP rooms cordoned off by velvet ropes, thin curtains.

More security staff milled about, T-shirts tightly stretched across barrel chests, rock hard abs, and arms the size of tree trunks. All human. Caleb discounted them. As impressive as they looked, none posed a serious threat to him.

Movement at the edge of his vision. One of the VIP rooms. The curtain fluttered and out stepped someone Caleb remembered. Young, long brown hair, leather jacket. The werewolf from the other night.

William.

They locked eyes. Caleb's lip curled slightly, his anger rising. William showed no outward emotion. He simply stood there, motionless.

All other distractions fell away. The music didn't hurt his ears anymore. The smells of conniving women and desperate men dissipated. Bouncing breasts and undulating hips no longer registered. His entire universe contracted, narrowed to a kind of tunnel vision. The only thing that mattered now was William, and whoever else waited beyond the curtain.

Caleb made his way past people, moving at angles both towards and away from William. His body twisted, turned, moved this way and that. His head always faced William. He never took his eyes off the impudent whelp.

God, how he hoped he would get the chance to kill this smug little fuck.

He stepped up the two steps to the elevated dais outside the VIP room. William grinned. Caleb failed to see the humor.

"We meet again," William said. Caleb did not respond. He added, "We're happy you came."

Caleb refused to respond to this bottom feeder.

William sighed, jerked a thumb over his shoulder. "In there. Please. Go on in."

Before William could do anything, Caleb stepped forward on one foot, grabbed William by one shoulder and yanked with tremendous force, spinning the whelp around. Caleb stiff-armed him in the middle of his back, spilling William through the curtains.

Caleb followed him in.

A small room, semicircular. A rounded booth seat, wide enough to hold three or four people, fit into the curve of the wall. A low table sat before it. In the booth sat two werewolves in human form. One Caucasian, yellow blonde hair, icy blue eyes so pale they were almost gray. Broad forehead, high cheekbones, pointy chin. Descended from European aristocracy. Beside him sat an imposing, powerfully built African man. Close-cut hair, a hint of gray. Dark brown eyes the shape of almonds, skin such a dark it appeared black under the subdued lighting.

Something familiar about them. Caleb's hackles rose. He had definitely met them somewhere before.

Furious, William spun around. He surged forward, screaming, "Motherfucker!"

Caleb's arm shot out in a millisecond, grabbed William by the esophagus. The hand closed in a viselike grip, strangling off all air. Caleb growled, his teeth longer, his nose flatter.

"Professor Jacobsen," Hans said.

Caleb's amber eyes moved to him, calmed down. He pushed and released, sending William backpedaling. He never took his eyes off Hans. He was aware of Francois of course, but Francois was not his main concern.

William coughed and sputtered, his embarrassment projecting as anger. He took a step towards Caleb. He froze in place when Francois snapped his fingers loudly.

"William. Sit." The carefully pronounced words, the clipped ending told Caleb this man most likely came from Western Europe. Maybe France or Belgium.

William paused for only the briefest of moments. Then he dropped all pretenses of violence, moved around the table and sat down beside Francois, sulking.

"Good boy," Francois said, patting William's leg.

Caleb continued to stare at Hans. His gaze floated over the jacket, the cable knit sweater (which had to be imported), custom slacks, Italian shoes. Hand stitched. Impressive.

"Nice clothes," Caleb said.

Hans nodded gratefully. "I am flattered, Professor Jacobsen. You are Professor Caleb Jacobsen?"

"I am he." He paused, then, "And you are?"

Hans grinned. "Of course. Where are my manners? I am Hans. This handsome devil beside me is Francois, my oldest and dearest friend. You already know William."

Caleb looked into Francois' eyes. Threats and violence boiled in there. Francois stared back, unblinking and unafraid, the silent promise of high-order violence lurking just seconds in the future.

It took Caleb everything he had to keep from killing François right there. Their gaze broke only when Hans cleared his throat.

"Hans," Caleb started, "May I call you Hans?" Hans nodded. "I must say I am surprised you wanted a sit-down. Why not just kill me?"

"It crossed our minds," Francois barked.

Hans patted François' hand. "Now, François. Civility, yes?" He looked back to Caleb. "You see, Professor, violence against you is not my goal. I'd rather resolve our differences with at least a modicum of gentility."

"Gentility?" Caleb almost laughed in Hans' face. "Then let us speak of gentility."

"We have much to discuss, you and I."

"Well, I didn't come here for the show."

"Care to sit?"

"I'll stand.

They stared at each other for a moment, each waiting for the other to start. Finally, Caleb sighed his impatience.

"Let's not waste each other's time."

"Indeed," said Hans. He pointed to William. "He is a babe, a newborn werewolf, drunk on newfound powers. He still has no idea of his potential."

"Muzzle him and keep him the hell out of my way," Caleb warned. "Or I'll put him down."

Hans knew Caleb meant what he said. He also knew Caleb would not warn them again. He smiled again, trying to put Caleb at ease.

"Let us speak of reason and logic, professor. There's no need for animosity between us. No need for bloodshed over a simple misunderstanding."

Caleb pretended to consider Hans' words. "Actually, sir, I think we understand each other perfectly," he said darkly.

"Men such as us are not like him." Hans pointed at William, who looked lost and confused. "We have had time to grow into our lupine selves."

Caleb stifled a laugh. What the hell was this? Self-help for werewolves?

"Our lupine selves?"

"Do you have a better term?" Francois challenged.

Caleb ignored him.

"We are not so different, you and I." Hans watched as Caleb simply lifted one eyebrow in response. "I believe we have much in common."

"How?"

"We have survived for centuries. We have grown into the Wolf, our 'lupine selves', as it were. We have seen the arrogance and weakness of man play out across the world time and time again with the same disastrous consequences."

"I can't argue with that. Those who fail to learn the lessons of history are doomed to repeat its mistakes."

"Quite so, Professor." Hans paused. "How far back does your history expertise go?"

"How far does it need to go?"

"To the beginning of time," Hans said, leaning forward for the first time. "Do you know why mankind's earliest ancestors had eyes placed in the front of their skulls?"

"They were becoming predators," Caleb answered. "They came out of the trees to hunt."

"Exactly," Hans praised. "Two eyes in front provides for binocular vision, depth perception. The ability to gauge the distance between themselves and their prey.

"Three-dimensional vision," Caleb shrugged. "All mammal predators have it. What's your point?"

"We are the true predators on this planet, Caleb. We have surpassed the humans. We have evolved."

"Into what?"

"A superior species. Certainly, superior to these weak pathetic humans." Hans' pale eyes turned a more intense blue. "We are the apex predators on this planet, Professor. Wolves amongst the sheep, hunters in a world filled with prey."

"Oh please," Caleb countered. I've heard that 'superior species' bullshit before. Only they called it the 'Master Race'. And look at how that turned out. Look at the death and destruction that one madman's twisted vision of racism and hatred inflicted upon this world." Caleb paused again, smiled wryly. "Lessons of history, Hans."

Hans seemed unfazed. "Unlike them, we are descended from the Ancient Ones. Humans exist to feed and to serve us, just as pigs and cattle exist to feed them. It is our divine right to step forward, emerge from the shadows and reestablish our rightful place."

"It's really a crime against nature if we don't, when you think about it," Francois agreed.

"A crime against nature?"

Francois looked at Caleb as if he should understand already.

"Look at the sorry state of the world as it is with humans at the helm," François said, spreading his arms wide. "Continuous war, continuous strife. Poverty, hunger. Crime. Political and social unrest. Pollution, climate change."

"To leave them in charge is insanity," Hans said.

"How so?"

"The definition of insanity is allowing the same thing to happen over and over and expect different results, Professor."

"And you're going to solve all these problems?"

"It's time to cull the herd," Francois glared.

Caleb glared back.

"Come Professor," Hans said. "Humans had their chance, and they've made a dastardly mess of things. Yet a global werewolf shadow society already exists," Hans continued. "Every pack all over the world. Organized, efficient, and all loyal to me, the Global Alpha."

"Global Alpha," Caleb repeated. He had to admit, it had a nice ring to it.

"Think of it! No more wars. The world economy stabilized. Peace. Prosperity. A true New World Order were poverty and hunger would no longer exist."

"Sounds like a werewolf utopia," Caleb said. "The problem with utopias is, they sound great in theory. But they don't work in the real world."

"Werewolves already infiltrated all segments of society. Banks, finance, business, energy, real estate, entertainment, news, social media influencers, you name it," Hans said. "We already have shadow control of Government, law enforcement, trade crafts like mechanics, carpenters, heavy equipment, the list goes on."

"So, your plan is to slaughter the humans?"

Hans shrugged, unconcerned. "Only about half."

Caleb's mind reeled. "Half is about three and a half *billion* people."

"A drop in the bucket," Francois said.

"We herd the rest."

"So, your plan combines the worst aspects of Nazism and Sharia law," Caleb pushed. "When you've gained control, who emerges as Supreme Ruler?"

Hans looked genuinely surprised. "I am Global Alpha. What more needs be said?"

"And do we call you? *Mein fuhrer?*"

"Do not sound so high and mighty," Francois growled. "You have no moral superiority here. Did you not fight in America's Civil War? Did you not fight for the South, to keep people of my color enslaved?"

"I fought for my land and my family. Nothing more," Caleb said.

Francois smirked. "You also love the hunt and the kill, yes?"

Caleb's instinct was to kill Francois right now. He bit down on the impulse.

"You and I are nothing alike," Caleb stated. "We didn't ask to be dealt this hand; it was dumped our laps. Fair point. But using our condition to justify atrocious crimes against humanity isn't noble. It's cowardly.

"You see, Hans it's like this."

"Oh," François sneered. "You're going to tell us how it is?"

Caleb kept his eyes on Hans. "How we conduct ourselves in this world, how we play the cards that Life deals us defines who and what we really are. Good or bad. Hero or villain. Brave or coward.

"I control the Beast," Caleb continued, "but the Beast controls you. It consumes you." Caleb shook his head. "It doesn't matter what form you take. You are the Beast.

"I kill in order to live. But you," Caleb pointed at Hans, "you live to kill."

Dead silence.

"You're the darkness, Hans. You're the evil within us all. You're the worst of what we are."

Francois had heard enough. "I told you he would never join us." He waved a hand. "Let me kill him now, like we should have back in Montana."

Caleb felt like he had been hit with a sledgehammer. His eyes popped wide. His jaw dropped, then slowly closed. Caleb remembered where they had crossed paths.

That smell.

"You," Caleb breathed, trembling with rage. "You."

Hans nodded. "I did not mean to Make you. I intended to kill you."

"I wish you had."

"Hold your tongue," Francois interjected. "You have been given a precious gift."

"There's nothing left to discuss," Caleb said, still ignoring Francois. "I will never join your pack or support your plan."

"Traitor," Francois rumbled lowly.

Caleb's glowing eyes stayed locked on Hans. "In the end, this will come down to you and me."

Hans sat there, said nothing.

"Next time we meet," Caleb rumbled, "one of us will die."

Francois leaned forward, barely holding his violent tendency in check. "You'll have to kill me first."

Caleb's gaze slowly drifted to Francois. Amber eyes glowing, a wicked smile spread across his lips.

"I'm looking forward to it."

Francois bristled. Hans placed a placating hand on Francois' forearm. Francois breathed, sat back.

"That's right, Big Dog," Caleb said, stepping back. "Sit. Heel. Good boy. Do what your Master says." He watched Francois' lip curl into a snarl. "Learn to roll over, maybe he'll give you a treat."

He paused just in front of the privacy curtain, making certain none of them were going to attack. Then he exited quickly. A mild flutter to the curtain was the only evidence he had ever been there.

Hans sat back and sighed, appearing fatigued. Perhaps he had been stressing about this meeting more than he had been letting on, Francois thought.

Francois picked up the drink on the table in front of him. "Well, we tried it your way, *mon ami*." He upended the glass, threw his head back. The amber liquid slammed to the back of his throat. "Now it is my turn."

Hans pulled his hands down his face. "Very well." He sighed again. "Proceed as you see fit."

"I already have."

Caleb fought hard keeping his emotions in check as he drove towards Port Orchard. While the initial meeting had not ended in bloodshed, nothing short of an all-out werewolf war would stop Hans.

As he crossed into Kitsap County, his disquiet grew. He was not afraid for himself. Death held no terror over him. But he was worried for people like Russell and Marla.

Especially Marla.

If he lost – if he got killed – Marla would be singled out, made an example of because she was his Beloved. Scenarios ran through his head, dark visions of screams and torture, pain and blood. None of it ended well for her.

Over his dead fucking body.

Details of the meeting replayed over and over in his mind on a continual loop. Every word, tone, voice inflection had significance. Every glance, every movement, every gesture carried weight. They had to be only days away, perhaps only hours from unleashing horror upon humankind the likes of which had never been seen.

Caleb would never buy into this dementia, but he would have to break the most ancient and fundamental rule of werewolf survival: werewolf on werewolf slaughter.

But these were obviously exigent circumstances. A global pack, operating as an umbrella organization, with all packs deferring to the Master. There was only one path to avert global genocide.

Caleb would have to kill the Master.

Part of him wondered if humankind didn't deserve to be put in check. Humans demonstrated every day what a savage species they were. Cruel and unfeeling, neglectful of strangers under the rationalization they were simply minding their own business. They murdered each other *en masse* for reasons like religious intolerance, skin color, or where a line needed to be drawn on some map.

Yes, perhaps humankind's arrogance, its hubris in the delusional belief that the evil and misery humans heap upon each other is justified needs to be nipped in the bud, challenged in a big way.

But not like this.

He took the Tremont exit, as he had done hundreds of times before. He turned left turn onto Port Orchard Boulevard, travelled down the hill, turned left again onto Bay Street.

Tension ratcheted up. Something was wrong. Terribly wrong. He bit his lower lip as he turned into the driveway.

He immediately noticed the wrecked front door. He hit the brakes hard, skidded to a stop. Barely daring to breathe, he stared into the darkness beyond the doorway. No movement detected. His head swiveled, eyes scanning.

Nothing.

He opened the door, climbed down. He sniffed the air, caught lingering scents of other werewolves. He moved around the front of his Jeep, crossed the distance to his porch. He crept up the steps, slipped inside.

The door lay in shards and splinters at his feet. Darkness and silence greeted him. He crept forward, alert, ready to make the Change in a millisecond. Chairs overturned, glasses broken, drinks spilled. He mentally reconstructed what had happened.

The onslaught had been swift, violent. By the time they realized what was happening, it was too late. The werewolves had control of the space.

Shock and awe.

Overwhelming force.

The unmistakable coppery odor of blood reached his nose, drilled into his brain. His head twisted, looked to the dark hallway.

Aw, shit.

Swallowing a lump in his throat, he took his first faltering steps across the room. He glanced at his computer as he passed. It looked to be untouched.

He paused at the beginning of the hallway, peering into the shadows. A half-naked body lay in a heap on the floor, thrown against the wall opposite the bathroom. Something resembling raspberry jam splattered across the wall above the body.

Caleb sniffed the air again. He had met this person before. Pablo the werewolf.

Then he heard heartbeat accompanied by choked respirations coming from the bathroom. He moved forward, the stench of the body becoming more apparent. So did Pablo's mechanism of death.

Half of Pablo's head had been blown away above his eyebrows. Caleb guessed he had been shot twice by a large caliber handgun. No amount of regeneration would fix that. He noticed his ruined bathroom door swinging limply by one hinge.

Just what in the actual hell did they have against his doors?

The shower curtain contained several bullet holes. He glanced around, noticed several bullet holes in the wall behind him, the bathroom ceiling, the bathroom wall.

In a panic, someone had fired wildly, probably emptying their magazine. And whoever had fired was still in the tub, hunkered down, waiting for reinforcements.

Maybe they had reloaded.

"Hey," he called out. "It's Caleb."

Something dark moved behind the curtain. A gun barrel inched out, hooked the edge of the curtain, pulled it back. It pointed at him.

"It's Caleb."

"Caleb?" Akin.

"Yeah. Don't shoot me." He edged past the doorway just as she pushed the curtain further back. Pale face, frightened eyes.

He flicked the overhead light on. Akin squeezed her eyes shut in response. He reached down, offering her a hand. She took it, used it to balance herself as she unfolded her legs, got her feet under her.

"Jose sent me in here," she said. She stepped out of the tub, then let go of his hand. "I heard everything. I couldn't do anything." Her voice went higher. Her eyes flooded. "I couldn't stop them, Caleb. I couldn't –"

"It's okay," he said.

"I should have –"

"Stop that. Don't second-guess yourself."

"I was so Goddamned scared." Tears spilled down her face.

"You survived," he told her. "You live to fight another day."

They exited the small bathroom, stepped over Pablo's remains, walked back into the living room. Akin had expected the living room to be absolutely trashed. All things considered, it looked pretty good.

"They came in there." He pointed to the front doorway. "More than a few. They took Russell and Marla."

"What about Jose?" she asked.

"He threw in with them."

"What does that mean?"

Caleb gazed into the distance, focused on nothing in particular. "I told him what would happen if he acted a coward." His head cranked around until he was looking the trembling detective in the eye.

"I can't let you kill him."

Caleb's amber gaze cut right through her. "Try and stop me."

Akin thought quickly. "Where would they take them?"

The distraction worked. She saw that lethal look fade a bit, replaced by the intellectual professor. She had to remind herself that he, like most people, had several facets to his personality.

"Someplace safe. Fortified."

"Oh great," she said, exasperated. "How are we supposed to find that?"

Caleb moved past her, going back into the hallway. He knelt beside Pablo's corpse. Somehow, his jeans had not been ripped apart when he last Changed.

Lucky me, Caleb thought as he rifled through the dead werewolf's pockets. In the left hip pocket, he found what he was looking for. He extracted it, walked back into the living room.

Akin looked his way. "Catch," he called out. He tossed something small, dark, compact towards her. She caught it, looked down at it. Confusion. She held it up.

"A cell phone? How does this help us?"

"GPS history."

Akin understood. "Having that kind of software on a home system is against departmental regulations."

"Are you fucking serious right now?"

Akin withered under the question. "Fine." She pulled out her own phone.

Caleb scanned the great room as Akin punched a number. A couple of new doors hung and a discrete disposal of a bullet-riddled body and everything would be good to go.

Akin waited as the phone rang on the other end. Then, "Jodie? This is Detective Akin. I need a favor… No, it can't wait…"

Caleb breathed, forcing himself to not fall prey to the panic that kept threatening to break free and overtake him. He rubbed his beard with one hand as Akin continued to talk.

She nodded as if Jodie could see her through the phone. "Yes. I know it's a huge fucking favor, and yes, I know that it's technically illegal."

Caleb turned her way just as she said, "Look, this is as real as it gets. This is life and death."

Caleb made out the question that Jodie asked on the other end. How many?

"About half of the entire human race," Akin replied. "Now are you going to help us or not?" A beat, then Akin took the phone away from her face, punched the END CALL button. "She's in."

"Good."

"So, what's the plan, then?"

"Asymmetrical warfare," he replied. "Whenever someone wants you to look down, be sure to look up."

"You're talking in riddles," she said. "Look, they control this situation."

"Do they?"

"They have Marla and Russell."

"And you think that dictates my actions?"

"Of course."

"Then that's your mistake," he said flatly. "More importantly, it's theirs."

"Huh?"

"They've made two mistakes," Caleb said. "They've overestimated themselves, and they've underestimated me."

Akin stood there, frowning in confusion. He was speaking in riddles again.

"They think they know what I'm going to do. Trust me, they don't."

He turned to look at Akin again. Those damned swirling amber eyes. When he spoke again, his voice was deeper. Huskier. "All they had to do was leave me alone. But no. They've pressured me, invaded my territory, kidnapped and threatened death to my mate." He snarled again. "No. They fucking started this. What's coming they've brought upon themselves. And they don't have the first motherfucking clue just how hard and how fast I'm about to deliver this fight to *their* door."

"But they're werewolves, too. Just like you. And there's a lot of them. No matter what you do, they'll see it coming."

Caleb stood up to his full height. A supreme confidence that bordered on arrogance.

A true Alpha.

A sadistic smile danced across his lips. Something truly frightening in the eyes. "No, Sandra," Caleb Jacobsen said. "They won't see *this* coming."

CHAPTER TWENTY-FIVE

Akin paced back and forth, occasionally glancing out the back windows at the black water. Caleb sat in an easy chair. Under ordinary conditions, he would be sitting there enjoying some TV.

"I'm completely out of my depth here," Akin admitted as she paced. "What do we do next? Wait for Jodi to call back?"

Caleb considered the tactical situation. There were still gaps that needed to be filled.

"Well?" she asked impatiently.

"We climb into your car." He glanced out across the waters himself. "We drive at a leisurely pace. Give Jodi time to work her magic."

"Why the police car?"

"So you can call for reinforcements."

"What about you?"

"I don't need reinforcements," he said. "I am the reinforcements. I will either live or die." He shrugged. "Most likely, die."

"How can you be so fucking casual about it?"

"I'm a hundred and eighty years old, Sandra." He stood from his chair. "God never meant for me to live this long." He exhaled through his nose, almost a snort. He looked at peace. "Everything that lives, dies." His eyes drifted up to her. "It's the nature of things. It has to end for me sometime."

"And what about your friends?"

"Russell has been my friend a long time. I haven't always agreed with his life choices, but I've always liked him. But Marla," he paused again, his eyes going soft. "If my death can ensure her survival, then so be it. Fair trade."

Akin's admiration for this noble creature known as Caleb Jacobsen swelled. She looked away to keep from tearing up. She busied herself, checked her weapon, dropped the old empty magazine out, slapped a fully loaded magazine in. She racked a round into the chamber, flicked the safety on.

"Well then," she finally said, "let's get going."

All quiet at Hans's compound. The skies had cleared in the last couple of hours, twinkling with stars. A full moon, tinted faint red and coppery orange, hung in the heavens above.

Blood Moons were a well-documented natural phenomenon caused by light refraction cast upon the moon during a lunar eclipse. But that night the overall effect created a chilling atmosphere to which even Hans was not immune.

The werewolves outside growled under their breaths. Agitated by something intangible in the air, they prowled their sectors. Amber eyes bounced malevolent fireflies in the darkness. They kept craning their necks, sniffing the air, looking skyward.

All spoiling for a fight.

William the werewolf was doubly agitated. After Caleb Jacobsen had left the strip club, he had wanted to stay. Have some drinks, see the show. Maybe even get laid right there in the VIP room. But Hans and Francois had stood to leave immediately. When he had voiced his suggestion, Francois had shut him down. Hard. Hans, the Master, had not even given it a second thought.

Man, that Francois was a real asshole, William thought as he patrolled the perimeter, hands flexing, claws clicking as he moved. Already chafed at being nothing more than a lap dog, William itched to move up the ranks. But Francois seemed determined to treat him in a dismissive, condescending manner. He clearly considered William replaceable. Expendable.

Well, if that's what Francois thought, he had another thing coming. William was neither replaceable nor expendable. Maybe that Frenchman needed to be taught that lesson. And maybe William was the one to teach him. He liked that idea. A lot.

But for the moment, he would bide his time and wait to make his move. Just a brief moment when Francois was vulnerable. Then he would strike.

They thought he had not been listening. Oh boy, were they ever so very fucking wrong. Francois underestimated him. Even the Master did not see his full potential. Well, he would show them. He would show them both.

He would show them all.

He moved away from the back of the house. The night was cold. The grass was wet. He smelled the salt air. He heard the faint thunder of waves lapping at the shore far below. He saw the Tacoma

Narrows Bridge in the distance. He could still make out the faint green color of the iron, along with the headlights of vehicles crossing back and forth.

He crept as close to the edge of the precipice as he dared. He did not understand why no safety fencing had ever been erected. He knew he could survive the fall, but he also knew it would hurt like hell. And recuperation would be a bitch.

He leaned out and looked down. Black and brown cliffside tumbled almost straight to the water. The thin strip of gravel beach below was punctuated by boulders that had become dislodged over time and had tumbled to the bottom.

The gentle surge and recession of the water continued to make a gentle slap and roar moving in, followed by a quiet hiss as it pulled back out. He could see the white foam slithering amongst the rocks, lit up in relief to its dithered surroundings.

What was the term for this? Effervescent? Bioluminescent? William didn't know. All he knew was that the foam glowed, and it looked cool.

Still clicking his claws together, feeling dread and not understanding why, he continued his patrol. As he trudged towards the far end of the property, he swung his head towards the house. All the curtains were drawn, doors and windows locked and secured.

Big things afoot.

Inside, the air crackled with tension. Everyone looked around, licking their lips. Perspiration dotted foreheads.

Russell and Marla both sat at the kitchen table. They were not bound or gagged, but they knew better than to bolt. A prison without bars was still a prison. They knew they were hostages.

"You guys want something to eat or drink?" Jose Martinez asked them pleasantly.

Russell glared at him, said nothing. Marla threw him a withering sneer.

"Hey," Martinez said in response, "just because you can't leave doesn't mean you have to starve."

"We're fine," Russell grumbled.

"Look at you," Marla spat. "Acting like we're all best friends."

"We are friends."

"Fuck you!" she shouted venomously. "You were never our friend. You're a goddamned traitor."

"Don't be so judgmental," Martinez said. "You don't know how tough a decision this was for me."

"You stood by and did nothing while those things grabbed us," Russell said. He looked up, daggers in his eyes. "Looked pretty fucking easy to me."

"Okay. You got me," Martinez said, shrugging. "Turns out, it was pretty easy."

"You're a traitor to your kind," Marla declared.

"We are his kind," Hans said as he strode into the kitchen from a second entrance. He was followed close behind by Francois and Diane. Marla noticed the heavy makeup on Diane's face in a futile attempt to hide facial bruises. No amount of makeup could cover up the swollen lip and jaw.

"Did you do that?" Marla demanded hotly.

"A minor misunderstanding," Hans grinned, looking like a Great White shark on two feet. "And completely irrelevant to the matter at hand."

"Killing us accomplishes nothing," Russell stated.

"Who said anything about killing you?"

Russell did not believe him. "Kidnapping us accomplishes nothing, either."

"I beg to differ, Professor Slater" Hans countered, holding up an index finger as he said, "it already has accomplished something."

"I don't follow."

"There's a surprise," Francois muttered under his breath.

"I've gone into his territory, invaded his Den, and taken his most prized possessions. I have shaken his ego and self-esteem to its core. He will be as you say, beside himself."

"Listen up, dipshit," Marla pointed at him. "You have no fucking idea what you've done, what kind of hell you've unleashed upon yourselves."

Still grinning Hans ran a hand over his face. "Really?"

"Caleb Jacobsen will track us down. He will find this place. And he will come for us."

Francois rolled his eyes. Diane simply stared glumly at the floor.

"I don't think you understand—"

"No, you don't understand," Marla interrupted. "You think you've shattered him? Think again. Right now, Caleb Jacobsen is

Death on two legs." She paused, then, "That's right. Death is coming, tonight, coming here, coming for all of you. And when he arrives, all Hell will follow in his wake."

"Well, now I'm scared," Francois quipped.

Hans ignored him. "I don't think so, Dr. Moreno. He wouldn't dare."

"And why is that?"

"Because I have my Pack," he said. "Not just here, but all over the world. He has no one. No Pack. No loyalty. No backup."

"He could bring the police," Russell said.

"We own the police. We own entire Governments. In every country, and on every continent on Earth." He paused briefly. "Even Antarctica. Let that one sink in."

The room was quiet for a moment. The defiant fires in Marla's and Russell's eyes faded.

"This is not a movie, young lady," Hans chastised. "Caleb Jacobsen is not some conquering hero in some mediocre novel written by a midlist author. He is isolated, alone, and worried sick about you two. He will do exactly what I tell him to get you two back."

"So, you do plan to give us back?" Russell asked

"Of course I do," Hans nodded. "Once my Plan is in motion, there's nothing Caleb can do to stop it. My victory will be complete."

Hans turned and exited the kitchen. Francois and Diane followed behind him. Outside in the open area right before the living room, Francois tapped Hans on the shoulder.

"You don't really intend to give them back, do you?"

"False hope now makes their final moments a much crueler fate."

In the kitchen, Martinez could not help but overhear. His eyes turned to his two charges. They had not heard anything. What a couple of saps.

"What's so funny?" Russell asked.

"Nothing," Martinez responded.

"So, is what he said true?" Marla asked.

"About what?"

"About werewolves positioned in all layers and all aspects of the human infrastructure, poised and ready to strike in one glorious global ascendance?"

"Probably."

"We trusted you," Marla said. "Caleb trusted you!"

"Then Caleb's a fool!" Martinez shot back, suddenly angry. "He knew me, knew my secret. He knew I couldn't kill them all if they attacked *en masse*, which is what they did. And you know what he told me?"

"What?"

"That he expected me to either protect you or die trying."

"And if you didn't?"

"He said he would kill me."

"Then you better worry, pal," Russell said. "I've known Caleb a long time. I've never seen him fail to keep a promise. If he says he's going to kill you, he will."

Martinez turned this over in his mind. Russell saw the confident façade slip. A brief instant of uncertainty, perhaps even fear floated across his face. Russell saw it. Bingo! Then it was gone.

"He's going to singlehandedly bring all this down?" He threw his arms wide, gesturing to everything around him. "I doubt it."

"You willing to bet your life on that?"

"Stay here," Martinez ordered. "I'll be right back."

He turned and disappeared around the corner. Russell got up, went to the refrigerator. He opened the door, leaned in, peered inside. Marla watched as he stood back up, closed the door. He turned around holding a soda in one hand, a beer in the other. He sat back down, placing the two beverages in front of him.

Without waiting, Marla reached out, grabbed the beer, pulled it towards herself. Russell watched in dismay as she popped the top, drank from the can. He had intended the beer for himself. He opened the soda, took a drag.

"I was thinking. The last words I said to him," she said. "They were cruel, spoken in fear and anger." She choked up.

"He understands."

"What if I never have a chance to make things right with him?" Her voice cracked.

"You will."

"You really believe that?"

Russell gestured with a wave of one hand. "I have to."

Outside, the Blood Moon still hung to the southeast. It slid higher in the sky, nearing its zenith. The eclipse would end soon, but for now the earth and moon were in a moment of synchronous orbit.

Jodi called. Seemed young Pablo had spent a lot of time at one particular address. Caleb memorized the street number, hung up.

"Exit nine," he said to Akin.

The unmarked police car exited the state highway, took the off-ramp to the traffic light. The car turned left, drove over the highway then descended following the winding road. Akin craned her neck, searching for intersections and address numbers in the dark.

"Turn here."

She yanked on the wheel suddenly, throwing Caleb into the side of his door.

"Sorry," she said.

He grunted. He kept staring out the passenger window. Patterns whizzed past, made by the thick bushes and tall trees, reflecting across the tinted glass. Ironic, really. Here he was, about to die within the hour, and he was calmer about it than she was. But then, she hadn't spent the last two centuries living every day, every minute in the shadow of Death, had she?

He looked down at the phone. "Turn around."

Akin braked, skidded in the middle of the roadway. "What?"

"Back to the last intersection."

She cranked the wheel, turned a slow wide arc, then went back the way they had come.

She slowed at the intersection. The road bent right almost immediately. She turned the wheel, making a smooth turn.

"This is it," Caleb announced.

She eased the car onto the soft dirt shoulder, keeping only the driver's side tires on the pavement. She killed the engine. He handed the phone back. They sat in silence for a beat.

Caleb leaned forward, craned his neck up. He scanned the sky, the trees. A night breeze ruffled the leaves, swayed the branches. The tops undulated to nature's rhythm.

She followed his eyes upwards. She also saw the trees swaying. So what?

"The wind is coming in off the Sound," he said, reading her mind. "Off the Sound, across the house, towards us."

She still didn't get it.

"We're upwind," he explained. He pointed to a huge, impressive wall down the lane. "They can't see me; they won't smell me. They won't know I'm there until it's too late."

"And what am I supposed to do while you're saving the world?"

"Nothing," he said emphatically. "Absolutely nothing. If you see werewolves coming over that wall or out that gate, burn rubber. Get the hell out of here."

"But—"

"No 'buts'. You see anything not human coming at you, you get the fuck out of Dodge. Got it?"

Before she could say anything else, he opened his door and stepped out. She watched him stand there a moment, then gently push the door shut only until it latched. A quiet sound, soft, easily overlooked. Then she watched him move fluid as water, smooth as smoke on a breeze, around the front of the car and to her side. She lowered the window halfway.

"But why you?"

"I'm the only one available."

"But why—"

He bent at the waist, his face close to hers, deadly serious. He paused a moment, then sighed, a man carrying the weight of the world on his shoulders.

"It is the responsibility of the strong to protect the weak from the evils of this world."

My God, Akin thought. I can see why she loves him.

"If I'm not back in an hour, head for the precinct," he whispered.

She nodded. Tears rimmed her eyes. She wanted to say something, knew she needed to say something, but had no idea what it was.

Caleb stood back up. "Detective Sergeant, it's been an honor."

Her breath caught in her throat. He knew he was going to his death. And yet here he was, taking time to tell her goodbye.

"The honor has been mine, sir."

For a beat, they simply stared at each other.

Akin opened her mouth to say something, to say anything, only to be stopped before she started by Caleb simply raising an index finger to his lips.

"Nothing left to say." He took a single step backwards, but never broke eye contact with her.

"One way or another," he said, "this ends tonight."

His finality struck her like a physical force. It pushed her back into her seat, knowing nothing would deter him from whatever suicide mission he had planned. She touched a button on the arm of her door. The window closed. Within the perceived safety of her unmarked car, she watched Caleb advance up the road. He loped away easily like he was going for a jog, using the shadows cast as camouflage.

She blinked, looked down, rubbed her eyes. Why the hell was she crying? By the time she looked back, he had disappeared completely. He was nearby, she knew. Getting ready to do the last thing they thought he would ever be brave enough or stupid enough to do – take the fight to them; to spill their own blood on their own doorstep, deep in their own territory.

Deep down, she knew she would never see him alive again.

Caleb moved quietly, keeping to darkness and shadow. The wind could shift any time. Surprise was crucial to attaining his first goal: getting over the wall undetected. Then he would savagely wade through the foot soldiers. Get inside. Rescue Russell and Marla. And like the Spartans of long ago, leave nothing but dead, broken bodies in his wake.

Not much of plan, but it was what he had.

Moving parallel to the compound, he picked up the werewolves' breathing, the light stamp of their feet on the ground. He stopped, squatted down in the tall grass, calmed himself. He closed his eyes, emptied his mind.

Then he pushed. His mind, his consciousness, his sense of awareness expanded outward from him in invisible waves. He concentrated harder, directing them, channeling them. Over the wall, across the lawn, into the house.

Marla in the kitchen.

Russell close to her.

Martinez.

Caleb opened his eyes, breaking contact. He moved backwards, working deeper into the blackness until his back touched the bottom of a cyclone fence. He leaned back, slid down, allowing his legs to unfold in front of him. He pulled his boots off, his socks. He stuffed a sock into each boot so he could find them later.

Assuming he didn't get killed.

He peeled off his jacket, his shirt. Placed them beside his boots. He stood, unbuckled his jeans, pushed them down, stepped out of them. Pulled his underwear off.

Cold air washed over bare skin. Goosebumps rose. Cremaster muscles contracted involuntarily, shrinking his scrotum and pulling his testicles closer to the warmth of his body.

But it was not just the cold air. Caleb admitted to himself that he was afraid. Not of dying, per se, but of dying before he could save them. He was afraid of failing. Of not being there for Marla.

And for Russell, of course.

Caleb pushed all self-doubt from his mind. He allowed his anger, his outrage to rise. These assholes had started this.

Caleb Jacobsen was going to Goddamned well finish it.

His back molars ground together. He steeled himself for what came next. The pain. He shook his head, determined.

Nothing to it but to do it.

Fangs sprouted. Hair grew. Muscles coiled like snakes under his skin, doubling in size and strength. Height and weight increased. Bones and ligaments snapped unpleasantly as they broke, reformed, healed. He winched as rib cage lengthened. Pain flashed as knee joints reversed and ankles strengthened. Hands and feet flattened, widened. Claws extended.

His nose flattened, blackened. His face narrowed, melted, extended as the fractured bones shifted underneath, lengthened, healed creating his muzzle.

Caleb's hairy chest rose and fell with his breathing. Fully transformed and ready for the fight of his life, he stood well over seven feet now, weighed over 350 pounds. All teeth, muscle, and bone. Plus, the cognizance, cunning, cruelty of a human along with the instincts, power, and primal savagery of the Wolf. Determination coursed through him like the blood in his veins. His hatred for them and everything they stood for seethed like a boiling cauldron, delivered to every cell.

Caleb stared at the wall directly across the street from where he now stood. His lip pulled upward into a snarl. He dropped to all fours, hands curled to sledgehammer fists on lengthened arms. He crouched back, summoning energy into his formidable leg muscles. He exploded forward, picking up speed and momentum. By the time he made it to the pavement, he was already moving at full speed, a fur-covered freight train barreling towards the wall.

Caleb Jacobsen was now a demon of vengeance.

Sandra Akin sat in the unmarked police car, paralyzed by indecision. She couldn't just sit here and do nothing. Yet every scenario she envisioned started with her getting out of her car and ended with her own death.

Movement caught her attention. Her eyes popped wide. An incredibly huge blur of an animal bolted from the darkness and bounded across the road. By the time she realized it was Caleb, he was already to the other side.

Then she witnessed something her rational mind could not reconcile. The incredible beast pushed off with massive hind legs and launched itself lithely into the air, easily clearing the high wall. It arced over and downward, disappearing from view.

Wind whistled past Caleb's ears as he sailed through the air. He extended his knees, pulled his feet up. He cleared the wall and immediately zeroed in on his first opponent, a werewolf sentry, his back to Caleb.

Too bad for him.

Caleb slammed into the hapless werewolf from behind. Both went tumbling to the ground. Caleb recovered first, rose to one knee and slashed, clawing through the other werewolf's throat just as the doomed sentry vocalized an alarm. The cry gurgled as Caleb ripped through the esophagus, cleaving vocal cords asunder.

Blood spurted from ruptured carotid arteries, sprayed in all directions. The dying werewolf clutched his throat with one hand, blindly slashed out with the other. Caleb stepped back and watched the young werewolf's legs go rubbery. By the time he collapsed, Caleb was already moving away.

William heard the commotion, the strangled yelp. An alarm! He growled and bolted, running towards the front.

In the front, Caleb was being challenged by another foot soldier. Growls and snarls, neither backing down. Caleb was about to attack when another werewolf came charging from around the far corner of the house. He recognized William.

Fine by Caleb. He had wanted to kill William from the first instant they met.

William launched himself into the air. Caleb ducked. As William sailed over Caleb's head, Caleb shoved one hand upwards, claws extended. He raked William's underside, rib cage to pubis.

William hit the ground hard. Grunting, he tried to stand. Gravity finished what Caleb had started. The four deep rents laced down his front flared open. Blood spilled onto the ground like black water.

Then William's intestines fell out.

Caleb, narrow eyes burning a deep orange, leapt upon William, bit into the side of his neck. He twisted violently to one side, snapping several of William's cervical vertebrae. A vertebral facet splintered, jammed into William's spinal cord, killing him instantly.

The second foot soldier, anonymous and inexperienced, watched in horror. What was he supposed to do against a monster like this?

Caleb rose, his fur peppered with the blood of fallen enemies. Eyes bright, teeth slimed red, muzzle dripping.

His gaze fell upon the foot soldier, who crouched, growling. The growls were not a prelude to attack. They communicated fear. The other werewolf was saying, *Please don't kill me.*

Caleb noted William's remains, a ruined mass of flesh and bone. Useless to anyone. But Caleb had a deliciously sadistic idea. He grabbed William by the ripped throat. He lumbered towards the cowering werewolf, dragging William's carcass alongside him.

The old bloodlust was back. Caleb did not fight it, didn't even try. He needed it to stay alive and save his friends. He gave himself to it, ancient hatred flooding his body. It had been a long time since he had experienced this.

He had forgotten how goddamned good this felt.

Inside the house, the atmosphere quickly went from tranquility to high tension. Foot soldiers inside the house made the Change and headed outside roaring, itching for the fight to come.

Both Marla and Russell noticed the commotion. So did Martinez. He turned towards the sounds, a worried look on his face.

"You look scared," Marla observed.

Martinez peeked out into the rest of the house. "You should be worried about yourself."

Francois stalked in from the opposite end of the kitchen. His face was set, his stride filled with purpose.

"Martinez." He kept stalking through, never breaking stride. He never looked at Marla or Russell as he walked out. Martinez fell in line behind Francois.

"They look worried," Russell said.

Marla's face lit up. "He's here." She shook her head in wonder. "He's risking his life, risking everything to save us."

"He's in love with you."

"I've treated him terribly."

"He doesn't hold grudges."

"I'd deserve it if he dumped me."

"Give the man some goddamned credit, will ya?"

Marla recoiled at Russell's chastisement. He had a point. Why couldn't she trust Caleb? So what if he was a werewolf, a mythical creature, a Beast of Legend? And so what if he was 180 years old? He didn't look a day over 40, and he had pledged his undying love and fidelity to her in such a way she knew he meant it.

So, what was her problem? Why couldn't she commit? Oh yeah, that's right. *Because he's a fucking werewolf!*

A tremendous commotion outside shattered the quiet. Thuds against the walls, crashes. Pottery breaking. Growls and roars like huge dogs in a fight. Yelps and howls of pain and fright, more roars and growls.

More people scrambled about inside. Voices, this time laced with fear, Marla and Russell temporarily forgotten. The commotion got louder, moving closer from outside. They dashed to the window, threw the curtains open and craned their necks, peering outside.

Russell went pale. His mouth dropped open.

"Oh my God," Marla muttered.

A fight to the death raged outside. One werewolf, already bleeding, backtracked in the face of another werewolf of enormous bulk, who appeared to be dragging something beside it along the ground. It took Marla a moment to realize what it was.

The disemboweled corpse of another werewolf.

Marla's breath caught in her throat. Her eyes bulged when she realized who that huge brutal bastard was.

"Caleb," she whispered.

Outside, the retreating werewolf's back slapped into the wall. Nowhere left to go. Desperate, he roared and sprang. Caleb brought one leg up and kicked. Hard. His gigantic foot struck the other werewolf square in the chest. The impact sent him sailing back against the wall, bouncing off like a rubber ball. Caleb heaved William's corpse high and over in a savage arc, crashing down on the head of the stunned werewolf in front of him. He used William's body as a bludgeon again.

Again…

And again.

He pummeled his enemy until the doomed whelp lay on the ground dazed, unable to fight back. Caleb dropped William's mutilated body, grabbed the stunned werewolf by the throat and hoisted him up off the ground. He slammed his victim into the wall relentlessly again and again. Dark blood splattered across the wall from the back of the werewolf's pulverized skull.

Caleb examined the misshapen head of the dead werewolf. He allowed himself a moment of grim satisfaction, then heaved the body away from him.

Caleb turned with surprising speed and scampered off around the corner of the house. He disappeared into the inky blackness.

Russell and Marla stood at the window, frozen in shock.

"Get away from the window."

Startled, they turned to see Martinez. He tried to put on a brave face, but they saw through it. He was scared shitless.

"What's it like to know you only have minutes to live?" Russell asked casually.

Martinez's eyes darkened. "You tell me."

"At least I won't die a coward."

Martinez snapped his teeth and growled. Behind him, Francois appeared in the doorway, looking displeased. He grabbed Martinez roughly by the shoulder.

"Time to earn your place in the Pack." He pointed at Marla. "Bring her." Without waiting for an answer, Francois turned and walked out.

Martinez motioned to Marla. "You heard the man."

"I don't take orders from murderers."

Martinez surged forward so fast it caught both Marla and Russell off guard. He brushed past Russell, grabbed Marla by the shoulder, pulled her towards him so hard she nearly fell.

Russell tried to intervene. "Now wait a minute—"

Martinez snarled and lashed out, knocking Russell back and onto the floor. He pulled Marla in front of him. He shoved the middle of her back, forcing her to either move forward or fall flat.

Half stumbling out of the kitchen, she took the scene in. A couple of young men raced towards the front door. To her left she saw huge French doors that opened to the back yard. Francois stood halfway up an ornate, winding staircase. Hans and Diane stood at the top of the second story landing. Hans rested one hand casually on the bannister, as if he hadn't a care in the world.

"They're fleeing," Martinez observed.

Hans spoke from on high. "We don't need them to kill Caleb Jacobsen. That's what we have you for."

Martinez gulped. Francois smirked. Jacobsen would rend Martinez in two without much effort. If by some miracle Martinez defeated him, so much the better. Either way, it was going to be entertaining.

Movement caught Marla's eye. More people scurrying out the front door into the night.

Rats fleeing a sinking ship.

She expected to hear screams, roars, the rending of flesh. All she heard was silence.

Martinez's eyes flitted in all directions. Francois sniffed, licked his lips. He leaned back against the wall, conserving his strength. He folded his arms across his muscular chest, checked his nails.

When this was over, he needed to get a manicure.

Hans ticked his head slightly, listening intently. He wondered if the markets would open up or down Monday morning. Diane stood sullen beside him. He did not need to read her thoughts. The honeymoon was over, and he could not have cared less.

The house, like the night outside, fell quiet. Oppressively so. Francois looked to Hans, wanting an answer to his unspoken question. Hans simply shrugged. Time stretched; seconds felt like minutes.

A deafening crash of breaking glass pierced the silence, followed by sparkling shards exploding inward at the back entrance. Something huge and brown and wet and red hurtled through, landed on polished hardwood floors. It slid several feet, leaving a slick red trail.

More silence as everyone recovered from the surprise. They all looked at the mangled thing that lay on the floor, broken, rent asunder, eyes glazed, mouth open, tongue lolling, intestines flopped across the floor.

William.

The violence visited upon him had been devastating. The mangled corpse had been ripped and twisted in unnatural directions. It was difficult to conceive this mountain of gruel had ever been a living being.

Which was exactly what Caleb had intended. *You like invoking terror, Hans? Surprise, motherfucker. Two can play that game.*

Both Marla and Martinez stood frozen in shock. Francois lifted one eyebrow. Impressive. Even Hans himself nodded his head in acknowledgement.

A low rumbling emanated from somewhere outside, wafted in on the night breeze. Something guttural. Primordial. Older than time itself. It reverberated throughout the room.

Martinez recognized it for what it was, for *who* it was. Ice gripped his spine. He fought to keep from pissing himself.

A shadow, starting low and rising up, stretched long across the floor until it reached Marla and Martinez. They looked up towards the doors just as the shadow inched upwards, covered them, enveloped them.

Caleb Jacobsen lumbered slowly up the steps onto the back porch. His body swayed, shoulders rolling as he moved. His legs lifted high, the extra joints pulling his feet close to him, just like the Wolf with whom he shared DNA. He paused at the entrance, completely filling the doorway. Orange eyes focused on Martinez the Traitor. Martinez the Coward.

Caleb's next kill.

"Good morning, Professor Jacobsen," Hans called out.

Caleb's ears twitched. He did not move. Not yet.

Hans gestured towards what had once been William. "We received your calling card. Please. Do come in."

CHAPTER TWENTY-SIX

They didn't need to ask twice.

Another low growl boiled out from deep within Caleb's chest. His eyes looked up, danced around the doorframe. Baring his teeth at Martinez, he reached out, slapped his palms on each side of the doorframe. He ducked his head, rolled one shoulder back. He stepped forward, squeezed his way through the shattered opening.

Once through, he took another step to get a better view. Francois on the staircase to the left. Threat. Hans at the top of the stairs. Threat.

Martinez in front of him.

No threat.

Caleb's eyes shifted right. Russell at the kitchen doorway. His eyes shifted back directly in front of him. Marla. And Martinez, holding her by the arm. Putting his filthy paws on Caleb's mate? His Alpha Female, his Beloved, his Queen?

HOW DARE HE!

Orange eyes darkened further as his fury built. He squared up on Martinez. Hands closed to fists. Upper lip lifted, exposing fearsome teeth. The pressure was building. Everyone knew it. Caleb trembled, unbridled hatred and boundless rage; a volcano ready to erupt.

In one swift movement, Caleb bent at the knee into a crouch, threw his arms wide, claws extended, thrust his head forward in front of his swelling chest. He opened his maw and ROARED his outrage, his hatred, his sense of betrayal. Marla and Martinez recoiled, his roar smashing them like a physical force.

A decorative vase sitting on a nearby console table shattered from the decibel level of Caleb's scream.

Caleb put one huge foot forward, then another. Hands flexing. Steak-knife claws clicking together. Eyes angry. Soul hating.

Martinez let go of Marla, took a step back. Looked left and right.

No escape.

"Time to get bloody, Detective," Hans called from the top railing.

Realizing his time had come, Martinez made the Change. His clothes stretched, then ripped and fell away as he grew. Fur almost black, eyes yellow. Younger in the Wolf, he was smaller than Caleb.

It was sink or swim time. Fight or die.

He extended his claws, growled in response. Caleb's lips pulled back, forming a menacing snarl – or perhaps just a malevolent grin. He had been looking forward to this.

"Marla," Francois called. "You might want to move."

She quickly complied.

Caleb smelled the fear wafting off Martinez. The smaller werewolf was ready to piss himself. It made no difference. The time for mercy had come and gone. Martinez had made his choice. Now he would suffer the consequences.

Caleb's massive legs coiled under him like taut springs. Martinez bared his teeth. His black hair stood on end, making him look bigger. Caleb was not intimidated. He sprung, flinging himself through the air.

Shocked, Martinez raised his hands and extended his claws as Caleb, all 350 pounds of him, slammed into Martinez with bone-crunching force. The impact lifted Martinez off his feet. They both went tumbling, sprawling and sliding across the polished floor.

All eyes watched as Caleb and Martinez bit, slashed, growled, yelped. Teeth flashed. Claws slashed. Skin split open. Blood flowed, mixing fresh with old.

Terror blinded Martinez. An inexperienced fighter, he slashed wildly. He landed a lucky downward strike. A single claw managed to cut a deep furrow on Caleb's forehead just over his left eyebrow. The furrow opened up ragged, following Martinez's fingernail. Blood spilled down Caleb's face.

That instant of hesitation as Caleb blinked was all Martinez needed. He managed to curl one leg up between them and kick. His foot impacted Caleb just below his ribcage and sent him flying.

Surprised his gambit worked, Martinez pushed forward. Strike a mortal blow before Caleb could recover. He had taken two steps when Caleb scampered to his feet. Blood stained his abdomen.

Francois watched the fight. He had no personal stake in it. If by some miracle Martinez vanquished Caleb, fine. But if, as he suspected, Caleb dispatched Martinez, then Francois would put Caleb out of everyone's misery himself.

His eyes drifted to the kitchen entrance. The fat human, what was his name? Russell. Yeah. Russell. He kept glancing around, occasionally looking over his shoulder.

What the hell was the puny mortal thinking about?

With all eyes on the incredible battle raging on the floor, Russell thought no one was watching him. He could not get to Marla. She was too far away, two warring werewolves between them. What to do?

The underlings had fled once the dying started. They were practically alone in the house. He had a clear route to the other kitchen entrance. Beyond that, a straight shot to the front door.

Make a run for it. Get help, call Detective Akin.

He shrunk back from the doorway, turned right. He crept along as quietly as he could. Once he made it to the front door, he'd haul his fat ass. Call in reinforcements—

Russell stopped in his tracks. His heart sank; the color drained from his face. In front of him, impossibly, stood Francois, leaning casually against the frame of the doorway.

"*Non, non, mon ami,*" Francois shook his head. "You can't leave now. Things are just getting interesting."

"Send me an email," Russell quipped. He moved to walk around Francois. Francois pushed off the frame, stood squarely in the doorway.

It was time for Francois to stop playing with his food.

Russell inhaled, as if to speak, then exhaled, sighing. His shoulders slumped in defeat. Francois smiled. He reached, put a comforting hand on the human's shoulder.

"Come. Let us watch your friend die together."

Russell came up swinging. Hard. He caught Francois completely by surprise with an uppercut that snapped Francois' head back and then back forward on the end of his neck. Russell followed that up immediately with a straight left that connected solidly with Francois' nose. The bone yielded with an audible pop.

Blood gushed. Francois staggered backwards, dropped to one knee. Russell charged him, kneed him in the chest. As he tried to slip past, Francois grabbed Russell's pant leg, yanked hard. Russell felt as if a giant force had just cut swept his feet out from under him. He smacked the floor hard.

Francois rolled over, grabbed Russell by the back of his shirt and pulled back, sending Russell's girth off the floor and sailing back into the kitchen area. He landed at a low angle and went sliding across the tiled floor.

Breathing heavily, Russell said, "Hey Francois. Looks like you got a Roman nose. It's roaming all over your fucking face!"

Francois staggered to his feet, touched his nose tenderly. Even the slightest touch resulted in blinding pain. His shirt was ruined, of course. Saturated now. Not even dry cleaning could salvage it.

Glaring at the stunned Russell sprawled across the floor, he grabbed his shirt with both hands, ripped it asunder. He pulled the pieces off his torso, threw them onto the floor.

"That was my favorite shirt."

Francois made the Change. His pants shredded and fell off as his massive bulk grew. Francois stood over seven feet tall. Thick black fur. Long snout. Gleaming teeth. Scalpel claws.

Russell backtracked deeper into the kitchen. Francois crept forward, a low rumble from his throat. Russell scanned the room. Think fast, he told himself. He couldn't fight Francois toe to toe. He couldn't outrun him.

What to do?

He had hung around Caleb long enough to know he did not want to go down without a fight. "Every man dies," he remembered Caleb once saying. "The best any man can hope for is to meet Death on his feet, not on his knees."

Russell yanked a kitchen drawer open, grabbed a butcher knife, spun around to Francois. He brandished the weapon in front of him.

The werewolf stopped. He had not expected this portly gent to possess a fighting spirit. Pleasantly surprised, his respect for this mortal raised just a bit. His lips pulled back into a wicked grin.

Adrenaline surging, Russell felt both mortal fear and exhilaration. He could hear Caleb's battle in the main room. He was only seconds away from dying, and he had never felt more alive. And somehow, perversely, this was... *fun*.

How could that be?

Martinez was proving to be a more determined foe than Caleb had anticipated. Both were bloodied and in pain, each determined to end the other's life.

Marla stood near the bottom of the staircase, giving the warring werewolves a wide berth. She watched with blank, unbelieving eyes. Suffering stimulus overload, her mind was threatening to shut down.

How had her life come to this?

Martinez lashed out, slicing horizontally, aiming for Caleb's nose. Caleb jerked back. The slash sliced only air. The arc sent arm wide, exposing one side of his abdomen and torso.

Caleb moved in a blur. He clawed across Martinez's abdomen, opening it up. He followed up by jamming his enormous hand up and into Martinez's open cavity.

Then he lifted up.

Martinez yelped as his feet rose off the floor. Using his claws like curved swords, Caleb jammed his free hand through skin and tissue on one side, penetrating a lung. Martinez's yelp strangled off as the lung collapsed, pushing in on his heart and his windpipe.

Caleb yanked back, bringing the dying Martinez near him. Inches away. Eye to eye. Nose to nose. Caleb's eyes emitted an evil gleam. He rumbled in satisfaction.

Then he bit sideways, crushing Martinez's throat. He chomped down, shook his head until he pulled out a chunk of flesh and underlying tissue the size of a grapefruit. He spat it onto the floor, then flung what was left of Martinez away from him like a bag of garbage.

Caleb's chest heaved. He sucked in great gulps of air. He looked down at his body. Between the blood of the werewolves he had killed and the multiple bites and lacerations he had suffered, most of his coat was slick and red. He pressed his huge hand over a wound on his side. The skin had been flayed open; the ribs beneath showed a dull white.

It hurt like hell.

"Caleb."

A soft word, floating on the air. He saw Marla standing by the staircase. His eyes lightened from orange to yellow. The lips came together, covering his fangs. The snarl left his face.

A single whimper escaped him, and Marla's heart broke. Remorse swept over her. How could she have treated him so badly?

A glass broke behind him from the kitchen. And just like that, the moment was over. Immediately back in the fight, Caleb's head swung in that direction. She gasped at the sight of his exposed ribs. His eyes darkened back to burnt orange.

A low rumble emanated from within his chest.

In the kitchen, Francois advanced on Russell who retreated, holding the knife out in front of him. He used the other hand to throw anything he could find at the towering monster. A glass vase. Yeah, that didn't faze him.

Russell looked around, grabbed a 10-inch iron skillet from its peg on the wall. He surged forward screaming in rage, swinging the skillet in one hand, slashing with the knife in the other.

The knife finally connected, slicing deep on Francois's left forearm. He roared in pain and fury. Emboldened, Russell pressed the attack and swung the skillet hard at Francois' enormous head. He planned to follow up with a slice to Francois' throat.

That never happened.

Francois grabbed Russell's skillet hand at the wrist in a viselike grip. He twisted back and down. The skillet flopped out of Russell's numb hand, clanged onto the floor. Russell bent backwards, twisted to the side to prevent his arm from breaking.

Francois lashed out so fast Russell never saw it coming. Claws raked horizontally across Russell's abdomen, shredding his shirt, slicing through skin with surgical precision.

Russell felt a strange sensation. Not pain exactly, more pressure than anything else. Then a hot wetness, spreading, red water spilling across his girth, down his legs.

Did he just piss himself?

Francois backhanded him so hard his feet left the floor. His three-hundred-pound frame sailed across the room, crashed full-force into the chef's stove. The impact shifted it backwards. In the space between the stove and the wall, the aluminum gas line bunched up, crimped.

Russell thudded to the floor, air whooshing out of his lungs. He tried to suck air but couldn't. It hurt too bad to breathe. He opened his eyes. Francois, grinning his toothy grin, stepped forward, arms folded across his chest. Fingers flexed. Claws clicked.

The deep wounds had sliced through skin but had not penetrated the abdominal cavity. Seeing heaps of yellow adipose tissue protruding through the gashes, Russell understood why. Francois' slash had simply rent flesh and fat, not the underlying muscle that guarded the internal organs.

For the first time in his life, Russell felt grateful he carried so much weight. It had saved him from what should have been certain death.

Irony.

He looked up as Francois advanced. Russell had only been given a few extra seconds. Francois would not miss the mark twice.

He sighed then, accepting the inevitable. He was not afraid.

Some impossibly large thing, all red and brown, all claws, muscle, and teeth charged into the kitchen. Roaring loudly, it slammed into Francois, a Sherman tank on two legs.

Caleb.

Thank God!

Caleb kept going, dynamo legs churning beneath him. He picked Francois up off the floor, pushed him across the room, then slammed him into the far wall. Plaster cracked from floor to ceiling. Francois yelped as his head bounced off the unyielding surface.

He slashed at Francois, opened four deep furrows across his muzzle. Caleb's index finger snagged a loose flap of skin on Francois' already torn nose, sliced it off. The wet piece flew off, landed with a splat.

Francois howled in pain, slashed blindly with both claws. Caleb stood at the ready, on the balls of his feet. Francois pawed at his face, blood pouring down his chest and belly, black fur staining bright red.

Arterial blood.

Caleb grinned.

Enraged, Francois sprang. Caleb responded. They slammed into each other, bouncing their skulls painfully off the other. They swooned momentarily, shaking their massive heads to clear the stars from their fields of vision. Caleb recovered first and plowed into Francois, once again lifting him off his feet. They slammed down onto the floor and slid into the chef's stove just as Russell tried to move aside.

The stove shook again, groaned as it slid, resettled further back. That extra quarter inch ruptured the thin aluminum metal pipe. Natural gas hissed softly as it escaped into the room.

Russell tried to get loose, but Francois's mass pinned him in place as the black werewolf battled Caleb. He tried pushing against Francois but to no avail.

"Get the fuck off me, Fang Face!" he yelled. He punched Francois in the side of the head near his ear.

Francois spun in a blur and slashed again, cutting deeply across Russell's chest. Blood spurted. Francois moved to bite, but Caleb wrestled him back. Teeth gnashing, claws slashing, they tumbled through the doorway, out of the kitchen and into the great room beyond.

Russell's head swam. He struggled back into a sitting position. He rested his head on the oven window behind him. He looked, saw fresh blood running, freely mixing with the old.

This was not good.

In the Great Room, all eyes were on Caleb and Francois as they scrabbled over the blood-slicked floor. Both werewolves were exhausted, bleeding, injured, and in agony. Neither would give an inch. They had hated each other from the beginning. Each knew the other represented everything he himself despised. They saw each other as an existential threat to life as they knew it.

And this was the only way werewolves resolved these matters.

Hans and Dianne watched the two combatants, each sapped of strength and panting, tongues lolling, doggedly continue their personal war. Diane had never seen Francois challenged by another werewolf clearly his equal. She glanced discretely at Hans. His eyes followed the action, but his face remained passive.

Caleb ducked under a savage slash and latched onto Francois shoulder near the neck. He bit down hard. He shook his head from side to side, turning his teeth into buzz saws, rending jagged flesh. He scooped Francois under the armpits and ran blindly forward, knowing he would eventually impact with –

The wall.

That hard, immovable thing that holds the roof up. They crashed into it full force. Francois yipped as the air rocketed out of his lungs. Caleb let go, allowed Francois to slide to the floor, stunned and semiconscious. Woozy, Caleb staggered back. He put a hand out, working hard to not fall down himself.

Diane turned to Hans. "Go down there."

"Why?"

"Francois is down. You need to end this."

"Francois takes his killing seriously," Hans said, looking back down. "Far be it for me to deny him his fun."

"Fun?" She pointed to Francois, slumped and breathing hard on the floor below. Blood spread slowly around his body. "You call that fun?"

"You don't understand."

Incensed, she turned. "I understand perfectly. You were never going to make me a werewolf, were you?"

Hans feigned innocence. "What?"

"You don't care about anything or anyone but yourself," she spat. "You don't care about me. You don't even care if Francois dies as long as your 'Plan' succeeds, right?"

Hans' hand whipped out, fingers closing in an iron grip around her throat. "You try my patience, dear."

"Fuck you," she croaked. She spat in his face.

Hans was proud of her. She had finally learned to stand up for herself, to quit being so goddamned passive.

Pity it was too late to do her any good.

He lifted her off her feet, flung her up and out. She sailed over the bannister, arced out into open space, and plummeted to the floor almost twenty feet below. Her neck snapped loudly. Her skull split open like an overripe watermelon dropped on a hot summer sidewalk. Blood and brains spilled across the already blood-stained floor.

Caleb's head spun around. He looked at Diane's broken body, then upwards at Hans. Had he thrown her at him? No matter. He would deal with Hans soon enough.

Francois was struggling to his feet. This was complicated by all the blood smeared all over the floor. But to his credit, Francois finally achieved it, leaning against the wall.

Eyes met. Chests heaved. Minds seethed.

Souls hated.

Depleted, bleeding, they sprang at each other at the same time. Arms flailed; claws cut. Hacked. Slashed. More wounds. More blood.

More pain.

Francois landed a blow along Caleb's left cheek. Skin splayed open cleanly, as if cut with a fillet knife. Caleb ignored it, stayed in the fight. Anything less meant instant death.

Francois coiled his legs, sprang with surprising speed and power, slammed into Caleb and rushed him backwards, clutching and clawing.

Caleb lost his balance. Francois' weight and momentum toppled them both. They slid along the slippery floor.

Francois recovered first, clambered onto Caleb. His jaws snapped and lathered as he pressed the attack. Caleb managed to get a forearm up across his face. He jammed it into Francois' throat, keeping him back, those lethal teeth just inches from Caleb's vulnerable neck.

Francois pressed further, moving millimeter by millimeter closer. Caleb turned his head, exposing his throat. Francois took the bait. He lunged and bit, just like Caleb had known he would.

Caleb spun his head to the other side and stabbed Francois in the side with his free hand, the claws penetrating all the way to the fingertips. As Francois ratcheted back, Caleb got one foot between them and kicked, sending Francois tumbling.

Caleb roared as he stabilized in a crouch. Francois tripped over William's corpse. He careened backwards and thudded against the wall.

Caleb pounced, roaring, arms wide, claws extended. Francois swung wildly, blindly, hoping to connect. All he slashed was air.

This proved to be Francois' final, fatal mistake.

Caleb ducked under the slashes obviously intended to either slice his face again or force him to retreat. He was too experienced for that.

When the enemy tries to keep you at a distance, close the gap. Get inside their defenses. Then go for the kill.

Caleb bellowed. All his pain. All his rage. All his hate. With the last of his waning strength he shot inside one last time. His arms coiled against his chest. His hands shot out like bullets. Caleb sunk all ten claws on into Francois' chest, plunging deep between the ribs, puncturing both lungs.

Francois had never felt pain or panic like this in his long life. He tried to scream but could not inhale. He wanted to cough but couldn't. He grabbed Caleb at the wrists, tried to force the claws out of his body. Why was it that suddenly he could not accomplish so simple a task?

Caleb curled his fingers inside Francois, gripping the ribs close to the sternum. He wrenched his entire body to one side, yanking Francois so hard it whiplashed the werewolf's neck from side to side. He drove François to the bloody floor, straddled him.

Game over, Francois.

Fingers curling tighter, Caleb growled, easing his body down so close his muzzle almost touched Francois' nose. He glared into his enemy's eyes, saw the light fading behind them.

But Caleb decided that in the final seconds of life, Francois should not be denied the experience of one last sensation.

Caleb wrenched his torso back, yanked hard with everything he had. Pink froth flung off his pain wracked body. Using his own momentum, he yanked upwards and outwards against the ribs.

HARD.

Francois' ribs separated from the sternum and snapped off. Erupting outward, they protruded through dark skin a millisecond before the entire chest cavity exploded open, spraying Caleb with rich arterial blood that geysered eight feet.

Francois spasmed, life draining quickly. But Caleb wasn't done. Not yet. He lunged downward, buried his snout into the spurting cavity. He located his prize, clamped down. Caleb whipped his head back and to one side, ripping Francois' bloody, dripping, still beating heart out of his chest with a terrible, wet tearing sound.

The last thing Francois LeCroix the Werewolf saw on this Earth was Caleb Jacobsen, his avowed enemy, bite down and begin to chew. How had this turned out so badly? How had he been defeated so utterly? He simply did not understand.

Francois's body relaxed; limbs flopped onto the floor. His bladder emptied.

Caleb the werewolf rose to his feet. He chewed a couple more times, then tilted his head high to straighten the path from mouth to stomach. He gulped, gravity helping him swallow the heart of his enemy in half-chewed chunks. He gobbled the last piece down, gulped, swallowed hard.

It went all the way down.

Looking down at the ruined carcass, euphoria enveloped him. He put one foot atop Francois' body, held his arms out wide, claws extended, tilted his head upwards again, and howled in triumph.

The howl carried, continued, got louder, crossed over into a roar. Like a lion broadcasting a successful kill, proclaiming dominance.

He stood there, primal, guttural, ancient. His entire body dripped blood as he screamed out this hard-earned, savagely fought victory so every living creature within earshot knew.

Finally, the roar retreated, became a howl again. Then the howl passed, died down, then died out.

Silence followed.

Caleb removed his foot from Francois, put it on the floor. The room spun. Fireworks sparked across his eyes. Suddenly dizzy, he staggered, slipped on Diane's brains, and fell to the floor flat on his back.

The burnt orange eyes dimmed. The color faded to amber, then to yellow. The rise and fall of his chest slowed, became less pronounced. In that moment, he didn't feel the pain anymore.

Was he dying? If so, this wasn't so bad. Maybe he'd just lay here for a minute.

He noticed Hans at the top of the stairs. He looked back at Caleb, a small, almost kindly smile on his face. That did not make any sense. What the hell was going through this lunatic's mind?

Marla.

He couldn't see her, but he felt her. He tried to move, and all the pain came back, threatening to drown him. He could not stand, so he clambered in her direction on his hands and knees.

Tears streamed down Marla's face as she watched her love work his way towards her, the effort becoming more Herculean with each passing second. Giant blood smears left in his wake tracked his progress.

Marla dropped to her knees, tried to catch him as he pitched face forward onto her, his enormous bulk pinning her. She pushed against him, grunting, struggling to get free.

Hans watched from above. "The sacrifices we make for those we love."

"Caleb. Get off me," Marla whispered.

Caleb grumbled, managed to roll to one side. Marla pulled free, squatted beside him. She threw a quick look at Hans to make sure he had not moved.

"Caleb. Look at me."

His yellow eyes focused on her. His head swung in the direction of the front door. Still open. He could smell the flowers outside. He grumbled, jerked his head in that direction.

Marla frowned, not understanding. He did it again. She still didn't get it.

Caleb pulled his hand away from a wound he had been protecting. Marla winced again when his ribs showed white through the blood and layers of jagged meat. Her eyes followed his arm movement. Time seemed to stand still as his elbow straightened and his fingers curled save for his index finger. The yellowish claw smeared red pointed towards the exit route.

The light bulb went on in Marla's head.

"But what about you?" she asked. "What about Russell?"

"Don't worry about me!" Russell's cracked voice crept in from the kitchen.

Caleb pointed more insistently. He allowed a low growl to escape. Just for emphasis.

Marla stood, looked over her shoulder at Hans. He had not moved.

"Caleb, do the world a favor. Kill that motherfucker at the top of the stairs."

She stepped around Caleb, then skirted around the various blood stains on the floor. She paused by the kitchen, was shocked at Russell's condition.

He looked at her, waved a tired arm. "Go. Now. Get help."

She hesitated, not wanting to leave him behind.

"Fucking go!"

His harsh tone spurred her to action. She bolted. She felt certain someone, or something would come crashing out of nowhere and pull her down.

Open doorway just a few feet ahead. She just might make it.

Marla burst from the house, leapt from the front porch at a dead run for the gate.

And she knew with every heavy thud of her jackhammer heart she would never see Russell or Caleb alive again.

Caleb lay on the bloody mess of a floor. Lacerations crisscrossed his body. Blood matted his fur.

Pushed beyond his limits, his head swam. Pain hit, wave after crashing wave, pummeling his body. His tongue flopped out of his mouth, spread like pink jelly on the floor. Breathing came in ragged gasps.

Caleb thought he knew what pain was.

Wrong.

This was pain on a whole new level. This transcended localized discomfort and encompassed his entire being, flooded his mind, his consciousness until there was no room for anything else. This was a pain that he knew might never go away.

Not much gas left in the tank, Caleb realized. Maybe if he just rested a bit more, he could still do this.

He just needed to catch his breath.

Russell sat in a puddle of coagulating blood. He knew what was happening. His body was performing a final inventory, preparing to shut down.

His head rolled to the left atop his shoulders. He saw that smug fuck Hans standing at the top of the stairs looking down from on high. He ignored the corpses. They were unimportant. What was important was Caleb's prostrate form, lying on the floor at the foot of the stair, legs splayed, one arm stretched out, hand resting on the first step of the stairway.

At first Russell thought Caleb was dead. Then he noticed the rise and fall of the torso. Then a foot moved. Then a hand.

That's right, Russell thought.

Sic 'em, boy.

From his perch atop the stairs, Hans watched as Caleb's eyes opened again, swirling amber. Then those eyes focused on him. The amber color coalesced, deepened, darkened back to their original burnt orange. A snarl crossed Caleb's ragged lip. An outstretched hand gripped the bottommost of the spindles that ran every eighteen inches, connecting the bannister rail into the steps themselves.

He watched as Caleb the werewolf struggled to get up and failed. Each time he tried to get a foot under him, it slipped away.

Hans began to think maybe Caleb was done. Killing him now would be so disappointingly easy.

Caleb gripped the spindle, used his elbow to inch along until his head was lying on the bottom step. He licked cut lips, ran a tongue over long teeth. He placed one palm flat on the step, pushed up while pulling himself closer to the bannister. He somehow got a knee under him, slid forward.

He let go of the first spindle, shot his hand out, grabbed another. He pulled with all his might, dragging his bulk out of the combined blood smears on the floor and onto the staircase itself.

Hans admired his passion. His tenacity. His grit.

Pity he was going to have to kill him, maybe eat his liver.

Caleb had pulled himself far enough to get one knee on the carpeted stair and grab both hands onto the rail above him. He struggled, pulled himself up. He got one foot under him and pushed. His upper body needed his lower body's help. He slowly inched higher, high enough to slap his other foot underneath him.

He grimaced through the pain and pulled himself up to standing. His took one hand off the rail, immediately went wobbly, gripped the rail again to steady himself. He finally found his balance. Then he stopped looking at his feet, brought his head up to see—

Hans. Waiting at the top of the stairs.

Old memories flooded back. That night in Montana. The terror. The pain. The fear. The victimization. Everything that had happened since. This asshole had robbed him of a normal life, had robbed him of being *human.*

As long as Hans was alive, the Plan was alive. Marla and Russell would never be safe. No one would be safe. Anywhere.

Ever.

Eyes narrowed. Lips pulled back. Wrinkled muzzle. Blood-slimed fangs. Adrenaline and endorphins pumped through his body. Flight for fight. No fucking way Caleb was going to run from the likes of Hans.

Only one thing left to do.

Fight.

Caleb pulled himself up to his full height. His chest expanded, his mouth opened, and Caleb roared so loudly it even surprised him. It died away into a low rumble. The message was clear.

Time to end this.

He stared upwards at Hans, hating him more than he had ever hated anyone before. But it was not just Hans the man. It was not even his ghastly, perverse Plan to enslave the human race, although that was horrific enough.

Caleb hated him for what he represented. Hans was the walking personification of racism, bigotry, false superiority. Because he was different, he thought that made him better than everyone else.

It did not.

Hans thought being different entitled him to rights and privileges he would deny and strip away from others not like him.

It did not.

Caleb had seen men like him all his life. Men like Hans carried their hatred within their hearts everywhere they went and spread it like a disease, a cancer infecting decent people insidiously, a little at a time. He had seen the rise of the Klan, the terror campaigns, the gangrapes, the lynchings.

He had witnessed the rise and fall of despots. Hitler, Stalin, Mussolini, Hirohito. The list went on and on. Men who believed their vision for the world was the only vision. Anyone who disagreed deserved to die.

And on it went. Still. Even today. In countries all over the world.

Stupid humans, he thought. They never fucking learn.

Caleb had been on the wrong side of history *once.*

Never again.

Because no matter who you are or where you come from, no matter your skin color, eye color, or hair color, no matter what God you pray to (or don't pray to!), the fact is we're all stuck on this spinning rock in space together, and there's no way out.

Better we work together in peace and respect each other, or at least mind our own damned business and leave other people alone.

Hans stood in the way of that. At the top of a simple staircase, he stood in the way of all that. He was the true immediate threat to life on the planet. He had to be knocked out of the box.

Still gripping the bannister, Caleb put his other arm out for balance. Glaring at Hans, his dark orange eyes bored through the core of his enemy.

His next kill.

And then Caleb Jacobsen raised his foot and stomped onto the next step going up the staircase.

CHAPTER TWENTY-SEVEN

Conflicting emotions clawed at Marla as she ran. Elation at getting away, dread at being killed any second, and remorse for leaving people she loved behind. Cold night air seared her lungs as the gate rushed up to meet her. A tiny glowing red light shone, a tiny dot against the blackness.

A control panel.

She skidded to a stop, felt the button beside the light. She made out the letters beneath the light: CLOSED. Her fingers crept laterally until she found the other one. She pushed it. The red winked out, replaced by green.

A motor clanged to life. The gate groaned as cold wet wheels rotated inside grooved tracks, opening. Marla shouldered her way through, caught her shirt on a protruding metal finger. She ignored the sharp pain across her back as she passed through. She broke into a run as blood seeped down her shoulder blades, staining her clothes.

She noticed a car parked across the street down the block. Someone got out of the driver's side, was waving her towards them.

Sandra Akin!

Nauseous with pain, semiconscious from blood loss, Caleb slugged his way up the staircase. Every lift of his feet required monumental effort. Every stair felt like climbing Mount Everest. Bloody footprints marked his path from the first-floor landing. Two footprints showed on the steps where he had stooped to rest, lest he pass out and fall to the bottom.

Hans remained at the top of the stairs. If only Caleb had joined them. Hans now had no choice but to kill him – if he didn't fall dead on his own. He could have forgiven Caleb's numerous indiscretions and offenses, even attacking the house, his Wolf Den, and killing several of his pack.

But there could be no forgiveness for killing Francois. Even for immortal beings such as them, there were some lines one did not cross. Killing Francois was a bridge too far. No coming back from that.

Blood continued to drip from Caleb's saturated coat, spattering each step beneath him. The anticoagulant properties of werewolf saliva kept his wounds from scabbing over. Woozy, he caromed off the side wall, left a huge red smear that swiped upwards as he advanced.

Pain exploded inside his head as his left shoulder dragged along the plaster wall. Stars went supernova behind his eyes. He had sustained a deep laceration to his left shoulder that would need stitches if he survived the night.

Caleb continued his seemingly never-ending climb towards the second-floor landing where his quarry waited. Eyes on Hans reminded him of his purpose, his outrage at what this bastard represented, what he wanted to do to the world.

Caleb continued his climb. Red footprints in his wake. More smears as he brushed against the wall. Fresh blood squished up between his fingers every time he grasped the next section of the bannister to keep from falling over.

Caleb clambered upwards, ever upwards, bringing him closer to his prey, his enemy, his next kill with each determined, deliberate, agonizing step.

Just one more, the Wolf reminded him. Then it's finished.

Marla trembled as she relayed what had happened. Akin steadied her by the shoulders.

"They're still in there," Marla finished. "They're dying."

"Okay," Akin soothed.

"We've got to help them!" Marla exclaimed, bordering on hysteria.

"We will," Akin assured her. She hustled Marla around the front of the car, put her in the front passenger seat. She retraced her steps and got in the driver's side.

Akin grabbed the radio, keyed the mic.

"Dispatch, Car 54. Come in."

"Car 54, this is dispatch. Where are you?"

Akin gave her location, requested backup. Dispatch informed her backup was already enroute. Neighbors had already called in a "disturbance" at that location.

Something caught Akin's eye. In the extreme distance, red and blue lights reflecting against the sky above. She could not hear the sirens yet. But she would. She pointed.

"What's that?" Marla asked.

"The Cavalry."

Russell felt strangely calm. Serene. Yes, that was word. He felt serene. Not a care in the world.

The blood around him had congealed into a gelatinous goo, cementing him in place. He was seriously fucked up. No way around that. But right in that moment as he sat propped against the stove, it didn't seem to matter too much.

He heard Caleb continue his struggling lurch up the staircase. What strength! What determination! He wished he could help, but he had been effectively sidelined, hadn't he?

He was cold, felt lethargic. His legs had become immovable. His arms weighed a ton, reduced to useless stumps. Fingers hung, curled gray, limp sausages.

I'm bleeding out, he realized. No way I'm leaving here alive.

A new, eerie calm descended over him. Marla had gotten out. Caleb was about to rip that blonde bastard apart. And Russell… well, Russell had nothing left to lose, did he?

He rolled his head left. He saw Caleb fighting his own fatigue, pain, and blood loss to overcome the last few stairs. He saw Hans push himself off the rail, take a step back.

Wait. An odor. Rotten eggs.

Was that gas Russell smelled?

Caleb forced himself up the last two steps. He planted both feet on the landing wide apart, still holding the bannister with one hand. He swayed slightly.

Hans smiled as Caleb the blood-soaked werewolf panted, pink tongue lolling, catching his breath.

"You are amazing," Hans said with genuine awe. "I do so wish things had been different for us."

Caleb growled, flicked his tongue across red wet teeth. His eyes locked on Hans once again, narrowed. The hatred radiating off his body was palpable.

"And here we are, at the end of all things. Just you and me."

Caleb was so sick of Hans' bullshit. He growled again, something primeval rumbling from his chest. He let go of the bannister, took one step forward.

Hans smiled again. "Yes. Let us meet destiny together."

Caleb clenched his fists, closed his eyes. He drew a breath in, held it. He trembled with the violent emotions and ancient, prehistoric impulses rushing through him.

Then a new tension built inside him. Pulling at him, straining like a wire stretched beyond its tensile strength. Threatening to snap. But this went beyond mere rage or hatred; transcended it. This was something else.

Something… more.

A compulsion to protect. To protect others. Protect Russell. Marla. Akin.

But it was more than that, too. He wanted to protect *everyone*.

Men, women, children.

Protect.

Old people. Young people.

Protect!

Babies, suckling at their mothers' breasts, snuggling inside warm blankets and loving arms.

PROTECT!

All those alive; all those yet to be born.

PROTECT!

Everyone now, and everyone that will ever be.

Everywhere.

For all eternity.

PROTECT!

Seven billion people currently living on planet Earth, a mostly water-covered blue and green rock spinning through space at twenty-four thousand miles per hour all while orbiting a medium-sized star. And at that moment in time, the immortal creature, that impossible Beast, the werewolf known as Caleb Jacobsen, loved and cherished them all.

Then this new pressure rose from deep within him, surging upwards, an ancient, profound power unlike anything Caleb had ever felt or experienced. It grew, pushing outwards, now, the pressure rising. All of it building for the inevitable eruption.

And erupt it did.

Caleb's eyes snapped open. Then they changed. Orange eyes deepened, darkened, until they glowed a deep, menacing red. His hands and feet widened. He twitched as he grew in height, gained weight, added muscle mass.

Caleb the werewolf now stood before Hans, forever transformed. Eight feet tall, four hundred pounds of primordial instinct and practically unlimited power.

Caleb thrust his head forward, jutting out in front of his body. He spread his arms wide, claws extended, opened his mouth and ROARED!

All that rage, all that pain all that hatred gushed out, Caleb's intent to utterly destroy Hans, to kill him, rip his goddamned throat out, eat his black heart right out of his chest just like he had Francois.

"Now you know what it is to truly hate," Hans observed. "Now you know what it takes to be Alpha."

Hans made the Change. His hair turned to golden fur, grew out, thickened. Fangs sprouted. Muscles developed, grew, stretched against the fabric of his clothes. He grabbed his shirt and shred it off his expanding chest. He reached down, grabbed the legs of his trousers, ripped them off his body as he kept growing. His shoes split apart, feet and toe claws bursting forth.

Hans opened his eyes, focused in Caleb. A true Alpha for over two centuries, his eyes glowed bright red as if they always had, as if he deserved it. He raised his arms outward, extended his claws. He crouched, ready.

Caleb exploded forward, somehow having found power in his legs. They churned underneath him, turning him into an eight foot, 400-pound blood-soaked unforgiving force of nature at its darkest.

He was pure animal now. The Wolf had been unleashed completely and ran free. The human side was gone, buried, resting. Rational thought obliterated, his body moved instinctively, independent of conscious thought.

Surprised by this onslaught, Hans slashed defensively. Blood spilled from Caleb as he slammed into Hans with the unstoppable force of a runaway tractor trailer. Claws slashed so fast they blurred. Jaws snapped. Teeth tore at flesh. Roars rattled the windows as these two elemental warriors locked in mortal combat.

Caleb pressed the advantage, kept Hans backing up. They grappled and tumbled, bit and clawed, lurching away from the landing and down the hallway towards Hans' quarters.

And towards that beautiful picture window at the end of the hall.

Russell was almost dead. He knew it. He only had minutes left. Maybe seconds.

He heard the battle erupt anew upstairs. The rotten egg smell twitched his nose. He frowned, the rudiments of an idea forming in his slowing brain.

He shoved his hand into one of his pants pockets. He fumbled around, numb fingers probing. He pulled something out, held it up a small box of matches.

A coughing spasm wracked him. His shattered abdomen felt like it was going to explode like a car bomb. Something thick, coppery flooded his mouth. He spat onto the floor. A thick plug of blood and mucus.

His lungs were filling up. God, I am so fucked, he thought.

He struggled with the simple task of opening the matchbox. He extracted a single match, concentrated on closing the box. Why was that so hard?

Oh yeah. Because I'm dying.

Another coughing spasm struck him like a Mack truck. His lungs exploded with unholy fire. The pressure caused some of his intestines to burst forth through the damaged muscular wall and out through the open lacerations.

The coughing passed. He sat there, bloody mucus stringing red and thick from his mouth, intestines protruding. Russell was completely wasted. Done. No gas left in the tank, as his friend Caleb would say.

Caleb.

Marla's lover. Her protector.

Russell's best friend. He smiled tiredly.

His own personal werewolf.

His best friend and personal werewolf who was upstairs right now, beaten, bloody, wounded, exhausted, fighting Evil to protect all mankind.

That 180-year-old werewolf upstairs was the most *human* being Russell had ever met.

No fucking way he was going to wuss out now and let his friend down. He was going to help Caleb, even if it killed him.

Why?

Because that what friends fucking do, that's why.

He held the box steady, concentrated hard on what he was doing. This would be his final act upon this earth. No way he would fuck it up. He pressed the phosphorus tip to the sandpaper strip.

"I love you, Marla," he whispered. Then he grinned. "Take care of her, Furball."

And then, in that moment, Russell Slater the college professor with the potty mouth, the pouchy belly, and the filthy mind of a horny fourteen-year-old finally became the selfless hero he had always hoped he someday could be. He closed his eyes, gritted his teeth, and flicked his hand, sending the match scratching along the sandpaper.

The phosphorus ignited.

At that moment upstairs, Hans and Caleb slashed and bit at each other. Caleb closed the distance and bit Hans deep on the shoulder. He tasted the satisfying flavor of his enemy's blood bubble into his mouth. Hans yelped, bit down on Caleb's shoulder. Caleb's legs continued working, moving towards the end of the hall.

Then came a rumble that shook the entire house. A shock wave heated their fur, followed by the blast, impossibly hot and overpowering. It picked them both up and hurled them through the window. Glass shards embedded in their skin. They both instinctively closed their eyes, protecting them.

Arms and legs flailing, they tumbled out the second story window and nose-dived into the cold night air.

Akin and Marla heard a great WHOOMPH! Through the open gate, they saw the huge orange fireball roil, boil, then expand outward. The entire first floor blew out in all directions. Weightbearing walls collapsed as the wooden columns inside snapped like twigs. With nothing underneath to support its weight, the second floor collapsed and fell into the inferno. The shock wave hit the wall, crumbled it. The wave rocked the car so violently Marla thought they might flip over.

Wailing sirens in the distance, getting closer. Flickering red and blue lights approaching.

Then Marla realized what had just happened. She was out the door before Akin could stop her.

"Russel! Caleb!" she screamed. Akin was out in a flash, grabbed her by the arm.

"Marla! You can't go in there."

"They're still in there!" Marla yelled.

"You can't help them now."

In the back yard, Caleb and Hans lay stunned in the grass. Singed fur, black on the tips. Hans tried to stand but fell back onto the grass. Caleb lay there, a piece of glass the size of a Bowie Knife embedded in his lower back. He grabbed it, yanked it out. More blood poured as he tossed the shard aside.

Hans rolled over onto his stomach, put his palms flat on the grass. He had a fight to finish. His head still swimming, he pushed himself up off the grass, pulled a knee underneath him. He turned to find his opponent. There he was, lying there, trying to keep from dying.

Trying to come kill him.

Hans bent the other leg, dragged the foot until it slapped flat on the ground beneath him, rose to his feet. He growled, bloodlust overpowering him. He stalked forward as his prey tried to stand.

Caleb was up on his knees when Hans kicked him savagely in the ribs. Bones crunched. Caleb fell back, pain blinding him. Hans kicked again, slashed Caleb across the face. He grabbed Caleb, picked him up off the ground and threw him towards the edge of the yard, near the sheer cliff and the black water below.

Caleb saw Hans closing in. He ignored the pain and scampered to his feet. Caleb moved laterally, circling right. He displayed his claws, growled at Hans.

No way Hans was going to take him. Either Hans died, or they both died.

Caleb moved on wobbly knees. He wished he could take time to throw up. But he lashed out with his claws instead. Hans twisted away, avoiding catastrophic injury. Hans spun around, planted his feet.

Was that the best this upstart had?

Caleb had put his weight into the strike. He fell forward, almost losing his balance. He panted, ribs on fire inside as lungs expanded and contracted. Hey, it only hurt when he breathed, right? His eyes found Hans.

What the hell?

Hans stood, bent at the knees, on the balls of his feet. Ready to attack or defend. But the precipice was directly behind him now. Golden fur stained red, some of it Caleb's blood, some of it his own. Instead of charging, he stood, arms bent in front of him. His lips pulled back, not in a snarl as Caleb might have expected, but into a distorted smile. His shoulders shook, grunts accompanied the shoulder shakes, rocking in concert.

The son of a bitch was *laughing* at him!

Caleb's fury boiled over. As long as Hans lived, Marla would never be safe. No one would be safe. Mankind would be butchered, enslaved, herded. Though flawed and weak, petty and selfish, as violent and savage as mankind could be, it did not deserve that fate.

Because mankind was also capable of love, kindness, compassion and mercy; capable of creating art and literature, of expanding culture and knowledge, of advancing technology; of negotiating peace and understanding; capable of goodwill and cooperation.

And as difficult as that could be at times, mankind had the right to keep trying, to figure it out for themselves.

Caleb's world spun in front of him, his vision dimming. He was dying. That was okay. He had cheated death so many times over the last 180 years. But sooner or later, death always wins the game. The only thing you can do is face it when your time comes.

Caleb's time had come.

He only had one thing left to do.

Knowing he had nothing left if he failed, he bent his legs, threw his arms wide, extended his claws. He thrust his head forward, red eyes glowing. He roared one last time and exploded forward, those powerful legs pumping under him.

Surprised, Hans took a half-step back. Expecting Caleb to hit high, he slashed with both arms where he thought Caleb's face would be.

Problem was, Caleb wasn't there.

Caleb ducked at the last second and streaked beneath Hans' lethal claws. He slammed low into Hans with monumental force. He rammed both hands into Hans' sides, high up under the armpits.

Roaring with rage, Caleb sunk his claws into Hans' lungs and lifted up, forcing Hans' feet off the ground.

Caleb's legs kept churning, pushing them away from the searing flames and burning ruins of what had once been a beautiful house. He heard Hans yelp in pain.

Take that, motherfucker!

Then the ground fell away beneath them and they arced out wide into the air. Caleb clamped his jaws around Hans' throat and bit down.

HARD!

He heard the hyoid bone crack, felt the esophagus collapse, the cartilaginous rings crush between his teeth. Hans' carotid artery gushed blood into Caleb's mouth as they plummeted two hundred feet, plunging down towards the narrow strip of rocky beach below. Grimly determined to make both his life and his death mean something, Caleb never let go until they hit the ground. The terrible impact was like nothing he had ever felt.

Then, mercifully, the werewolf known as Caleb Jacobsen felt nothing at all.

The sun lay hidden behind heavy gray clouds. The street in front of the decimated house was blocked off, filled with police cars from various jurisdictions. Ambulances waited. Firetrucks squatted on the property, firefighters recoiling firehoses. Thick black smoke hung in the air, stirred by smoldering rubble.

Akin walked the perimeter, her arm around a stunned Marla. Her eyes looked vacant, her face slack. Realizing she had lost both her cousin and the man she loved had simply been too much. Her mind had shut down. Psychogenic shock. She stumbled blankly along as they circled around the firefighters.

A young uniformed officer, a rookie still in her first full year, tread carefully, looking to flag evidence for the detectives. She edged closer to the cliff, noticed the blood trail that led right up to the edge. She peered cautiously over the edge. Then she did a double-take, peered again.

What the hell?

Impossible!

Mouth open and eyes wide, she turned and looked around. She saw Akin, raised her hand and waved.

"Detective! Over here!"

Akin turned towards the gesturing police officer. "What?"

The rookie pointed. "There's two bodies down there!"

Akin left Marla with the paramedics, vacant eyes staring, seeing nothing. Akin keyed the mic in her car, arranged for a police boat to meet her at the nearby marina.

Twenty minutes later, Akin stepped off the patrol boat's bow and onto the gravel beach. The tide was coming in. She didn't have much time.

This was now part of the crime scene. She crept closer. The first body was that of a large, naked blonde man. His throat had been ripped out, almost decapitating him. Cervical vertebrae shown white and fractured through the gaping hole in his neck, head twisted at an impossible angle. Blue eyes stared upwards, seeing nothing Rocks around him shone black with blood.

The other body lay on his back, face turned away from her. But that luxurious long brown hair, that physique, was unmistakable.

Caleb.

She sighed, dreading what would come next. But she was a professional. She squared her shoulders, picked her way across the rocks.

His torso looked like someone had taken a Ginsu knife to it. Enormous lacerations crisscrossed his body. Deep bites on his shoulders. Face swollen. Broken ribs protruding through pale skin.

Pained by his death, she squatted beside him. "Oh Caleb."

Caleb's eyes fluttered open. He gasped loudly, taking a huge, agonizing breath. Akin recoiled, fell backwards on her butt. He winced, grabbed his torso and squeezed as if that would make things feel better.

It didn't.

She scrambled to him. "Caleb. You're alive."

"Really?" he closed his eyes, sighed. "I thought I'd died and gone to hell." He spat something thick and pink out of his mouth.

Akin stood up, cupped her hands around her mouth. "Get Life Flight out here!" she screamed at the boat. "We have a survivor!"

She squatted back down beside Caleb. "What happened?"

"I killed them. I killed them all." He winced. "Marla?"

"She's safe."

He looked relieved. "Russell?"

"He didn't make it."

Caleb winced again, this time in grief.

"Caleb. What about the plan? The plan to take over the world?"

"Gone. Died with Hans and Francois. No one else who knew all aspects of it."

"So, the world is safe then?"

"For now." Caleb's head swooned, like he was going to pass out.

Akin grabbed him by the shoulders, shook him.

"Stay with me."

His eyes opened once more.

"Caleb." She gulped. "What about the rest of them? All the other werewolves out there?"

He coughed, spat out another thick red blob. It hit the rocks, stuck like gory spackle. He stared at her with his one good eye.

"We're still out there," he croaked. "We're everywhere. We're around you every day, everywhere you go. Bus driver, schoolteacher, doctor, lawyer, movie star, cop. We bump into you at the store, stand in line with you at the movies.

"We can smell you a hundred feet away. We can hear your heartbeat across the room." He swallowed. "And we can tear the scream right out of your throat.

"For as much as you've seen, trust me, you've seen nothing. We're more dangerous and more powerful than you can ever imagine.

"Sandra, beware of us."

EPILOGUE

July in the PNW. Warmer days, mild nights. Sunrise by 5 a.m., full dark around 10 p.m. Today, blue skies, scant clouds, temps in the mid-sixties. Marla had not returned to Port Orchard since everything that happened.

She had been in the ambulance when word came someone had survived the inferno and a two-hundred-foot fall. Her first emotion was terror.

Hans?

She learned minutes later that Caleb had survived. With such grievous and extensive injuries, she was not sure if even a werewolf with regenerative powers could ever recover. She watched the Life Flight helicopter rise from the water's edge then accelerate southward towards St. Clare's in Tacoma, the closest trauma center.

Even now, she felt no sense of time of the following days. It was all an emotional blur. Akin had driven her home, said something about sleeping. Marla had absorbed about every third or fourth word.

She had given an official statement a few days later. She had no idea how much Akin could use in her report. Probably none.

Russell's tattered remains had been transferred to a local mortuary and placed in a casket, along with enough weight to equal one hundred and fifty pounds.

No open casket funeral for Russell Slater.

Marla flew home to Kentucky. Both Russell's and Marla's mothers, along with various other family members, had make the trek to the airport in Louisville. They had welcomed her with open arms and unrestrained tears.

Russell's funeral was quiet, staid. Dignified. It was a funeral befitting the hero he was, but not what Russell would have wanted. He would have preferred everyone getting shitfaced, telling funny stories of him while listening to Lynyrd Skynyrd and Bob Seger. Marla kept that to herself.

Funerals are for the living, not the dead.

She found herself alone in her old room in the rusty single-wide where she had grown up. She sat down on her squeaky twin bed, smelled the musty quilt, looked at the sad veneer wood paneling.

Sitting there smelling the same dank air and looking through the same dirt-streaked window screen, she remembered why she had left home and had never come back.

The next day at lunch, Marla's mother had initiated the conversation she had dreaded.

"So. What are your plans?" she asked from behind her eyeglasses.

"I have to go back."

"Why?"

"I still have a job there. Commitments," Marla said. "My research is woefully behind schedule. I've already missed a deadline."

"I thought it might have something to do with that man you told me about."

"Caleb."

Her mother nodded, sipped iced tea from a mason jar. "There's a lovely zoo in Louisville, you know."

"Mom…"

"You'd be closer to home."

"I don't really work for the zoo. I work for Global BioTech."

"I just thought—"

"Global BioTech is a Seattle-based company, Mom, and my contract is with them. That's where the work is."

Her mother had smiled slyly. "That's where Caleb is, too. Right?"

The flight back had been just as interminable as the flight out. It was not until she saw the familiar snowcapped peak of Mt. Rainier that her spirits lifted her out of her depression and allowed her to just feel numb.

She had collapsed onto her bed when she got home and slept eighteen hours straight. Then she had showered and forced herself to eat something. Then it was back to work. She needed to lose herself in something all-encompassing, and her work certainly qualified.

She endured explaining to her superiors what exactly had happened the night Ty had been killed. She told them as much truth as possible. They were happy she had helped the police close out a case regarding a band of serial killers but were aghast at Ty's demise. Both the company and the zoo were facing legal liability from his family.

Personally, Marla didn't give a shit.

And that was really the thing, wasn't it? She had been sleepwalking through life, looking at people she passed, idly wondering which ones were werewolves. Knowledge of their existence proved burdensome. She considered seeing a shrink but decided against that. If she started talking about werewolves, she would wind up in a padded room somewhere.

Akin proved to be invaluable. She alone understood the weight Marla carried. Akin kept her up to date on the aftermath, about how Martinez had been hailed a hero killed in the line of duty.

Sometimes a false narrative worked better when the truth would threaten a complete breakdown of civilized society.

Caleb had been in a medically induced coma until the intracranial pressure resolved, Akin told Marla. He had sustained a fractured skull, shattered pelvis, broken femur, several broken ribs. His spleen was surgically removed, and he had suffered a collapsed lung.

His doctors were amazed at his recovery. His neurologists were astounded that not only was his skull fracture healing at an incredible rate, but according to his EEG results, he had suffered no brain damage. They continued clucking over him, calling him a miracle.

Marla had not gone to see Caleb. She never called, emailed, or texted. He had called after he had regained consciousness, left messages. He even sent a couple of texts. She did not answer; he eventually stopped.

After everything she had been through, after all the death, dismemberment, and destruction, after all the terrible things he had endured to save her, what was she supposed to say to him? In the end, she allowed her own insecurities to dictate her actions, and stayed away.

But here she was on a lovely early summer day, driving down Bay Street, heading into downtown Port Orchard. She passed the used car dealership, City Hall, and had crept along until she got to the intersection of Bay and Sidney Avenue.

She turned left with the light. Inching along, she saw the blue water of Sinclair Inlet, the terminal for the Foot Ferry to Bremerton, the totem pole. She turned into the parking lot, found a spot.

Walking past the corner antique store, she turned left. She found the coffee shop, entered. The smell of fresh roasting coffee and hot panini sandwiches made her smile.

She ordered espresso, headed towards the back. Wooden tables, chairs lined both sides. Old, threadbare easy chairs and a torn leather sofa littered the back. She eased herself down into a surprisingly comfortable wingback. She gazed at the low coffee table in front of her. Scarred, dinged up, lusterless. It looked like it had been there for decades.

Movement caught her attention. The person she had come to see stepped inside. They paused at the counter, ordered, paid. Her fear rising, she tore her gaze away, looked right. A side exit just beyond the bathroom. If she bolted now, she could leave without being seen. Maybe…

Too late. Already seen, already walking towards her. Nervous, she gulped. Where the hell was her espresso?

The person, a male, moved around the coffee table, sank into the leather sofa. He crossed his legs at the knee, stretched an arm out across the back of the sofa. Completely at ease, not a care in the world.

"So. How about this weather, huh?"

No hiking boots today. He had dressed up. Cowboy boots. Black, polished, silver tips. Faded green canvas pants. Blue denim shirt, two buttons unbuttoned at the top. He looked so comfortable she wondered how he kept from falling asleep.

A young brunette barista approached, Marla's espresso in her hands. She greeted Marla, carefully placed the steaming cup on the coffee table.

"Enjoy," she said, and turned away, giving the man on the couch an extra-long once over. She smiled at him, obviously liking what she saw.

Marla pressed her lips together, unable to speak. She placed her palms around her cup, feeling the heat.

"I hate espresso. I don't know why I ordered it."

They sat there in silence. This had been her idea.

Just as she was about to speak, the pretty young brunette barista approached again, this time placing a large mug of coffee in front of him. She smiled at him again, stayed bent over so he could get a good glimpse down her shirt if he wanted. But he seemed uninterested in the teen. She stood up, turned and walked back. He grabbed his mug, drank.

"The food's kinda pricey here," he said, "but I come anyway."

"Why?"

"Some of the money goes to help homeless teens."

She noticed the differences. The hair was longer now, over his ears and past his collar. The beard thicker. Gray now at the temples. Hints of silver in the beard around the mouth, at the chin. Crow's feet. Scars ran along the jawline, under one eye. A vertical scar on the forehead, going down through the eyebrow, ending on the skin under the eye. A hoop earring sparkled from his left earlobe.

"I… I didn't know if you'd come."

He sipped his coffee.

"After all that's happened," she began, "the way I've acted…" She did not know how to finish.

Her mind was a whirlwind, threatening to twist her out and away. She felt like she was falling apart. She sighed, squeezed her eyes shut. Was this a dream? Was she not really here?

What if he wasn't really here?

But when she dared to open her eyes again, she knew.

Caleb Jacobsen was still there, watching her from the sofa. His face filled with compassion. His eyes shined bright with love.

"I am so sorry," she blurted, tears coming. "I'm sorry for everything. For not visiting you in the hospital, for not talking to you since, I –" she choked, swallowed, then continued, "I'd understand if you never wanted to see me again."

Caleb moved his arm off the sofa, leaned forward. Marla saw thick muscles working underneath the denim as he reached out, gently cupped his hands around hers as she held her cup on the table.

She looked at his hands encircling hers, hands she had seen twice their current size. Hands that were capable of a level of violence, cruelty, and barbarity that few people could ever comprehend.

And yet now, here they were, warm, gentle, comforting. Conveying tenderness and compassion. In that moment, she felt flooded by a peace that passed all understanding.

Then he stretched across the remaining expanse and kissed her. Deeply. It ignited a passion she had feared was gone forever. Suddenly, all was right with the world. There was hope for a brighter future. She was now a spiritual being, floating through space and time, spanning the cosmos, at one with the universe whenever this man – yes, this *man* - kissed her.

He sat back down, his hands still cupping hers. Swirling colors in his eyes promised pleasures ahead she had never contemplated.

"Nothing short of Death will ever keep me away from you again," Caleb Jacobsen said.

ABOUT THE AUTHOR

Mark Allen was born in Jacksonville, Texas. After graduating high school in 1980, he joined the United States Navy and served as a Navy Hospital Corpsman. He was a Fleet Marine Force Warfare Specialist, and eventually became an Independent Duty Hospital Corpsman. He retired in May 2001.

Mark had been writing story stories and attempting novels since he was ten years old and had always had a deep abiding love for horror, thanks to the old black and white Universal Classic Monsters and the "big-bug" movies of the 1950s that he watched on TV. In the early 2)00s, he wrote and directed the no-budget feature film DELIRIUM, and wrote and co-produced the feature film, EARLY GRAVE.

Then a Stage 4 Throat Cancer knocked him out of the box in February 2014. He and eventually emerged victorious years later, but was badly beaten, bent, weakened. It has taken years for him to scratch and claw his way back. It was in the dark days of his cancer that he began writing what would become his critically acclaimed debut novel, NOCTURNAL.

Mark now lives in a small town in Northwestern Washington state with his wife, published author and award-winning photographer Fiona Young. He is currently working on JUST BEFORE DAWN, which will be a sequel to NOCTURNAL.

He writes every day.

Printed in Great Britain
by Amazon

10078731R00200